THE IMAGE
of CHEKHOV

THE IMAGE
of CHEKHOV

*Forty Stories by Anton Chekhov
in the Order in Which
They Were Written*

NEWLY TRANSLATED, AND WITH AN INTRODUCTION,
BY ROBERT PAYNE

ALFRED A. KNOPF  *New York 1979*

L.C. catalog card number: 62–15559

THIS IS A BORZOI BOOK,
PUBLISHED BY ALFRED A. KNOPF, INC.

*Copyright © 1963 by Alfred A. Knopf, Inc.
All rights reserved under International and
Pan-American Copyright Conventions. Published in the United States by Alfred A.
Knopf, Inc., New York, and in Canada by
Random House of Canada Limited, Toronto.
Manufactured in the United States of
America and distributed by Random House,
Inc., New York.*

PUBLISHED APRIL 15, 1963
REPRINTED SIX TIMES
EIGHTH PRINTING, NOVEMBER 1979

FOR

Patricia

CONTENTS

CONTENTS

The Image of Chekhov

I

WE KNOW this image well, for it is usually reproduced as a
frontispiece to his works or stamped on the bindings—the image
of a solemn, elderly man with lines of weariness deeply etched on
his thin face, which is very pale. The accusing eyes are nearly
hidden by pince-nez, the beard is limp, the lips pursed in pain. It
is the image of an old scholar or the forbidding family doctor
who has brought too many children into the world.

We know him well, but what we know bears little resemblance to the real Chekhov. This portrait of Chekhov is based on
a painting made by an obscure artist called Joseph Braz in 1898,
when Chekhov was already suffering from consumption. He was
restless while sitting for his portrait, and had little confidence in
the artist's gifts, and the best he could say of the portrait was that
the tie and the general configuration of the features were perhaps
accurate, but the whole was deadly wrong. "It smells of horse-
radish," he said. Five years later, when the portrait was solemnly
hung on the walls of the Moscow Art Theater, he wrote to his
wife that he would have done everything in his power to prevent
the painting from being hung there. He would have preferred to
have a photograph hanging in the Moscow Art Theater—anything but that abomination. "There is something in it which is
not me, and something that is me is missing," he wrote, but that
was one of his milder criticisms. His rage against the portrait in-

creased as time went on. It became "that ghastly picture," and he would lie awake thinking about the harm it would do. The painting has a fairly academic quality: he may have guessed that posterity would take it to its heart.

Chekhov had good reason to hate the picture, for he knew himself well and possessed a perfectly normal vanity. In his youth and middle age he was quite astonishingly handsome. The writer Vladimir Korolenko, who met Chekhov in 1887, speaks of his clean-cut regular features which had not lost their characteristically youthful contours. His eyes were brilliant and deep-set, thoughtful and artless by turns, and his whole expression suggested a man filled with the joy of life. His face was never still, and he was always joking. Even in his later years, when he was afflicted with blindness and hemorrhoids and consumption, and perhaps half a dozen other diseases, he continued to crack jokes like a schoolboy. There are still a few people living who can remember the sound of his infectious laughter.

Let us imagine Chekhov entering a room about the year 1889, when he was nearly thirty and had already written most of the stories he would ever write. "A Dead Body," "Heartache," "Anyuta," "Vanka," "Sleepyhead," and countless others are already behind him, and he is at the height of his fame. He has received the Pushkin Prize from the Imperial Academy of Sciences, and he has been elected a member of the Society of Lovers of Russian Literature. He is already aware that he is a great writer with a certain place in Russian literature, and he is dressed accordingly in a silk shirt with a necktie made of colored strings and a fawn-colored coat which offsets the ruddy color of his face. He is over six feet tall, but the narrow shoulders make him seem even taller. He wears a thin beard pointed in the Elizabethan manner, and there is something of the Elizabethan in his calm assumption of power, in his elegance and the nervous quickness of his movements. His thick brown hair is brushed straight back from a clear forehead. He has thick brown eyebrows, and his eyes too are brown, though they grow darker or brighter according to his mood, and the iris of one eye is always a little lighter than the other, giving him sometimes an expression of absent-mindedness when he is in fact all attention. His eyelids are a little too heavy, and sometimes they droop in a fashionable aristocratic manner, but the real explanation is that he works through the night and sleeps little. He is nearly always smiling or breaking out into huge peals of laughter. Only his hands trouble him: they are the hands of a peasant, large, dry and hot, and he does not always know what to do with them. Excessively handsome, slender and elegant, he knew his power over people and drew them to him like a magnet.

This young and handsome giant was without any trace of arrogance. He treated his gifts with a kind of careless disdain. "Do you know how I write my stories?" he said once to Korolenko. "Look!" His eyes moved across the table until they fixed upon an ash tray. "There's the story," he said. "Tomorrow shall I bring you a story called 'The Ash Tray'?" Korolenko had the curious feeling that vague images were already swarming over the ash tray, and already situations and adventures were beginning to shape themselves, while the light of Chekhov's humor was already playing on the absurdities and ironies of an ash tray's existence. When the veteran writer Dmitry Grigorovich, the friend and mentor of Dostoyevsky, complimented him on the classical perfection of his short story "The Huntsman," Chekhov was genuinely surprised, and wrote back that he had written the story to pass away the time in a bathhouse and had thought nothing more of it. He could write under any conditions, but he seems to have written best when he was surrounded by his friends.

He was tireless in his attention to his friends—nothing was too good for them. He had a passion for entertaining them, and his hospitality was princely. The severe, accusing doctor of the Braz portrait vanishes in the actor, the mimic, the clown, who would amuse himself by going to a hotel with a friend, pretending to be a valet, and proclaiming in a loud voice all the secret vices of his master, until the whole hotel was in an uproar. He adored buffoonery. He liked putting on disguises. He would throw a Bokhara robe round his shoulders and wrap a turban round his head and pretend to be some visiting emir from the mysterious lands of the East. On a train journey he was in his element. If he was traveling with his mother he would pretend she was a countess and himself a very unimportant servant in her employ, and he would watch the behavior of the other passengers toward the bewildered countess with wide-eyed wonder and delight. He had a trick of making a walk in the country an adventure in high drama. Everything excited him. He was fascinated by the shapes of clouds, the colors of the sky, the texture of fields, and it amazed him that each person walking along a country path contained so many improbable miracles in his soul. The world abounded in miracles, and he rejoiced in all of them with an unself-conscious and devouring eagerness.

Even in his last years Chekhov bore very little resemblance to the Braz portrait. No one could guess from looking at that portrait that this was a man who was always laughing and joking, who was gay and carefree and confident of his powers, who was kind and gentle and generous and very human. What distinguished him from other people was precisely what the portrait left out—the flame of eagerness in the eyes, the wild appetite for experience, the sense of sheer enjoyment which accompanied him everywhere. Men felt doubly men in his presence, and women were continually falling in love with him. There was nothing of the puritan in him. He yearned for only one thing—that people should live in the utmost freedom, perhaps because very early in his own life he had acquired all the freedom he wanted.

By the time he was thirty Chekhov had traveled across the whole length of Russia, visited Hong Kong, Singapore, and Ceylon, and half the great cities of Europe. He makes one of his characters say: "I long to embrace, to include in my own short life, all that is accessible to man. I long to speak, to read, to wield a hammer in a great factory, to keep watch at sea, to plow. I want to be walking along the Nevsky Prospect, or in the open fields, or on the ocean—wherever my imagination ranges . . ." "I want to go to Spain and Africa," he wrote at another time. "I have a craving for life." He imagined himself leading great caravans of his friends across the whole world, and since this was impossible he was always inviting them to come and stay with him, so that his various houses in the country came to resemble circuses with all the visitors assigned to play out their comic roles. He wrote to the vaudeville writer Bilibin: "I tell you what: get married and come down here, wife and all, for a week or two. I assure you it'll do you all a world of good, and you'll go away marvelously stupid." The venerable Grigorovich came to stay with him, and some time later, remembering the strange things that had happened to him, he lifted his arms in mock horror and exclaimed: "If you only knew what went on at the Chekhovs'! A saturnalia, a regular saturnalia, I tell you!"

What went on, of course, was nothing more than an experiment in furious good humor, with Chekhov playing his usual conspiratorial role. The wonder is that he was able to write so many stories in a life given over to so many friendships. He never stinted his friends, and gave money away recklessly. At those famous house parties there would be poets and novelists and musicians, some high officials, an ecclesiastical dignitary or two, a handful of circus folk, but there were also other people who were not so easily categorized, and these would turn out to be horse thieves, ex-convicts, piano tuners, or prostitutes, anyone in fact that he had met in the course of his travels. He had an especial fondness for pretty young women and homely priests, and he loved all animals except cats, which he abominated. What he sought for in people was that eagerness for life and experience which he regarded as man's birthright, and his hatred of poverty arose from the despairing knowledge that poverty saps unendurably at human vitality. He had no liking for the government, and he had even less liking for the revolutionaries attempting to overthrow the government. He loved life, and regarded politics as death.

Chekhov was *l'homme moyen sensuel* raised to the level of genius. He worked prodigiously hard at his medical practice and over his stories and plays, but even at the moments of greatest tension good humor kept creeping in. Everything about him was phenomenal—his charm, his courage, his capacity for work, his thirst for experience—but what he prized most was his ordinary humanity. He enjoyed and often celebrated the animal pleasures of life, and he was something of a connoisseur of wine and women. He had his first sexual experience at thirteen, and this love affair was followed by countless others. The legend of the remote, detached analyst of the human soul with a faintly ironical smile dies hard, and is not yet dead. The Braz portrait and some of the later photographs showing him in the throes of consumption, white as a sheet, with his coat buttoned to the neck, have helped to give credence to the legend. But those who knew him best remember his stupendous gaiety.

Even today, nearly sixty years after his death, there are still a handful of people who can remember him. A Russian now living in New York remembers meeting him as a boy in Yalta. "Chekhov was always cracking jokes," he said recently. "He was an actor, a clown. He would sweep off his pince-nez and gaze at you with a quizzical expression, telling you some perfectly impossible story with a straight face. He had a habit of walking with one arm curled round his back, pretending to be very old and tired, and very sad, and then he would straighten up and howl with laughter. In those days he was very ill, and his voice was the hoarse voice of a consumptive, but you soon forgot his illness. And what an actor he was! He could do the most extraordinary things with his pince-nez. He used them as actors use props. He was always sweeping them on and sweeping them off. He looked so young without them, and so old when they were on, that it was like seeing two different people. He would look down on me from his immense height, and I had the feeling that all his attention, all his humor, all his kindness, were being given to me."

In the hot summer of 1904 Chekhov, accompanied by his actress wife, arrived in the German watering place of Badenweiler. He was already dying, but he was in good spirits. He sent off gay messages to his friends, telling them how delighted he was with the small villa where he was staying, and how he was looking forward to a trip to Italy, a country he had loved ever since he had journeyed through it after his return from the Far East. And then after Italy there would be a leisurely cruise through the Mediterranean, and so to the Black Sea and his house in Yalta. At seven o'clock on the evening of July 1 the dinner bell rang, but for some reason neither Chekhov nor his wife heard it. A few minutes later, when they realized their mistake, Chekhov characteristically invented a story on the theme of the unheard dinner bell.

The story he told concerned a fashionable watering place full of fat, well-fed bankers and ruddy-faced Englishmen and Americans, all of them hurrying back to dinner from their sight-seeing expeditions in the country, all of them exuding animal vigor and thinking only of their stomachs. But when they arrived at the hotel, there was no dinner bell, for there was no supper— the cook had fled. Then, gaily and happily, Chekhov went on to describe all those pampered visitors as they confronted the awful fact that there would be no supper. He described their horror, their stratagems, their mounting impatience, and he told the story kindly, as he had told so many similar stories in the past. His wife sat curled up on a sofa, laughing as one comic invention followed on another. He died shortly after midnight, falling suddenly on his side, and it was observed that in death he looked very young, contented, and almost happy. Through the wide windows the wind brought the scent of new-mown hay, and later into the terrible stillness of the night there came, like a messenger from another world, a huge black moth which burst into the room like a whirlwind and kept beating its wings madly against the electric lights.

The funeral took place a week later in Moscow. Gorky and others have related the strange circumstances of the funeral, usually with bitterness. They tell how the body arrived in Moscow in a freight train labeled with the words FOR OYSTERS in large letters, and how part of the crowd waiting for Chekhov followed the coffin of General Keller, who had been brought from Manchuria, and they were a little surprised that Chekhov was being buried with full military honors. When the confusion was straightened out, a sad little procession of about a hundred people accompanied Chekhov's coffin to the Novodevichy Cemetery through the heat and dust of a Moscow summer. "I recall particularly two lawyers," wrote Gorky. "They were both wearing new boots and spotted neckties, and I heard one of them discoursing on the intelligence of dogs and the other on the comforts of his country home and the beauty of the landscape all round it. Then there was a lady in a lilac dress with a lace-fringed umbrella who was trying to convince an old gentleman in large spectacles about the merits of the deceased. 'Ah, he was so wonderfully charming, and so witty,' she said, while the old gentleman coughed incredulously. At the head of the procession a big, fat policeman rode majestically on a fat white horse. It all seemed cruelly common and vulgar, and quite incompatible with the memory of a great and subtle artist."

But was it so incompatible? Chekhov laughed gaily throughout his life, and he would have laughed at the human absurdities which accompanied his funeral. FOR OYSTERS would have pleased him, and it would have delighted him that he should have been mistaken for General Keller, and he would have listened entranced to all the inane conversations of the people following the coffin, and it would have rejoiced his heart to see the fat policeman on the fat horse. He would have swept off his pince-nez, thrown back his head, and hooted with joy when he

XVI

discovered that he was being buried next to "the Cossack widow Olga Kookaretnikov," a name as improbable as any he invented in his stories. Chekhov loved the absurd, and he loved all the splendors and inanities of the human condition.

II

Chekhov was born on January 16, 1860, a year before the freeing of the serfs. He was the son of a man born into slavery, and would himself have been born a serf if it had not been that his grandfather, who managed the vast Chertkov estates, was able to buy his freedom for 3,500 rubles. Chekhov's father was a heavy-set, deeply religious man, with a talent for painting icons and violin playing, who made his living as a grocer in the small seaport town of Taganrog. At home the father was gruff and unbending, a stern disciplinarian, loving his children but keeping at a distance from them. Chekhov's mother was the daughter of a cloth merchant, a quiet, beautiful woman, very gentle with the six children, five boys and a girl, born of the marriage. She made all the children's clothes, and she liked to tell them stories of the days when she traveled with her father in a carriage over the length and breadth of Russia. She had a deep feeling for the Russian countryside, and for people. Chekhov inherited from her his tenderness and sweetness of character, and from his father he inherited his artistic gifts and a formidable capacity for hard work and a kind of stubbornness which enabled him to overcome any obstacles in his path. He had his father's forehead and eyes, and his mother's mouth and chin. And they said that in his way of walking and talking he was most like his grandfather, the estate manager who pulled himself out of slavery.

In later years Chekhov would often talk of his childhood, which was neither happy nor unhappy, but curiously somber. Life revolved around the shop and the church. Outside the shop a sign announced in gold letters: "Tea, coffee, soap, sausage, and other colonial products are sold here." The "colonial products" referred to imports from Turkey—Turkish delight, halva, and dried currants—but in fact the shop sold very nearly every kind of grocery: herbs, dried fish, macaroni, olive oil, vodka, wine, beer, small packets of tea: everything in fact except livestock. Herring swam in barrels of pickling brine. In summer there were flies everywhere, and in winter it was strangely dark and menacing. As soon as he could walk Chekhov had to help out. He hated the long hours and the beatings he received from his father when he was inattentive, but it was in this dark and squalid room, with its overwhelming smell of fish, with strings of peppers and sweetmeats hanging from the roof, with the sacks of flour and meal crowding the wall, and the religious medallions sold to pilgrims glinting in the candlelight, that Chekhov came in contact with men and women of all classes, seeing them pass in an endless procession through the shop as later they were to pass through his stories. He came to know their faces, their smells, the way they dressed and quarreled and haggled and got drunk, and very early in his life, employing the defense mechanism of sensitive children everywhere, he learned to mimic them. Deeply impressed on his imagination were the faces and characters of two or three hundred Russian types.

There was a Greek colony in Taganrog, and for some reason he was sent to the local Greek school, where he learned Latin and ancient Greek, and modern Greek well enough to speak it, but he showed no particular brilliance in his studies. There was talk of sending him later to Athens University, but nothing came of it. Chekhov's father seems to have had little business sense, and when the family finances became increasingly precarious, there occurred a marked change in the character of the shopkeeper. He became more obsequious to the Greek merchants and began writing begging letters to important dignitaries; and from being a father he became a toadying, wheedling shopkeeper with a reverence for uniforms and an incapacity to think of anything except money. With disgust and fury Chekhov watched his father decline into a kind of senility.

Meanwhile the boy was developing his gifts of mimicry and acting. One day, dressed as a beggar, he walked through the streets of Taganrog and entered the house of his uncle Mitrofan, who failed to penetrate his disguise and gave him three kopecks. This success elated him. Thereafter he began to think seriously of a life as an actor, or perhaps as a clown in one of the traveling circuses. He wrote sketches and plays and acted them out in a barn with his brothers and his sister, taking the part of a bishop or a pompous official or a bearded professor delivering a ludicrous and incomprehensible lecture. He adored false beards and mustaches, and he fell hopelessly in love with the stage when he was thirteen and attended a production of Offenbach's *La Belle Hélène* at the local theater. He was also developing as a writer, and stories written when he was twelve show him already in full command of the Russian language, with a style as direct and simple as the works of his maturity. He edited the family magazine, which he characteristically called *The Stammerer.* Many of the stories and sketches written in his early teens were later reworked—"Surgery," one of the most famous of his early stories, was a reworking of some clownish nonsense performed when he was scarcely more than ten years old, with Chekhov himself playing the role of a dentist extracting with a pair of tongs an enormous tooth, made of cork, from his brother's mouth.

Many of Chekhov's stories are quips, jokes, *boutades*, which can be traced back to the events of his childhood and the days when he was studying medicine. When the stories were printed in book form, he usually omitted the slighter anecdotes, but a surprisingly large amount of purely anecdotal material was retained, perhaps because these casual stories represented an important element in his character. He was happy in his impudence. He reveled in telling stories which are not very far removed from "shaggy dog" stories, and he especially enjoyed farce. He would tell a story about a visit to a graveyard, joking prodigiously, and while still laughing he would suddenly unfold a landscape where the laughter mysteriously changes, becomes frozen, dies on a clap of thunder, but before the story was over he would be laughing again. The great comedians laugh *for the sake of* tragedy, and Chekhov was of their number. How he would have laughed at Charlie Chaplin!

True comedians can usually be recognized by their tragic air, but there was nothing in the least tragic about Chekhov's life until he contracted tuberculosis. Though he raged against his father, and remembered with painful accuracy every whipping he received, his childhood was immensely satisfying. He grew up tall and straight, handsome and popular, with a gift for telling stories to admiring schoolboys and schoolgirls. He enjoyed a succession of love affairs, including one with the wife of a teacher, and he remembered later that these love affairs were all "happy and gay." He was growing quickly, too quickly for his strength. Once he dived into the sea and cut his head on a rock, and the scar remained for the rest of his life. He was fifteen when he caught a chill while bathing, and peritonitis set in. For a few days his life was despaired of. A German doctor who attended him during his convalescence told him about a doctor's life; and from wanting to be a clown he changed direction and determined to be a doctor. A few words from an obscure German doctor changed his whole life.

In the following year his father's business, which had been failing for many years, suddenly collapsed, and the father fled to Moscow to escape a debtors' prison. The two older brothers were already in Moscow before the collapse. Chekhov remained in Taganrog to finish his schooling. He was perfectly cheerful, and perhaps glad to be alone. Earning a pittance from tutoring, he sent every ruble he could spare to Moscow, and with the money went letters full of jokes to keep them amused. He made some extra money by capturing goldfinches and selling them in the market. Soon he was making money by selling short sketches to the newspapers. Long before he left school and enrolled in the faculty of medicine at Moscow University, his writing career had begun.

Most of the early sketches are lost, hidden in obscure news-papers under a baffling array of pseudonyms. He continued to write as a medical student, and he continued to invent more and more pseudonyms depending on his mood at the moment. A teacher in Taganrog had given him the name of Antosha Chekhonte, and this name with its variations (A. Ch-te, Anche, A. Chekhonte) was largely reserved for the stories which gave him the greatest pleasure. He signed lesser stories with sardonic descriptions of himself—Blockhead, A Man Without a Spleen, My Brother's Brother, A Quick-Tempered Man, A Prosaic Poet, A Doctor Without Patients, Ulysses, Starling. About thirty pseudonyms are known, and there are perhaps thirty more which remain to be discovered. He was writing stories nearly every day to pay for his tuition fees and to provide for his family, which soon came to accept him as its perennial benefactor, and since Chekhov was the soul of generosity, he accepted the burden of providing for them with astonishing gaiety.

He matured quickly, and his early full-length stories published in Moscow while he was struggling with the first year of his medical course have the gay, sardonic, impudent, passionately human quality of the stories he wrote in the last years of his life. There is always the sharp cutting edge, like the bright gleam of a plow breaking through the soil. There is always laughter, and the trace of melancholy. He sets his scenes in the cloudy afternoons, or in the evenings when the lights are coming up, or in the dead of night when his characters are warming themselves over a fire. After spending the day in the anatomy laboratory, he would spend his evenings writing about the quiet villages of southern Russia and the country estates where he sometimes spent his holidays during the last years of his schooling. Gaiety and impudence keep creeping in. "The Little Apples," written in 1880, when he was twenty, describes a landlord and a farm bailiff who discover two young peasant lovers stealing apples in an orchard; to punish them the landlord makes the boy flog the girl and the girl flog the boy. The story is not in the least sadistic. Chekhov is amused, and only a little horrified, for the young lovers can do no harm to each other, and the landlord is a grotesque vaudeville character blundering among the windfalls. "St. Peter's Day," written in the following year, is an excursion into the wilder shores of lunacy, with the author bubbling with good humor as he describes a perfectly ridiculous shooting party, where nothing happens as the hunters expect it to happen, and everyone is at odds with everyone else. "Green Scythe," written in 1882, is a more serious matter, for though it deals with the lighthearted escapades of a group of young people staying on the estate of a Georgian princess of impeccable ancestry, Chekhov for the first time created characters in three dimensions: the bullying matriarchal princess, the young and beautiful Olya, and Lieutenant Yegorov are all completely credible, and these characters, or characters very similar to them, will appear again and again in his stories. There is a sense in which "Green Scythe" is the first of his stories of character, and in its background and development it is oddly similar to "The Bride," the story Chekhov was writing in the last year of his life. Once more we see the bullying matriarch and the beautiful daughter and the young suitors vying for her hand, but now the chill of winter has set in, the gardens are fading, and there is very little laughter.

Chekhov put himself into "Green Scythe," and indeed he put himself into most of his stories. He is present in a surprisingly large number of them, perhaps all the more present because he was so determined to be absent. He is the boy in the shop, the keeper of goldfinches, the peasant wandering across the plain, the family doctor, the dying bishop. We see him in his various disguises, and more often than not the disguise is transparent. Very few of the current translations of Chekhov give the stories in their proper order. Once they are printed in the order of development, we become aware of the autobiographical thread running through them. Far from being the neutral observer, Chekhov was a man who portrayed himself endlessly.

But while Chekhov is abundantly present in the stories, so that we can nearly always detect one person who wanders through the story like a representative of the author, taking the author's part, he never insists upon himself. Dostoyevsky and Tolstoy continually portrayed themselves and gave themselves the more important roles. Chekhov gives himself comparatively unimportant roles. Very often he is content to watch, delighting in the people of his invention, his wit blending with his profound sympathy for his fellow men, without rancor and without remorse, hating only obsequiousness and human indignity. Early in 1879 his brother Mikhail wrote a letter which he signed: "Your worthless and insignificant little brother." In cold fury Chekhov replied: "Do you know where you should be conscious of your worthlessness? Before God, if you please, before the human intellect, beauty, and nature, but not before people. Among people one must be conscious of one's human dignity. You are not a swindler, but an honest fellow! Then respect the honest fellow in yourself and remember that no honest man is ever insignificant." So he wrote when he was nineteen, and nine years later he announced his credo to his friend the poet Alexey Pleshchev: "My Holy of Holies are the human body, health, intelligence, inspiration, love, and the most absolute freedom from violence and lying in whatever forms they may manifest themselves." Against human indignity, and against those who would build walls around human freedom, he waged implacable war.

Mostly he waged war with weapons of laughter and mockery, with lighthearted rapier thrusts against the pomposity and silliness of officials. In 1883 he wrote over a hundred short descriptive pieces, most of them satirical, and nearly all of them directed against officialdom. Chekhov was inclined to regard uniforms as badges of servility. He had no patience with the government clerks who were always attempting to catch the eyes of their superiors in order to humble themselves publicly and perhaps receive a promotion if they bowed deeply enough, and in "Death of a Government Clerk" he wrote the classic story of the fawning official in the presence of an exalted and godlike superior. We are not, of course, intended to believe the story. The poor wormlike clerk is no more credible than Gogol's Ivan Yakovlevich, who found the nose of the Collegiate Assessor Kovalyov in a loaf of bread. "Death of a Government Clerk" is a grotesque and glorious parody until we reach the last word of the story, and then quite suddenly, with shattering effect, the life of this obscure clerk, whose one offense was that he sneezed at the wrong time, comes into sharp and final focus. It is a trick which Chekhov uses often. A paragraph, a phrase, a sentence, sometimes only a word, has the effect of raising the story to another plane, one which we had never suspected and could hardly have hoped for. With that word, that paragraph, Chekhov isolates a fragment of experience and casts such a blinding light on it that the rest of the story shines in its light.

Chekhov was a conscious artist from the beginning. It amused him to say that he wrote easily, but the evidence of the surviving manuscripts suggests that he often wrote with extreme care, continually revising and amending, his quick mind working hurriedly to destroy any impression of speed. A few sketches and quips written in 1883 and 1884 when he was taking his final medical examinations seem to have been dashed off in a few minutes, but generally his stories are carefully worked over. "At the Post Office," which has almost nothing to do with a post office, is a devilishly cunning evocation of an entire social landscape in two startling pages. There is not a word too many. Those odd and wonderful creatures attending the funeral feast are outrageously funny in the same way that the government clerk is funny: they are grotesque, but they are also desperately human. These stories written while he was studying at Moscow University are often dismissed as juvenilia, and until recently they were rarely included in collections of his works. But Chekhov was not a writer who developed in a normal tentative fashion. From "The Little Apples" onward we are aware of a constant and steady power, and a mind already formed. The light does not flicker or flare up: it is strong from the beginning.

Yet sometimes it happened that he produced in a single year so many stories of great and undeniable brilliance that he gives the impression of a man tapping unsuspected sources of strength. 1885 was the *annus mirabilis*. In that year he produced at least four masterpieces—"The Huntsman," "The Malefactor," "A Dead Body," and "Sergeant Prishibeyev." "The Huntsman" simply tells the story of a meeting along a forest pathway of a man and the wife he had discarded long ago. The man is sketched in lightly. His shoulders, his red shirt, his patched trousers, the white cap perched jauntily on the back of his head —this is all we are told, but it is enough. The woman is sketched in even more lightly. She is a pale peasant woman of thirty with a sickle in her hand. In a few pages the whole absurd, lamentable history of these people is revealed: the indifference of the husband, the yearning of the wife, the infinite spaces which separate them even when they are standing together. The wife is intoxicated with joy at the sight of her husband. In describing her happiness, Chekhov adds the simple sentence which is like the moment of truth, illuminating all that has gone before and all that comes afterward—*Ashamed of her happiness, she hid her smiles with her hand.* It is with such simple means that he succeeds in conveying a whole character. He gives us no indication of what she looked like, or what she was wearing, or what gestures she made. The color of her eyes and her hair are never mentioned. He is utterly uninterested in all the details of her physical appearance; instead, he is able to suggest the quivering life within her, and her human grandeur. At the end the husband thrusts a crumpled ruble in her hand and wanders down the forest path until his white cap is lost among the green of the trees.

Chekhov uses an astonishing economy of means. It is the same in "The Malefactor," where the peasant Denis Grigoryev is put on trial for stealing nuts from railroad ties to use as sinkers for his fishing lines. Clearly the peasant has endangered the lives of hundreds of people traveling on the trains. Chekhov tells the story without taking sides, amused by the confrontation of the baffled peasant and the armed might of justice, uninterested as always in the political implications of his stories. Gorky relates that a lawyer made a special visit to Chekhov to determine whether Denis Grigoryev was guilty or innocent in the eyes of his creator. The lawyer made a long speech about the necessity of punishing those who damaged state property and asked Chekhov what he would have done to the prisoner if he were the judge.

"I would have acquitted him," Chekhov replied. "I would say to him: 'You, Denis, have not yet ripened into a deliberate criminal. Go—and ripen!' "

In "Sergeant Prishibeyev" Chekhov described once and for all the type of the officious prosecutor. There is no malice in the story. He laughs quietly at the besotted sergeant who is always arresting people for infractions of the rules, but even that inane sergeant is given a human dimension. There is no cracking of the whip, no flicker of hatred. In the end the sergeant became a legend, his name repeated all over Russia whenever an officious policeman or magistrate appeared, for everyone had read the story and recognized the beast when he saw it.

We can very rarely pinpoint the precise origin of a Chekhov story. The incidents which made up the story derived from ancient memories, anecdotes told to him long ago and then forgotten, the face of a girl coming across a room, the way a man stepped out of a carriage on a busy street. Chekhov was perfectly aware that he wrote out of his memories. He said: "I can only write from my memories, and I have never written directly from nature. The subject must first seep through my memory, leaving as in a filter only what is important and typical." We know some of the memories which were later shaped into stories, and it is instructive to observe what he took from them and what he left out.

"A Dead Body," written in the late summer of 1885, clearly

derives from an incident which took place the previous year, when Chekhov had to conduct an autopsy in an open field near the city of Voskresensk. Here is the account he wrote the same day to his friend Nikolay Leikin:

Today I attended a medico-legal autopsy which took place ten versts from V. I drove in a valiant troika with an ancient examining magistrate who could scarcely draw breath and who was almost entirely useless, a sweet little gray-haired man who had been dreaming for twenty-five years of a place on the bench. I conducted the post-mortem in a field with the help of the local district doctor, beneath the green leaves of a young oak tree, beside a country road . . . The dead man was no one the villagers knew by name, and the peasants on whose land the body was found entreated us tearfully, by the Lord God, not to conduct the post-mortem in their village. "The women and children will be too terrified to sleep. . . ." At first the examining magistrate made a wry face, because he was afraid it would rain, but later, realizing that he could make out a rough draft of his report in pencil, and seeing that we were perfectly prepared to cut up the body in the open air, he gave in to the desires of the peasants. A frightened little village, the witnesses, the village constable with his tin badge, the widow roaring away fifty yards from the post-mortem, and two peasants acting as custodians near the corpse. Near these silent custodians a small campfire was dying down. To guard over a corpse day and night until the arrival of the authorities is one of the unpaid duties of peasants. The body, in a red shirt and a pair of new boots, was covered with a sheet. On the sheet was a towel with an icon on top. We asked the policeman for water. There was water all right —a pond not far away, but no one offered us a bucket: we would pollute the water. The peasants tried to get round it; they would steal a bucket from a neighboring village. Where, how, and when they had the time to steal it remained a mystery, but they were terribly proud of their heroic feat and kept smiling to themselves. The post-mortem revealed twenty fractured ribs, emphysema, and a smell of alcohol from the stomach. The death was violent, brought about by suffocation. The chest of the drunken man had been crushed with something heavy, probably by a peasant's knee. The body was covered with abrasions produced by artificial respiration. The local peasants who found the body had applied artificial respiration so energetically for two hours that the future counsel for the defense would be justified in asking the medical expert whether the fracture of the ribs could have been caused by the attempts to revive the dead man. But I don't think the question will ever be asked. There won't be any counsel for the defense and there won't be any accused. The examining magistrate is so decrepit that he would hardly notice a sick bedbug, let alone a murderer. . . .

Such is Chekhov's account in a letter which is evidently written hurriedly, but with total recall and with a purely medical fascination for the details of death. The scene is crowded, and the characters are painted in swiftly. The pond, the village, the oak tree, the policeman with the tin badge and the crowds of villagers, the local doctor and the decrepit examining magistrate, would all, it would seem, find their proper place in any story he wrote about the dead body. But what did Chekhov do? He deliberately threw away all the superficially interesting details, and reduced the scene to its simplest proportions—the dead body and the two guardians. The autopsy took place in daylight; in the story it takes place in the dead of night. The oak tree remains, but the country road becomes a path along the edge of a forest. In fact there was very little mystery about the dead peasant. Deliberately in the story Chekhov creates a mystery—the appalling mystery of a dead body lying abandoned in a field.

By deliberately cutting away the dead wood, by reducing his characters only to the essential, and by creating a mood of profound uneasiness and disquiet, Chekhov prepared the stage for a story which is at once tragic and exceedingly comic. The comedy comes from the invention of a wandering lay brother who blunders upon the corpse and is frightened out of his wits, so frightened indeed that he dare not continue his journey in the dark unless one of the guardians accompanies him. (The lay brother may be a projection of Chekhov himself.) So Chekhov tells a story which seems at first sight to have only a remote connection with the scene he had described in the letter to Leikin, but afterward we come to realize that he has in effect told almost the same story, only now it is stripped to the bone. "The subject must first seep through my memory, leaving as in a filter only what is important and typical."

"A Dead Body" in its final form becomes a wrily amusing fable, but not all Chekhov's stories are amusing. "Heartache" lives up to its title, and "Vanka" is a heart-rending study of a child caught in a trap. Chekhov had a horror of cruelty, a horror closely connected with his conviction that violence and lies were sins against the Holy of Holies. Confronted by cruelty in any form, he would leap to the defense of the victim. The thought of convicts languishing forgotten on the island of Sakhalin tormented him so much that in 1890 he abandoned his medical practice and set off to make a tour of inspection of the prison camps, hoping in this way to call attention to their sufferings. He was thirty years old, but after Tolstoy he was the most famous living Russian writer. Honors had been showered on him. He had won the Pushkin Prize, and everywhere he went he was pointed out as the writer who would endure when most of the others were forgotten. He was already ill with tuberculosis when he went to the Far East, and he may have known he was signing his death warrant.

Chekhov had almost no interest in social problems; he did not go to the Far East to test any social theories, and he kept apart from the radicalism of his age. He had no messianic belief in the healing power of flames or firing squads, and he loathed the thought of a revolution overwhelming Russia. For most of his working life his greatest friend was his publisher, Alexey Suvorin, a former serf who had raised himself by intelligence and business sense to a commanding position in the world of publishing, owning newspapers, magazines, and printing houses. Suvorin had "a devilish literary scent"; he had been the friend and publisher of Dostoyevsky; he knew everybody of importance, and he remained oddly humble. Chekhov liked him as a man in spite of his reactionary sympathies, and went on liking him until they quarreled over the Dreyfus case. Chekhov could not understand why anyone should defend those who cruelly abused Dreyfus, and Suvorin could not understand why Chekhov could be so foolish as to defend a lost cause.

It would seem that all the great Russian writers of the nineteenth century were defending lost causes. The cause which Chekhov defended was perhaps the most precarious of all, for he defended the ordinary humors and frailties of ordinary men. He rarely wrote about exceptional people. His men and women are of the earth, earthy, and usually they desire nothing more than to be left in peace. There are no Fyodor Karamazovs saturated with hate, no Anna Kareninas endlessly communing with their consciences; there are no violent intrigues, almost no dramas. There is life endlessly renewing itself, the bright rings of a tree, and there is the figure of a man walking in majesty down a lonely road.

III

Tolstoy said that Chekhov would have been a better writer if he had not been so good a doctor. Chekhov himself regarded his medical training as the salvation of himself as a writer, for medicine gave him an intimate contact with people he would otherwise never have known. Even when, after his return from the Far East, he settled down on a small country estate at Melikhovo with the surviving members of his family, he was unable to escape from medicine. He built a clinic and attended the peasants from miles around, usually forgetting to charge them any fees. He threw himself into a plan for building more clinics in Moscow. 1891, the year of the great famine, found him traveling in western Europe, but immediately on his return to Russia, when he realized the extent of the suffering in the famine-stricken provinces, he was away again, organizing relief, pouring his time, his money, and his affection on those who were suffering wherever he found them. There was something in him of the dedicated priest. He was continually coughing up blood, continually wracked by hemorrhoids, but he accounted his sufferings a small price to pay for the honor of being a human being shaped in the likeness of God. It was a phrase which was often on his lips, and often encountered in his stories.

He was changing a little. He had grown a full beard, and there was a grayness about his face which sometimes startled his friends. Two heavy vertical lines of worry appeared on his forehead. But the humor shone through, and his eyes crinkled with amusement, and his deep voice, very soft and musical and curiously veiled with hoarseness, would explode in ringing laughter whenever he heard or told a good story. He was as gregarious as ever, inviting hordes of friends to stay with him on the estate, taking part in charades, and playing practical jokes; and then he would be off again, traveling from village to village in a broken-down carriage, curing bodies and healing souls, driving himself so furiously that, as he once complained, he had become a kind of cupboard which was falling apart.

There was gaiety in Chekhov always, but there was also despair—the despair of a man who could no longer conceal from himself the knowledge that he was dying at an absurdly early age. The intensity of his despair was equaled only by the intensity of his gaiety.

Among the surviving fragments of Chekhov's notebooks there are some lines of a play he once contemplated on the life of Solomon. He speaks about the play very briefly in his letters, but whether it was to be a full-length play or simply a monologue is never made clear, and perhaps Chekhov himself never really knew. All we have is the fragment which seems to have been written in his heart's blood on one of those long nights when he suffered from insomnia and gave himself up to despair. He wrote:

SOLOMON (*alone*): Oh how dark life is! No night since the days of my childhood has terrified me so much as this darkness terrifies me in my incomprehensible existence. Dear God, Thou who gavest to my father David the gift of assembling words and music, and the gift of song and of praising Thee on the harp, and of sweet weeping and of compelling tears to arise in strangers' eyes and of smiling upon beauty, why hast Thou given me a soul fatigued unto death and oppressed by interminable hungry thoughts? Like an insect born of the dust, I hide in darkness, in terror and despair, given over to trembling and shivering, and everything I see and hear is an incomprehensible mystery to me. Why this morning? Why did the sun come out from behind a temple and gild the palm tree? Why the beauty of women? Where is the bird hurrying and what is the meaning of its flight if it and its young and the place to which it hastens must like myself turn to dust? Oh, it were better if I had never been born or were a stone to whom God had given neither eyes nor thoughts. In order to tire out my body by nightfall, all day yesterday like a mere workman I carried marble to the Temple, and now the night comes and I cannot sleep. I shall go and lie down. Phaorses tells me that if I imagine a flock of sheep running and refuse to think about anything else, then my thoughts will become confused and I shall sleep sound. I'll do this. (*He goes out.*)

Nowhere else in Chekhov's notebooks is there any passage comparable with this in its fierce elegiac beauty. It is a passage of sustained eloquence, the words ringing like iron on stone, and though the subject is the futility of life on earth, the prose moves with a kind of urgency which is itself a denial of futility. Writing this, Chekhov is like a man hurled back by the horror he has seen, but a moment later he catches his breath and sings a song in honor of the dying world. He is writing about himself, his own vision and his own fears, and he is himself the "mere workman" who wearies himself unendurably by carrying marble to the Temple.

Here and there in Chekhov's notebooks we find equally disturbing fragments. Usually they are short and spare, and seem to have been dashed off at night in the intervals of nightmares. "Perhaps the universe is suspended on the tooth of some monster," he wrote once. On another page he wrote: "Russia is an enormous plain over which wander mischievous men," a statement which is harmless enough until we remember that he also wrote in a letter to a friend: "I am a sort of Potemkin who appears from the depths of devastation." There was savagery in him, and he knew it. He was far from being the gentle ironist. Like Dostoyevsky, he was one of those who believe that man is a mystery which needs to be solved "even if you pass your entire life solving it." "I occupy myself with this mystery because I want to be a man," Dostoyevsky wrote, and there is little doubt that Chekhov occupied himself with the mystery for the same reason.

The "Solomon" fragment stands alone in the notebooks, but that peculiar tone, that ringing elegiac music soaring triumphantly over the chasms of futility, can be heard again in many of his stories. We hear it at the end of "Gusev," where an old soldier dies at sea and his body is tossed overboard with hardly more ceremony than if he were a dead fish, and suddenly Chekhov summons a full orcestra to describe the perfect majesty of sunset as it impassively offers its benediction on the dead soldier. It is a passage very close in feeling and texture to the concluding words of Melville's *Billy Budd*, written in the same year. Such passages are marked by an intensity which betrays the author's deepest feelings, and usually they come at the very end of a story with a sudden flowering into another and more permanent world, into another dispensation of time altogether. When Billy Budd is lifted into the rosy dawn light, he is utterly transformed, and his death is an intimation of immortality: he becomes the accomplice of the serene and beautiful heavens. So it is with the dead soldier in Chekhov's story, as the indifferent heavens gaze down on him.

We know how the story "Gusev" came to him from a wonderful letter he wrote on his return from the Far East:

When we left Hong Kong our steamer began to roll. She was sailing without ballast, and sometimes she had a list of 38°, so that we were afraid she would capsize. I was not seasick, and this discovery came as a pleasant surprise. On the way to Singapore we threw two bodies into the sea. When you watch a dead man, wrapped in sailcloth, flying head over heals into the water, and when you realize that the sea is a couple of miles deep, you are overwhelmed with fear, and for some reason you begin to think that you, yourself, will die and be cast into the sea.

I remember very little about Singapore, for when we passed it I felt sad and was close to weeping. Then we arrived in Ceylon, and Ceylon was Paradise, and here I traveled more than seventy miles by train and had my fill of palm groves and bronze-hued women. When I have children I'll say to them, not without pride: "You sons of dogs, in my day I made love to a dark-eyed Indian girl, and where? In a forest of coconut palms, in moonlight." From Ceylon we sailed for thirteen days and nights without a single stop and grew dazed with boredom. I stand the heat well. The Red Sea is dismal. Looking at Mount Sinai, I was deeply moved.

The Lord's earth is beautiful. Only one thing is not beautiful, and that is us. How little there is in us of justice and humility, and how poorly we understand the meaning of patriotism. A drunken, worn-out, good-for-nothing husband loves his wife and children, but what good is this love? The newspapers tell us we love our great country, but how does this love express itself? Instead of knowledge—immeasurable arrogance and conceit; instead of hard work—laziness and filth. There is no justice, and the conception of honor does not go beyond "the honor of the uniform," a uniform which is too often seen in the prisoners' dock. What is needed is work: everything else can go to the devil. The main thing is to be just, for if we are just all the rest will come of itself.

In this extraordinary letter written to his friend Suvorin, a man whom Lenin later characterized as "the running dog of the Tzar," Chekhov came closer than ever again to defining his ultimate beliefs. His attitude toward life was poetic and practical, as a child is poetic and practical, but at the same time he spoke with a strange authority which came from his vast knowledge of suffering. Sometimes he seems to be talking like those old peasants who sit round the campfires in his stories, but his voice remained young and vibrant to the end.

His last years were spent at Yalta in the white house he built facing the sea. He had mellowed a little, and the stories tended to become longer and slower, as though he took even greater enjoyment in mulling them over, sipping them like wine. Now at last he could afford to write without any sense of being dogged by time. For fifteen years he had been dreaming of writing "The Bishop," and in March 1901 he began writing it, but it was not finished until a year later. It is one of the most autobiographical of his stories, though he liked to say that it came about after he had seen a photograph of a certain Bishop Mikhail Gribanovsky in a bookshop in Yalta. He bought the picture, made a few discreet inquiries about the bishop's life, and sat down to write the story. But in fact the photograph was no more than the catalytic agent. In the portrait of the dying bishop he painted himself.

"The Bishop," "The Lady with the Pet Dog," and "The Bride" were all written in Yalta. There is no falling off of strength: there is the same calm, the same mastery, the same flickering gaiety. But what is especially noticeable is that the language has been stripped bare of ornaments: in those last stories he writes close to the bone.

Once in "Gusev" Chekhov spoke of "the huge bull without eyes," the ultimate horror, the symbol of all that was confused and terrible and final in life. Unlike Dostoyevsky and Tolstoy, he showed no rage, no presumptuousness: he would confront the evil calmly, gaily, refusing to be overwhelmed by it, remembering always that his first task was to celebrate life, celebrating it all the more fervently because so little life remained in him.

Sometimes it amused him to wonder how long his works would last. One day, talking with the writer Ivan Bunin, he said he thought that people might go on reading him for seven years.

"Why seven?" asked Bunin.

"Well, seven and a half," Chekhov replied. "That's not so bad. I've got six years to live. Mind you, don't tell the Odessa reporters about that."

He was dead a few months later, making quips and jokes to the end.

Chekhov made a gross mistake in calculating the extent of his fame. His real fame is only just beginning, and it is likely that he will be read hundreds of years from now, for he was one of those who, in the words of Boris Pasternak, "are like apples plucked green from the trees, ripening of themselves, mellowing gradually and always increasing in meaning and sweetness."

IV

It is perhaps Chekhov's very greatness as a writer which makes him so impossibly difficult to translate. He writes, of course, in the idiom of the nineteenth century with a certain deliberate diffuseness, and with a feeling for the balanced phrase and for rising and falling periods. Dostoyevsky writes in a harsh journalese; he is nearly always the hammer raining down blows on the souls of men and on recalcitrant paragraphs. Chekhov remains the musician, charming his audience, sometimes introducing melodies for no better reason than that it pleases him to listen to the music. He is Mozart to Dostoyevsky's Beethoven, and like Mozart, he is the master of many moods and many instruments.

So one translates him as best one can, knowing that there are no precise equivalents, and that nothing is to be gained by making him speak in the modern manner. His precision is not our precision, and we do him a disservice if we put him into crisp English, for his language is essentially romantic. He will speak of "the sweet May-time," and think nothing of it. He rejoices in the pathetic fallacy, and goes to considerable trouble to make his landscapes reflect the moods of his characters. And since this is as much a part of him as his gaiety and his impudence, we must accept him as he is. To modernize him is to destroy him completely.

The difficulties of translating Chekhov are endless. It is not only that he speaks in the manner of his time; he is continually describing a way of life which has vanished from the earth. The Russians no longer speak as Chekhov spoke. Time after time he describes events which are unthinkable in modern Russia. His peasants fall into colloquialisms which must have been completely intelligible to Russians living at the end of the last century, though they are almost beyond understanding today, with the result that modern texts of Chekhov published in Russia are often provided with explanatory footnotes. More than once I have been baffled by a phrase, and consulted a Russian, only to discover that he was equally baffled. To translate Chekhov adequately, one should have a vast knowledge of church ritual, the social customs of the nineteenth century, the dialects of Moscow and half a dozen other towns in Russia. Ideally, he should be translated by a group of churchmen, sociologists, and experts on dialect, but they would quarrel interminably and the translation would never be done.

Though we can no longer recapture precisely what Chekhov

meant by "the sweet May-time," for too many cruel Aprils have intervened, there is no mystery about his way of looking at the world, or the value he placed on human freedom. The texture of the language changes, but the human heart remains oddly unchangeable, though various. Chekhov celebrated the human variety, and while his peasants and princes have vanished, they are closer to us than we know.

That is why of all Russian writers Chekhov, the archconservative, is the most subversive. He is dynamite for children, for he proclaimed the utmost freedom and gave to the human heart the place of sovereign eminence. His stories are hosannas in praise of freedom, of the wanderings of the human heart in search of its own peace. And so, with the insidious power of genius, he prepares us for the revolutions of the future.

ROBERT PAYNE

А. Чехов

TRANSLATOR'S NOTE

These translations have been
made from the twelve-volume
edition of Chekhov's *Collected
Works*, edited by V. V. Yermi-
lov and published by the Bi-
blioteka Ogonyok (Moscow,
1950).

The Little Apples

BETWEEN the Black Sea and the Solovetsky Islands, at such
and such degrees of latitude and longitude, the landowner Trifon
Semyonovich had been living on his own black earth for a long
time. His surname was as long as a barge pole, and derived from
a very resounding Latin word designating one of the innumerable human virtues. He owned an estate comprising about 8,000
acres of black earth. This estate, being in his full possession, had
been mortgaged and offered for sale. The "For Sale" notices were
put up before he acquired his bald spot, but the estate has never
been sold, thanks to the gullibility of the bank manager and the
skill of Trifon Semyonovich, and so the worst has not befallen
him. One day, of course, the bank will fail, because Trifon
Semyonovich and all those others whose names are legion take
bank loans without paying the interest. Indeed, whenever
Semyonovich did pay a little interest on his loan, he always made
a great ceremony of it, as a man does when he offers a penny for
the repose of the souls of the dead or for the building of a cathedral. If this world were not this world, and if things were called
by their proper names, then Trifon Semyonovich would be called
by another name than Trifon Semyonovich: he would be given a
name usually reserved for horses and cows. Frankly, Trifon
Semyonovich is nothing more than a beast. I am sure he would
agree with me. If he ever hears of this (for he sometimes reads
The Dragonfly), he will probably not burst a blood vessel, for he

3

is a man of considerable intelligence and is likely to be in complete agreement with my thesis, and he might also send me a dozen of his Antonovka apples in the autumn as an act of gratitude for my not revealing his surname, for on this instance I have confined myself to the use of his Christian name and patronymic. I shall not describe all his virtues: it would be very tedious. To describe Trifon Semyonovich in his entirety would demand a volume as thick and heavy as *The Wandering Jew* of Eugène Sue. I shall not mention his cheating at cards, or his politics, which have enabled him to avoid paying his debts and the interest on his mortgage, nor shall I mention the tricks he plays on the old priest and the deacon, or how he rides through the village streets in a costume contemporary with Cain and Abel. I shall confine myself to a single incident characteristic of his attitude towards his fellow creatures, in praise of whom, after three quarters of a century of continuing experience of their affairs, he once composed the following quick-firing couplet:

All fools, clodhoppers, simpletons,
Ruin themselves by playing at dunce.[1]

One perfectly beautiful morning at the end of summer Trifon Semyonovich found himself walking down a long and narrow pathway in his magnificent orchard. Whatever it is that inspires their excellencies the poets was here generously strewn around in great profusion, seeming to say: "Pluck me! Pluck me! Enjoy yourselves, for the autumn will soon come!" But Trifon Semyonovich was not enjoying himself that morning, partly because he was far from being a poet, but also because his soul had suffered a particularly uncomfortable night, as always happened whenever the soul's owner lost heavily at cards. Behind Trifon Semyonovich marched his faithful servant Karpushka, who was about sixty years old and who kept looking suspiciously from

---

[1] An untranslatable pun. *Durachki* ("dunces") is also the name of a card game.

side to side. The virtues of this Karpushka almost surpassed those of Trifon Semyonovich. He had a wonderful talent for shining boots, a still greater talent for hanging unwanted dogs; he stole everything he could lay his hands on, and as a spy he was incomparable. The clerks in the village call him "a bloody dragoon." Hardly a day passes but some peasants or landowning neighbors of Trifon Semyonovich lodge a complaint about the atrocious behavior of Karpushka, but nothing is ever done, for the good reason that Karpushka is irreplaceable. When Trifon Semyonovich goes for a walk, the trusty Karpushka always accompanies him: this way it is safer and more pleasant. Karpushka possesses an inexhaustible treasure of anecdotes of varying vintages, tall stories, quaint sayings, and fairy tales, and he never stops telling them. The flow of his conversation is never dammed, at least until the time comes when he hears something of interest to himself. On this particular morning he was walking behind his master, telling a long story about two schoolboys wearing white caps who had made their way into the orchard with weapons in their hands, and they had implored him, Karpushka, to let them go hunting, and even tried to bribe him with fifty kopecks, but he, knowing his true master, had rejected their proffered bribes with ignominy and contempt, and set the two dogs Chestnut and Gray on them. And having finished this story, he began to paint in bold colors a picture of the revolting behavior of the local medical orderly, but the picture was never finished, for at that moment there came to his ears a suspicious rustling in a nearby clump of apple and pear trees. So he stopped talking, pricked up his ears, and listened intently. And having convinced himself that he recognized the sound and that it had a suspicious origin, he tugged at his master's coat and then hurried off quick as a shot in the direction of the rustling sound. Trifon Semyonovich, anticipating some pleasant excitement, went hurrying after Karpushka with an old man's slow mincing steps.

On the edge of the orchard, under an old spreading apple

tree, stood a peasant girl slowly chewing on an apple, while not far from her a broad-shouldered peasant boy crawled on his hands and knees, picking up windfalls. He tossed the unripe apples into the bushes, but the ripe ones were tenderly presented to his Dulcinea in his broad and dirty hands. Dulcinea showed not the slightest alarm over the condition of her stomach, but kept on chewing the apples with a fierce appetite, while the boy continued to collect them, crawling over the ground, taking no thought for himself, concentrating his entire attention on his Dulcinea, and no one else.

"Take one off a tree," the girl whispered, deliberately provoking him.

"I wouldn't dare."

"What are you frightened of? The bloody dragoon? Most likely he's tippling in the pothouse. . . ."

The boy jumped up, sprang into the air, plucked a single apple from the tree, and handed it to the girl. But like Adam and Eve in ancient days, the boy and girl suffered disastrously with their apple. No sooner had she bitten off a small piece of it, and given this piece to the boy, no sooner had they both tasted the sharp acid flavor of the apple than their faces became contorted and they turned pale . . . not because the apple was sour, but because they had observed the stern features of Trifon Semyonovich and Karpushka's little snout lit with a smile of pure malignance.

"Good day to you, my dears," Trifon Semyonovich said, advancing on them. "So you're enjoying the little apples, eh? I hope I am not disturbing you."

The boy took off his cap and his head hung low. The girl looked down at her apron.

"Well, Gregory, how are you these days?" Trifon Semyonovich went on, addressing himself to the boy. "How are things going, me lad?"

"I only took one," the boy muttered. "I picked it off the ground."

Trifon Semyonovich turned his attention to the girl.

"How are you, my little darling?"

She found herself paying even more passionate attention to her apron.

"Well now, we haven't celebrated your wedding yet, have we?"

"No, sir, we haven't. . . . I swear to God we only took one apple, and that one wasn't . . ."

He turned to the boy.

"Good, good. Fine fellow. Learned how to read yet?"

"No, sir. We only took one apple, sir, and we found it on the ground. . . ."

"You don't know how to read, but you do know how to steal, eh? Well, that's fine! You're not burdened down with the weight of learning. When did you start stealing?"

"I wasn't stealing, sir."

"Then what about your pretty little sweetheart?" Karpushka interrupted his master, and turned to the boy. "Why is she looking so down-in-the-mouth? Is it because you are not showing her enough love?"

"Shut up, Karpushka!" Trifon Semyonovich exclaimed. "Gregory, I want you to tell me a story."

Gregory coughed and gave an odd smile.

"I don't know any stories, sir. I don't need your apples either. When I want apples, I'll go and buy them!"

"It's a great joy to me that you're rich, my boy. But still—I want you to tell me a story. I'll listen, and Karpushka will listen. Your little sweetheart will listen, too. Don't be shy. Be brave. 'Brave is the heart of a thief.' Isn't that true, my dear fellow?"

Trifon Semyonovich let his malicious eyes rest on the boy, who had fallen into the trap. On the boy's forehead sweat was dripping down.

"Sir, sir—" Karpushka interrupted in his unpleasantly thin tenor voice. "Why don't you let him sing a song instead? He's too much of a silly fool to tell us a story!"

7

"Shut up, Karpushka. He has to tell us a story first. Now, my boy, do as you are told!"

"I don't know any stories."

"What do you mean—you don't know any stories! You know how to steal! How does the Eighth Commandment go?"

"Why are you asking me, sir? How should I know! God is my witness, we only took one apple, and we took it off the ground."

"Tell me a story!"

Karpushka began to gather nettles. The boy knew very well why the nettles were being gathered. Like all his tribe, Trifon Semyonovich had beautiful ways of taking the law into his own hands. If he found thieves, he shut them up in a cellar for twenty-four hours, or flogged them with nettles, or sent them away after stripping them stark naked. Is this news for you? There are people with whom such behavior is as stale and commonplace as a farm cart. Gregory gazed at the nettles out of the corner of his eyes, hesitated, coughed a little, and instead of telling a story he began to give vent to completely nonsensical statements. Groaning, sweating, choking, blowing his nose ever so often, he began to make up some sort of tale about the days when the Russian knights cut down the evil ogres and married beautiful maidens. Trifon Semyonovich stood there listening, never taking his eyes from the storyteller.

"That's enough!" he said, when the boy finally lost the thread of his story and uttered driveling nonsense. "You're good at telling tales, but you're better at stealing. And now, my pretty one—" He turned to the girl. "Say the Lord's Prayer."

The pretty one blushed and recited the Lord's Prayer in a muffled voice, scarcely breathing.

"Now recite the Eighth Commandment."

"You think we took a lot of apples, don't you?" the boy said, throwing up his arms in despair. "I'll swear it on the cross, if you don't believe me."

"It's a sad thing, my dears, that you don't know the Eighth Commandment. I'll have to give you a lesson. Did he teach you to steal, my beauty? Why so silent, my little cherub? You have to answer! Speak! Keep your mouth shut—that means you agree. And now, my little beauty, I'll have to ask you to give your sweetheart a beating because he taught you to steal!"

"I won't!" the girl whispered.

"Oh, just beat him a little bit! He's a fool, and has to be taught a lesson! Give him a beating, my dear. You don't want to? Then I'll have to order Karpushka and Matvey to give you a taste of the nettles. . . . You still don't want to?"

"No, I don't!"

"Karpushka, come here!"

At that moment the girl flew headlong at the boy and gave him a box on the ears. The boy smiled stupidly, while tears came to his eyes.

"Wonderful, my dear! Now pull his hair out! Go at it, my darling! You don't want to? Karpushka, come here!"

The girl clutched at her sweetheart's hair.

"Don't stand still! Make it hurt! Pull harder!"

The girl really began to pull at her sweetheart's hair. Karpushka was in ecstasies, bubbling over with good humor and roaring away.

"That's enough now!" Trifon Semyonovich said. "Thank you, my dear, for having given wickedness its due. And now"—he turned to the boy—"you must teach your girl a lesson. She gave it to you, and now you must give it to her!"

"Dear God, how could you think of such a thing? Why must I beat her?"

"Why? Well, she gave you a beating, didn't she? Now beat her! It will do her a lot of good! You don't want to? Well, it won't help you! Karpushka, call for Matvey!"

The boy spat on the ground, hawked, grabbed his sweetheart's hair in his fist, and began to give wickedness its due. As he was punishing her, without realizing it he was carried away, and in his transports of joy he forgot that he was thrashing his sweetheart: he thought he was thrashing Trifon Semyonovich.

The girl was screaming at the top of her voice. He kept on beating her for a long time. I don't know how this story would ever have come to an end if Sashenka, Trifon Semyonovich's charming daughter, had not at that moment popped up from behind the bushes.

"Papa, come and have tea!" she exclaimed, and when she saw what was happening she burst out into peals of laughter.

"That's enough!" said Trifon Semyonovich. "You may go now, my dears. Good-by! I'll send you some little apples for the wedding."

And Trifon Semyonovich bowed low to the offenders.

The boy and the girl recovered their composure and went away. The boy went to the right, the girl to the left, and to this day they have never seen each other. If Sashenka had not suddenly appeared out of the bushes, they would probably have been whipped with the nettles. This is how Trifon Semyonovich amuses himself in his old age. His family is not far behind him. His daughters are in the habit of sewing onions into the caps of visitors "belonging to the lower orders," while drunks belonging to the same category have "Ass" and "Fool" chalked on their backs in enormous letters. His son, Mitya, a retired lieutenant, outdid his own father last winter. With the help of Karpushka he smeared the gates of a former private soldier with tar because the soldier refused to give him a wolf cub, and also because he was thought to have warned his daughters against accepting candy and gingerbread from the hands of the retired lieutenant.

After this, call Trifon Semyonovich—Trifon Semyonovich.

August 1880

St. Peter's Day

~~~~~~~~~~~~~~

CAME the long-awaited morning, the long-dreamed-of day —
Tallyho! — Came June 29 — Came the day when all debts,
dung beetles, delicacies, mothers-in-law, and even young wives
are forgotten — Came the day when you are free to thumb your
nose a dozen times at the village constable, who forbids you to
go hunting!

The stars paled and grew misty. Somewhere voices could be
heard. From the village chimneys poured pungent dark-blue
smoke. To the gray bell tower came the drowsy sexton, tolling
the bell for mass. From the night watchman stretched out beneath a tree came a snore. The finches woke, stirred, flew from
one end of the garden to the other, and filled the air with their
tedious and insufferable chirping. An oriole sang from a thorn
brake. Starlings and hoopoes hurried over the kitchens. The
free morning concert had begun.

Two troikas drove up to the house of the retired Cornet of
the Guards Yegor Yegorich Optemperansky. The tumble-down
steps of his house were picturesquely overgrown with thorn
nettles. A fearful uproar arose, both inside and outside the
house. Every living thing in the neighborhood of Yegor Yegorich
began to walk, rush, and stomp up and down the stairs and
through the barns and stables. They changed one of the shaft
horses. The coachmen's caps flew off; a red lantern of a boil appeared under the nose of the footman who haunted the house-

11

maids; someone called the cooks "carrion," and the names of Satan and his angels were overheard. . . . In five minutes the carriages were loaded with furs, rugs, gun cases, and sacks full of food.

"It's all ready, sir!" Avvakum thundered.

"Well, thank you. Ready, eh?" Yegor Yegorich squeaked in his thin, syrupy voice, while a mob gathered on the house steps.

The first to jump into the carriage was the young doctor, followed by old Kuzma Bolva, a small trader of Archangel, who wore boots without heels, a carrot-colored top hat, and yellow-green spots on his neck. He was carrying a twenty-five-pound double-barreled shotgun. Bolva was a plebeian, but out of respect for his advanced years (he was born at the turn of the century), and because he could shoot down a twenty-kopeck piece in mid-air, the gentry were not overly squeamish about his origins, and they took him out hunting.

"Be so good as to get in, Your Excellency!" said Yegor Yegorich to a small stout gray-haired man, who was wearing his white summer uniform with its glittering buttons, and the Cross of Anna round his neck. "Move over, Doctor!"

The retired general groaned, stood with one foot on the carriage step, while Yegor Yegorich lifted him up. With his stomach the general pushed the doctor over and sat down heavily beside Bolva. Then the general's puppy Idler, and Yegor Yegorich's setter Music Maker, jumped in after him.

"Vanya! Hey, there, young fellow!" the general addressed his nephew, a schoolboy with a long single-barreled shotgun slung over his back. "You can sit here beside me! Come here! That's right! Sit right here! Don't play any tricks, my friend! You might frighten the horse!"

After once more blowing cigarette smoke up the nose of the shaft horse, Vanya jumped into the carriage, pushed Bolva and the general to one side, looked round, and finally sat down. Yegor Yegorich crossed himself and sat down beside the doctor.

On the coachman's box beside Avvakum sat a tall man who taught physics and mathematics at Vanya's school. His name was Mange.

When they had filled the first carriage, they began loading up the second.

"Are we ready?" Yegor Yegorich shouted when, after long arguments and much running around and about, eight more men and three dogs were loaded onto the second carriage.

"Ready!" shouted the guests.

"Shall we start now, Your Excellency? Well, God save our souls! Let's get going, Avvakum!"

The first carriage swayed, lurched, and drove on. The second, which contained the most ardent hunters, swayed, lurched, gave an awful scream, swerved slightly to one side, and then overtook the first and drove to the gate. The hunters were all smiles, clapping their hands in an access of joy. They were in their seventh heaven when . . . Oh, cruel fate!—they had no sooner left the courtyard than a ghastly accident occurred.

"Stop! Wait for me! Halt!" a piercing tenor voice called from somewhere behind.

The hunters looked back, and turned pale. Stumbling after the carriages was the most insufferable man in the world, a brawler and roughneck, as was well known to everyone in the entire province, a certain Mikhey Yegorich Optemperansky, brother of Yegor Yegorich, and a retired naval captain, second class. He waved his hands wildly. The carriage came to a halt.

"Well, what's up?" asked Yegor Yegorich.

Mikhey Yegorich hurled himself at the carriage, climbed the step, and shook his fists at his brother. The hunters were all shouting at once.

"What's going on?" Yegor Yegorich shouted, his face turning crimson.

"What's going on?" shouted Mikhey Yegorich. "I'll tell you what's going on! You're a Judas, a beast, a swine! Yes, a swine, Your Excellency! Why didn't you wake me, you fool? What a

13

scoundrel you are! Why didn't you wake me? Excuse me, gentlemen, I never . . . I only want to teach him a lesson! Why didn't he wake me? Don't you want your brother to come with you? Would I be in the way? You purposely made me drunk yesterday evening, thought I would sleep till noon! Fine fellow you are! Excuse me, Your Excellency . . . I only want to hit him once . . . only once! . . . Excuse me!"

"You mustn't come in!" the general said, spreading out his hands. "Don't you see there is no room? It's really too much!"

"You won't get anywhere by cursing, Mikhey!" Yegor Yegorich said. "I didn't wake you because there's no reason why you should come with us! . . . You don't know how to shoot! So what's the point of coming? You'll only get in the way! You just don't know how to shoot!"

"I don't know how to shoot, eh?" Mikhey Yegorich shouted so loud that Bolva flung his hands up to his ears. "If that's so, then why the devil is the doctor going? He doesn't know how to shoot either! So you think he's a better shot than I am?"

"He's right, gentlemen," said the doctor. "I don't know how to shoot. I don't know how to handle a gun. I can't stand shooting! . . . I don't know why you take me with you. The hell with it! Let him take my place! I'll stay behind. Here's a place for you, Mikhey!"

"Did you hear that? Why should we take him along?"

The doctor rose with the evident intention of climbing out of the carriage. Yegor Yegorich tugged at his coattails and pulled him down.

"Don't tear my coat! It cost thirty rubles! Let go! Really, gentlemen, I must ask you to spare me your conversation today! I'm not in a good mood, and might do something unwise, even something I didn't want to do! Let go, Yegor Yegorich! I'm going home to get some sleep!"

"No, you've got to come with us," Yegor Yegorich said, not letting go of the coat. "You gave me your word you would come!"

"That's right. I gave you my word—you forced it out of me! Why do I have to come?"

"Why?" squeaked Mikhey Yegorich. "Why? Because otherwise you would be left behind with his wife, that's why! He's jealous of you, Doctor! Don't go, dear fellow. Don't go, in spite of him! Lord God, he's jealous, that's what it is!"

Yegor Yegorich turned a thick scarlet and clenched his fists.

"Hey, you!" voices shouted from the other carriage. "Mikhey Yegorich, stop all that fiddle-daddle! Come over here! We've got a place for you!"

Mikhey Yegorich smiled his malicious smile.

"Listen, you swine!" he said. "What's come over you? Didn't you hear them? They've found a place for me, so I'm coming to spite you! I'll get in your way! I give my word I'll get in your way! Devil take you, you won't shoot anything! And don't you come, doctor. Let him crack wide open with his jealousy!"

Yegor Yegorich got up and shook his fists. His eyes were bloodshot.

"You good-for-nothing!" he said, turning to his brother. "You're no brother of mine! Our poor dead mother was right to put a curse on your head! Our poor dead father died before his time, because of all the things you did!"

"Gentlemen," interrupted the general. "I think it can be said we have all had enough! Remember, you are brothers both born from the same mother!"

"He's the brother of an ass, Your Excellency—no brother of mine! Don't come, doctor, don't come!"

"Let's get going!" the general shouted, thumping Avvakum in the back with his fist. "Devil take you all! God knows what it is all about! Come on! Let's go!"

Avvakum lashed out at the horses and the troika drove on. In the second carriage Captain Kardamonov, a writer, took the two dogs on his knees and made room for the explosive Mikhey Yegorich.

"Lucky for him you found room," said Mikhey Yegorich as he

15

settled down in the carriage. "Otherwise I might have . . . Kardamonov, won't you describe that highway robber of yours?"

It happened that the previous year Kardamonov had sent to the magazine *Niva* an article entitled "An Interesting Case of Fertility among the Peasant Population," and receiving a reply which reflected unfavorably on his pride as an author, he complained bitterly to the neighbors, thus earning the reputation of being a writer.

According to the predetermined plan of action, their first stop was to be at the hayfields where the peasants were busy mowing —the fields were about four miles away from Yegor Yegorich's estate—and there they would shoot quail. At the hayfields the hunters stepped out of their carriages and divided into two groups: one group, headed by the general and Yegor Yegorich, turned to the right; the other, with Kardamonov at the head, went off to the left. Bolva remained behind and went off on his own. He liked to hunt in peace, in complete silence. Music Maker ran on ahead, barking, and a minute later he raised a quail. Vanya fired a shot and missed.

"Aimed too high, dammit!" he muttered.

Idler, the puppy, had been taken along "to learn the ropes." For the first time in his life the puppy heard gunfire, set off a howl, and went running back to the carriages with his tail between his legs. Mange aimed at a lark and hit it.

"I enjoy that bird," he said to the doctor, pointing to the lark.

"Go to hell!" the doctor said. "It's no use talking to me! I'm in a bad mood! Leave me alone!"

"You're a skeptic, doctor."

"Eh, what's that? What does skeptic mean?"

Mange thought for a while.

"A skeptic is a man . . . a man who is . . . a person who doesn't love . . ."

"Wrong! Don't use words you don't understand! Leave me alone! I might do something unpleasant, something I don't want to do! I'm in a bad mood! . . ."

Music Maker began pointing. The general and Yegor Yegorich turned pale and held their breaths.

"I'm shooting this one," the general whispered. "I . . . I . . . Excuse me, this is the second time you have . . ."

But nothing came of the dog's pointing. The doctor, with nothing to do, threw a pebble, which struck Music Maker between the ears, and immediately the dog set up a howl and leaped in the air. The general and Yegor Yegorich looked round. They heard a rustling sound in the grass, and a large bustard flew up. The members of the second group were making a lot of noise and pointing at the bustard. The general, Mange, and Vanya fired. Mange missed. Too late! The bustard flew over a mound and vanished in a field of rye.

"I put it to you, doctor, this is no time for a joke!" the general said, turning sharply on the doctor. "Not the right time, is it?"

"What?"

"It's no time for a joke."

"Stupid of you, doctor," Yegor Yegorich observed.

"Well, they shouldn't have brought me along. Who told you to bring me? I don't want to explain anything. I'm in a bad mood today."

Mange killed another lark. Vanya aimed at a young rook, fired, and missed.

"Aimed too high, dammit!" he muttered.

Two shots were heard in quick succession. Bolva, on the other side of the mound, had shot down two quail with his heavy double-barreled shotgun, and he put them in his pocket. Yegor Yegorich aimed at a quail and fired. The quail, wounded, fell in the grass. Yegor Yegorich triumphantly retrieved the quail and presented it to the general.

"In the wing, Your Excellency. Still alive, too."

"True, she's still alive. Ought to have a summary execution!"

Saying this, the general lifted the quail to his lips and bit through her neck with his eyeteeth. Mange killed a third lark. Music Maker began pointing again. The general flung his cap away and took aim. "Take that!" A big quail flew up, but at that moment the good-for-nothing doctor somehow got into the line of fire, being almost directly in front of the muzzle of the shotgun.

"Get out of here!" the general exploded.

The doctor jumped to one side, the general fired, but as it happened the shot was fired too late.

"Young man, that's a bloody awful thing to do!" the general roared.

"What did I do?" the doctor asked.

"You got in my way! Who told you to get in my way? I missed the bird, thanks to you! God knows what's happening, but whatever it is, it's all an unseemly mess!"

"What are you shouting for? Pfui! I'm not afraid of you! I'm not afraid of mere generals, Your Excellency! I'm especially not afraid of retired generals! So please shut your mouth!"

"What an extraordinary fellow he is! Walks around and messes everything up! It's enough to try the patience of an angel."

"Stop shouting, general! If you have to shout at someone, shout at Mange. He's afraid of generals. You can't unnerve a real huntsman! You might as well admit you don't know how to fire a gun!"

"Enough, sir! One word from me, and there's a dozen thrown back in my face!" the general said, and then he turned to Vanya. "Vanya, dear boy, give me my powder horn!"

"What made you ask that soldier of fortune to go hunting with you?" the doctor asked Yegor Yegorich.

"Had to, my dear fellow," replied Yegor Yegorich. "Simply had to take him. I owe him eight thousand. . . . Yes, my dear boy, all those accursed debts of mine . . ."

Yegor Yegorich left the sentence unfinished and waved his hand.

"Is it true you are jealous of me?"

Yegor Yegorich turned away and aimed at a high-flying kite.

"Lost it, you little whippersnapper!" came the rumbling roar of the general. "Lost it, and it cost a hundred rubles! You're a little pig, that's what you are!"

Yegor Yegorich went over to the general and asked what the matter was. It appeared that Vanya had lost the general's cartridge bag. A search was undertaken, and the hunt was broken off. The search lasted an hour and a quarter, and was crowned with success. With the cartridge bag recovered, the hunters sat down for a rest.

The second group of quail hunters was also having its troubles. Within this group Mikhey Yegorich behaved as badly as the doctor, and perhaps worse. He knocked the guns out of their hands, quarreled violently, thrashed the dogs, scattered powder around, and in a word—the devil knows what he wasn't up to! After some unsuccessful shooting at quail Kardamonov and his dogs went after a young kite. They winged it, but were never able to retrieve it. Captain Kardamanov, second class, killed a marmot with a stone.

"Gentlemen, let us dissect the marmot," suggested Nekrichikhvostov,[1] clerk to the marshal of the nobility.

So the hunters sat down in the grass, took out their penknives, and began to dissect the creature.

"I can't find anything in this marmot," Nekrichikhvostov complained when the marmot had been cut to ribbons. "It doesn't have a heart. It has entrails, though. Know what, gentlemen? Let us go on to the marshes. What can we shoot here? Quail isn't game. We ought to be going after woodcock and snipe. Shall we go?"

The hunters rose and wandered lazily in the direction of their carriages. When they were close to the carriages, they fired a volley at the local pigeons and killed one.

"Tallyho! Your Excellency! Yegorich!" shouted the members of the second group when they caught sight of the first group sitting down and resting.

[1] The name means "not-screaming-tail."

The general and Yegor Yegorich looked round. The second group were waving their caps.

"What on earth are you doing that for?" Yegor Yegorich shouted.

"Success! We've killed a bustard! Come quickly!"

The first group simply refused to believe they had killed a bustard and went straight off to the carriages. Once inside the carriages, they decided to leave the quail in peace and agreed to follow an itinerary which would take them three miles farther on —into the marshes.

"I get all burned up when I'm hunting," the general confided to the doctor when the troikas had brought them a mile or so away from the hayfield. "I get all burned up! I wouldn't spare my own father! Please forgive an old man, eh?"

"Hm."

"Sweet old rogue," Yegor Yegorich whispered into the doctor's ear. "He says that because it's the fashion nowadays to marry off your daughter to a doctor. He's a sly excellency, he is! Hee-hee-hee! . . ."

"We're coming to the wide-open spaces," Vanya said.

"So we are. Plenty of 'em."

"What's that?"

"Gentlemen, where is Bolva?" Mange said, wondering where he had gone.

They all stared at one another.

"He must have been in the other troika," Yegor Yegorich suggested, and he began shouting: "Gentlemen, is Bolva with you?"

"No, he's not," Kardamonov shouted back.

The hunters pondered the matter.

"Devil take him," the general decided. "We're not going to turn back for him!"

"Really, we ought to go back, Your Excellency. He's not strong. He'll die without water. He couldn't walk that far."

"He could if he wanted to."

"It would kill the old man. He's ninety years old!"

"Nonsense!"

When they came to the marshes, our hunters pulled long faces. The marshes were crowded with other hunters: it was therefore hardly worth their while to emerge from their carriages. After a little thought they decided to go on a little farther to the state forest.

"What will you shoot there?" the doctor asked.

"Thrushes, orioles, maybe some grouse . . ."

"That's all very well, but what will my poor patients be doing in the meantime? Why did you bring me along, Yegor Yegorich? Why? Why?"

The doctor sighed and scratched the back of his neck. When they came to the first parcel of forest, they got out of their carriages and fell to discussing who should go left, who right.

"Know what, gentlemen?" Nekrichikhvostov suggested. "In view of the law, or should we say the guiding principles, of nature, the game won't leave us in the lurch. Hm. The game won't leave us in the lurch. So I suggest we fortify ourselves before anything else! A nip of wine, and vodka, and caviar, and sturgeon won't do any harm. Right here on the grass! What do you think, doctor? You know best—you're a medical man. Shouldn't we fortify ourselves?"

Nekrichikhvostov's suggestion was accepted. Avvakum and Firs spread out two rugs, and round these were arranged the bottles and sacks full of food. Yegor Yegorich sliced the sausages, cheese, and sturgeon, while Nekrichikhvostov opened the bottles and Mange cut the bread. The hunters licked their lips and lay down on the rugs.

"Come, come, Your Excellency . . . Let us each have a little . . ."

The hunters ate and drank. The doctor immediately poured himself another drink and drank it down. Vanya followed his example.

"I wouldn't be surprised if there were wolves here," Kardamonov announced after a period of deep meditation, throwing a sidelong glance at the forest.

The hunters pondered, discussed the matter at length, and at the end of ten minutes came to the conclusion that one might be quite safe in saying there were no wolves.

"Well, now, shall we have another? Drink up, eh? Yegor Yegorich, what are you staring at?"

They drank another round.

"What are you thinking about, young fellow?" Yegor Yegorich turned to Vanya.

Vanya shook his head.

"When I'm here," said the general, "you can drink, but when I'm not here . . . So let's have a little nip!"

Vanya filled his wineglass and drank it down.

"What about a third round, Your Excellency?"

They drank a third round. The doctor drank his sixth.

"Young fellow!"

Vanya shook his head.

"Drink, Amphiteatrov!" said Mange, patronizingly.

"When I'm here you can drink, but when I am not here . . ."

Vanya drank another glass.

"Why is the sky so blue today?" asked Kardamonov.

The hunters pondered the problem, discussed it, and at the end of a quarter of an hour they came to the conclusion that no one really knew why the sky was so blue.

"A rabbit! A rabbit! . . . Steady there!"

A rabbit appeared on the other side of the mound. The rabbit was being pursued by two mongrels. The hunters jumped to their feet and grabbed their guns, while the rabbit ran past them and vanished into the forest with Music Maker, the two mongrels, and still other dogs hot on its trail. Idler pondered for a moment, threw a suspicious glance at the general, and then hurried after the rabbit.

"It's a big one! We ought to have brought him down, eh? How did he get away?"

"True! But there's a bottle here, and what's to be done with it?

You didn't finish your drink, Your Excellency? Well, well, that's fine!"

So they drank a fourth round. The doctor drank his ninth, quacked loudly, and then he too vanished into the forest. He found a dark shady spot, lay down on the grass, put his coat under his head, and proceeded to make snoring noises. Vanya was fuddled. He drank another glass of wine, and then became wildly excited. He fell on his knees and declaimed twenty verses of Ovid.

The general observed that Latin shared many remarkable similarities with French. Yegor Yegorich agreed, and observed that anyone who wanted to learn French should absolutely know Latin, which was a very similar language. Mange did not agree with Yegor Yegorich. He emphasized that this was not the proper occasion for discourses on languages, since there was a physics and mathematics teacher present, and a goodly number of bottles; and he added that his own gun had cost a fortune when he bought it some time ago, and now you couldn't buy a gun like that for love or money. . . .

"An eighth round, gentlemen?"

"Wouldn't that be a bit too much?"

"Get on with you! Eight too much? It's clear to me you've never done any drinking!"

They drank their eighth round.

"Young fellow!"

Vanya shook his head.

"Drink it down, boy, like a soldier! I see you shoot well. . . ."

"Drink up, Amphiteatrov!" said Mange.

"It's all right when I'm here, but when I'm not here . . . Well, let's have a little drink. . . ."

Vanya put his beer aside and drank another shot of vodka.

"A ninth round, gentlemen? What did you say? I hate the number eight. My father died on the eighth day. . . . I mean Ivan . . . Fyodor . . . Yegor Yegorich! Fill the glasses!"

So they drank a ninth round.

"You might say it is a hot day. . . ."

"So it is, but it's not going to prevent us from drinking a tenth round, is it?"

"But . . ."

"I spit on the heat! Gentlemen, let us show the elements we are not afraid of them. Young fellow! Make us ashamed of ourselves. Put your old uncle to shame! We're not afraid of the heat or the cold!"

Vanya drank down a glass of wine. The hunters shouted "Hurrah!" and followed his example.

"This way we might get sunstroke," the general observed.

"Quite impossible!"

"Impossible! In our climate? Hm . . ."

"Still, cases have been known. My godfather, for example, died of sunstroke. . . ."

"Well, doctor, what do you think? Can a man get sunstroke, eh, in our climate? Eh, doctor?"

There was no response.

"You haven't had to treat any cases, eh? We're discussing sunstroke. Doctor! Where's the doctor?"

"Where the devil is the doctor?"

The hunters looked all round: the doctor had gone.

"Where's the doctor? Faded away? Like wax in the presence of flame! Ha-ha-ha!"

"He's gone to see Yegor's wife," Mikhey Yegorich said maliciously.

Yegor Yegorich turned pale and let the bottle fall to the ground.

"Yes, gone to see his wife," Mikhey Yegorich went on, nibbling on some sturgeon.

"Why do you have to tell lies?" Mange asked. "Did you see him go?"

"Of course I saw him! A peasant went by in a cart, and he jumped on and drove away. I swear to God! Shall we have an eleventh round now, gentlemen?"

Yegor Yegorich jumped up and shook his fists.

"That's right," Mikhey Yegorich went on. "I asked him where he was going. 'I'm going after strawberries,' he said, 'and to sweeten the horns of a cuckold. I planted 'em, and now I'm going to sweeten 'em.' And then he said: 'Good-by, Mikhey Yegorich, dear boy. Give my love to Yegor Yegorich!' and then he winked at me. Well, here's to your health, hee-hee-hee!"

"Horses!" shouted Yegor Yegorich, and he ran staggering in the direction of the carriage.

"Hurry, or you'll be too late!" Mikhey Yegorich shouted after him.

Yegor Yegorich dragged Avvakum onto the box, jumped in the carriage, and drove home, shaking his fists at the other hunters.

"What's the meaning of this, gentlemen?" the general asked when Yegor Yegorich's white cap had vanished out of sight. "He's gone, devil take it, but how am I to get home? He went off in my carriage. Not in mine, of course, but in the one I'm supposed to go home in. Strange behavior! Ill-mannered of him!"

Vanya felt ill. Vodka and beer conspired to act as an emetic. They had to take him home. After the fifteenth round, they decided to let the general have the troika, but only on condition that as soon as he reached his home he would send fresh horses immediately to take them back.

The general began his good-bys.

"You can tell him from me, gentlemen," the general said, "that only swine behave like that!"

"You should protest his bill of exchange, Your Excellency," Mikhey Yegorich suggested.

"What's that? Bill of exchange? Why, yes, he shouldn't take advantage of my kindness, should he? I've waited and waited, and now I'm tired of waiting. Tell him I'm going to pro— Good-by, gentlemen! Come and visit me. Yes, he's a swine all right!"

The hunters bade farewell to the general and put him in the carriage alongside the sick Vanya.

"Let's go!"

And the general and Vanya drove away.

After the eighteenth round of drinks the hunters went into the forest and spent some time shooting at a target before lying down and going to sleep. Towards evening the general's horses came. Firs handed Mikhey Yegorich a letter addressed to "that brother of mine." The letter contained a demand which would result in legal proceedings if not promptly carried out. After the third round of drinks (when they woke up, they started a new count), the general's coachmen put them into the carriages and took them home.

When Yegor Yegorich at last reached his own house, he was met by Idler and Music Maker, whose rabbit hunt had only been a pretext for going home. Yegor Yegorich threw a threatening look at his wife, and started to search the house. He searched every storeroom, cupboard, closet, and wardrobe: he never found the doctor. But he did find the choirmaster Fortunov hiding under his wife's bed.

It was already dark when the doctor awoke. For a while he wandered about the forest, and then, remembering that he had been out hunting, he cursed and began shouting for help. Of course, his cries remained unanswered, and he decided to make the journey back on foot. It was a good road, safe, and quite visible. He covered the sixteen miles in under four hours, and by morning he reached the district hospital. He gave a tongue-lashing to the orderlies, the patients, and the midwife, and then he began to compose an immensely long letter to Yegor Yegorich. In this letter he demanded "explanations for your unseemly conduct," said some injurious things about jealous husbands, and swore on oath that he would never go hunting again—not even on the twenty-ninth of June.

June 1881

Green Scythe

A SHORT NOVEL

CHAPTER 1

ON the shores of the Black Sea, in a small village which my diary and the diaries of my heroes and heroines call Green Scythe, there is a most charming villa. Architects and those who have a fondness for fashionable and rigorous styles would perhaps derive little pleasure from it, but your poet or artist would find it delightful. For myself, I particularly admire its unobtrusive beauty, which never overwhelms the pleasant surroundings, and I like, too, the absence of cold, intimidating marble and pretentious columns. It has warmth, intimacy, a romantic charm. With its towers, spires, battlements, and flagpoles, it can be seen looming behind a curtain of graceful silver poplars, and somehow it suggests the Middle Ages. When I gaze upon it, I am reminded of sentimental German novels full of knights and castles and doctors of philosophy and mysterious countesses. This villa is on a mountain; around the villa are rich gardens, pathways, little fountains, greenhouses. At the foot of the mountain lies the austere blue sea. Moist coquettish winds hover in the air, every conceivable bird utters its songs, the sky is eternally clear, and the sea translucent—a ravishing place!

The owner of the villa, Maria Yegorovna Mikshadze, the widow of a Georgian or perhaps Circassian princeling, was about fifty. She was tall and well fleshed, and no doubt had once been a beauty. She was well-disposed, good-tempered, and hospitable, but altogether too strict. Perhaps "strict" is not the word; let us say she was capricious. She always gave us the best food and fine wines, she lent us money with openhanded generosity, and she was a dreadful torment to us. She had two hobbyhorses: one was etiquette, the other was being the wife of a prince. Driven by these hobbyhorses, she had a mania for carrying things too far. For example, she never permitted herself to smile, perhaps thinking a smile would be out of place on her face, or on the face of any *grande dame*. Anyone younger than she, even if he was only younger by a single year, was regarded as a whippersnapper. She held that nobility was a virtue in comparison with which everything else was sheer poppycock. She hated frivolity and lightheadedness, she honored those who kept their mouths shut, and so on. Sometimes, indeed, she could be quite insupportable. Had it not been for her daughter, probably none of us would be cherishing our memories of Green Scythe. The old lady was well-disposed to us, but she threw a dark shadow over our lives. Her daughter Olya was the pride and joy of Green Scythe. She was small and well formed, a pretty nineteen-year-old blonde, quite lively and not at all stupid. She knew how to draw, she was a student of botany, spoke excellent French and poor German, read a great deal, and danced like Terpsichore herself. She had studied music at the conservatory, and played the piano passably well. We men loved the little blue-eyed girl, but we were not in love with her. She was dear and precious to us, and Green Scythe would have been unbearable without her. This charming creature stood out against a charming landscape—I am myself little enamored of landscapes without human figures in them. The whisper of the waves and the rustling of the leaves were pretty enough in themselves, but when Olya sang soprano to a piano accompaniment and our own basses and tenors, then the sea and the garden became an earthly Paradise. We loved the little princess, for it was impossible not to love her. We called her the daughter of our regiment. And Olya in turn loved us, gravitating towards us, her male companions, feeling in her natural element only when she was with us. Our little band consisted of house guests, summer visitors, and some of the neighbors. Among the house guests were Doctor Yakovkin, the journalist Mukhin from Odessa, Fiveysky the former physics instructor, now a professor, three students, the artist Chekhov, a Kharkov baron who practiced law, and myself. (I had been Olya's tutor—I taught her to speak bad German and how to catch goldfinches.)

Every May we descended upon Green Scythe, taking over all the spare rooms and wings of the medieval castle for the entire summer. Every March we received two letters inviting us to stay at the house—one letter was stern and pompous, full of reprimands: this one came from the Princess. The other one was very long and gay and full of madcap projects: this came from her daughter, who found time hanging heavy on her hands in our absence. So we would come and stay until September. Then there were the neighbors who joined us every day. Among them were the retired lieutenant of artillery Yegorov, a young man who had twice taken the entrance examination for the Military Academy and had twice failed, a personable and cultivated fellow; and then Korobov, the medical student, and his wife Ekaterina Ivanovna; also Aleutov, a landowner; also a considerable number of landowners, some active, some retired, some gay, some dull, some good-for-nothings, some dregs from the vat. All summer long, all day and all night, these people drank and ate and played and sang and set off fireworks and quips. Olya was passionately fond of them. She shouted happily and whirled around and made more noise than any of us. She was the heart and soul of the company.

Every evening the Princess summoned us to her drawing room, and purple with anger, she would scold us for our "unconscionable behavior," putting us to shame, as she declared that she had a splitting headache and it was all our fault. She loved to reprimand us. Her reprimands were utterly sincere, and she deeply believed that they were delivered for our benefit. She was harder on Olya than on anyone else. It was the Princess's belief that Olya was the most deserving of punishment. Olya was afraid of her mother. She idolized her, and would stand quite still, silent and blushing, while her mother lectured her. The Princess regarded Olya as a child. She even made her stand in a corner and go without lunch and dinner. Interceding for Olya would only have poured oil on the flames. If it had been possible, the Princess would have put us in the corner, too. She made us attend vespers, commanded us to read the Lives of the Martyrs, counted each article of our laundry, and interfered in all our affairs. We were always being sent to fetch and carry for her, and we were always losing her scissors, smelling salts, and thimbles.

"Clumsy fool!" she would say. "You made me drop it when you came blundering along, and now you won't even pick it up! Pick it up! Pick it up this moment! God sent you to punish me! You are in the way!"

Sometimes we would commit small crimes for fun. Inevitably we would be brought before the old lady for an interrogation.

"So it is you who stepped on my flower bed?" the judge would say. "How dare you? . . ."

"It was only an accident. . . ."

"Shut up! I am asking you how you could dare to step on my flower bed!"

Such trials always ended with a free pardon, the kissing of the Princess's hands, and the withdrawal of the culprit to the sound of Homeric laughter from behind the door. The Princess never spoiled us: she reserved her kinder words for old ladies and little children.

I never saw her smile. There was an old general who came over to play piquet with her on Sundays, who was once the recipient of her whispered confidence that every one of us—all these doctors, professors, artists, writers, and baronial lawyers—would have come to a bad end if it had not been for her good of-

fices. We did not try to make her change her mind. Let her
think as she pleased! We would have tolerated the Princess
more if she had not made us get up no later than eight o'clock in
the morning and go to bed no later than midnight. Poor Olya
had to go to bed at eleven o'clock. Useless to contradict her. But
we derived a good deal of fun from her illegal attempts to en-
croach upon our freedom! The whole crowd of us would go up to
her and beg her pardon, or we would address complimentary
verses to her in the style of Lomonosov, and we would draw up
the genealogical tree of the Mikshadze princes, and so on. The
Princess would accept all these offerings as pure gold, while we
roared with laughter. She loved us, and there was nothing in the
least insincere about her deep-throated sighing over the fact that
we were not princes. She grew accustomed to us, as one grows
accustomed to children.

The only one of us she did not love was Lieutenant Yegorov.
She cordially disliked him, and nourished an unwavering an-
tipathy toward him. She only let him come to Green Scythe because they had some financial dealings together, and for reasons
of etiquette. There was a time when the lieutenant had been her
favorite. He spoke rarely, was handsome and witty, and was
"army": the Princess held the Army in high regard. Sometimes
Yegorov behaved strangely. He would sit down, prop his head in
his hands, and start saying the most awful things. He would say
them about anyone and anything, sparing neither the living
nor the dead. The Princess would be beside herself, and whenever he said these awful things she would send us all packing
from the room.

One day at lunch Yegorov propped his head in his hands and
for no reason at all he embarked on a speech about Caucasian
princes, and then he pulled a copy of *The Dragonfly* from his
pocket, and in the presence of the Princess he had the effrontery
to read the following passage: "Tiflis is a grand city. Among
the merits of this beautiful city, where the 'princes' are street-
sweepers and hotel bootblacks, must be included . . ." The

Princess rose from the table and left the room in silence. Her hatred for him was all the more inopportune and unfortunate because the lieutenant dreamed of marrying Olya, and Olya herself was in love with him. The lieutenant dreamed furiously, but had little hope that his dreams would come true. Olya loved him secretly, stealthily, imperceptibly, keeping her love to herself. It was contraband love, on which a cruel veto had been placed. She was not permitted to love.

CHAPTER 2

This medieval castle was very nearly the scene of the most absurd medieval drama.

It happened that seven years before, when Prince Mikshadze was still living, his boon companion Prince Chaikhidzev came to stay at Green Scythe. He was a landowner from Ekaterinovslav, and very rich. His whole life had been spent in dissipations of the most abominable kind, but he had somehow retained his fortune, and indeed he retained it to the end of his life. Prince Mikshadze was his drinking companion. Together they had once abducted a girl from her home, and the girl later became Chaikhidzev's wife. For this reason the princes found themselves bound together with indissoluble ties of friendship. Chaikhidzev visited Green Scythe with his son, a bug-eyed, dark-haired boy still at school. For old times' sake the princes set about drinking, while the boy flirted with Olya, who was then thirteen. The flirtation did not pass unnoticed. The parents winked at it and concluded that Olya and the boy were not unsuitably matched. The princes, quite drunk, ordered the children to kiss each other, and then the princes themselves shook hands and kissed each other. Mikshadze wept with emotion. "It's God's will," said Chaikhidzev. "You have a daughter, I have a son! It's God's will!"

The children were each given rings and were photographed together. The photograph hung in the salon, and was long a source of particular irritation to Yegorov, who made it the target for countless barbed remarks. Princess Maria Yegorovna herself had solemnly blessed the betrothed. Their fathers' idea pleased her, but only because she was bored. A month after the departure of the Chaikhidzevs, Olya received a most impressive present through the mail, while equally impressive presents arrived each year thereafter. The young Chaikhidzev treated the matter more seriously than anyone expected. He was a rather shallow-brained young man. He used to come to Green Scythe every year, staying for a whole week, during which time he never uttered a word, but remained in his room writing love letters to Olya, who read these letters with a feeling of embarrassment. She was intelligent, and it puzzled her that a big boy should write such stupidities, for in fact he wrote nothing but stupidities. Then two years ago Prince Mikshadze died. As he lay on his deathbed, he told Olya: "Be careful! I don't want you marrying some fool! Marry Chaikhidzev—he's an intelligent fellow, and worthy of you!" Olya knew all about Chaikhidzev's intelligence, but she did not contradict her father. She gave her word that she would marry Chaikhidzev.

"It's what Papa wanted," she would tell us, saying this with a certain pride, as though performing a heroic act. She was pleased that her vow had accompanied her father to the grave. It was such an unusual, romantic vow.

But nature and good judgment claimed their own. The retired Lieutenant Yegorov was constantly before her eyes, while with each passing year Chaikhidzev became, in her eyes, sillier and sillier.

Once when the lieutenant boldly hinted of his love, she begged him never to speak about it again, reminded him of the promise given to her father, and she spent the whole night weeping.

Every week the Princess wrote a letter to Chaikhidzev in Moscow, where he was studying at the university. She commanded him to complete his studies as quickly as possible. "Some of my guests," she wrote, "have not such thick beards as you have, but they earned their diplomas long ago." Chaikhidzev replied most respectfully on rose-tinted note paper, explaining the impossibility of acquiring a diploma without studying for the required length of time. Olya, too, wrote to him. Her letters to me were far more interesting than the ones she wrote to her fiancé. The Princess firmly believed that Olya intended to marry Chaikhidzev, for otherwise she would not have allowed her daughter to run around and "fiddle-daddle" with swashbucklers, madcaps, atheists, and "non-princes." On this subject there could hardly be any doubt. Her husband's wishes were sacred to her. And Olya, too, believed the time would come when she would sign herself with the Chaikhidzev name.

But it did not happen in that way. The plan formed by the two fathers failed just at the moment when it was about to reach fruition. Chaikhidzev's romance miscarried. It was destined to end in pure farce.

Last year Chaikhidzev arrived at Green Scythe towards the end of June. This time he was no longer a student, but a graduate. The Princess welcomed him with a solemn and majestic embrace followed by a long lecture. Olya wore an expensive dress bought specially for this meeting with her fiancé. Champagne was ordered from the city, fireworks were set off, and on the following morning all Green Scythe was buzzing with rumors of the wedding, believed to be set for the end of July. "Poor Olya!" we murmured as we wandered aimlessly about the house, sometimes staring angrily at the windows of the room overlooking the garden, which was occupied by this detestable man from the East. "Poor Olya!" A pale, thin, only half-alive Olya was walking in the garden. "Papa and Mama wanted me to," she said, when we started to offer friendly advice. "But it's absurd! It's idiotic!" we shouted at her. She shrugged her shoulders and turned her sad little face away, while her fiancé remained in his room, sending her tender love letters by way of the footman. He would look out of the windows and see us and grow alarmed by the liberties we took with Olya. He never left his room except to eat. He ate in silence, looked at no one, and answered all questions curtly. Only once did he so far forget himself as to tell an anecdote—a hoary one, and the stupidest imaginable. After dinner the Princess would make him sit beside her. She taught him piquet, which he played with an air of gravity and concentration, his lower lip jutting out, sweat pricking up on his skin. His attitude towards piquet pleased the Princess.

One evening after dinner Chaikhidzev suddenly abandoned the game of piquet and went running after Olya, who was wandering alone in the garden.

"Olya Andreyevna!" he began. "I know you don't love me! Our betrothal is really quite strange and stupid. But I . . . I hope you will come to love me. . . ."

Having uttered these words with great confusion, he made his way sideways out of the garden and went back to his own room.

All this time Lieutenant Yegorov remained on his estate and never once showed himself. He simply could not bear the sight of Chaikhidzev.

One Sunday—the second Sunday after the arrival of Chaikhidzev, which must have been July 5—a student, a nephew of the Princess, came to our wing early in the morning, and gave us our orders. These orders from the Princess were to the effect that we had to prepare for the evening: dark suits, black ties, gloves; show ourselves serious, clever, intelligent, obedient, our hair curled like a poodle's; we must make no noise, and we must tidy up our rooms. Apparently there was to be some sort of engagement ceremony at Green Scythe. Wine, vodka, and *hors d'oeuvres* had been ordered from the city. Our own servants were being commandeered to help in the kitchen. Guests began to arrive after dinner, and they kept on arriving until late in the evening. At eight o'clock, after a boat ride, the ball began.

Before the ball we men had a small meeting. At this meeting we unanimously resolved that Olya must be saved from Chaikhidzev at all costs, even at the cost of a fearful scandal. The meeting over, I went in search of Lieutenant Yegorov. His estate was about fifteen miles away. I found him at home, but in what a condition! He was drunk, and dead to the world. I shook him, washed him, dressed him, and in spite of his profanity and wild kicking I dragged him back to Green Scythe.

At ten o'clock the ball was in full swing. They were dancing in four rooms to the music of two fine pianos. During the entr'actes a third piano played on a little hill in the garden. Even Olya went into ecstasies over our fireworks. We set them off in the garden, along the shore, and from boats far out to sea. From the castle roof we fired a succession of many-colored Bengal rockets, lighting up all the village of Green Scythe. At two buffets heavy drinking was going on. One buffet was set up in the summer house in the garden; the other was inside the house. Quite clearly Chaikhidzev was the hero of the evening. Squeezed into a tight frock coat, with red spots on his cheeks and sweat running down his nose, a painful smile on his lips, acutely aware of his awkwardness, he was dancing with Olya. All the time he kept watching his feet. He had a terrible desire to shine in some way, but there was no way for him to shine. Olya told me later she felt very sorry for the poor princeling that evening. He was so pathetic, and he seemed to have a presentiment that he was about to lose his fiancée—that fiancée of whom he had dreamed while listening to lectures at the university, who was in his thoughts when he fell asleep and when he awoke. Whenever he caught sight of us, there was a pleading look in his eyes. He sensed we were strong and merciless rivals.

When the long-stemmed glasses were set out, and the Princess could be seen looking at the clock, we knew that the great and solemn moment was about to arrive: in all probability Chaikhidzev would be permitted to embrace Olya at midnight. We had to act fast. At half past eleven I rubbed powder into my face to make myself look pale, pulled my tie to one side, mussed up my hair, assumed a troubled expression, and went up to Olya.

"Olya Andreyevna!" I said, taking her by the hand. "For God's sake! . . ."

"What is it?"

"Oh, for God's sake! . . . But you mustn't be frightened, Olya Andreyevna! . . . It had to be! We should have known it would happen!"

"What happened?"

"Promise not to be frightened. For God's sake, my dear. . . . Lieutenant Yegorov is . . ."

"Yes? . . ."

Olya turned pale and gazed at me with wide-open, trustful, and friendly eyes.

"Yegorov is dying. . . ."

Olya staggered and drew her fingers across her pale brows.

"The thing I dreaded has come to pass," I went on. "He is dying! Save him, Olya Andreyevna!"

Olya took me by the hand.

"He is . . . Where is he?"

"He's in the garden, in the summer house. It's terrible, my dear. . . . But people are looking at us. Let's go to the terrace. He doesn't blame you. He knows that you have . . ."

"How is he?"

"Very poorly."

"Let me go to him! I don't want him to think that I've . . . that I've done anything . . ."

We went out on the terrace. Olya's knees were shaking. I pretended to wipe away a tear. Members of our group kept running past us on the terrace, looking pale and alarmed, fear and anxiety written all over their faces.

"The bleeding has stopped," the physics professor murmured, just loud enough for Olya to hear.

"Let's hurry!" Olya whispered, taking my hand.

We hurried down the terrace steps. The night was silent, very bright. The music of the piano, the whispering of the dark trees, the rustling of cicadas, caressed our ears. From below came the gentle splashing of the sea.

Olya could scarcely walk. Her legs failed her, entangled in the heavy skirt. Trembling with fear, she leaned against my shoulder.

"It's not really my fault," she whispered. "I swear it's not my fault! It's what Papa wanted. He should understand that. Is something terrible going to happen?"

"I don't know. Mikhail Pavlovich has done everything possible. He's a good doctor, and loves Yegorov. We're nearly there, Olya Andreyevna. . . ."

"I . . . I couldn't face seeing it. . . . I'm frightened. . . . Really I couldn't look. . . . Why did he have to do a thing like that?"

Olya burst into tears.

We had come to the summer house.

"Here it is!" I said.

Olya closed her eyes and threw both arms round me.

"I can't . . ."

"Don't be frightened. Yegorov, you're not dead yet, are you?" I shouted in the direction of the summer house.

"Not yet? . . . Why?"

At the gate of the summer house the lieutenant appeared, brilliant in the moonlight. He was pale from his drinking bout, his waistcoat was unbuttoned, and his hair disheveled.

"Why?" he repeated.

Olya lifted her head and saw Yegorov. She looked at me, and then at him, and then at me again. I laughed, and her face lit up. She stepped forward, a cry of joy on her lips. I thought she would be angry with us, but it was not in her to be angry. She made another step forward, thought for a moment, and then threw herself on Yegorov, who had quickly buttoned up his waistcoat and opened wide his arms. Olya fell against his chest. Yegorov broke out into peals of laughter, but he turned his head to one side so as not to breathe on her, and he murmured all kinds of wonderful nonsense.

"You shouldn't have done it. . . . It's not my fault, though," Olya stammered. "It was what Papa and Mama wanted. . . ."

I turned round and strode back to the brilliantly lit castle.

There, in the castle, the guests were making preparations for congratulating the betrothed pair. They kept glancing impatiently at the clock. In the hallway the waiters were carrying trays and jostling one another: there were bottles and glasses on the trays. Chaikhidzev was impatiently squeezing his right hand with his left, and his eyes were searching for Olya. The Princess was wandering through all the rooms of the castle, looking for Olya, bent on giving her instructions—she should know how to conduct herself towards her mother, and so on, and so on. And we laughed.

"Have you seen Olya?" the Princess asked me.

"No."

"Then go and find her."

I went out into the garden and twice circled the castle, my hands behind my back. Our artist blew a note on a trumpet. It was the signal that meant: "Hold her! Don't let her escape!" From the summer house Yegorov answered with an owl's cry, which meant: "All's well! Am holding her!"

I wandered around for a little while and then returned to the house. In the hallway the waiters had put their trays down on the tables and stood empty-handed, staring dully at the guests. The guests themselves were gazing at the clock with perplexed looks on their faces. The pianos were silent. A dull and brooding silence reigned oppressively in all the rooms.

"Where's Olya?" the Princess asked me. She was purple.

"I don't know. She is not in the garden."

The Princess shrugged her shoulders.

"Doesn't she realize she is long overdue?" she asked, pulling at my sleeve.

I shrugged my shoulders. The Princess moved away and whispered something to Chaikhidzev, who also shook his shoulders. The Princess pulled at his sleeve.

"Complete idiot!" she muttered, and went running through all the rooms.

The maids and some schoolboys who were related to Olya ran noisily down the steps and went searching for the vanished fiancée in the depths of the garden. I, too, went into the garden. I was afraid Yegorov would not be able to keep Olya much longer: and our carefully contrived plot would come to nothing. I went straight to the summer house. My fears were unfounded. Olya was sitting beside Yegorov, gesticulating with her little hands, whispering, whispering. . . . Whenever Olya stopped whispering, Yegorov would begin murmuring. She was explaining her "ideas," as the Princess would call them. He sweetened each word with a kiss. When he spoke to her, not a moment passed without a kiss, and somehow he succeeded in holding his mouth sideways so that she would not smell his vodka-laden breath. They were both completely happy, oblivious of the world, and of time passing. For a moment I stood rejoicing at the gate of the summer house, and then, having no desire to disturb them, I returned to the castle.

The Princess was almost out of her wits, inhaling her smelling salts. She was full of wild conjectures, but before Chaikhidzev and the assembled guests she felt angry and ashamed. She was a woman who had never had recourse to violence, but when a maidservant came to tell her there was no sign of Olya, she slapped the maidservant on the face. The guests, weary of waiting for the champagne and the congratulations, exchanged smiles and the latest gossip, and began dancing again.

The clock struck one, and still no sign of Olya. The Princess was close to madness.

"This is one of your tricks," she hissed, passing by one of our group. "She'll hear about this! Where is she?"

Finally she found a benefactor who revealed Olya's hiding place. This benefactor was her nephew, a small potbellied schoolboy, who came running out of the garden like someone possessed, hurled himself at the Princess, jumped on her lap, pulled her head down, and whispered into her ear. The Princess turned pale and bit her lip so hard that she drew blood.

"In the summer house?" she asked.

"Yes."

The Princess rose, and with a grimace which somehow resembled the smile of officialdom, she informed the guests that Olya was suffering from a headache and had begged to be excused, et cetera, et cetera. The guests expressed their regrets, quickly finished supper, and began leaving.

At two o'clock—Yegorov had excelled himself by keeping Olya all this time—I was standing at the entrance to the terrace behind some oleanders, waiting for Olya's return. I wanted to see how her face would express at one and the same time her love for Yegorov and her fear of the Princess; and which was stronger, her love or her fear. For a little while longer I breathed the scent of the oleanders. Then Olya appeared, and I feasted my eyes on her face. She walked slowly, holding up her skirt a little, revealing her tiny slippers. Her face was brilliantly clear in the light of the moon and of the lanterns hanging on the trees, the glow of the lanterns somehow spoiling the pure radiance of the moon. Her face was solemn, very pale, with the ghost of a smile playing around her lips. She was gazing thoughtfully on the ground with the expression of one pondering a particularly difficult problem. When Olya climbed the first step I saw that her eyes were troubled, darting restlessly to and fro, as she remembered her mother. For a moment her hand went up to her disheveled hair, and then for a while she stood on that first step undecided. At last, with a toss of her head, she marched bravely to the door. And then I saw an extraordinary thing. The door was flung open suddenly, and Olya's white face was lit with a fierce light. She shuddered, stepped back, and her knees trembled under her. *On the threshold, head held high, stood the Princess, scarlet-faced, quivering with shame and rage. For two whole minutes there was silence.*

"So the daughter of a Prince and the betrothed of a Prince goes to see a mere lieutenant!" she began. "A man with a common name like Yegorov! What an abominable creature you are!"

Olya was completely annihilated. She was shivering feverishly as she made a serpentine glide past the Princess and flew to her own room. All night long she sat on her bed and stared at the window with terror-stricken eyes.

At three o'clock that morning we had another meeting. At this meeting we had a good laugh at Yegorov, drunk with happiness, and we appointed our baronial lawyer from Kharkov as an ambassador to Chaikhidzev. The prince was still awake. The baronial lawyer from Kharkov was to explain "in the most friendly fashion" the delicacy of Chaikhidzev's position, and to beg his pardon for our interference in his affairs, all this, of course, "in the most friendly fashion," as one intelligent man speaks to another. Chaikhidzev informed the baron that "he understood perfectly," that he attached no importance to the paternal vows, but he was in love with Olya and that was why he had been so persistent. . . . With deep feeling he shook hands with the baron and promised to retire from the scene the next day.

The next morning Olya appeared at the breakfast table looking wan, annihilated, terribly apprehensive, fearful and ashamed. But her face lit up when she saw us in the dining room and heard our voices. The whole group of us stood before the Princess, shouting. We shouted in unison. We had removed our masks, our very small masks, and we loudly insinuated into the mind of the old Princess certain "ideas," which were the same as those Yegorov had been insinuating into the ears of

Olya the previous evening. We spoke of the "personality" of women, and of their right to choose freely their own husbands, and so on, and so on. The Princess listened in gloomy silence, and then she read out a letter which had been sent to her by Lieutenant Yegorov—in fact, the letter had been written by the entire group and abounded in phrases like "being of immature years," "owing to inexperience," "by your favor," et cetera. The Princess heard us to the end, read Yegorov's letter to the end, and said:

"How dare you young whippersnappers teach an old woman like me! I know exactly what I am doing! Finish your tea, and then get out of here, and turn someone else's head for a change! You are not the proper people to live with an old woman! You're all so clever, and I'm only a fool! So good day, my dears! I'll be grateful to you to the end of my days!"

The Princess threw us out of the house. We all wrote her a bread-and-butter letter, kissed her hand, and that same day we regretfully moved on to Yegorov's estate. Chaikhidzev left the castle at the same time. At Yegorov's we embarked on a course of dissipation; we missed Olya, and we consoled Yegorov. In this way two weeks passed. Then, during the third week, our baronial lawyer received a letter from the Princess asking him to come to Green Scythe to draw up some legal documents. The baron left us, and two or three days later we followed, pretending to come and fetch him. We arrived just before dinner. We did not go into the house, but wandered around the garden, gazing up at the windows. The Princess saw us from a window.

"So you're here?" she shouted at us.

"Yes, we're here!"

"What brought you here?"

"We've come for the baron."

"The baron hasn't any time to fool around with gallows birds like you! He's writing!"

We removed our hats and approached the window.

"How do you do, Princess," I said.

"Well, what are you gadding about for?" the Princess replied. "Go back to your rooms!"

So we went to our rooms and sat down humbly in our chairs. Our humble airs must have gratified the Princess, who had grown terribly bored without us. She made us stay for lunch. There, at lunch, when one of us dropped a spoon, she castigated him for being a clumsy fool, and she excoriated us all for our lack of table manners. We went for a walk with Olya and stayed the night there. The following night we were still at Green Scythe, and indeed we remained there until September. Peace had been declared.

Yesterday I received a letter from Yegorov. The lieutenant wrote that he had spent the winter "buttering up" the Princess, and he had finally succeeded in taming her anger and resentment. She has promised to let them marry in the summer.

Soon I shall receive two letters—one will be stern and official, from the Princess; the other will be a long one from Olya, full of gaiety and madcap schemes. In May I shall be going back to Green Scythe again.

1882

Joy

IT WAS twelve o'clock at night when a young man called Mitya Kuldarov, disheveled and blazing with excitement, burst into his parents' apartment and ran wildly through all the rooms. His mother and father were already in bed. His sister, too, was in bed, finishing the last pages of a novel. His younger brothers, the schoolboys, were fast asleep.

"What happened?" his parents asked, surprised out of their wits. "What on earth is the matter?"

"Oh, don't ask me! I never thought it would happen! Never expected it! It's . . . it's absolutely beyond belief!"

Mitya exploded with laughter and fell into a chair, because so much joy had weakened his legs.

"It's beyond belief!" he went on. "You simply couldn't imagine it! Just look!"

His sister jumped out of bed and, pulling a blanket round her shoulders, went in to see her brother. The schoolboy brothers also woke up.

"What on earth is the matter with you? You look as though you had gone completely out of your mind!"

"It's because I am so happy, Mama. Today, all over Russia, people know me! Everyone! Until today you were the only ones who knew such a person as Dmitry Kuldarov, collegiate registrar, existed. Now everyone knows! Oh, Mama! Oh, Lord!"

Mitya jumped up and once more ran through all the rooms, and then he fell into a chair.

"Well, tell us what happened! Please get some sense into your head!"

"You—you live like wild animals! You don't read the newspapers, and popular fame has no meaning for you! Very remarkable things are recorded in newspapers! Whenever anything important happens, everyone knows about it: nothing is left out. I'm so happy. Oh, Lord! You know newspapers only print things about celebrities! Well, they've printed something about me!"

"How? Where?"

Papa turned pale. Mama glanced at the icon, and crossed herself. The brothers jumped out of bed and ran to their elder brother as they were, in their attenuated nightshirts.

"Yes, indeed! They have printed something about me! Now all of Russia knows about me! Mama, please keep this number as a souvenir! You can look at it from time to time. Just look!"

Mitya pulled a newspaper from his pocket and handed it to his father. He pointed to a place marked with a blue pencil. "Read that!"

His father put on his spectacles.

"Go on! Read it!"

Mama gazed at the icon and crossed herself. Papa cleared his throat and began to read:

"December 29, at eleven o'clock in the evening, the collegiate registrar Dmitry Kuldarov . . ."

"See? See? Go on!"

". . . the collegiate registrar Dmitry Kuldarov, coming out of the tavern situated at the Kozikhin house on Little Armorer Street, being in an intoxicated condition . . ."

"That's right! I was with Semyon Petrovich. . . . It's absolutely correct! Go on! Read the next line! Listen, all of you!"

". . . being in an intoxicated condition, slipped and fell under a horse belonging to the cabman Ivan Drotov, a peasant from the village of Durikina in the Yuknovsky district. The terrified horse jumped over Kuldarov, dragging the sleigh after it: in which sleigh sat Stepan Lukov, merchant in the Second Guild of Moscow Merchants. The horse galloped down the street until brought to a halt by house porters. Kuldarov, after being unconscious for some moments, was removed to a police station for examination by the appropriate medical officers. A blow sustained by him at the back of the neck . . ."

"That was from the shaft, Papa. Go on! Read further down!"

". . . A blow sustained by him at the back of the neck was pronounced to be slight. The victim was given medical assistance."

"They put bandages soaked in cold water round my neck. Read it! There you are! All of Russia knows about it! Give me the newspaper!"

Mitya took the newspaper, folded it, and slipped it into his pocket.

"I'll have to run to the Makarovs and show it to them. . . . And then the Ivanitskys. Natalia Ivanovna and Anisim Vasilich must see it, too. . . . I must run now! Good-by!"

Then Mitya crammed the cap with the cockade on his head, and ran joyously, triumphantly, down the street.

January 1883

The Ninny

JUST a few days ago I invited Yulia Vassilyevna, the governess of my children, to come to my study. I wanted to settle my account with her.

"Sit down, Yulia Vassilyevna," I said to her. "Let's get our accounts settled. I'm sure you need some money, but you kept standing on ceremony and never ask for it. Let me see. We agreed to give you thirty rubles a month, didn't we?"

"Forty."

"No, thirty. I made a note of it. I always pay the governess thirty. Now, let me see. You have been with us for two months?"

"Two months and five days."

"Two months exactly. I made a note of it. So you have sixty rubles coming to you. Subtract nine Sundays. You know you don't tutor Kolya on Sundays, you just go out for a walk. And then the three holidays . . ."

Yulia Vassilyevna blushed and picked at the trimmings of her dress, but said not a word.

"Three holidays. So we take off twelve rubles. Kolya was sick for four days—those days you didn't look after him. You looked after Vanya, only Vanya. Then there were the three days you had toothache, when my wife gave you permission to stay away from the children after dinner. Twelve and seven makes nineteen. Subtract. . . . That leaves . . . hm . . . forty-one rubles. Correct?"

Yulia Vassilyevna's left eye reddened and filled with tears. Her chin trembled. She began to cough nervously, blew her nose, and said nothing.

"Then around New Year's Day you broke a cup and saucer. Subtract two rubles. The cup cost more than that—it was a heirloom, but we won't bother about that. We're the ones who pay. Another matter. Due to your carelessness Kolya climbed a tree and tore his coat. Subtract ten. Also, due to your carelessness the chambermaid ran off with Varya's boots. You ought to have kept your eyes open. You get a good salary. So we dock off five more. . . . On the tenth of January you took ten rubles from me."

"I didn't," Yulia Vassilyevna whispered.

"But I made a note of it."

"Well, yes—perhaps . . ."

"From forty-one we take twenty-seven. That leaves fourteen."

Her eyes filled with tears, and her thin, pretty little nose was shining with perspiration. Poor little child!

"I only took money once," she said in a trembling voice. "I took three rubles from your wife . . . never anything more."

"Did you now? You see, I never made a note of it. Take three from fourteen. That leaves eleven. Here's your money, my dear. Three, three, three . . . one and one. Take it, my dear."

I gave her the eleven rubles. With trembling fingers she took them and slipped them into her pocket.

"*Merci*," she whispered.

I jumped up, and began pacing up and down the room. I was in a furious temper.

"Why did you say '*merci*'?" I asked.

"For the money."

"Dammit, don't you realize I've been cheating you? I steal your money, and all you can say is '*merci*'!"

"In my other places they gave me nothing."

"They gave you nothing! Well, no wonder! I was playing a trick on you—a dirty trick. . . . I'll give you your eighty rubles, they are all here in an envelope made out for you. Is it possible for anyone to be such a nitwit? Why didn't you protest? Why did you keep your mouth shut? Is it possible that there is anyone in this world who is so spineless? Why are you such a ninny?"

She gave me a bitter little smile. On her face I read the words: "Yes, it is possible."

I apologized for having played this cruel trick on her, and to her great surprise gave her the eighty rubles. And then she said *"merci"* again several times, always timidly, and went out. I gazed after her, thinking how very easy it is in this world to be strong.

February 1883

The Highest Heights

The Height of Credulity

A FEW days ago K., a man of considerable local importance, rich and well connected, shot himself in the town of T. The bullet entered his mouth and lodged in his brain.

In the poor man's side pocket a letter was found, with the following contents:

"I read in the Almanac today there will be a bad harvest this year. For me a bad harvest can only mean bankruptcy. Having no desire to fall victim to dishonor, I have decided to put an end to my life in advance. It is my desire, accordingly, that no one should be held responsible for my death."

The Height of Absent-mindedness

We have received from authentic sources the following distressing item from a local clinic:

"The well-known surgeon M., while amputating both legs of a railway switchman, absent-mindedly cut off one of his own legs, together with one of the legs of his assistant. Both are now receiving medical care."

51

The Height of Citizenship

"I, the son of a former honorary citizen, being a reader of *The Citizen*,[1] wearing the clothes of a citizen, contracted a civil marriage with my Anyuta. . . ."[2]

The Height of Conformity

We are informed that a certain T., one of the contributors to *Kievlyanin*,[3] having read the greater portion of the Moscow newspapers, suffered an attack of self-doubt and searched his own home for illegal literature. Finding none, he nevertheless gave himself up to the police.

April 1883

[1] *The Citizen* was a conservative St. Petersburg newspaper, owned by Prince Meshchersky and edited for a while by Dostoyevsky. Chekhov loathed *The Citizen* and pilloried it on many occasions.

[2] This is a joke. There were no civil marriages in Russia before 1917.

[3] A conservative newspaper published in Kiev.

Death of a Government Clerk

ON a beautiful night the no less beautiful government clerk
Ivan Dmitrich Chervyakov [1] sat in the second row of the stalls
watching *Les Cloches de Corneville* through opera glasses. He
was gazing at the stage and thinking himself the most blessed
among mortals when suddenly . . . (Very often in stories you
come upon this word "suddenly," and this is all very proper,
since authors must always concern themselves with the un-
expectedness of life.) Suddenly, then, his face puckered up,
he rolled his eyes, his breathing stopped, the opera glasses fell
from his eyes, he collapsed into his seat, and . . . *at-choo!* As
the reader has observed, he sneezed.

There are, of course, no laws promulgated against sneezing.
It is done by peasants, police inspectors, even by privy council-
ors. Everyone sneezes. Chervyakov was not in the least embarrassed. He wiped his nose with a handkerchief, and like any
well-behaved man, he looked round to see whether he had in-
convenienced anyone. He was acutely embarrassed when he saw,
sitting in the front row of the stalls just in front of him, an old
man who was carefully wiping his bald head and neck with a
pair of gloves and muttering something under his breath. The
old man, as Chervyakov recognized, was General Brizzhalov, a
very high official in the Ministry of Communications.

"I splashed him!" thought Chervyakov. "He's not my boss,

[1] Chervyak means "worm."

but still—it's devilishly awkward! I shall have to apologize."

Chervyakov coughed, leaned forward, and whispered in the general's ear: "I'm afraid, Your Excellency, I sneezed . . . quite unintentionally. . . ."

"Don't mention it."

"Forgive me, for God's sake. I really didn't intend . . ."

"Sit down and keep quiet! Let me listen!"

Chervyakov was embarrassed. He smiled stupidly, and began to turn his attention to the stage. Watching the actors, he no longer felt he was the most blessed among mortals. He was suffering torments of anxiety. During the entr'acte he sought out Brizzhalov, hovered around him for a while, and at last, gaining courage, he murmured: "Excellency, I sneezed over you. Forgive me. I didn't . . . I really haven't . . ."

"Oh, this is too much!" the general exploded, his lower lip twitching with impatience. "I'd forgotten all about it."

"He's forgotten all about it, but there's a mean look in his eyes," Chervyakov thought, glancing suspiciously in the general's direction. "He refuses to talk to me. I'll have to explain I had absolutely no intention of . . . Why, it's a law of nature! . . . He may even think I spat on him deliberately. Maybe not now, but later that's what he'll think."

As soon as he got home, Chervyakov told his wife about this unfortunate happening. It occurred to him that his wife took the news with altogether too much levity. There was a moment when she seemed alarmed, but when she understood that Brizzhalov belonged "to another bureau," she regained her composure.

"Still, I think you should go and apologize," she said. "Otherwise he may think you don't know how to behave in public."

"That's just it! I've already apologized, but he behaved so strangely. . . . His words didn't make sense. He gave me no time to explain. . . ."

The next day Chervyakov put on his new frock coat, had a haircut, and went to offer his excuses to Brizzhalov. He found

the general's reception room full of petitioners, the general himself standing there and listening to the petitions. He listened to
quite a few of them before he raised his eyes and recognized
Chervyakov.

"Yesterday, Your Excellency . . . if you remember . . .
at the Arcadia Theater . . . I sneezed, sir . . . and quite ac-
cidently splashed a little . . ."

"Balderdash!" snapped the general. "God knows what's going
to happen next! What can I do for you?" he went on, addressing
the next petitioner.

"He won't talk to me," Chervyakov thought, turning pale.
"He's furious with me. I can't possibly leave it like that. I'll
have to explain to him . . ."

When the general had finished talking with the last of the
petitioners and was turning to enter his private apartments,
Chervyakov hurried after him, muttering: "Your Excellency,
may I presume to trouble you for a moment . . . feelings dic-
tated, you might say, by a deep regret . . . not intentionally
. . . extremely sorry . . ."

The general looked as though he were about to break out in
tears, and waved him away.

"You're making fun of me, my dear sir!" the general said,
before shutting the door in his face.

"So I am making fun of him, am I?" Chervyakov thought.
"It's not a laughing matter! He's a general, and knows nothing.
Well, I won't bother to apologize any more to that brazen old
fool! Devil take him! I'll write him a letter, and never set eyes
on him again. God in heaven, I'll never trouble him again."

So Chervyakov thought as he made his way home. But he did
not write a letter to the general. He thought and thought, but
he could never put the words in the right order. On the following
day he again visited the general to offer his excuses.

"Yesterday I ventured to trouble Your Excellency," he murmured, as soon as the general turned a questioning glance in
his direction. "I assure Your Excellency I never intended to

make fun of you. I've come to apologize for sneezing, for splashing a little . . . Making fun of Your Excellency was the last thing on my mind. I wouldn't dare to—I really wouldn't. If we made fun of people, I ask you, what would happen to respect for the individual?"

"Get out of here!" the general roared, livid and shaking with rage.

"What were you saying, sir?" Chervyakov whispered.

"Get out!" the general repeated, and he stamped his foot.

In the living body of Chervyakov something snapped. He neither heard nor saw anything as he backed towards the door, went out into the street, and shuffled slowly away. Mechanically he put one foot before the other, reached his home, and without taking off his frock coat he lay down on the divan and died.

July 1883

At the Post Office

A FEW days ago we attended the funeral of the beautiful young wife of our postmaster, Sladkopertsov. According to traditions handed down from our forefathers, the burial was followed by the "commemoration," which took place at the post office.

While the pancakes were being offered round, the old widower was weeping bitterly.

"Those pancakes are just as pink as my poor darling," he said. "So beautiful she was. Indeed she was . . ."

"Well, that's true enough," we all chanted in unison. "She really was beautiful—no doubt about it."

"True, true. Everyone was amazed when they saw her. Oh, but, gentlemen, I did not love her for her beauty or her gentle disposition alone. It's natural for women to have these qualities, and many times one finds them in this world below. I loved her for another quality entirely. The truth is I loved my poor darling—may God grant her to enter the Kingdom of Heaven— because in spite of her playfulness and *joie de vivre* she was always faithful to her husband. She was faithful to me though she was only twenty, and I shall soon be past sixty. She was faithful to her old man!"

The deacon, who was sharing our meal, expressed his disbelief by means of an eloquent, bellowlike cough.

"Why, don't you believe me?" The widower turned in his direction.

"It's not that I don't believe you," the deacon said in some confusion. "But you know . . . young wives nowadays . . . what is it called? . . . rendezvous . . . *sauce proven-çale* . . ."

"Then you don't believe me! Well, I'll prove it! I kept her faithful to me by means of certain strategical efforts on my part—you might call them fortifications. Because of what I did, and because I am a very cunning man, it was absolutely impossible for my wife to be unfaithful to me. I employed craft to protect my marriage bed. I know some magic words. I have only to say these words, and—*basta!*—I can sleep in peace as far as unfaithfulness goes."

"What were the words?"

"Very simple. I spread a terrible rumor round the town. I am sure you know the rumor. I told everyone: 'My wife Alyona is sleeping with Ivan Alexeyevich Zalikhvatsky, the Chief of Police.' These words were enough. Not a single man dared to make love to Alyona for fear of the wrath of the Chief of Police. And if anyone so much as caught a glimpse of her, he would soon be running away for dear life, for fear of what Zalikhvatsky might think of him. Hee-hee-hee. Try having anything to do with that whiskered pisspot! You'll get no satisfaction from him! He'll write out five official reports about your sanitation, and if he so much as saw your cat wandering about in the street, he would write a report which would make it look as though a herd of cattle were wandering abroad."

"So your wife didn't live with Ivan Alexeyevich?" we said in amazement, the truth slowly dawning on us.

"No, of course not! That was where I was clever! Hee-hee. I played the fool with you, eh? Clever, wasn't I?"

Three minutes passed in silence. We sat and said not a word, and we felt insulted and ashamed for having been so successfully cheated by that fat, red-nosed old man.

"May God grant you to marry again," the deacon said.

October 1883

Surgery

IN the zemstvo hospital the patients were received by the medical orderly Kuryatin in the absence of the doctor, who had gone away to get married. Kuryatin, a stout man, about forty, was wearing a shabby pongee jacket and frayed woolen trousers, and his expression was one of amiability and devotion to duty. Between the index and middle finger of his left hand, there was a terrible-smelling cigar.

The sexton Vonmiglasov [1] entered the waiting room. He was an old man, tall and thickset, and wore a cinnamon-colored cassock with a wide leather belt. He had a cataract in his right eye, and there was a wart on his nose which from a distance resembled a large fly. For about a second the sexton searched for an icon, and not finding one, he crossed himself in front of a bottle of carbolic acid, and then removed the communion bread from his red handkerchief and with a deep bow laid it before the medical orderly.

"Ah-ha . . . Well, how are you?" the orderly yawned. "What brings you here, eh?"

"May the Lord be upon you, Sergey Kuzmich. I've come because I have need of you. Verily hath the Psalmist said: 'Thou givest them tears to drink in good measure.' The other day I sat down to drink tea with my old woman, and dear God, not a drop, not a swallow could I take, though I lay me down and die. . . . Not even for one little sip did I have the strength!

[1] Vonmiglasov means "Listen-to-my-voice."

59

And not just the tooth alone, but the whole side of the face. And how it aches! How it aches! Excuse me, it goes right into my ear, as though a nail or something like that was being driven in! Such pain, I could die! I have sinned and transgressed against the law of God. . . . Such sins have I committed, my soul is like unto ice, and all the days of my life have been passed in slothfulness. It's because of my sins, Sergey Kuzmich, because of my sins! The priest rebuked me after the liturgy: 'You are tongue-tied, Yefim,' he said. 'You warble through your nose. You sing, and no one can understand a word you utter!' Tell me, please, how can I sing, how can I open my mouth which is all swollen, and not having had any sleep last night? . . ."

"M'yes . . . Sit down. . . . Open your mouth!"

Vonmiglasov sat down and opened his mouth.

Kuryatin knit his brows, peered into the mouth, found among all those teeth yellowed by age and tobacco one which was ornamented with a yawning cavity.

"Father deacon recommended an application of vodka and horse-radish, but it didn't help. Glyceria Anasimovna, God grant her health, gave me a little thread from Mount Athos to wear and recommended rinsing the tooth in warm milk, and I must confess I wore the little thread, but as for the milk there was a difference of opinion—I'm a God-fearing man, and I keep the fast. . . ."

"Such superstition," said the orderly, and there was a considerable pause. "We'll have to pull it out, Yefim Mikheich."

"You know best, Sergey Kuzmich. You are properly trained, and you understand what has to be done: whether to pull it out, or use drops, or something else. . . . You are my benefactor, and this is your situation in life, and so God grant you health, so that day and night, until we drop into our graves, we should pray for you, our father. . . ."

"A mere bagatelle," said the orderly modestly, going to a cupboard and rummaging among the instruments. "Surgery is a mere nothing. . . . The important thing is a steady hand. . . . Quick as you can spit! . . . A few days ago the landowner Alexander Ivanich Yegipetsky came to the clinic, just like you . . . also about a tooth. . . . He's a cultivated man, asks all kinds of questions, goes into everything, is concerned with the how and the what. He shook me by the hand and addressed me in the proper manner. . . . He lived in Petersburg for seven years and went around with all the professors. . . . I spent a long time with him. . . . He said: 'For God's sake, pull it out for me, Sergey Kuzmich!' Well, why not? It can be pulled. Only you have to understand this business, and nothing happens without this understanding and knowledge. There are all kinds of teeth. Some are pulled with pincers, some with forceps, and others with monkey wrenches. . . . To each according . . ."

The orderly took up the pincers, looked at them for a moment dubiously, then put them down and took up the forceps.

"Now, open your mouth wide!" he said, advancing on the sexton with the forceps. "We'll get rid of him . . . quick as you can spit! We'll have to cut underneath the gum a bit . . . to acquire leverage on the vertical axis." He cut under the gum. "That will be all."

"You are our benefactor. As for us, we are fools and poor idiots, while the Lord has enlightened you . . ."

"Don't start a conversation just because you have your mouth open. . . . We'll pull this one easily, it's not like those which are all roots. . . . This one will be quick as you can spit. . . ." Here he put down the forceps. "Don't tremble! Keep still! In the twinkling of an eye. . . ." Here he acquired leverage. "The important thing is a very strong grip"—here he pulled at the tooth—"in order not to break the crown."

"Our Fathers . . . Blessed Mother! . . . Oh-oh-oh!"

"Don't do that! What's come over you? Don't hold my hands!" Here he pulled again. "Coming now—now! I suppose you think it is easy?"

"Fathers! Blessed saints!" the sexton screamed. "Angels in heaven! Oh-oh! Pull! Pull! Why do you have to take five years to pull a tooth?"

"You must understand . . . surgery is required. . . . Can't be done quickly! . . . Now, now—"

The sexton jerked his knees up to his elbows, his fingers twitched, his eyes bulged, his breath came in spasms. Perspiration broke out on his purple face, and tears filled his eyes. Kuryatin made loud breathing noises, wavered in front of the sexton, and pulled. There passed an agonizing half minute— and the forceps slipped off the tooth. The sexton jumped off the chair, and his fingers flew to his mouth. And feeling around in his mouth, he discovered that the tooth was in the same place.

"So you really pulled it!" he exclaimed, and his voice was complaining and at the same time full of derision. "Let's hope they pull you like that in the world to come! Our most humble thanks! If you don't know how to pull a tooth, then you shouldn't try! I can't see anything . . ."

"You shouldn't have grabbed me!" the orderly said angrily. "I was pulling, and at the same time you were pushing me away and saying stupid things! You're a fool!"

"You're a fool yourself!"

"I suppose you think, peasant, that it is an easy thing to pull a tooth? Well, it's not like going up in the bell tower and ringing bells!" Here he teased the sexton. " 'You don't know how to do it!' So an expert has come on the scene? Who is the expert? You? When I pulled for Mr. Yegipetsky—Alexander Ivanich Yegipetsky—he didn't utter a single word. . . . He's a better man than you are . . . didn't grab hold of me. . . . Sit down! Sit down, I'm telling you!"

"I can't see anything. . . . Let me catch my breath. . . . Oh!" The sexton sat down. "Don't take a long time, get it out quick! Just get it out—pull it right out!"

"Teaching the teacher, eh? Oh Lord, how ignorant can you get? Live with people like that, and you're fit for the madhouse!

Open your mouth!" At this point he inserted the forceps. "Surgery is no joke, brother. . . . It's not like reading the Scriptures from the pulpit." Here he acquired leverage. "Don't jerk your head back. . . . That tooth has been neglected for a long time and has deep roots. . . ." Here he pulled. "Don't tremble so much! . . . There . . . there. . . . Don't move. . . . Now—" A crunching sound was heard. "I knew it!"

For a brief moment Vonmiglasov sat motionless, as though all feeling had gone from him. He was stunned. . . . His eyes gazed blankly into space, and his face became pale and covered with sweat.

"Perhaps I should have used the pincers," the orderly murmured. "What a horrible mess!"

Coming to himself, the sexton explored his mouth with his fingers, and in the place of the diseased tooth he found two sharp stumps.

"You rotten devil!" he exploded. "You Satan, sent on earth to destroy us!"

"Curse as much as you like!" the orderly murmured, putting the forceps back in the cupboard. "Poor little innocent lamb! They should have given you more strokes of the birch rod in the seminary! . . . Mr. Yegipetsky—Alexander Ivanich Yegipetsky—spent seven years in Petersburg . . . a cultured man . . . he didn't mind spending a hundred rubles on a suit of clothes . . . and he didn't swear. . . . What a little peacock you are! Nothing to worry about! You won't die!"

The sexton took up the communion bread from the table, and holding his hand to his cheek, he went on his way.

August 1884

In the Cemetery

> *Where be your gibes now?*
> *your gambols? your songs? your*
> *flashes of merriment?*
>
> HAMLET

"GENTLEMEN, the wind is rising, and it is growing dark. Wouldn't it be better all round if we left now?"

The wind was playing among the yellow leaves of the ancient birch trees, and from the leaves heavy raindrops came showering down on us. One of us slipped in the mud, and to prevent himself from falling he grabbed at a large gray cross.

"Titular Councilor and Chevalier Yegor Gryaznorukov,"[1] he read. "I knew that gentleman. . . . He loved his wife, wore the order of St. Stanislas, and never read a single word. . . . His stomach punctually digested his food. . . . Why is he dead? It would appear he had no reason to die, but—alas!—fate watched over him. The poor fellow fell a victim to curiosity. He happened to be listening behind a door when the door opened, and he received a blow on the head which caused a shock to his brain (he had a brain), and so he died. The man who lies beneath this monument abhorred verses and epigrams from the cradle, and so the monument is derisively dotted all over with verses. . . . Well, someone is coming!"

A man wearing a worn coat, and with a shaved bluish-purple face, came up to where we were standing. There was a bottle

[1] Gryaznorukov means "muddy hands."

under his arm and a sausage in its wrappings was sticking out of his pocket.

"Where is the tomb of the actor Mushkin?" he asked hoarsely.

We led him in the direction of Mushkin's tomb. The actor died two years ago.

"Are you a government official?" we asked him.

"No, gentlemen, I am an actor. Nowadays it is hard to distinguish actors from ecclesiastical functionaries, as you rightly observed. Quite characteristic, of course, though not altogether flattering to the functionaries."

We had some difficulty finding the tomb of the actor Mushkin. It had collapsed, weeds grew over it, and it no longer resembled a tomb. The little cheap cross, falling to pieces, coated with green moss and blackened by frost, gazed at us with an old man's despondent look, and seemed to be ill.

We read: ". . . forgettable friend Mushkin." Time had destroyed the "un," and corrected the human lie.

"Some actors and journalists collected money to buy him a monument, but the dear fellows drank it all up," the actor sighed, making a low bow, falling to his knees and bending so that his hat touched the damp earth.

"What do you mean—they drank it all up?"

"Very simple. They collected the money, put an announcement in the newspapers, and drank it all up. I'm not standing in judgment over them, but that's how it was. . . . Angels, to your health! Here's to your health, and eternal remembrance!"

"As for that, drinking is bad for the health, and eternal remembrance—there's grief for you! God gives us temporary memories. Who wants an eternal accounting?"

"True, true! Mushkin was a celebrated man. A dozen wreaths followed his coffin, and already he is forgotten! Those he favored have forgotten him, and those who were ill served by him remember him. Myself, I shall never, never forget him, because I never received anything but harm from him. I have no love for the dead man."

"What harm did he do you?"

"A great deal of harm," sighed the actor, and an expression of bitterness and outrage spread over his face. "He was a man who sinned against me, a great malefactor, God have mercy on him! Looking at him and listening to him, I became an actor. His art enticed me from my parental home, seduced me with vain artifices, promised much, and left me in tears, sorrowing. An actor's lot is a bitter one. I lost my youth, I lost sobriety, I lost the divine image. Without a penny in my pocket, down at heels, wearing trousers frayed and patched like a chessboard, and with a face which looked as though it had been gnawed by dogs . . . My head filled with wild thoughts and inanities . . . Yes, that robber robbed me of my faith! Maybe there was some talent in me, but I lost all for something not worth a cent. It is cold, gentlemen. You want none of it, eh? Well, there's enough for everyone! Brrrr . . . Let us drink to the dear departed! Though I have no love for him, and though he is dead, he's all I have left in the world. This is the last time I'll ever pay him a visit. The doctors say I'll soon be dead from alcoholism, and so I have come to bid him my last farewell. One should forgive one's enemies!"

We left the actor holding converse with the dead Mushkin, and went on. A fine cold rain was beginning to fall.

At a turning in the main road through the cemetery, a road entirely strewn with rubbish, we encountered a funeral procession. Four pallbearers with white calico sashes round their waists, dead leaves glued to their muddy boots, were carrying a dark-brown coffin. It was growing dark, and they were hurrying and stumbling under the weight of the coffin.

"We have been walking about here for two hours, gentlemen, and already this is the third funeral we have seen. Shall we go now?"

October 1884

Where There's a Will, There's a Way

〜〜〜〜〜〜〜〜〜

1st: Take off your hat! Wearing hats is forbidden here!

2nd: It's not a hat! It's a silk topper!

1st: It's all the same thing. . . .

2nd: I assure you it is not the same thing. . . . You can buy a hat for fifty kopecks, but just try to buy a silk topper . . .

1st: Hats, toppers . . . all of them . . .

2nd (removing topper): Explain yourself more clearly. (Provokingly.) Hats, hats, I say!

1st: Please be quiet! You are preventing the others from hearing!

2nd: It's you who are talking and preventing them from hearing, not me! My dear fellow, I was keeping my mouth shut! In fact, I would have been absolutely quiet if you hadn't annoyed me!

1st: Shushshsh . . .

2nd: How dare you shush me? (After a silence.) I, too, can say shush. You don't have to gape at me, either! . . . You can't frighten me! . . . I've seen others like you. . . .

Wife of 2nd: Keep quiet now! You've said enough!

2nd: Why does he have it in for me? I wasn't disturbing him, was I? Didn't say anything, did I? Then why does he have to crawl all over me? Or maybe you think I should complain to his superior?

1st: Later, later . . . Now keep quiet! . . .

2nd: You can see I've got him scared. Just as they say, the devil catches his tail, or the tail catches the devil. . . .

Voice from public: Shushshshsh . . .

2nd: Even the public has noticed it! His job is to keep order, but instead he creates disorder. (*Smiles sarcastically.*) And all those medals on his chest! Sword, too! . . . Well, dear public, you'll soon see sparks flying.

(*The 1st leaves for a moment.*)

2nd: He was ashamed of himself—that's why he went away. It would appear that he is not entirely without honor, seeing that he was overcome with shame by his words. . . . If he had delivered himself of one word more, I assure you I would have given him a mouthful. I know how to make fellows like that run off with their tails between their legs.

Wife of 2nd: Please keep quiet! They are all staring at you!

2nd: Let them stare at me! I paid for my seat with my own money, not with someone else's. . . . And if I have to unburden myself, you don't have to nag! . . . He's gone now. . . . Well, I won't say another word. . . . If he hadn't sailed into me, I wouldn't have started talking, would I? Wouldn't have any reason for talking. . . . I know that. . . . (*Applauds.*) *Bis! Bis!*

1st, 3rd, 4th, 5th, and 6th (as though they had sprung out of the ground): Come on now! Out you go!

2nd: Why? Where? (*Turning pale.*) What's the reason for all this?

1st, 3rd, 4th, 5th, and 6th: Come on now! (*They take him by the arms.*) Don't kick out with your legs! Forward, march! (*They drag him off.*)

2nd: I paid with my own money, didn't I? . . . It's a rotten shame! . . .

Voice from public: Seems they just arrested a thief.

October 1884

To His Excellency
The Commissioner of Police
of the Second Class
A Report

I have the honor to inform Your Excellency that in the Mikhalkovo Woods, not far from the Old Ravine, while crossing the footbridge I observed the hanged body of a dead man showing no signs of life, bearing the name, according to documents found in his possession, of Stepan Maximov Kachagov, 51 years old. From the state of his wallet and his rags, he was clearly in an impecunious condition. Except for the rope I found no other marks on his body, while all his effects were still in his possession. No motive for the suicide was disclosed, but these things happen from vodka. The peasants of Zhabrovo saw him leaving the pothouse. Should I make an official report, or await the coming of Your Excellency?

Policeman Denis Ch.

March 1885

The Threat

A NOBLEMAN'S horse was stolen. The next day the following announcement appeared in all the newspapers: "Unless the horse is returned to my possession, I shall be forced to have recourse to the extreme measures formerly employed by my father in similar circumstances." The threat was effective. The thief, not knowing exactly what was in store, but supposing he would fall victim to some extraordinary and fearful punishment, became panic-stricken, and he secretly returned the horse. The nobleman rejoiced in the successful issue of the affair, and told his friends how very glad he was that he would not have to follow his father's example.

"What did your father do?" they asked him.

"You are asking me what my father did, eh? Well, I'll tell you. He was staying in lodgings when they stole his horse. He threw the saddle over his shoulders and walked home on foot. I'd swear I would have had to do the same thing, if the thief had not been so obliging."

May 1885

The Huntsman

NOON, hot and stifling, with no clouds in the sky. The sun-burned grass had a dismal, hopeless look. Even if the rains came, it was doubtful whether the grass would ever be green again. The forest was silent, motionless, as though gazing out from the treetops or waiting for something to happen.

At the edge of the clearing a tall, narrow-shouldered man of forty, wearing a red shirt, patched trousers which had evidently once belonged to a gentleman, and high leather boots, was sauntering along a pathway with lazy, shambling strides. To the right was the green of the clearing, to the left a golden sea of ripened rye stretching to the horizon. His face was ruddy and sweating. A white cap with a straight visor, like those worn by jockeys, perched jauntily on his handsome blond head—the cap must have been the gift of a generous young nobleman. Over his shoulder hung a game bag with a crumpled woodcock lying in it. The man was holding a double-barreled shotgun in his hand, both barrels cocked, and he was screwing up his eyes as he followed the ancient and lean hunting dog which was running on ahead, sniffing at the bushes. There was silence all round, not a sound anywhere. Every living thing had taken refuge from the heat.

"Yegor Vlassich!" The huntsman suddenly heard a soft voice.

He was startled and turned round, knitting his brows. Beside him, as though she had sprung out of the earth, stood a pale

peasant woman of thirty, with a sickle in her hand. She was trying to peer into the face, and she was smiling shyly.

"Oh, it is you, Pelageya!" said the huntsman, and he stopped
and slowly uncocked the gun. "Well, how do you happen to be
here?"

"The women from our village have come to work here, and so
I came with them. . . . I'm working with them, Yegor Vlassich."

"Ah," Yegor muttered, and walked slowly on.

Pelageya followed him. They went on in silence for twenty
paces.

"It's a long time since I saw you, Yegor Vlassich," Pelageya
said, gazing tenderly at the movement of his shoulders and
shoulder blades. "I remember you dropped into our hut during
Easter week for a drink of water, and then I never saw you
again. . . . You dropped in for a moment at Easter, and
then God knows what was the matter . . . you were quite
drunk . . . you swore at me, and gave me a beating, and then
you went away. . . . I've waited and waited. . . . I've worn
out my eyes waiting. . . . Ah, Yegor Vlassich, Yegor
Vlassich! If only you'd come back just once in all that time!"

"What would I be doing in your place?"

"No use. . . . Still, there's the house to look after . . . seeing about things. . . . You are the master there! . . . So you
shot a woodcock, Yegor? Why don't you sit down and rest
awhile. . . ."

Saying this, Pelageya smiled like an idiot and looked up
into Yegor's face. Her own face was glowing with happiness.

"Sit down? Well, if you want me to . . ." Yegor said in a
tone of indifference, and he chose a spot in the shade between
two fully grown fir trees. "Why are you standing, eh? You sit
down, too!"

Pelageya sat down a little way away in the full sunlight.
Ashamed of her happiness, she hid her smiles with her hand.
Two minutes passed in silence.

"You might come back to me just once," Pelageya said softly.

"Why?" Yegor sighed, and he removed his cap and wiped his red forehead with his sleeve. "I don't see any need for it. There's no sense in coming for an hour or two—it will only upset you! And as for living all the time in your village, well, it's beyond endurance! You know yourself how I have been spoiled. . . . I have to have a bed, and good tea, and fine conversations. . . . Me, I want all the fine things of life, and as for you—you enjoy the poverty and smoke of your village. . . . I couldn't stand it for even a day. Imagine there came an order saying I must live permanently with you—well, I'd rather set fire to the cottage or lay hands on myself! Ever since I was a boy, I was always spoiled—there's no getting away from it!"

"Where are you living now?"

"With Dmitry Ivanich, a fine gentleman, and I'm his huntsman. I furnish his table with game . . . and there it is . . . he keeps me more for his own pleasure than for anything else."

"That's not proper kind of work, Yegor Vlassich! . . . People call that fooling around—there's only you who thinks of it as an occupation, a real job of work. . . ."

"You don't understand, stupid," Yegor said, gazing dreamily at the sky. "Ever since you were born, you've never understood what kind of man I am, and you never will. . . . According to you I'm just a crazy half-cocked sort of fellow, but anyone with an ounce of understanding knows that I'm the best shot in the whole district. The gentry know that, and they've even written me up in a magazine. There isn't a man who can be compared with me as a huntsman. . . . And it isn't because I am spoiled and proud that I despise the work of your village. From the time when I was a child, as you know, I never had to do with anything except guns and dogs. If they took my gun away, I'd go out with a fishing rod, and if they took my rod away, then I'd find some way to busy myself with my hands. I went in for horse trading and I'd go to fairs when I had money, and you know yourself that when a peasant goes in for hunting and horse trading, then it's good-by to the plow. Once freedom catches hold of a man, you can never hammer it out of him! In the same way a gentleman who takes up acting or goes in for the arts will never be of any use as an official or a landowner. You're a peasant girl, and you'll never understand that, but it's something you've got to know!"

"I do understand it, Yegor Vlassich."

"You obviously don't understand, seeing that you're about to cry."

"I . . . I'm not crying," Pelageya said, turning her head away. "It's a sin, Yegor Vlassich! You ought to come and spend a bit of time with me. I'm so miserable! We've been married for twelve years . . . never once was there any love between us. . . . I . . . I'm not crying."

"Love," Yegor muttered, scratching his arm. "There couldn't be any love between us. It's only on paper we're husband and wife—the truth is we are really nothing at all, eh? You think of me as a wild sort of fellow, and I think of you as a simple peasant girl who doesn't understand anything. We are not much of a pair! I'm a free man, and I've been spoiled, and I go where I please. And you're a laboring woman wearing bast shoes, living in filth, and your back is bent low to the ground. I know all about myself—I know I'm the best huntsman around, and you look at me with pity. . . . There's a fine pair for you!"

"We were married in church, Yegor Vlassich," sobbed Pelageya.

"It wasn't my fault we got married. . . . Have you forgotten? You have Count Sergey Pavlich to thank for it . . . and you had some responsibility, too. He was full of envy for me because I was a better shot than he was, and he kept me drinking for a whole month, and when a fellow is drunk, you can make him do anything—get married, change his religion, anything! Out of revenge he married me to you when I was drunk. . . . A huntsman marrying a cow girl! You saw I was drunk, so why did you marry me? You were not a serf—you could have refused! Sure, it is a lucky thing for a cow girl to marry a huntsman, but you have to use your brains. Now you are making yourself miserable, and crying. The count thought it was a joke, but you went right on crying . . . beating your head against a wall. . . ."

Silence followed. Three wild ducks flew over the clearing. Yegor watched them, following them until they became three barely perceptible dots, and then they vanished on the other side of the forest far away.

"How do you live?" he asked, no longer looking at the ducks, but at Pelageya.

"This time of year I go out and work, and in the winter I take a baby from the foundling hospital and bring it up on the bottle. For that they give me a ruble and a half a month."

"So . . ."

Again there was silence. From a field which had been reaped there came the first soft notes of a song, which broke off abruptly. It was too hot for singing.

"They say you built a new hut for Akulina," said Pelageya. Yegor was silent.

"Are you fond of her?"

"It's just your luck, it's fate!" said the huntsman, stretching himself. "You have to suffer, poor orphan! Good-by! I've been chattering too much! .   . I have to reach Boltovo by evening."

Yegor rose, stretched himself, and threw his gun over his shoulder. Pelageya got up.

"When are you coming to the village?" she asked softly.

"No reason for me to come. I won't come sober, and I won't be much use to you if I come drunk. I'm mean when I'm drunk. Good-by!"

"Good-by, Yegor Vlassich."

Yegor put his cap on the back of his head, made a clicking noise with his tongue to summon the dog, and went on his way. Pelageya stood there and watched him going. She followed the movement of his shoulder blades, the vigorous young neck, the lazy and careless gait, and her eyes were full of melancholy and tender affection. . . . Her eyes ran over the tall, lean figure of her husband, and caressed and fondled him. As though he felt the force of her gaze, he stopped and looked back. . . . He did not speak, but from his face and the thrust of his shoulders Pelageya knew he wanted to say something to her. She went up to him timidly, gazing at him imploringly.

"Take it," he said, and he turned away.

He gave her a crumpled-up ruble note, and walked on quickly.

"Good-by, Yegor Vlassich," she said, mechanically taking the ruble.

He went down the long road, which was as straight as a taut strap. She stood there pale and motionless as a statue, following closely each one of his footsteps. Soon the red color of his shirt melted into the dark color of his trousers, and she could no longer follow his footsteps, and the dog became indistinguishable from his boots. At last she could see only his cap, and suddenly Yegor turned sharply to the right into a clearing, and the cap vanished in the green depths.

"Good-by, Yegor Vlassich," whispered Pelageya, and she stood on tiptoe, hoping to see the white cap.

July 1885

The Malefactor

THE tiny and extraordinarily skinny peasant, wearing patched drawers and a shirt of striped linen, stood facing the investigating magistrate. His hairy face was pitted with smallpox, and his eyes, scarcely visible under thick overhanging brows, conveyed an expression of sullen resentment. He wore his hair in a tangled unkempt thatch which somehow emphasized his sullen spiderlike character. He was barefoot.

"Denis Grigoryev!" the magistrate began. "Step closer, and answer my questions. On the morning of July 7 the linesman Ivan Semyonov Akinfov, while performing the duty of examining the tracks, found you in proximity to the one-hundred-and-forty-first mile post unscrewing one of the nuts from the bolt securing the rail to the tie. The nut is here. He thereupon arrested you with the nut in your possession. Do you testify to the truth of this statement?"

"Wha-at?"

"Did all this happen as stated by Akinfov?"

"Sure—yes, it did."

"Excellent. Now why were you unscrewing the nut?"

"Wha-at?"

"Stop saying 'what' and answer the question! Why were you unscrewing the nut?"

"I wouldn't have unscrewed it, would I, if I hadn't wanted it?" Denis said hoarsely, squinting up at the ceiling.

"What on earth was the good of the nut to you?"

"The nut, eh? Well, we make sinkers out of 'em."

"Who is 'we'?"

"We—the people in the village. The peasants of Klimovo. . . ."

"Listen, fellow. Don't play the fool with me. Learn to talk sense. Don't tell me any lies about sinkers!"

"Me, tell lies? All my life I haven't told any lies, and now . . ." Denis muttered, his eyes blinking. "Your Honor, I ask you, what can you do without sinkers? Now, if you put live worms on the hook, how do you think it touches bottom without a sinker? So I'm lying, am I?" he smirked. "Then what is the good of live bait floating on the surface? The perch and pike and eelpout always go along the bottom, while if the bait floats on the surface there's only the snapper will bite, and that doesn't happen often. . . . And there are no snappers in our part of the country. . . . Our fish like a lot of space. . . ."

"What's all this talk about snappers?"

"Wha-at? Why, you asked me that yourself! I'm telling how the gentry catch fish, but the very stupidest child wouldn't try to catch anything without a sinker. Maybe a man without a brain in his head might try to catch a fish without a sinker, but there's no accounting for people like that!"

"According to you, the nut was unscrewed so you could use it as a sinker. Is that right?"

"Well, it couldn't be anything else, could it? I wasn't playing knucklebones with it, was I?"

"Instead of a nut, you could have used a bit of lead or a bullet —perhaps a nail would have served the same purpose?"

"Well, Your Honor, as for that, you don't find lead lying about in the street, and it has to be paid for, and a nail—a nail's no use at all. There's nothing better than a nut. . . . It is heavy, and has a hole in it. . . ."

"The witness is determined to convince us he is out of his wits —pretends he was born yesterday or fell out of the sky! Really, you miserable blockhead, don't you understand what happens when you unscrew these nuts? If the linesman had not seen you at work, the train could have gone off the rails, people could have been killed, and the responsibility for killing them would have been yours!"

"Oh, God forbid, Your Honor! No! Why should I kill anybody! Do you think we are criminals or heathen, eh? Ah, good gentlemen, we thank God we have lived our lives without ever letting such an idea as killing people enter our heads! Save us and have mercy on us, Queen of Heaven! What were you saying, sir?"

"How do you suppose train wrecks happen? Doesn't it occur to you that if a few nuts are unscrewed, you can have a train wreck?"

Denis smirked and screwed up his eyes incredulously at the magistrate.

"Why, Your Honor, we peasants have been unscrewing nuts for a good many years now, and the good Lord has protected us, and as for a train wreck and killing people, why, nothing at all. . . . Now, if I took up a whole rail or put a big balk of timber across the track, maybe I could smash up a train. . . . But just an ordinary nut, pfui! . . ."

"Can you get it into your head that the nut holds the rail to the tie?"

"Of course, Your Honor. We understand that. That's why we don't unscrew all of them. We leave some of them. We've got heads on our shoulders. . . . We know what's what. . . ."

Denis yawned and made the sign of the cross over his mouth.

"Last year a train went off the rails here," the magistrate said. "Now we know how it happened."

"Beg pardon?"

"I said, now we know why the train went off the rails last year. It's all clear now."

"Good kind gentlemen, God gave you understanding, and He gives it to whom He pleases. You know about things, how it happened, what happened, and all, but the linesman, he was a peasant, too, not a man with an education, and he took me by the collar and carted me off! He ought to know about things before dragging people off! A peasant has the brains of a peasant—that's what they say. And write down, too, Your Honor, that he hit me twice—once in the jaw and once in the chest."

"Listen, when they searched your place, they found another nut. . . . Now, where and when was that one unscrewed?"

"You mean the one they found under the little red chest?"

"I don't know anything about where it was. I only know they found it. When did you unscrew that one?"

"I didn't unscrew it. It was given to me by Ignashka, the son of one-eyed Semyon. I'm talking about the one under the chest. The one they found in the yard, on the sleigh—that one was unscrewed by Mitrofan and me."

"Which Mitrofan?"

"Mitrofan Petrov. Do you mean to say you've never heard of him? He's the one who makes nets in our village and sells them to the gentry. He needs a lot of nuts. Every net, I reckon, must have about ten nuts."

"Listen. According to Article 1081 of the Penal Code, every willful act leading to the damage of a railroad and calculated to jeopardize the passage of trains, shall, if the perpetrator knows the act will cause an accident—*knows*, you understand?—and for that matter you couldn't help knowing the consequences of unscrewing the nut—such a man is liable to exile with hard labor. . . ."

"Oh, well, you know best. We ignorant people, we don't know anything. . . ."

"You do know! You're lying and shamming ignorance!"

"Why should I lie? Ask in the village if you don't believe me! Only the bleak fish can be caught without a sinker, that's true! There's no fish worse than a gudgeon, and even he won't bite without a sinker."

"You'll be talking about snappers next," the magistrate smiled.

"I told you, we don't have snappers in our part of the country.
. . . Now, if we cast our lines on the surface without a sinker,
with a butterfly for bait, we might maybe catch a mullet, but it
don't happen often."

"Shut up!"

Then there was silence, while Denis shifted from one foot to
the other, stared at the table covered with a green cloth, and
violently blinked his eyes. He was like someone gazing, not at
the green cloth, but at the sun. The magistrate was writing
rapidly.

"May I be getting along now?" Denis asked a moment later.

"No, you'll be kept in custody and sent to prison."

Denis stopped blinking. Raising his thick eyebrows, he looked
inquiringly in the direction of the magistrate.

"What do you mean, prison? Your Honor, I haven't the time
for prison! I've got to go to the fair—there's Yegor, who owes me
three rubles for the lard he . . ."

"Keep your mouth shut, and don't disturb me!"

"Prison, eh? Now, listen. If I'd done anything wrong, then
I'd go . . . but there's neither rhyme nor reason in sending
me . . . What for should I go to prison? I haven't stolen anything so far as I know. I haven't been fighting. . . . If there's
any question in your mind about the arrears, well, Your Honor,
you shouldn't believe the village elder. . . . Ask the permanent
member of the board. . . . The elder, he hasn't been bap-
tized. . . ."

"Silence!"

"All right, I'll be silent," Denis murmured. "But I'll take
my oath the elder lied about the assessment. There are three of
us brothers—Kuzma Grigoryev, then Yegor Grigoryev, and then
Denis Grigoryev . . ."

"You're a nuisance," the magistrate shouted. "Hey, Semyon!
Take him away!"

"We're three brothers," Denis went on muttering, while two
husky soldiers took hold of him and led him out of the room. "A

brother doesn't have to answer for a brother, does he? Kuzma won't pay. So it's up to you, Denis. . . . Judges, indeed! Our late master, the general, is dead, may God rest his soul, or he would have shown you what's what. . . . You ought to judge sensibly, not in a cockeyed way. . . . Flog a man, you understand, but only when he deserves it. . . . Understand? . . ."

July 1885

A Dead Body

A CALM August night. The mist rose slowly from the fields, covering everything within view with a dull-colored winding sheet. When lit by the moon, the mist gave the impression of a quiet and limitless expanse of ocean, and at another time it resembled an immense white wall. The air was damp and chilly, and the morning still far away. There was a fire blazing a step or two beyond the pathway running along the edge of the forest. Near the small fire, under a young oak, lay a dead body covered from head to foot with a clean white linen sheet, and there was a small wooden icon lying on the dead man's chest. Beside the dead body, almost sitting in the pathway, were "the watchers," two peasants who were performing one of the most disagreeable and uninviting tasks ever given to peasants. One was a tall youngster with a faint mustache and thick black bushy eyebrows, wearing bast shoes and a tattered sheepskin jacket, his feet stretched out in front of him, as he sat in the damp grass. He was trying to make time go faster by getting down to work. His long neck was bent, and he wheezed loudly while he whittled a spoon from a big curved chunk of wood. The other was a small, thin pock-marked peasant with an ancient face, a scant mustache, and a little goatee beard. His hands had fallen on his knees, and he gazed listlessly and motionlessly into the flames.

The small pile of faggots that lay between them blazed up and threw a red glare on their faces. It was very quiet. The only sound came from the scraping of the knife on the wood and the crackling of the damp faggots in the flames.

"Don't fall asleep, Syoma," the young man said.

"Me? No, I'm not falling asleep," stammered the man with a goatee.

"That's good. It's hard sitting here alone, I'd get frightened. Talk to me, Syoma."

"I wouldn't know . . ."

"Oh, you're a strange fellow, Syomushka! Some people laugh, invent stories, and sing songs, but you—God knows what to make of you. You sit there like a scarecrow in a potato field and stare at the flames. You don't know how to put words together. . . . You're plain scared of talking. You must be getting on for fifty, but you've no more sense than a baby. Aren't you sorry you are such a fool?"

"Reckon so," said the man with a goatee gloomily.

"Well, we're sorry too. Wouldn't you say so? There you are, a good solid fellow, don't drink too much, and the only trouble is that you haven't a brain in your head. Still, if the good Lord afflicted you by making you witless, there's no reason why you shouldn't try to pick up some glimmerings of intelligence, is there? Make an effort, Syoma. . . . If someone speaks a good word and you don't understand it, you ought to try to fathom it, get the sense of it somehow, keep on thinking and concentrating. If there's anything you don't understand, you should make an effort and think over exactly what it means. Do you understand me? Just make an effort! If you don't get some sense into your head, you'll die an idiot, you'll be the least important man in the world."

Suddenly a long-drawn-out moaning sound was heard from the direction of the forest. There was the sound of something being torn from the top of a tree, slithering down and rustling among the leaves, and falling to the ground, followed by a dull echo. The young man shuddered and looked searchingly at his companion.

"It's only an owl running after little birds," Syoma said gloomily.

"I'd have thought it was time for the birds to be flying to warm countries now."

"Yes, that's true."

"And the dawns are getting cold now—there's a chill in the air. Birds, too—cranes, for example—they feel the cold, they're delicate things. When it's cold like this, they die. Me, I'm not a crane, but I'm frozen. Put some more wood on!"

Syoma rose and vanished in the dark undergrowth. While he was wandering through the undergrowth, snapping off dry twigs, his companion shielded his eyes with his hands, shivering at every sound. Syoma brought back an armful of wood and threw it on the fire. Little tongues of flame licked the black twigs uncertainly, and then suddenly, as though at a word of command, the flames leapt up and enveloped their faces in a deep purple glow; and the pathway, and the white linen sheet which showed the dead man's hands and feet in relief, and the icon, all these shone with the same deep purple glow. The watchers remained silent. The young man bent his neck still lower and went back to work more nervously than ever. Meanwhile the old man with the goatee sat motionless, never taking his eyes from the fire.

"Oh, ye that love not Zion shall be ashamed in the face of the Lord!"—the silence of the night was suddenly broken by a high falsetto voice, and soft footsteps.

Into the purple firelight there emerged the dark figure of a man wearing a broad-brimmed hat and the short cassock of a monk, carrying a birch-bark sack on his shoulders.

"Thy will be done, O Lord! O Holy Mother!" he sang in a voice grown hoarse. "I saw the fire in the depths of night, and my soul leapt for joy! At first, I told myself they were keeping watch over horses, and then I told myself, it cannot be so, for there are no horses. Then, said I, they were thieves waiting to pounce upon some rich Lazarus, and then it crossed my mind they were gypsies preparing to sacrifice victims to their idols. My soul again leapt for joy! I said to myself: Go then, Theodosy, thou servant of God, receive a martyr's crown! So I flew to the fire on the gentle wings of a moth. Now I stand before you, and examine your physiognomies, and judge your souls, and I conclude you are neither thieves nor heathens! Peace be upon you!"

"Good evening to you."

"Dear brethren in God, pray tell me where I can find Makukhinsky's brickyard?"

"It's not far. Straight down the road, and after a mile and a half you'll come to Ananova, which is our village. Turn right at the village, Father, follow the riverbank, and keep on going till you reach the brickyard. It's two miles from Ananova."

"God give you health! . . . Tell me, why are you sitting here?"

"We are keeping watch. Look over there—there's a dead body."

"Eh, what's that? A dead body! Holy Mother!"

When the stranger saw the white sheet and the icon, he shivered so violently that his legs involuntarily made little hopping motions. This unexpected sight produced an overwhelming effect. He shrank within himself and was rooted to the spot, his eyes glazed, his mouth wide open. For three minutes he remained completely silent, as though he could not believe his eyes, and then he muttered: "O Lord, O Holy Mother! I was wandering abroad and giving offense to none, and now am I consigned to punishment. . . ."

"What are you?" the young man asked. "Are you a member of the clergy?"

"No, no . . . I wander from one monastery to another. Do you know by chance Mikhail Polikarpich? He runs the brickyard, and I'm his nephew. . . . Thy will be done, O Lord! . . . What are you doing here?"

"We are the watchers. They told us to watch him."

"Yes, yes," muttered the man in the cassock, running his hands over his eyes. "Tell me—the dead man—where did he come from?"

"He was passing by."

"Well, such is life! So it is, dear brethren, and now I must go on my way. I'm all confused. I tell you, I'm more frightened of the dead than of anything else. And it comes to me that when he was living, no one paid any attention to him, and now that he is dead and delivered over to corruption, we tremble before him as though he were a great conqueror or a high official of the Church. . . . Such is life! . . . Tell me, was he murdered?"

"Christ knows! Maybe he was murdered, maybe he just died."

"Yes, yes. So it is! And who knows, dear brethren, even now his soul may be tasting the delights of Paradise."

"No, his soul is still clinging close to his body," the young man said. "It doesn't leave the body for three days."

"Hm, yes! How cold it is, eh? My teeth are chattering. . . . How do I go? Straight ahead, eh?"

"Till you reach the village, and then you turn to the right, by the river."

"By the river, eh? Why am I standing here? I must get going. Good-by, dear brethren!"

The man in the cassock took four or five steps along the path, and then stood still.

"I forgot to give a kopeck for the funeral," he said. "You are good religious people. May I—is it right for me to leave the money?"

"You should know best, since you go about from one monastery to another. Suppose he died a natural death—then it will go for the good of his soul. If he didn't, then it's a sin."

"That's true. Maybe he killed himself, and so I had better keep the money. Oh, so much evil in the world! Even if you gave me a thousand rubles, I wouldn't stay here. . . . Farewell, brothers!"

Slowly the man in the cassock moved away, and again he stood still.

"I don't know what to do," he muttered. "It's terrible to be staying here by the fire and waiting for daybreak, and it's terrible to be going along the road. I'll be haunted by him—he'll come out of the shadows! God is punishing me! I've walked for four hundred miles, and nothing ever happened to me, and now I am close to home, and there's all this misery. I can't go on. . . ."

"You're right. It's terrible."

"I'm not afraid of wolves. I'm not afraid of robbers, or the dark, but I'm afraid of the dead. I'm terrified, and that's the truth! Dear good religious brethren, I beg you on my knees to see me to the village."

"We have to stay with the body."

"Dear brethren, no one will ever know. Truly, no one will see you coming with me. God will reward you a hundredfold. You with a beard—come with me! Do me that kindness! Why doesn't he talk?"

"He hasn't got much sense," the young man said.

"Come with me, friend. I'll give you five kopecks!"

"I might, for five kopecks," the young man said, scratching the back of his head. "It's against orders, though. If Syoma, the poor fool, will stay here, then I'll come. Syoma, do you mind staying here alone?"

"I don't mind," the fool said.

"All right. Let's go."

So the young man rose and went with the man wearing a cassock, and soon the sound of their steps and the talk died away into the night.

Syoma closed his eyes and fell into a gentle sleep. The fire gradually went out, and soon the dead body was lost among great shadows.

September 1885

Sergeant Prishibeyev

"SERGEANT Prishibeyev! You are charged with using insulting language and committing assault and battery upon the persons of Police Officer Zhigin, the village elder Alyapov, Patrolman Yefimov, the witnesses Ivanov and Gavrilov, and six other villagers on the third of September. The three first-named were insulted by you during the performance of their official duties. Do you plead guilty?"

Prishibeyev, a shriveled-up non-commissioned officer, whose face was all bristles, came to attention and replied in a hoarse, choked-up voice, forming each word as though he were on the parade ground:

"Your Honor, Mr. Justice of the Peace! . . . In accordance with the articles of the law it stands to reason that testimony must be taken mutually and severally with regard to all the circumstances of any and every case. No, it's not me that's guilty—it's the rest of them. I may say the whole business started with that dead body—may God give him rest! On the third day of the aforesaid month I was quietly and respectably taking a promenade with my wife Anfisa. Then what do I observe but a mob of people standing there on the shore. I ask myself: Do they possess a legal right of assembly? I ask myself: What on earth are they up to? Is it permissible for people to crowd around like cattle? So I shout at them: 'Break it up there, all of you!' Then I barge into them and send them off packing

90

to their homes, and I order the patrolman to give them a taste of the stick!"

"Listen to me. You are not the village elder, nor the patrolman —is it your business to break up crowds?"

"It's not his business—no, it isn't!" people shouted from all over the room. "No one can live in the same world with him, Your Honor! Fifteen years we've had to endure him! Ever since he came back from the Army, we've felt like running away from the village. He only torments us—that's all he ever does!"

"Just so, Your Honor," says the village elder. "The whole village—everyone—complains about him. No one can breathe while he's around. Whenever we march in procession with the icons, or there's a wedding, or any kind of occasion, he's always there shouting, making noises, and ordering everyone about. He pulls the children's ears, and spies on the womenfolk in case they are up to mischief—he's like a father-in-law. . . . The other day he went round all the houses ordering us not to sing songs and not to burn lights!"

"Wait a bit," said the magistrate. "You'll be given an opportunity to testify later. For the present Prishibeyev may proceed. Proceed, Prishibeyev!"

"Oh yes, sir!" the sergeant croaked. "Your Honor, you've been pleased to say it's not my business to disperse the crowd. Very good, sir. But supposing there is a breach of the peace. You can't permit people to behave in an unbecoming manner. What law says people can be free? I won't permit it. If I don't run after them and punish them, who will? No one here knows anything about law and order, and in the whole village, Your Honor, there's only me who knows how to deal with the common folk, and, Your Honor, there isn't anything I don't know. I'm not a peasant. I'm a non-commissioned officer, a retired quartermaster sergeant! I did my service in Warsaw attached to headquarters, and later on, may it please Your Honor, upon receiving an honorable discharge I was seconded into the fire brigade, and then, seeing as how I was retired from the fire brigade due to in-

firmities consequent to illness, I served for two years as doorkeeper in a junior high school for boys. . . . I know all the
rules and regulations, sir. Take an ignorant peasant who doesn't
understand anything—he has to do what I tell him to do, because it's for his own good. Then there's this little trouble we're
talking about. Well, it is quite true I broke up the crowd, but
right there on the shore, lying on the sands, there was a dead
body, see. Man drowned. So I says to myself: What right does he
have to lie there? What's right and proper about it? What's the
officer doing there, gaping away? So I address myself to the
officer, and I say: 'You ought to notify the authorities. Maybe
the drowned fellow drowned himself, or maybe there's a smell
of Siberia about the business. Maybe it's a question of criminal
homicide. . . .' Well, Officer Zhigin didn't pay any attention to
me; he only went on smoking a cigarette. 'Who's giving orders
here?' he says. 'Where does he come from, eh? Don't we know
how to behave without him butting in?' 'You're a damned fool!'
says I. 'The truth is you don't know what you're doing. You
just stand there and don't pay attention to anything.' Says he:
'I notified the district police inspector yesterday.' 'Why,' says I,
'did you notify the district police inspector? Under what article of
what code of law? In such cases, when it's a matter of drowning
or hanging or something of the sort, what is the inspector expected to do? Here we have what is properly speaking a criminal
matter,' says I. 'A matter for the civil courts,' I says. 'Best
thing you can do is to send an express to His Honor the examining magistrate and the judges. And then,' says I, 'before you do
anything else, you have to draw up a charge and send it to the
justice of the peace.' And would you believe it, the officer hears
me quite well and bursts out laughing. And the peasants
laughed, too. They were all laughing, Your Honor. I testify to
my aforesaid statement under oath. See that fellow over there—
he was laughing. And that fellow, too. And Zhigin. All laughing. 'So why do you show me the color of your teeth?' says I.
'Cases of this sort,' says the officer, 'don't come under the juris-

diction of justices of the peace.' That made my blood boil. 'Didn't you say those very words, Officer?' " the sergeant said, turning and confronting Officer Zhigin.

"Yes, that's what I said."

"Of course you did! The whole mob of people heard you. You said: 'Cases like this don't come under the jurisdiction of the justices of the peace. . . .' Your Honor, my blood boiled! I was stunned. 'Say that again, you so-and-so,' says I. 'Just you repeat it. . . .' And so I said to him: 'How can you bring yourself to say those words about His Honor? You, a police officer, dare to set yourself in opposition to constituted authority? Do you realize,' says I, 'that for speaking in that fashion His Honor can have you brought up before the provincial gendarmerie on the grounds of gross misconduct? Do you realize,' says I, 'that for those political observations His Honor could have you summarily dismissed?' And then the village elder interfered and said: 'His Honor can't settle anything outside his powers—only minor cases come within his jurisdiction.' That's what he said, and everybody heard him. 'How dare you set the authorities at nought?' says I. 'Don't go playing jokes on me, brother, or you'll come to grief. Why, when I was at Warsaw and later when I was appointed doorkeeper at the junior high school for boys, as soon as I heard about anything that wasn't quite proper, I'd take a look down the street and see whether there was a policeman in sight. 'Come along here, Officer,' I'd say, and I'd make a full report to him. But here in the village, who does one report to? So my blood was boiling. I was outraged by the way people nowadays assert their rights and commit acts of insubordination. So I belted him—oh, I didn't use undue force, just a gentle tap, you understand, to remind him not to talk about Your Honor in that way. The officer jumped to the side of the village elder. So, of course, I belted him, too. . . . That's how it all began. I was in a rage, Your Honor. It's understandable. You have to belt people sometimes. If you don't sometimes belt one of those mugwumps, why, you have a sin on your conscience. Especially when, as it happens, he deserves it, and there's a disturbance of the public peace."

"Wait a moment. There are some people charged with the duty of keeping public order. The officer, the patrolman, the village elder . . ."

"The officer can't keep an eye on everything. The officer just doesn't understand things as I do."

"Does it occur to you that it is none of your business?"

"What's that, sir? None of my business? Why, that's a queer thing to say. People can go on a rampage, and it's none of my business! Am I supposed to pat them on the head? They are complaining because I won't let them sing songs. . . . What's the good of songs? Instead of getting on with something useful, they sing songs. And recently they've been sitting up at night, keeping the lights burning. They should be in bed. Instead of that they're sitting up and talking and joking. I made a report about that."

"What did you say in the report?"

"They sit up and keep their lights burning."

Prishibeyev removed a greasy scrap of paper from his pocket, put on his spectacles, and read:

"The following peasants were seen sitting up with the lights on—Ivan Prokhorov, Savva Mikiphorov, Pyotr Petrov. The soldier's widow Shustrova lives in sin with Semyon Kisslov. Ignat Sverchok practices witchcraft, and his wife Mavra is a witch who goes out milking other people's cows at night."

"That will do!" said the judge, and he began to examine the witnesses.

Sergeant Prishibeyev pushed his spectacles up on his forehead and gazed with amazement at the justice of the peace, who plainly was not on his side. The sergeant's protruding eyes gleamed, and his nose began to turn scarlet. He looked at the judge, at the witnesses, and he could not understand why the judge was so perturbed or why there was so much suppressed laughter, so many whispers coming from all corners of the courtroom. And the verdict, too, was incomprehensible: one month in jail.

"Why? Why?" he asked, flinging out his hands in bewilderment. "What law said so?"

And it was clear to him that the world had changed, and it was utterly impossible for him to go on living. He was oppressed by melancholy thoughts. When he left the courtroom and saw the peasants wandering about and talking about nothing in particular, he drew himself to attention and barked in his hoarse, ill-tempered voice:

"Move along there! Stop crowding! Go on back to your homes!"

October 1885

A Blunder

ILYA SERGEICH PEPLOV and his wife Cleopatra Petrovna
stood outside the door, listening closely. In the small room on the
other side of the door someone was quite obviously making a declaration of love: this declaration was being made by the district
schoolmaster Shupkin to their daughter Natasha.

"Well, he's hooked now," Peplov whispered, shuddering with
impatience and rubbing his hands together. "Listen, Petrovna, as
soon as they start talking about their feelings for one another,
take the icon from the wall and we'll go in and give them our
blessing. . . . A blessing with an icon is sacred and can't be
broken. . . . Also, he won't be able to wriggle out of it, even
if he goes to court!"

On the other side of the door the following conversation was
taking place:

"Really you'll have to change your character," Shupkin was
saying as he struck a match on his checkered trousers. "I've
never written you any letters in my life!"

"What a thing to say! As though I didn't know your handwriting!" The young woman laughed in an affected manner
while gazing at herself in a mirror. "I recognized it at once!
How funny you are! A teacher of handwriting, and your handwriting is nothing but a scrawl! How can you teach handwriting
when you yourself write so badly?"

"Hm. That's not important. The really important thing in

handwriting is that the children don't drop off to sleep. Of course, you can give them a little rap on the head with a ruler, or a rap on the knees. . . . That's handwriting! . . . Quite simple, really. Nekrasov was a writer, but it is shameful to see *how* he wrote. There are examples of his handwriting in his collected works."

"Nekrasov is one thing, and you are another." Here she gave a sigh. "I would marry a writer with the greatest pleasure. He would be continually writing poems in my honor."

"I would write poems for you, if you wanted me to."

"What would you write about?"

"About love . . . about my feelings for you . . . about your eyes. . . . When you read them, you would be out of your mind. . . . You would be moved to tears! And if I really wrote some poetical verses for you, would you allow me to kiss your little hand?"

"What a lot of fuss! Here, kiss it!"

Shupkin jumped up, his eyeballs protruding, and he took her plump little hand, which smelled of scented soap.

"Take down the icon!" Peplov whispered, turning pale with emotion. He jostled his wife with his elbow, and buttoned up his coat. "Well, here we go!"

And without any further delay he threw open the door.

"Children!" he muttered, raising his hands and screwing up his eyes tearfully. "May God bless you, my children. . . . Live . . . be fruitful . . . multiply . . ."

"I, too, bless you," the girl's mother repeated, weeping with joy. "Be happy, my dears. Oh, you are taking away my only treasure!" she added, turning to Shupkin. "Love my daughter, and be good to her!"

Shupkin gaped in astonishment and fright. The sudden descent of the parents was so unexpected and so awesome that he was unable to utter a single word.

"I'm caught! I'm trapped!" he thought, near fainting with terror. "The roof's falling in on you, brother! No use to run!"

And he lowered his head in humility, as though he were saying: "Take me! I have been vanquished!"

"Bless you, bless you!" the father went on, and tears filled his eyes. "Natasha, my daughter, stand beside him. . . . Petrovna, hand me the icon."

Suddenly there was an end to his tears, and his face became contorted with rage.

"Idiot!" he shouted angrily at his wife. "Stupid blockhead! Is this an icon?"

"Oh, God in heaven . . . !"

What had happened? The writing master cautiously looked up and saw that he was saved. In her haste, instead of the icon, the mother had taken from the wall the picture of the writer Lazhechnikov. Cleopatra Petrovna stood there with the portrait in her hands, and she and old Peplov presented an appearance of utter confusion, for they had no idea what to do or say. The writing master profited from their confusion by taking to his heels.

January 1886

Heartache

To whom shall I tell my sorrow?

EVENING twilight. Thick flakes of wet snow were circling lazily round the newly lighted street lamps, settling in thin soft layers on rooftops, on the horses' backs, and on people's shoulders and caps. The cabdriver Iona Potapov was white as a ghost, and bent double as much as any human body can be bent double, sitting very still on his box. Even if a whole snowdrift had fallen on him, he would have found no need to shake it off. The little mare, too, was white, and quite motionless. Her immobility, and the fact that she was all sharp angles and sticklike legs, gave her a resemblance to one of those gingerbread horses which can be bought for a kopeck. No doubt the mare was plunged in deep thought. So would you be if you were torn from the plow, snatched away from familiar, gray surroundings, and thrown into a whirlpool of monstrous illuminations, ceaseless uproar, and people scrambling hither and thither.

For a long while neither Iona nor the little mare had made the slightest motion. They had driven out of the stableyard before dinner, and so far not a single fare had come to them. The evening mist fell over the city. The pale glow of the street lamps grew brighter, more intense, as the street noises grew louder.

Iona heard someone saying: "Driver—you, there!—take me to Vyborg District!"

99

Iona started, and through his snow-laden eyelashes he made out an officer wearing a military overcoat with a hood.

"Vyborg!" the officer repeated. "Are you asleep, eh? Get on with it—Vyborg!"

To show he had heard, Iona pulled at the reins, sending whole layers of snow flying from the horse's back and from his own shoulders. The officer sat down in the sleigh. The driver clucked with his tongue, stretched out his neck like a swan, rose in his seat, and more from habit than necessity, he flourished his whip. The little horse also stretched her neck, crooked her sticklike legs, and started off irresolutely. . . .

"Where are you going, you fool!" Iona was being assailed with shouts from some massive, dark object wavering to and fro in front of him. "Where the devil are you going? Stay on the right side of the road!"

"You don't know how to drive! Stay on the right side!" the officer shouted angrily.

A coachman driving a private carriage was swearing at him, and a pedestrian, running across the road and brushing his shoulder against the mare's nose, glanced up at him and shook the snow from his sleeve. Iona shifted about on the box, as though sitting on needles, thrust out his elbows, rolled his eyes like a madman, as though he did not understand where he was or what he was doing there.

"They're all scoundrels," the officer laughed. "All trying to shove into you, or fall under your horse. Quite a conspiracy!"

The driver turned towards the officer, his lips moving. He appeared about to say something, but the only sound coming from him was a hoarse wheezing cough.

"What is it?" the officer asked.

Iona's lips twitched into a smile, and he strained his throat and croaked: "My son, sir. He died this week."

"Hm, what did he die of?"

Iona turned his whole body round to face his fare.

"Who knows? They say it was fever. . . . He was in the

hospital only three days, and then he died. It was God's will!"

"Get over, damn you!" came a sudden shout out of the darkness. "Have you gone blind, you old idiot? Keep your eyes skinned!"

"Keep going," the officer said. "This way we won't get there till tomorrow morning. Put the whip to her!"

Once more the driver stretched his neck, rose in his seat, and with heavy grace flourished the whip. Several times he turned to watch his fare, but the officer's eyes were closed and apparently he was in no mood to listen. And then, letting off the passenger in the Vyborg District, the driver stopped by a tavern, and again he remained motionless, doubled up on his box. And again the wet snow splashed him and his mare with its white paint. An hour passed, and then another.

Then three young men came loudly pounding the sidewalk in galoshes, quarreling furiously among themselves. Two were tall and slender, the third was a small hunchback.

"Driver, to the Police Bridge!" the hunchback shouted in a cracked voice. "The three of us for twenty kopecks!"

Iona tugged at the reins and smacked his lips. Twenty kopecks was not a fair price, but he did not care any more. Whether it was a ruble or five kopecks no longer mattered, so long as he had a fare. The young men, jostling and cursing one another, came up to the sleigh, and all three of them tried to jump onto the seat, and then they began to argue about which two should sit down, and who should be the one to stand up. After a long, fantastic, and ill-natured argument they decided that the hunchback would have to stand, because he was the shortest.

"Let's go!" cried the hunchback in his cracked voice, taking his place and breathing down Iona's neck. "Get going! Eh, brother, what a funny cap you're wearing. You won't find a worse one anywhere in St. Petersburg!"

"Hee-hee-hee," Iona giggled. "Yes, it's a funny cap."

"Then get a move on! Are you going to crawl along all this time at the same pace? Do you want to get it in the neck?"

"My head's splitting!" said one of the tall ones. "Yesterday at the Dukmassovs', I drank all of four bottles of cognac with Vaska."

"I don't know why you have to tell lies," the other tall one said angrily. "You lie like a swine!"

"May God strike me dead if I am not telling the truth!"

"A flea coughs the truth, too."

"Hee-hee-hee," Iona giggled. "What a lot of merry gentlemen. . . ."

"Pfui!" the hunchback exclaimed indignantly. "Damn you for an old idiot! Will you get a move on, or won't you? Is that how to drive? Use the whip, dammit! Go on, you old devil, give it to her!"

Iona could feel at his back the hunchback's wriggling body, and the tremble in the voice. He heard the insults which were being hurled at him, he saw the people in the street, and little by little the feeling of loneliness was lifted from his heart. The hunchback went on swearing until he choked on an elaborate six-story-high oath, and then was overcome with a fit of coughing. The tall ones began to talk about a certain Nadezhda Petrovna. Iona looked round at them. He waited until there was a short pause in the conversation, and then he turned again and murmured: "My son died—he died this week. . . ."

"We all die," sighed the hunchback, wiping his lips after his fit of coughing. "Keep going, eh? Gentlemen, we simply can't go any further like this. We'll never get there!"

"Give him a bit of encouragement. Hit him in the neck!"

"Did you hear that, old pest? You'll get it in the neck all right. One shouldn't stand on ceremony with people like you—one might just as well walk. Do you hear me, you old snake? I don't suppose you care a tinker's damn about what we are saying."

Then Iona heard rather than felt a thud on the nape of his neck.

"Hee-hee-hee," he laughed. "Such merry gentlemen! God bless them!"

"Driver, are you married?" one of the tall men asked.

"Me, am I married? Hee-hee-hee. You're all such merry gentlemen. There's only one wife left to me now—the damp earth. Hee-ho-ho. The grave, that's what's left for me. My son is dead, and I'm alive. Strange how death comes by the wrong door. It didn't come for me, it came for my son. . . ."

Iona turned round to tell them how his son died, but at that moment the hunchback gave a little sigh of relief and announced that, thank God, they had come to the end of the journey. Having received his twenty kopecks, Iona gazed after the revelers for a long time, even after they had vanished through a dark gateway. Once more he was alone, once more silence fell on him. The grief he had kept at bay for a brief while now returned to wrench his heart with still greater force. With an expression of anxiety and torment, he gazed at the crowds hurrying along both sides of the street, wondering whether there was anyone among those thousands of people who would listen to him. But the crowds hurried past, paying no attention to him or to his grief. His grief was vast, boundless. If his heart could break, and the grief could pour out of it, it would flow over the whole world; but no one would see it. It had found a hiding place invisible to all: even in broad daylight, even if you held a candle to it, you wouldn't see it.

There was a doorman carrying some kind of sack, and Iona decided to talk to him.

"What time is it, my dear fellow?" he asked.

"Ten o'clock. What the devil are you standing there for? Get a move on!"

Iona drove along the street a bit. His body was bent, and he was surrendering to his grief. He felt it was useless to turn to people for help, but in less than five minutes he had straightened himself up, shaking his head as though he felt a sharp pang of pain, and then he pulled at the reins. He could bear it no longer.

"Back to the stables," he thought. "Back to the stables."

The little mare, as though she read his thoughts, started off at a trot.

An hour and a half later Iona was sitting by a large dirty stove. On the stove, on the floor, on benches, men were snoring. The air was noisome, suffocating. Iona found himself gazing at the sleeping people. He scratched himself, and he was sorry he had come back so early.

"I haven't earned enough even for the hay," he thought. "There's grief for you. But a man who knows his work, and has a full belly, and a well-fed horse besides, he's at peace with the world all his days."

From one of the corners a young driver rose, grunting sleepily as he reached for the water bucket.

"You thirsty?" Iona asked him.

"Reckon so."

"Well, it's a good thing to be thirsty, but as for me, brother, my son is dead. Did you hear me? This week, at the hospital. . . . Such a lot of trouble!"

Iona looked to see whether the words were producing any effect, but saw none—the young man had covered up his face and was asleep again. The old man sighed and scratched himself. Just as the young man wanted to drink, so he wanted to talk. Soon it would be a week since his son died, and still no one had let him talk about it properly. He would have to tell it slowly, very carefully. He would tell them how his son fell ill, how he suffered, what he said before he died, how he died. He would have to describe the funeral, and how he went to the hospital to collect his son's clothes. His daughter Anissya was still in the country. He wanted to talk about her, too. Yes, there was so much to talk about. And the listener would have to gasp and sigh and bewail the fate of the dead man. And maybe it would be better to talk about it to women. Even though women are so foolish, you can bring the tears to their eyes with a few words.

"Now I'll go and look at my horse," Iona thought to himself. "There's always time for sleep—nothing there to be afraid of."

He threw on his coat and went down to the stable to look after her, thinking about such things as hay, oats, and the weather. Alone, he dared not let his mind dwell on his son. He could talk about him to anyone, but alone, thinking about him, conjuring up his living presence, no—no, that was too painful for words.

"Filling your belly, eh?" he said, seeing the mare's shining eyes. "Well, eat up! We haven't earned enough for oats, but we can eat hay. Oh, I'm too old to be driving. My son should be driving, not me. He was a real cabdriver, and he should be alive now. . . ."

Iona was silent for a moment, and then he went on: "That's how it is, old girl. My son, Kuzma Ionich, is no more. He died on us. Now let's say you had a foal, and you were the foal's mother, and suddenly, let's say, the same little foal departed this life. You'd be sorry, eh?"

The little mare munched and listened and breathed on his hands.

Surrendering to his grief, Iona told her the whole story.

January 1886

Anyuta

IN one of those very cheap rooms in the Lisbon rooming house, Stepan Klochkov, a third-year medical student, was pacing up and down as he applied himself zealously to cramming from a medical textbook. The strain of memorizing the words made his mouth dry, and sweat dampened his forehead.

Anyuta, who roomed with him, sat on a stool by the window, where the edges were white with icy tracery. She was a small, thin brunette, twenty-five years old, very pale, with gentle gray eyes. Head bent, she was embroidering the collar of a man's shirt with red thread. She was working hurriedly, against time. It was afternoon, and the clock in the passageway outside drowsily struck two o'clock, but the room was still in disorder. Rumpled bedclothes, pillows scattered everywhere, books, clothes, a large filthy washbasin filled with soapy slop water in which cigarette butts were floating, filth on the floor—everything seemed to have been hurled down in a heap, crumpled, deliberately thrown into confusion.

"The right lung consists of three lobes . . ." Klochkov recited. "Boundaries! Upper lobe on anterior wall of the chest reaches fourth or fifth rib, on the lateral surface, the fourth rib . . . behind up to the *spina scapulae* . . ."

Klochkov tried to visualize what he was reading, and raised his eyes to the ceiling. Unable to form a clear picture, he began to feel his upper ribs through his waistcoat.

"These ribs resemble the keys of a piano," he said. "To avoid being confused by them, you simply must make a mental picture of them. You have to study them on the skeleton and on the living body. Come here, Anyuta! Let's get this thing straight!"

Anyuta put down her sewing, removed her jacket, and straightened her shoulders. Kluchkov sat down facing her, frowned, and began to count her ribs.

"Hm! The first rib can't be felt. . . . It's behind the collarbone. This must be the second rib. . . . Oh yes, and here is the third, and the fourth. . . . Hm . . . Well, why are you shivering?"

"Your fingers are cold!"

"Nonsense, it won't kill you! Don't wriggle about so much. This must be the third, and here's the fourth. . . . You're so thin, and yet I can hardly feel your ribs. . . . Here's the second. . . . Here's the third. . . . No, you are getting confused. You don't see the thing clearly. I shall have to draw it. Where is my piece of charcoal?"

Klochkov took the charcoal crayon and began to sketch some parallel lines corresponding to the ribs on Anyuta's chest.

"Wonderful! Now everything is clear as daylight. Now let me sound your chest. Stand up!"

Anyuta stood up, raising her chin. Klochkov began to tap her chest, becoming so deeply immersed in the task that he did not notice that her lips, nose, and fingers were turning blue with cold. She shivered, and then she was afraid the student would see her shivering, stop drawing lines on her chest, stop tapping her, and then perhaps he would fail miserably in the examinations.

"Now it's all clear," Klochkov said, and he stopped tapping her. "Just sit there, don't rub off the charcoal, and I'll learn some more."

Once again the student began pacing up and down the room, memorizing. Anyuta had black stripes across her chest, and looked as though she had been tattooed. She sat there thinking, huddled up, shivering with cold. She was never talkative, always silent, thinking, thinking. . . .

In six or seven years of wandering from one furnished room to another, she had known five students like Klochkov. Now they had finished their courses, had gone out into the world, and being respectable people, they had put her out of their minds. One of them lived in Paris, two were doctors, a fourth was an artist, and they said the fifth was already a professor. Klochkov was the sixth. Soon he too would leave the medical school and go out into the world. No doubt a beautiful future awaited him, and no doubt he would become a great man, but the present prospects did not look promising. He had no tobacco, no tea, and there were only four lumps of sugar left. She must hurry up with her embroidery, take it to the woman who had ordered it, and then with the quarter ruble she would get for it buy tea and tobacco.

"Can I come in?" said a voice from the door.

Anyuta quickly pulled a woolen shawl round her shoulders.

Fetissov, an artist, walked in.

"Do me a favor," he began, addressing Klochkov and glaring like a wild beast through the hair hovering over his forehead. "Do me the kindness of lending me that pretty woman of yours for an hour or two! You see, I am painting a picture, and I can do nothing without a model."

"With pleasure," the student said. "Go along, Anyuta."

"What I have to put up with," Anyuta murmured softly.

"That's enough! He wants you for the sake of his art, not for some nonsense or other. Why not help him when you can?"

Anyuta began dressing.

"What are you painting?" Klochkov said.

"Psyche. Wonderful subject. It's not going along well, though. I have to keep working with different models. Yesterday there was one with blue legs. I asked how the legs got blue, and she said it was the dye from her stockings. Still learning away, eh? Happy man, with all that patience!"

"Medicine is one of those things you have to keep pegging away at."

"Hm . . . Excuse me, Klochkov, but you are really living in a terrible pigsty. The devil alone knows how you live!"

"What do you mean? I can't live any other way. I only get twelve rubles a month from my father, and it's difficult to live decently on that money."

"Well, so it is," the artist said, knitting his brows with an air of disgust. "Still, you should be able to live better. A civilized man should have some measure of aesthetic taste, surely? Only the devil knows what this room is like! The bed's not made. Slops, filth . . . Yesterday's porridge still in the plates! Pfui!"

"It's true enough," the student said, embarrassed. "Anyuta did not wash up today. All her time was taken."

When Anyuta and the artist had left, Klochkov threw himself down on the divan and went on with his lessons, lying down. Unexpectedly he fell asleep, waking up an hour later. He propped his head in his fists and gave himself up to gloomy reflections. He remembered the artist saying that all civilized men were obliged to have a measure of aesthetic taste, and yet here in the room everything was revolting and loathsome. In his mind's eye he saw himself as he would be in the future: receiving patients in his consulting room, drinking tea in a vast drawing room with his wife, a very proper woman, beside him—and now here was the washbasin with cigarette butts swimming around, and it was unbelievably nauseating. He thought of Anyuta—ugly, unprepossessing, pitiful. He decided to get rid of her at once, whatever the cost.

When she returned from the artist, she took off her coat. He got up and spoke very seriously: "My dear, sit down and listen to me. We have to separate. I don't want to live with you any longer."

Anyuta came back from the artist worn out and close to fainting. From long standing in a suitable pose, her face looked thin and sallow, her chin sharper than ever. She did not reply to the student, but her lips trembled.

"You knew it would have to come sooner or later," the student said. "You're a good, fine person, and you're nobody's fool. You'll understand."

Anyuta put on her coat again. Silently she wrapped up her embroidery in a sheet of paper, gathered up needles and thread, and picked up the four lumps of sugar she had left by the window. These she put on the table next to his books.

"There's your sugar," she said softly, and turned away to hide her tears.

"Why are you crying?" Klochkov said.

He walked confusedly around the room, and said: "Really you are a strange woman. You knew yourself we would have to separate one day. We can't live together forever."

She had already bundled together all her belongings. She was turning to say good-by when he felt sorry for her.

Perhaps I could let her live here for another week, he thought. After all, she might as well stay. In another week I'll tell her to go.

Annoyed by his own weakness, he shouted roughly: "What are you standing there for? If you are going, go! If you don't want to go, take off your coat and stay! Stay if you want to!"

Slowly, silently, Anyuta removed her coat, then blew her nose very softly, sighed, and quietly returned to her familiar place on the stool by the window.

The student drew up his textbook to him, and once again he began to pace up and down the floor.

"The right lung consists of three lobes," he read slowly. "The upper lobe on the anterior wall of the chest reaches the fourth or fifth rib . . ."

In the passageway someone was shouting at the top of his voice: "Gregory! The samovar!"

February 1886

The Proposal

A STORY FOR GIRLS

Valentin Petrovich Peredyorkin, a handsome young man, put on a frock coat, laced his patent-leather boots with their sharp toe-caps, clapped an opera hat on his head, and then, hardly able to restrain his excitement, he drove off to the house of Princess Vera Zapiskina.

How sad, dear reader, that you have never met the Princess. She is a gentle and enchanting creature with soft heavenly-blue eyes and hair like a silken wave.

The waves of the sea break on rocks, but the waves of her hair, on the contrary, would shatter and crumble into dust the hardest stone. Only an insensitive nincompoop could resist her smile or the soft charms of her very small and perfectly formed bust. Only a blockhead could fail to register feelings of absolute joy when she speaks or smiles or shows her dazzling white teeth.

Peredyorkin was received. . . .

He sat down facing the Princess, and he was beside himself with excitement when he said: "Princess, would you listen to something I have to say?"

"Oh, yes."

"Princess, forgive me. I don't know where to begin. It will be so sudden for you . . . so extempore. . . . Promise me you won't be angry. . . ."

He put his hand in his pocket, pulled out a handkerchief, and began to mop his face. All the while the Princess was smiling gently and gazing inquiringly at him.

"Princess!" he went on. "From the moment I set eyes on you, my soul . . . yes, my soul has been filled with unquenchable desires. These desires give me no peace during the day or during the night . . . and if these desires are to remain unfulfilled, I will be utterly miserable. . . ."

The Princess lowered her gaze meditatively.

Peredyorkin was silent for a moment, and went on: "Oh, my dear, it will come as a surprise to you. . . . You are above all earthly concerns, but . . . I regard you as the most suitable. . . ."

A silence followed.

"Most especially," Peredyorkin sighed, "because our estates are contiguous. . . . I am rich. . . ."

"Yes, but what is all this about?" the Princess asked in a soft voice.

"What is it all about? Oh, Princess!" Peredyorkin exclaimed impetuously, rising to his feet. "I entreat you, do not refuse me. . . . Do not ruin my plans with your refusal. My dear, permit me to propose to you . . ."

Valentin Petrovich suddenly sat down, leaned over toward the Princess, and whispered: "I am making the most profitable proposal possible. . . . This way we shall be able to sell a million poods of tallow in a single year. . . . Let us start on our adjoining estates a limited liability company dedicated to tallow boiling!"

The Princess reflected for a moment, and then she said: "With great pleasure!"

The feminine reader, who expected a melodramatic ending, may relax.

October 1886

Vanka

NINE-YEAR-OLD Vanka Zhukov, who was apprenticed three months ago to the shoemaker Alyakhin, did not go to bed on Christmas Eve. He waited till the master and mistress and the more senior apprentices had gone to the early service, and then he took a bottle of ink and a pen with a rusty nib from his master's cupboard, and began to write on a crumpled sheet of paper spread out in front of him. Before tracing the shape of the first letter, he looked several times fearfully in the direction of the doors and windows, and then he gazed up at the dark icon, flanked on either side by shelves filled with cobbler's lasts, and then he heaved a broken sigh. With the paper spread over the bench, Vanka knelt on the floor beside it.

"Dear Grandfather Konstantin Makarich," he wrote. "I am writing a letter to you. I wish you a Merry Christmas and all good things from the Lord God. I have no father and mother, and you are all I have left."

Vanka raised his eyes to the dark windowpane, on which there gleamed the reflection of a candle flame, and in his vivid imagination he saw his grandfather Konstantin Makarich standing there. His grandfather was a night watchman on the estate of some gentlefolk called Zhivaryov, a small, thin, unusually lively and nimble old man of about sixty-five, his face always crinkling with laughter, and his eyes bleary from drink. In the daytime the old man slept in the servants' kitchen or cracked jokes with the cooks. At night, wrapped in an ample sheepskin coat, he made the rounds of the estate, shaking his clapper. Two dogs followed him with drooping heads—one was the old bitch Brownie, the other was called Eel from his black coat and long weaselly body. Eel always seemed to be extraordinarily respectful and endearing, gazing with the same fond eyes on friends and strangers alike; yet no one trusted him. His deference and humility concealed a most jesuitical malice. No one knew better how to creep stealthily behind someone and take a nip at his leg, or how to crawl into the icehouse, or how to scamper off with a peasant's chicken. More than once they just about broke his hind legs, twice a noose was put round his neck, and every week he was beaten until he was only half alive, yet he always managed to survive.

At this very moment Grandfather was probably standing by the gates, screwing up his eyes at the bright red windows of the village church, stamping about in his felt boots and cracking jokes with the servants. His clapper hung from his belt. He would be throwing out his arms and then hugging himself against the cold, and, hiccoughing as old men do, he would be pinching one of the servant girls or one of the cooks.

"What about a pinch of snuff, eh?" he would say, holding out his snuffbox to the women.

Then the women would take a pinch and sneeze, and the old man would be overcome with indescribable ecstasies, laughing joyously and exclaiming: "Fine for frozen noses, eh!"

The dogs, too, were given snuff. Brownie would sneeze, shake her head, and walk away looking offended, while Eel, too polite to sneeze, only wagged his tail. The weather was glorious. The air was still, transparently clear, and fresh. The night was very dark, but the whole white-roofed village with its snowdrifts and trees silvered with hoarfrost and smoke streaming from the chimneys could be seen clearly. The heavens were sprinkled with gay, glinting stars, and the Milky Way stood out as clearly as if it had been washed and scrubbed with snow for the holidays.

Vanka sighed, dipped his pen in the ink, and went on writing: "Yesterday I was given a thrashing. The master dragged me by the hair into the yard and gave me a beating with a stirrup strap because when I was rocking the baby in the cradle, I misfortunately fell asleep. And then last week the mistress ordered me to gut a herring, and because I began with the tail, she took the head of the herring and rubbed it all over my face. The other apprentices made fun of me, sent me to the tavern for vodka, and made me steal the master's cucumbers for them, and then the master beat me with the first thing that came to hand. And there's nothing to eat. In the morning they give me bread, there is porridge for dinner, and in the evening only bread again. They never give me tea or cabbage soup—they gobble it all up themselves. They make me sleep in the passageway, and when their baby cries, I don't get any sleep at all because I have to rock the cradle. Dear Grandfather, please for God's sake take me away from here, take me to the village, it's more than I can bear. . . . I kneel down before you. I'll pray to God to keep you forever, but take me away from here, or I shall die."

Vanka grimaced, rubbed his eyes with his black fists, and sobbed.

"I'll grind your snuff for you," he went on. "I will pray to God to keep you, and if I ever do anything wrong, you can flog me all you like. If you think there's no place for me, then I'll ask the manager for Christ's sake to let me clean boots or take Fedya's place as a shepherd boy. Dear Grandfather, it's more than I can bear, it will be the death of me. I thought of running away to the village, but I haven't any boots, and I am afraid of the ice. If you'll do this for me, I'll feed you when I grow up, and won't let anyone harm you, and when you die I'll pray for the repose of your soul, just like I do for my mother, Pelageya.

"Moscow is such a big city. There are so many houses belonging to the gentry, so many horses, but no sheep anywhere, and the dogs aren't vicious. The boys don't go about with the Star of Christmas, and they don't let you sing in the choir, and once I saw fishhooks in the shopwindow with the fishing lines for every kind of fish, very fine ones, even one hook which would hold a skate fish weighing forty pounds. I've seen shops selling guns which are just like the master's at home, and each one must cost a hundred rubles. In the butcher shops they have woodcocks and partridges and hares, but the people in the shop won't tell you where they were shot.

"Dear Grandfather, when they put up the Christmas tree at the big house, please take down a golden walnut for me and hide it in the green chest. Ask the young mistress, Olga Ignatyevna, and say it is for Vanka."

Vanka heaved a convulsive sigh, and once more he gazed in the direction of the window. He remembered it was Grandfather who always went to the forest to cut down a Christmas tree for the gentry, taking his grandson with him. They had a wonderful time together. Grandfather chuckled, the frost crackled, and Vanka, not to be outdone, clucked away cheerfully. Before chopping down the fir tree Grandfather would smoke a pipe, take a long pinch of snuff, and make fun of Vanka, who was shivering in the cold. The young fir trees, garlanded with hoarfrost, stood perfectly still, waiting to see which of them would die. . . . Suddenly out of nowhere a hare came springing across the snowdrifts, quick as an arrow, and Grandfather would be unable to prevent himself from shouting: "Hold him! Hold him! Hold that bobtailed devil, eh!"

When the tree had been chopped down, Grandfather would drag it to the big house and they would start decorating it. The young mistress, Olga Ignatyevna, Vanka's favorite, was the busiest of all. While Vanka's mother, Pelageya, was alive, serving as a chambermaid, Olga Ignatyevna used to stuff him with sugar candy, and it amused her to teach him to read and write, to count up to a hundred, and even to dance the quadrille. But when Pelageya died, they relegated the orphan Vanka to the servants' kitchen to be with his Grandfather, and from there he went to Moscow to the shoemaker Alyakhin. . . .

"Come to me, dear Grandfather," Vanka went on. "I beseech you for Christ's sake, take me away from here! Have pity on me, a poor orphan, they are always beating me, and I am terribly hungry, and so miserable I can't tell you, and I'm always crying. The other day the master hit me on the head with a last, and I fell down and thought I would never get up again. It's worse than a dog's life, and so miserable. I send greetings to Alyona, to one-eyed Yegor, and to the coachman, and don't give my harmonica away. I remain your grandson Ivan Zhukov, dear Grandfather, and come soon!"

Vanka twice folded the sheet of paper and then he put it in an envelope bought the previous day for a kopeck. He reflected for a while, dipped the pen in ink, and wrote the address:

To Grandfather in the Village

Then he scratched his head and thought for a while, and added the words: *Konstantin Makarich*. Pleased because no one interrupted him when he was writing, he threw on his cap, and without troubling to put on a coat, he ran out into the street in his shirt sleeves.

When he talked to the clerks in the butcher shop the previous day, they told him that letters were dropped in boxes, and from these boxes they were carried all over the world on mail coaches drawn by three horses and driven by drunken drivers, while the bells jingled. Vanka ran to the nearest mailbox and thrust his precious letter into the slot.

An hour later, lulled by sweetest hopes, he was fast asleep. He dreamed of a stove. His grandfather was sitting on the stove, bare feet dangling down, while he read the letter aloud to the cooks. Eel was walking round the stove, wagging his tail.

December 1886

Who Is to Blame?

〰〰〰〰〰〰

MY uncle Pyotr Demyanich, a lean and bilious collegiate councilor, who bore a close resemblance to a stale smoked catfish with a stick through it, was just about to leave for the high school where he taught Latin when he saw that the binding of his grammar book had been nibbled by mice.

"Good heavens," he shouted, and ran to the kitchen, where he addressed his remarks to the cook. "Listen, Praskovya, how did the mice get in? God save my soul, yesterday they nibbled at my top hat, and today, if you please, they have begun to ruin my grammar book! Soon enough they will be having a feast on my clothes!"

"I did not bring them here," Praskovya said. "What do you expect me to do?"

"Well, I expect you to do something. Why don't you get a cat?"

"We already have a cat, but he is no good."

Praskovya pointed to a corner in the kitchen where a white kitten, thin as a matchstick, lay curled up asleep beside a broom.

"Why isn't he any good?" asked Pyotr Demyanich.

"Because he's only a silly little baby. He's less than two months old."

"Hm . . . Then he must be trained. Training is better than doing nothing."

Saying this, Pyotr Demyanich sighed with a preoccupied air and left the kitchen. The kitten looked up, surveyed the world with a lazy glance, and then closed his eyes again.

The kitten was not sleeping, but deep in thought. What was he thinking about? He knew absolutely nothing about real life and possessed no store of accumulated impressions: therefore he could only think instinctively and picture life according to concepts inherited, like his flesh and blood, from his ancestors, the tigers (*vide* Darwin). His thoughts possessed the character of daydreams. In his imagination he saw something resembling the Arabian desert, over which there hovered shadows resembling Praskovya, the stove, the broomstick. Among these shadows a saucer of milk would suddenly appear. This saucer would grow paws, it would move and display a tendency to run away, and the kitten would therefore leap up, give way to a bloodthirsty sensuality, and dig his paws into it. Then the saucer would vanish among the misty clouds, and suddenly there would appear a piece of meat dropped by Praskovya. The meat would give forth a timid little squeak before darting to one side, but the kitten would leap after it and dig his claws into it. Everything that rose up in the imagination of this young dreamer had its origin in sudden leaps, claws, and teeth. . . . The soul of another lies in darkness, and a cat's soul more than most, but how near these visions I have just described are to the truth may be seen from the following circumstance: under the influence of his reveries the kitten suddenly jumped up, gazed at Praskovya with glittering eyes, fur bristling, and suddenly hurled himself at the cook, digging his claws into her skirt. Clearly he was born to be a hunter of mice, worthy of his bloodthirsty ancestors. Clearly he was destined by fate to be the terror of cellars, storerooms, and cornbins, and had it not been for education . . . But nothing is to be gained by anticipating.

When he returned from high school, Pyotr Demyanich went to a local store and bought a mousetrap for fifteen kopecks. After dinner he hung a small morsel of cutlet on the hook and set the trap under the divan, where there was a litter of old exercise books which Praskovya would sometimes use for her own domestic purposes. Exactly at six o'clock that evening, when our worthy Latinist was sitting at table and correcting his students' exercises, he heard a sudden *clop!* coming from under the divan —the sound was so loud that my uncle jumped up in the air and dropped his pen. Without any hesitation he marched over to the divan and drew out the mousetrap. In it he found a sleek and tiny mouse, about the size of a thimble, sniffing at the wire cage and shivering with fear.

"Aha!" muttered Pyotr Demyanich, and he gazed at the mouse with the expression of a man about to give it a bad mark. "I've caught you now, you little devil! Just you wait! I'll teach you to eat my grammar book!"

For a while Pyotr Demyanich continued to feast his eyes on the spectacle of his little victim, then he put the mousetrap on the floor and shouted: "Praskovya, the mouse hasn't got away! Bring the kitten in here!"

"Coming at once!" Praskovya answered, and a few moments later she walked in, carrying in her arms the descendant of tigers.

"Very good," Pyotr Demyanich murmured, rubbing his hands together. "Now we'll teach him a lesson. Put him down facing the mousetrap. . . . That's right. Let him sniff at it, and have a good look. That's right."

The kitten looked wonderingly at my uncle and then at the armchair, and then he sniffed the mousetrap with a look of complete bewilderment. Perhaps it was because he was frightened by the glare of the lamp and the attention he was receiving: suddenly he was off to the door, scampering away in fear and trembling.

"Stop!" shouted my uncle, seizing him by the tail. "Stop, you little idiot! Fool, he's afraid of the mouse! Look at the mouse! Look hard! I told you to look, didn't I?"

Pyotr Demyanich lifted the kitten by the scruff of the neck and pushed his nose against the mousetrap.

"Vile, stupid creature! . . . Praskovya, take him and hold him. Hold him opposite the door of the trap! When I let the mouse out, let the kitten go after him at once. Are you listening? Let him go at once!"

My uncle assumed a mysterious expression and lifted the door. The mouse emerged, uncertain and frightened; it sniffed the air, and then flew quick as an arrow under the divan. When the kitten was let go, he lifted his tail and ran under the table.

"He's got away! He's got away!" Pyotr Demyanich shouted, assuming a ferocious expression. "Where is the kitten, the little horror? Under the table, eh? Just you wait!"

My uncle dragged the kitten from under the table and gave him a good shaking.

"What a rascal you are, eh?" he muttered, smacking the kitten across the ear. "Take that! Take that! Will you just stand there gawking the next time? You r-r-r-rascal, you!"

The following day Praskovya heard him shouting for the second time: "Praskovya, we've caught a mouse! Bring the kitten here!"

After the abuse he had received the previous day the kitten had taken to hiding under the stove, where he remained throughout the night. When Praskovya pulled him out and carried him by the scruff of the neck to the study, he was trembling all over and mewing pathetically. He was put in front of the mousetrap.

"You see, he has to feel at home," Pyotr Demyanich said. "Let him look and sniff a bit. Look and learn!" And when he saw the kitten backing away from the trap, he shouted: "Stop, dammit! I'll tear you to pieces! Hold him by the ear! . . . That's right, and now set him down opposite the door."

My uncle slowly lifted the door. The mouse dived under the kitten's nose, threw itself against Praskovya's hand, and then

121

dived under a cupboard, while the kitten, feeling relieved, decided upon a sudden desperate leap in the air and scuttled under the divan.

"That's the second mouse he has let go!" Pyotr Demyanich roared at the top of his voice. "Do you call that a cat? It's a silly idiot, that's what it is, and deserves a thrashing. That's right—give him a thrashing in front of the mousetrap."

When the third mouse was caught, the kitten shivered uncontrollably in full view of the mousetrap and its occupant, and dug his claws into Praskovya's hand. . . . After the fourth mouse my uncle was beside himself with rage, kicked out at the kitten, and shouted: "Take the filthy thing away! Get it out of the house! Throw it out! The hell with it!"

A year passed. The lean and frail kitten became a wise and sedate tomcat. One day he was making his way through the back yard in search of amatory adventure and was very close to finding what he wanted to find when he suddenly heard a rustling sound and saw a mouse running between the water trough and the stables. My hero's fur bristled, he arched his back, he hissed, he trembled all over, and ignominiously ran away.

Alas, I sometimes feel I am in the same ludicrous position as this cowardly cat. Long ago, like the kitten, I had the honor of receiving lessons in Latin from my uncle. Now, whenever someone mentions an ancient classic, instead of being moved with eager enthusiasm, I remember my uncle's gray and sallow face. irregular verbs, *ut consecutivum*, *ablativus absolutus*. . . . I grow pale, my hair stands on end, and like the kitten I take refuge in ignominious flight.

December 1886

Typhus

YOUNG Lieutenant Klimov sat in a smoking compartment on the mail train from Petersburg to Moscow. Opposite him was an elderly man with the clean-shaven face of a ship's skipper, to all appearances a well-to-do Finn or Swede; he kept sucking at his pipe and spoke in broken Russian. He had only one subject of conversation throughout the entire journey.

"Ha! So you are an officer, eh? Well, my brother is also an officer, but he is in the Navy. He's a sailor serving at Kronstadt. Why are you going to Moscow?"

"I'm stationed there."

"Ha! Are you married?"

"No, I am living with my aunt and sister."

"My brother is also an officer, but he's in the Navy, and he's married and has a wife and three children. Ha!"

The Finn seemed puzzled by something, but smiled broadly and idiotically whenever he said "Ha!" Every now and then he blew through his evil-smelling pipe. Klimov was feeling unwell, had no desire to answer questions, and hated the skipper with all his heart. He was thinking how good it would be to snatch that noisy, grumbling pipe out of the man's hands and hurl it under the seat, and then to order him into another car.

"Those Finns . . . and Greeks," he thought. "They're all loathsome. They're completely useless, good-for-nothing, rotten people. They only fill up the earth's space. What good do they do?"

The thought of Finns and Greeks overwhelmed him with a kind of nausea. He tried to compare them with the French and Italians, but for some reason he could only conjure up images of organ-grinders, naked women, and the foreign oleographs which hung over the chest of drawers in his aunt's house.

The officer was beginning to feel some abnormal symptoms. There seemed to be no room at all for his arms and legs on the seat, although he had the whole seat for himself. His mouth was dry and sticky; a heavy fog weighed down his brain; his thoughts seemed to be straying not only within but also outside his skull, among the seats and the people muffled up in the misty darkness of the night. Through the turmoil of his brain, as through a dream, he heard the murmur of voices, the clattering of wheels, the slamming of doors. The clanging of bells, the guards' whistles, people running up and down the platform—these sounds seemed more frequent than usual. Time flew by quickly, imperceptibly, and it seemed that never a minute passed but the train stopped at a station, and at each stop there could be heard metallic voices saying:

"Is the mail ready?"

"Ready!"

It seemed to him that the man in charge of the heating was continually coming in to look at the thermometer, and the roar of approaching trains and the rumbling of the wheels over bridges never ended. The noise, the whistles, the Finn, tobacco smoke . . . all these things, mingled with the menacing and trembling shapes of mist in his brain, those shapes which healthy men can never afterwards remember, weighed down on Klimov like an unendurable nightmare. In awful agony he lifted his heavy head and gazed at the lamp, whose light was encircled with shadows and misty blurs. He wanted to ask for water but his tongue was excessively dry and could hardly move, and he had scarcely enough strength to answer the Finn's questions. He tried to lie down more comfortably and go to sleep, but he could not. Several times the Finn fell asleep, then woke up, lit his pipe, turned and said "Ha!" and went to sleep again; but the lieutenant could not find room for his legs on the seat, and still the menacing shapes came hovering over his eyes.

At Spirov he went out into the station and drank some water. He saw people sitting at a table, eating hurriedly.

"How can they eat?" he thought, trying not to inhale the smell of fried meat, trying not to observe the way they chewed their food—both of these things nauseated him.

A pretty woman was talking loudly with an officer in a red cap. She smiled, showing splendid white teeth. The smile, the teeth, the woman herself, produced on Klimov exactly the same feeling of repulsion as the ham and the fried cutlets did. He could not understand how it was that the officer in the red cap could endure to be sitting beside her and gazing at her healthy smiling face.

After drinking the water he went back to the compartment. The Finn was still sitting there, smoking away. The pipe gurgled, making a sobbing noise like a galosh full of holes on a rainy day.

"Ha! What station is this?" he wondered aloud.

"I don't know," Klimov replied, lying down and shutting his mouth so as not to inhale the acrid tobacco smoke.

"When do we reach Tver?"

"I don't know. I'm sorry. I can't talk to you. . . . I am not well. I've caught a cold."

The Finn knocked out his pipe against the window frame, and began talking of his brother, the sailor. Klimov no longer listened to him; he was miserably dreaming about a soft, comfortable bed, a carafe of cold water, and his sister Katya, who knew so well how to tuck him up and how to soothe him and bring him water. He was smiling when the image of Pavel, his orderly, flashed through his mind: Pavel was removing the master's heavy, stifling boots and putting water on the table. It seemed to him if he could only lie on his own bed and drink water, then the nightmare would give place to a sound, healthy sleep.

"Is the mail ready?" a hollow voice could be heard in the distance.

"Ready!" came a bass voice close to the window.

Already they were at the second or third station from Spirov.

Time passed, galloping along at a furious pace, and there seemed to be no end to the stops, the bells, the whistles. In despair Klimov buried his face in a corner of the seat, clutched his head in his hands, and once again found himself thinking of his sister Katya and his orderly, Pavel; but his sister and the orderly got mixed up in the misty shapes whirling around his brain, and soon they vanished. His hot breath, reflected from the seat cushions, scalded his face; his legs were uncomfortable; a draft from the window poured over his back. In spite of all these discomforts he had no desire to change his position. Little by little a heavy nightmarish lethargy took possession of his limbs and chained them to the seat.

When at length he decided to lift up his head, the compartment was flooded with daylight. The passengers were putting on their fur coats and moving about. The train was standing still. Porters in white aprons with badges were bustling about among the passengers and carrying off their trunks. Klimov slipped on his greatcoat and mechanically followed the other passengers out of the carriage, and it seemed to him that it was not himself who was walking, but someone else entirely, a stranger, and he felt he was being accompanied by his fever and the heat of the train and by all those menacing images which all night had prevented him from sleeping. Mechanically he found his luggage and engaged a cab. The driver charged a ruble and a quarter to take him to the Povarskaya, but he did not haggle and without any protest at all he took his seat. He could understand that he was paying too high a price, but money had ceased to have any meaning for him.

At home Klimov was met by his aunt and his sister Katya, a

girl of eighteen. While Katya greeted him, she was holding a copybook and a pencil in her hands and he remembered that she was preparing for her teacher's examination. He paid no attention to her questions and her greetings, but gasped in the heat and walked aimlessly through all the rooms until he reached his bedroom, and then he threw himself down on the bed. The Finn, the red cap, the lady with the white teeth, the smell of fried meat, the shifting blurs of light in the compartment, filled his consciousness, and he no longer knew where he was, and did not hear the frightened voices near him.

When he recovered consciousness he found he was in his bed, and undressed. He could see Pavel and the carafe of water, but the bed was no cooler, no softer, and no more comfortable. His legs and arms felt just as cramped as before. His tongue was clinging to the roof of his mouth, and he could hear the groaning of the Finn's pipe. . . . Beside the bed a stout, black-bearded doctor was bustling about and brushing against Pavel's broad back.

"It's all right, me lad," the doctor murmured. "Wery good! Yies indeed!"

The doctor called Klimov "me lad," and said "wery" instead of "very," and "yies" instead of "yes."

"Yies, yies, yies," he said. "Wery good, me lad! Don't take it too much to heart!"

The doctor's quick, careless way of speaking, his well-fed face, and the condescending way he said "me lad" infuriated Klimov.

"Why do you call me 'me lad'?" he moaned. "What familiarity! Go to hell!"

And he was frightened by the sound of his own voice. It was so dry, so weak, so muted, that he could not recognize it.

"Excellent, excellent," murmured the doctor, not in the least offended. "No use to get angry now. Yies, yies . . ."

At home, time flew by with the same startling speed as in the train. In the bedroom, daylight was continually giving place to shadowy darkness. The doctor seemed never to leave the bedside; and every minute he could be heard saying: "Yies, yies . . ." A continual stream of faces plunged across the room—the doctor, the Finn, Pavel, Captain Yaroshevich, Sergeant-Major Maximenko, the red cap, the lady with the white teeth. They were all talking and waving their arms, smoking and eating. Once in broad daylight Klimov saw Father Alexander, his regimental chaplain, standing by the bed. The priest was wearing a stole and holding a prayer book in his hands, and he was muttering something with a grave expression such as Klimov had never encountered before. The lieutenant remembered that Father Alexander, in the most friendly way possible, had the habit of calling all the Catholic officers Poles, and to amuse him the lieutenant cried out: "Father, the Pole Yaroshevich has climbed up a pole!"

But Father Alexander, usually so jolly and lighthearted, did not laugh, but instead looked graver than ever as he made the sign of the cross over Klimov. And then at night two shadows came flitting silently across the room, one after another. They were his aunt and his sister. The sister's shadow knelt and prayed. She bowed low before the icon, and her gray shadow on the wall also bowed low: both shadows were praying to God. And all the time there was the smell of fried meat and the Finn's pipe. Once Klimov detected the strong smell of incense. He shuddered with nausea, and began shouting: "The incense! Take the incense away!"

There was no answer. He heard only the subdued chanting of priests and the sound of someone running up the stairs.

When Klimov recovered from his delirium there was no one in the bedroom. The morning sunlight streamed through the window and through the drawn curtains, and a quivering sunbeam, thin and keen as a sword edge, trembled on the carafe of water. He could hear wheels rattling: this meant there was no more snow on the streets. The lieutenant gazed at the sunbeam, at the door and all the familiar furniture in the room, and his first impulse was to laugh. His chest and stomach trembled with a sweet, happy, tickling laugh. From head to foot his whole body was filled with a sensation of infinite happiness, such as the first man must have felt at the moment of creation and when for the first time he looked out upon the world. The lieutenant felt a passionate desire to know people, to talk with them, to see things moving. His body was nothing more than a motionless lump: only his hands stirred, and he was scarcely aware they were stirring, for his whole attention was concentrated upon unimportant things. He was happy to be breathing, to be laughing: the existence of the carafe, the ceiling, the sunbeam, the ribbon on the curtain, all these made him rejoice. God's world, even in the narrow space of the bedroom, seemed beautiful, various, and immense. When the doctor appeared, the lieutenant was thinking how delicious his medicine was, how charming and sympathetic was the doctor, and how good and interesting people were on the whole.

"Yies, yies, yies," said the doctor. "Excellent! . . . Now we are much better, eh? Wery good, wery good!"

The lieutenant listened and laughed happily. He remembered the Finn, the lady with the white teeth, and the train. He wanted to eat and smoke.

"Doctor," he said, "tell them to give me a crust of rye bread and some salt . . . and sardines."

The doctor refused. Pavel did not obey the order and refused to go for the bread. The lieutenant could not bear it and began to cry like a child in a tantrum.

"What a baby!" the doctor laughed. "Hush-a-bye, baby!"

And then Klimov began to laugh, and when the doctor left, he fell into a deep sleep. He woke up with the same joy and happiness he had known before. His aunt was sitting by the bed.

"Well, aunt!" he said happily. "What has been the matter with me?"

"Typhus."

"Good heavens! But I'm well now. Where's Katya?"

"She's not at home. She must have gone out somewhere after her examination."

The old woman said this, and then bent over her stocking. Her mouth began to tremble, she turned her face away, and suddenly broke into sobs. She was so overcome with grief that she forgot the doctor's orders and cried out: "Oh, Katya, Katya! Our angel has gone away! Our angel has gone!"

She dropped her stocking and bent down to pick it up, and as she did so her cap fell from her head. Klimov found himself gazing at her gray hair, understanding nothing. He was alarmed for Katya's sake, and asked: "Where is she, aunt?"

The old woman had already forgotten Klimov and remembered only her grief.

"She caught typhus from you, and died. She was buried the day before yesterday."

This terrible, unexpected news took deep hold of Klimov's consciousness, but however frightening and shocking it was it could not entirely overcome the animal joy which flooded through him in his convalescence. He cried and laughed, and soon he was complaining because he was being given nothing to eat.

A week later, supported by Pavel, he walked in his dressing gown to the window and looked out at the gray spring sky and listened to the horrible rattle of old iron rails as they were being carried away in a cart. His heart was aching and he burst into tears, leaning his forehead on the window frame.

"How miserable I am!" he murmured. "My God, how miserable I am!"

And joy gave way to the weariness of daily life and a feeling of irreparable loss.

1887

Sleepyhead

NIGHT. Varka, the nursemaid, a girl of about thirteen, **was**
rocking the cradle and singing in an almost inaudible voice to **the**
baby:

Hush-a-bye, hush-a-bye,
I'll sing you a song . . .

A green lamp was burning in front of the icon, and there was
a rope stretching from one corner of the room to the other, with
diapers and an enormous pair of black trousers hanging down
from it. A great stain of green light, reflected upward from the
lamp, glowed on the ceiling. The diapers and trousers threw
heavy shadows on the stove, on Varka, and on the cradle. When
the lamp flame flickered, the green stain and the shadows
moved in unison and seemed to be buffeted by a wind. There
was a suffocating smell of soup and old boot leather.

The baby was crying. For a long time he had been hoarse
and weak from crying, but nevertheless he continued to cry and
showed no sign of stopping. Varka wanted to sleep. Her eyelids
were glued together, her head ached, her neck throbbed. She
could scarcely move her eyes or her lips; her face felt stiff **and**
dry, and her head seemed to have shriveled to the size of a pin-
head.

"Hush-a-bye, baby," she sang softly. "You shall be fed **bye**
and bye."

A cricket chirped in the stove. Behind the door, in the next room, Varka's master and the journeyman Afanasy were snoring. The cradle creaked plaintively and Varka sang her songs; and these two noises mingled together in a soft, lulling night music sweet to the ears of those who lie in bed. But now this music only irritated and depressed her, for it made her sleepy and sleep had become impossible. God forbid that Varka should fall asleep, for if she did her master and mistress would beat her unmercifully.

The lamp flickered. The green stain and the shadows wandered about the room, falling upon the half-open motionless eyes of Varka, creating images in her drowsy, half-awakened brain. She saw dark clouds chasing each other across the sky and crying like the child. When the wind rose, the clouds vanished, and then she saw a wide highway covered with liquid mud: along this highway she saw baggage trains stretching into the distance, and men crawled after them with knapsacks on their backs, and the shadows hovered over them. On both sides of the highway were forests, which could be seen emerging out of the raw and chilling mists. Suddenly the men with the knapsacks and the shadows fell in the liquid mud. "Why did this happen?" Varka asked, and the reply came: "Go to sleep! Go to sleep!" So they slept sweetly and soundlessly. Crows and magpies perched on the telegraph wires, and they were weeping like children, trying to awaken those who had fallen by the wayside.

"Hush-a-bye, hush-a-bye," Varka sang softly. "I'll sing you a song." And then she found herself in a dark and suffocating hut.

Her dead father, Yefim Stepanov, was sprawled over the floor. She could not see him, but heard him tossing about and moaning. He used to say: "My hernia is acting up!" and so it was. The pain was so fierce that he was unable to speak a single word. He just sucked in the air and expelled it from his mouth with a sound like the rolling of drums.

"*Bu, bu, bu, bu . . .*"

Her mother, Pelageya, ran off to the farmhouse to tell the

master that Yefim was dying. She had been gone for a long while, and Varka wondered whether she would ever return. She lay on the stove, unable to sleep, growing accustomed to her father's voice, the interminable "*Bu-bu-bu-bu* . . ." She heard someone coming up to the hut. The master had sent the young doctor: he was a guest from a neighboring town and was staying at the master's house. The doctor came into the hut. The shadows were so thick that he remained invisible, but she heard his cough and the creaking of the door.

"Let me have a light!" the doctor said.

"*Bu-bu-bu-bu* . . ." Yefim muttered.

At that moment Pelageya sprang to the stove and began to search for the crock with the matches. A whole minute passed in silence. The doctor, diving into his pocket, produced a match and struck it.

"I'm coming straight away, *batyushka!*" Pelageya said, running out of the hut and returning a moment later with a candle end.

Yefim's cheeks were flushed, his eyes glittered, and his gaze was very penetrating, as though he could see right through the hut and right through the doctor.

"How do you feel?" the doctor said. "Has it been going on a long time?"

"Eh, what's that? My time's up, Your Honor. I'm on my way out. . . ."

"Fiddlesticks! We'll have you cured in no time!"

"Just as you say, Your Honor. . . . We thank you humbly. . . . Only we understand, if it comes to dying, then there's nothing we can do about it."

For a quarter of an hour the doctor stayed with Yefim, and then he rose and said: "There's nothing more I can do for you. You'll have to go to the hospital, and they'll operate on you. You have to go now, make no mistake. It's a bit late. They'll all be asleep at the hospital, but that's all right. I'll give you a note. . . . Can you hear me?"

"*Batyushka*, how can they take him there?" Pelageya said. "We don't have a horse to our name."

"Don't worry about that. I'll speak to the master, and he'll lend you a horse."

The doctor went away, and then it grew dark, and once more she heard: "*Bu-bu-bu-bu* . . ." Half an hour later someone drove up to the hut. It was the small cart sent by the master to take Yefim to the hospital. Yefim got ready, and then he went away in the cart.

The next morning rose fine and clear. Pelageya was not at home: she had gone to the hospital to see her husband. Somewhere a baby was crying, and Varka was surprised to hear someone singing in her own voice:

> *Hush-a-bye, baby, hush-a-bye,*
> *Nurse will sing for you bye and bye . . .*

When Pelageya returned from the hospital, she crossed herself and whispered: "He was operated on last night, but early this morning he gave up his soul to God. Heavenly kingdom, eternal rest . . . They say he went too late to the hospital. We should have taken him earlier. . . ."

Varka slipped away into the forest and gave herself up to weeping, and suddenly someone hit her across the nape of the neck with such force she cracked her forehead against a birch tree. Then she looked up, and saw it was her master, the shoemaker.

"What do you think you are doing, stupid!" he shouted. "The baby is crying, and you let yourself fall asleep."

He smacked her across the ears. It hurt, but she only shook her head and went on rocking the cradle and murmuring her song. The green stain, the shadow of the diapers and the trousers waved and winked at her, and once again penetrated into her brain. Once again she saw a highway covered with liquid mud. Men with knapsacks on their backs, dark with shadow, lay down in the mud and slept soundly. And while she gazed at them, Varka passionately wanted to sleep. She could have thrown herself down on a bed with perfect happiness, but at that moment her mother, Pelageya, came and hurried her away, and together they went to the town to look for work.

"Give us something for the love of Christ!" her mother called to everyone she met. "Dear good people, be merciful to us!"

The well-known voice was saying: "Give me the baby! Give him to me!" The same voice said angrily, with a sharp cutting edge: "So you are sleeping again, you little wretch!"

Varka jumped up and looked around her. She remembered now where she was. There was no highway, no Pelageya, no passers-by: only her mistress standing there in the middle of the room, coming to feed her baby. She was a stout, heavy-shouldered woman, and while she was feeding and soothing the baby, Varka stood quite still, gazing at her and waiting until she had finished. Outside the windows darkness was giving place to blue sky, and all the shadows and the green stain on the ceiling were visibly turning pale. Soon it would be morning.

"Now you take him," the mother said, buttoning the top buttons of her nightgown. "He's still crying. Someone must have put a spell on him!"

So Varka took the baby and laid him in the cradle, and once more she began to rock the cradle. Slowly the shadows and the green stain faded to nothing, and there was no teeming darkness, nothing at all, to keep her brain in turmoil. She wanted so terribly to sleep. She laid her head on the edge of the cradle and rocked it with her whole body in order to overcome the desire for sleep; but soon her eyelids were glued together and her head grew heavy.

"Varka, light the stove!" Her master's voice came from behind the door.

This meant it was time to get up and start the day's work. She abandoned the cradle and ran into the woodshed. This made her happy, for while she was running or walking, she had no desire for sleep: that desire which overcame her whenever she was sitting down. She gathered up the sticks of wood and lit the stove, and her face no longer felt stiff, and her thoughts were coming clear.

"Varka, get the samovar ready!" her mistress shouted.

Varka split the fagots into small pieces, and she had scarcely put fire to them and pushed them into the samovar when there came another order: "Varka, clean your master's galoshes!"

Varka sat on the floor, cleaned the galoshes, and thought how wonderful it would be if she could hide her head in those big, deep galoshes and go to sleep for a while. Before her eyes the galoshes began to grow and swell up and fill the whole room. She let the cleaning brush fall from her hands, and she shook her head from side to side. Her eyes were bulging, and she was gazing at objects as though they had not grown larger and were not continually moving in front of her eyes.

"Varka, wash the outside steps! They're an insult to our customers!"

Varka washed the steps, tidied up the room, lit another stove, and ran into the shop. There was so much work to be done: not a single moment left free for herself.

There is nothing in the world so tiring as to stand in one spot beside a kitchen table peeling potatoes. Her head fell forward, the potatoes made her eyes ache, the knife dropped from her hand, and the stout, ill-tempered mistress strode about the room with her sleeves rolled up, complaining in a loud, menacing voice which set Varka's ears ringing. It was sheer torture for her to wait at table, and do the washing up and sewing. There were moments when, in spite of everything that was happening around her, she wanted only to throw herself on the floor and fall asleep.

The day passed. While gazing at the darkening windows, Varka pressed her fists against her numbed temples and smiled, scarcely knowing why she was so happy. The evening shadows caressed her drooping eyelids, promising her that she would soon sleep sound.

That evening visitors came flocking to the shoemaker's house. "Varka, get the samovar ready!" her mistress shouted.

It was a small samovar, and before the visitors had drunk all the tea they wanted, it had to be warmed up five times. After the tea Varka had to stand in one place for a whole hour, gazing at the visitors and attending to their wishes.

"Varka, go out and buy three bottles of beer!"

Varka tore herself away, running faster than ever so as to drive sleep away.

"Varka! Get the vodka! Where's the corkscrew? Varka, gut the herrings!"

At last the visitors left. The fires were put out, and the master and mistress went off to bed.

"Varka! Rock the cradle!" This was the last of the orders she received.

A cricket chirruped in the stove. Once again the green stain on the ceiling and the shadows of trousers and diapers penetrated her half-closed eyelids, beckoned to her, and darkened her brain.

"Hush-a-bye, baby," she murmured softly. "I'll sing you a song . . ."

The baby went on crying, though the effort exhausted him. Once more Varka saw the muddy highway, the people with knapsacks, Pelageya and her father, Yefim. She knew them all; recognized them all; but in her drowsy state of mind she was far from understanding the power which bound her hand and foot, suffocated her, and prevented her from being alive. She gazed round the room, searching for that power in order to push it away from her. She could not find it. At last, worn out beyond endurance, she exerted all her strength, all her gift of sight; and while gazing at the green and beckoning stain, she heard the baby crying and discovered the enemy who was destroying her.

Her enemy was the baby. She laughed aloud. She was astonished how simple it all was! It seemed to her that the shadows, the cricket, the green stain—all of them were smiling in astonishment.

A strange idea took possession of her. She rose from her low chair, smiling broadly, and with wide-open eyes she began pacing up and down the room. It pleased her, and she was also amused, by the thought that she would soon be free of the baby, which had bound her hand and foot. To kill the baby, and then to sleep—

Smiling, her eyes sparkling, she made a threatening gesture with her finger at the green stain, and then she crept up to the cradle and bent over the baby. She strangled him. Then she fell on the floor, laughing with joy because now at last it was given to her to be able to sleep. A moment later, she was fast asleep.

January 1888

The Princess

A CARRIAGE drawn by four plump, beautiful horses drove through the so-called Red Gate of the N—— Monastery, and the monks and lay brothers crowding round the rooms of the hostel reserved for the gentry recognized the coachman and the horses from afar, and they knew that the lady sitting in the carriage was their own dear, familiar Princess Vera Gavrilovna.

An old man in livery jumped off the box and helped the Princess down. She raised her dark veil, and without hurrying went up to the priests to receive their blessing, and then with a gracious nod to the lay brothers she made her way into the hostel.

"I suppose you have missed your Princess," she said to the monk who brought in her things. "I haven't come to see you for a whole month! Well, here I am! Behold your princess! And where is the archbishop? Dear God, I am burning with impatience to see him. Such a wonderful, wonderful old man! You should be proud to have such an archbishop!"

When the archbishop came to see her, the Princess uttered an excited squeal, crossed her hands over her breasts, and went up to him to receive his blessing.

"No, no! Let me kiss your hand!" she said, seizing his hand and greedily kissing it three times. "How glad I am, holy father, to see you at last! No doubt you forgot your Princess, but I assure you not a moment passed when I was not thinking about your dear monastery. How good it is to be here! This surrender of life to God, far from the vanities of the world, has a special charm of its own, holy father, and I feel this with all my soul, though I cannot put it into words!"

The Princess's cheeks reddened, and tears came to her eyes. She went on talking fervently while the archbishop, an old man of seventy, grave, homely, and timid, remained silent, only occasionally interrupting with some abrupt soldierlike sentences: "Certainly, Your Highness . . . Quite so . . . I understand . . ."

"Will Your Highness deign to spend some time with us?" he asked.

"I shall stay the night with you, and tomorrow I'm going to stay with Claudia Nikolayevna—it's a long time since I've visited her—and the day after tomorrow I shall come back to you for three or four days. I want to rest my soul among you, holy father."

The Princess loved to stay at the N—— Monastery. For the last two years it had been her favorite resort, and every summer she spent some part of every month there, sometimes staying for two or three days, sometimes for a whole week. The gentle lay brothers, the silence, the low ceilings, the smell of cypresses, the unpretentious meals, the cheap curtains on the windows—all these things touched her, moved her, and disposed her to contemplation and good thoughts. It was enough for her to spend half an hour in the hostel and then she would feel that she too was weak and unassuming and that she smelled of cypress wood; and the past vanished into the distance, losing its significance. Although she was only twenty-nine, it occurred to the Princess that she resembled the archbishop and that, like him, she was not created for the enjoyment of wealth or of love or of earthly splendors, but for the sake of a tranquil, secluded life, as full of shadows as the hostel.

So it happens that quite suddenly and unexpectedly a ray of light will gleam in the dark cell of a monk given over to fasting and absorbed in prayer, or a bird will alight on the window of his cell and sing its song, and the stern monk will find himself involuntarily smiling, and there will flow into his heart, from underneath the heavy burden of his sorrows for all the sins he has committed, a joy which is entirely without sin, just as a silent fountain will flow from beneath a stone. The Princess believed that she was the vehicle of just such consolations from the outside world as the ray of light or the bird. Her gay, inviting smile, her benignant gaze, her voice, her jokes—in fact everything about her, even her small well-formed figure in a simple black dress, was meant to arouse in simple austere people a feeling of joy and tenderness. Everyone looking at her must think: "God has sent us an angel." And feeling that everyone must inevitably think in this way, she smiled still more invitingly and tried to look like a little bird.

After drinking tea and taking a rest, she went for a walk. The sun was already setting. From the monastery gardens there came to the Princess the moist fragrance of freshly watered mignonettes, and from the church came the soft singing of men's voices, which seemed very charming and melancholy when heard from a distance. It was the time of vespers. In the dark windows where the flames of the icon lamps shed their gentle glow, in the shadows, and in the figure of the old monk sitting on the church porch with a collection box in his hands, there was such tranquillity and peace that the Princess felt moved to tears.

Outside the gate there were benches set along the avenue which lay between the birch trees and the monastery wall. On these the evening had already descended, and every moment the light was growing darker. . . . The Princess walked along the avenue, sat down on a bench, and fell to thinking.

She thought how good it would be if she could spend the rest of her days in the monastery, where life was as quiet and tranquil as a summer evening; and how wonderful if she could completely forget her dissolute and ungrateful husband, the Prince, and her vast estates, and the creditors who came to torment her every day, and her misfortunes, and her maid Dasha, who had given her a particularly impertinent look that very morning. How good it would be to sit there on the bench for the remainder of her days, looking past the birch trees to the tufts of evening mist flowing at the foot of the mountains, or watching the rooks flying away to their nests far, far above the forest like a black cloud or a veil set against the sky, and the two lay brothers— one astride a piebald horse, the other on foot—who were driving out the horses for the night, rejoicing in their freedom and frolicking like children, their young voices ringing out clearly and musically in the motionless air, so that she could distinguish every word. How good to be sitting there, listening to the silence, while the wind stirred and stroked the tops of the birch trees, and a frog rustled the leaves of another year, and the clock high on the wall struck the quarter. . . . One could sit there for hours without moving, thinking, thinking. . . .

An old woman carrying a sack over her shoulder came along the path. It occurred to the Princess that it would be good to stop her and say something friendly and sincere, to help her on her way. . . . But the old woman did not once turn her head, and she vanished round the corner.

Not long afterward a tall man with a gray beard and a straw hat came along the avenue. As he passed the Princess, he took off his hat and bowed, and from the large bald spot on his head and the sharp, crooked nose the Princess recognized him as the doctor, Mikhail Ivanovich, who had been in her service five years before on her estate at Dubovki. Someone had told her, she remembered, that the doctor's wife had died the previous year, and she wanted to tender her sympathy and comfort him.

"I am sure you don't recognize me, Doctor," the Princess said with her inviting smile.

"Of course I recognize you, Princess," the doctor replied, and once again he took off his hat.

"Oh, thank you, I was so afraid you had forgotten your Princess. People only remember their enemies, and forget their friends. Have you come here to pray?"

"I come here every Saturday night, because it is my duty. I'm the doctor here."

"Well, how are you?" the Princess asked, sighing. "I heard about the death of your wife. How terrible it must have been for you!"

"Yes, Princess, it was a terrible misfortune for me."

"What can we do? We must bear our misfortunes humbly. Not a hair falls from a man's head but by the will of eternal Providence."

"True, Princess."

To the Princess's sweet and friendly smiles and sighs the doctor answered coldly and dryly: "True, Princess." And the expression of his face was cold and dry.

"What else can I say to him?" the Princess wondered.

"It is such a long time since we met," she went on. "Five years! Think of all the water which has flown under the bridges in that time! So many changes have taken place, it is terrible to think about them! You know I am married now? . . . I'm not a countess any more, but a princess. And I have separated from my husband."

"Yes, I heard about it."

"God has sent me many trials. I am sure you have heard that I am almost ruined. My Dubovki, Kiryakovo, and Sofino estates have been sold to pay the debts of my miserable husband. There is only Baronovo and Mikhaltsevo left. It's a terrible thing to look back over the past! So much has changed, so many misfortunes, and so many mistakes!"

"Yes, Princess, many mistakes."

The Princess was a little put out. She knew she had made mistakes, but they were of such an intimate character that she thought she alone could think about them, or speak about them. She could not resist asking: "What mistakes were you thinking about?"

"You mentioned them, and you know them," the doctor said, and smiled. "Why should we talk about them?"

143

"Do tell me, Doctor. I should be so grateful to you. And please don't stand on ceremony with me. I love hearing the truth."

"I am not judging you, Princess."

"Not judging me indeed! What a tone you have! Then you really must know something! Tell me!"

"If you want me to, then I shall have to. Only I regret I am not a man with a clever tongue, and people do not always understand me."

The doctor thought for a moment, and said: "There were a great number of mistakes, but in my opinion the most important was the spirit . . . the spirit prevailing on all your estates. As you see, I don't know how to express myself very well. Chiefly I mean the lack of love, the loathing of people in general which could be felt as a positive force on all of them. Your entire way of living was built upon that loathing. Loathing the human voices, the faces of people, the scruffs of their necks, the way they walked . . . in a word, loathing everything that went to make up the human condition. At all the doors and on the stairways stand well-fed, ill-mannered, lazy grooms in livery who refuse to allow ill-dressed people into the house. In the hallway there are chairs with high backs especially placed there so that whenever you give balls or entertain, the servants won't dirty the tapestries on the walls with the back of their heads; and in all the rooms there are thick carpets so that no human footsteps can be heard; and everyone who visits you is invariably commanded to speak softly and as little as possible, and never to say anything which would produce the least unpleasantness on your mind or on your nerves. And in your private sitting room you don't shake hands with people or ask them to sit down—just as you don't shake hands with me or ask me to sit down. . . ."

"Oh, please do sit down, if you wish," the Princess said, holding out her hands and smiling. "Tell me, why are you so angry about such utterly unimportant things?"

"Why should I be angry?" The doctor laughed, but his face

144

reddened, and he removed his hat and waved it about as he went on hotly: "To tell you the truth, I have been waiting for a long time for the opportunity to say these things to you. . . . I wanted to tell you that you have the Napoleonic way of regarding mankind—men are just cannon fodder. At least Napoleon had some ideas. You—you have nothing except your loathing!"

"Do I have a loathing for people?" The Princess smiled, shrugging her shoulders in amazement. "Do I?"

"Yes, you do! You want facts? Very well! At Mikhaltsevo there are three former cooks of yours living on charity—they went blind in your kitchens from the heat of the stoves. All the health, strength, and beauty that pours from your tens of thousands of acres is given over by you and your parasites to your grooms and footmen and coachmen. All these two-legged animals are brought up to become flunkies, stuffers of food, vulgarians, men who have departed from 'the image and likeness of God.' . . . They might have been young doctors, agricultural experts, teachers, intellectuals, but, God in heaven, you tear them away from honest work, and for the sake of a crust of bread you make them play in your puppet shows, and that's enough to make any decent man ashamed. Men like that can't remain in your service for three years without becoming hypocrites, slanderers, and flatterers. . . . Is that good? Your Polish overseers, those scoundrels and spies, with names like Kasimir and Gaëtan, prowl from morning to night over your tens of thousands of acres and to please you they try to skin every ox three times over! Excuse me if I speak at random, but it doesn't matter. You don't regard the simple folk on your estates as though they were living people. And even the princes, counts, and bishops who used to visit you—you never regarded them as anything more than decoration. They were not living people. But the most important thing—the one that revolts me most of all—is that you possessed a fortune of more than a million rubles, and you did nothing for the people—nothing at all!"

The Princess sat there with a look of amazement, shock, and

fear. She did not know what to say or how to behave. No one had ever spoken to her in that tone of voice. The doctor's unpleasantly angry voice, his fumbling and stuttering, came like a harsh grating sound on her ears and on her brain: until she felt that the gesticulating doctor was beating her around the head with his hat.

"It's not true at all," she answered softly in an imploring voice. "I've done a lot of good things for people, and you know it!"

"Stuff and nonsense!" the doctor shouted at her. "Can you possibly maintain that your philanthropic works were undertaken for a serious purpose—weren't they just puppets being pulled on strings! They were nothing more than a farce from beginning to end! You were playing a game of loving your neighbor—such an obvious game that even children and stupid peasant women understood what you were doing! Take your—what do you call it?—rest home for homeless old women, of which I was appointed a kind of head doctor, and in which you played the role of honorary patroness. God have mercy on us, what a wonderful institution that was! You built a house with parquet flooring, and there was a weather vane on the roof, and a dozen old women were rounded up from the villages and made to sleep under blankets of some woolen stuff and sheets of Dutch linen, and given candy to eat!"

The doctor laughed maliciously into his hat, and went on speaking rapidly, stammering out the words.

"What a game, eh? The lower-ranking officials in the rest home kept the sheets and blankets locked up, because they were afraid the old women would spoil them—'Let the devil's pepperpots sleep on the floor!' The old women didn't dare sit on the beds, or put on their jackets, or walk on the smooth parquet floors. Everything was arranged for display purposes only, and everything was hidden away from the old women as though they were thieves; and so they had to be clothed and fed on the sly by charitable persons. Day and night these old women prayed God to deliver them from their prison as soon as possible, and they prayed to be delivered from the edifying discourses of the fat swine into whose care they had been entrusted by you. And what did the higher-ranking officials do? It was perfectly charming! Twice a week, during the evening, there would descend upon us about thirty-five thousand messengers announcing that the Princess—you—would pay us a visit on the following day. That meant that on the next day I had to abandon my patients, dress up, and go on parade! Very well! I arrive. The old women are drawn up in a row to await your arrival. They wear their new, clean clothes. Around them marches the old garrison rat —the inspector—smiling his sweet, fawning smile. The old women yawn and exchange glances, but they are afraid to grumble aloud. We wait. The junior director comes hurrying up. Half an hour later he is followed by the senior director, and after him comes the director-in-chief of the finance department, and then another, and then another. . . . An endless crowd of them comes galloping up. They all have mysterious solemn faces. We wait, we wait. We shift our weight from one leg to the other, we look at the clock—all this happens in the silence of the grave because we hate each other to the death. An hour passes, then another, and finally the carriage is seen in the distance, and . . . and . . ."

The doctor went off into peals of shrill laughter, and continued in a high-pitched voice: "Well, you descend from your carriage, and at that moment the old hags, having heard the word of command from the garrison rat, begin to sing: 'The Glory of our Lord in Zion the tongue of man cannot convey . . .' Not bad at all, eh?"

The doctor chuckled in a deep voice and waved his hand about, as though indicating that he was so overcome with laughter that he could not utter another word. He laughed heavily, harshly, his teeth powerfully locked together—you find evilly disposed people laughing like that—and from his voice, his face, his glittering, rather impertinent eyes, it was evident that he had a profound contempt for the Princess, the old women, and the hostel itself. There was nothing in the least charming or amusing in those coarse, brutal descriptions of his, but he kept laughing with great joy and satisfaction.

"And the school?" he went on, breathing heavily because he was still laughing. "Do you remember how you wanted to teach the children of the peasants? You must have taught them very well, because the boys ran away so fast they had to be flogged and bribed to come back to you! Remember how you wanted to offer bottled milk to the breast-fed children whose mothers worked in the fields? You went about the village complaining because the children were not being placed at your disposal— the mothers were taking them to the fields. Then the village elder gave orders that the mothers should take turns leaving their babies with you—for your delectation. And what a wonderful thing that was! The women ran away from your charities like mice from a cat! Why? It was very simple! Not because our people were ignorant and ungrateful—that was the explanation you gave—but because in all your capricious behavior, if you'll pardon the expression, there was never a kopeck's worth of love or real kindness! There was only your desire to amuse yourself with living puppets, nothing more! . . . Someone who doesn't know the difference between living people and lap dogs shouldn't go in for works of charity. I assure you there's a great difference between people and lap dogs!"

The Princess's heart was beating wildly, and there was a roaring in her ears. She still had the feeling that the doctor was beating her around the head with his hat. The doctor was speaking in an ugly way, rapidly and fiercely, all the time stuttering and gesticulating far too frequently. All she knew was that a spiteful, ill-mannered, ill-bred, and ungrateful person was talking to her, but she could not understand what he wanted of her and what he was talking about.

"Go away!" she said in a tearful voice, raising her hands to protect her head from the doctor's hat. "Go away!"

"And then there's the way you treat your servants!" the doctor went on, surrendering to his indignation. "You don't look at them as people! You treat them as though they were the lowest kind of rogues! For example, permit me to ask why you dismissed me. For ten years I served your father, and then I served you, always honestly, never taking a holiday or a leave of absence, and I was loved and respected for miles around, and then one fine day I am suddenly informed that my services are no longer required! Why? To this day I have never understood why. I am a doctor, a gentleman by birth, a graduate of Moscow University, the father of a family—that is, I am a paltry, insignificant creature, and so you can kick me in the teeth for no reason at all! Why do you stand on ceremony with me? It came to my knowledge that my wife, secretly, without asking my permission, approached you three times in order to intercede for me, and not once did you let her come near you! They tell me she wept in your hallway! To the day I die I shall never forgive her for that—never!"

The doctor grew silent and clenched his teeth, making an intense effort to think of something else to say—something very unpleasant and spiteful. Then he remembered something, and his cold, frowning face suddenly brightened.

"Take this attitude of yours toward the monastery," he said eagerly. "You have never shown any mercy to anyone! The holier the place, the more chance there is of things getting hopelessly out of hand as a result of your charity and angelic meekness. Why do you come here? Excuse me for asking this, but what do you want from the monks? What is Hecuba to you, or you to Hecuba? It's just another sport, another game, another sacrilege against human dignity, that's all! You don't believe in the God of the monks, you have your own God in your heart—a God who popped into your brain when you were attending spiritualistic séances. You have only a condescending attitude toward the ceremonies of the Church. You don't go to mass or vespers. You sleep till midday. . . . Why do you come here? . . . You come with your own God into a monastery which is foreign to you, and you imagine the monastery regards it as a tremendous honor to have you here. Of course it does! Ask the monks what your visit costs them! You were graciously pleased to arrive here this evening, but two days ago a messenger on horseback arrived from your estate to spread the news of your coming. All day yesterday they were getting the hostel ready for you, and waiting upon your arrival. This morning the advance guard arrived in the shape of an impudent maidservant, who kept running around the courtyard making a rustling sound with her skirts, demanding answers to her questions, and issuing orders. . . . I can't bear it any longer! All day today the monks have been on the lookout—there would be trouble if you were not met with the proper ceremony! You would complain to the archbishop: 'Your Holiness, the monks don't approve of me! I don't know what I have done to harm them! It's true I'm a great sinner, but I'm so unhappy!' Already one monastery has suffered as a result of your visits. The archbishop is a busy, learned man, he doesn't have a moment for himself, but you keep on sending to him to come to your rooms. No respect for an old man's dignity! It wouldn't be so awful if you had given large sums to the monastery, but all this time the monks have not received a hundred rubles from you!"

Whenever the Princess was troubled or offended or misunderstood, and whenever she did not know what to say or do, she usually gave way to tears. Now at last she hid her face in her hands and wept in a thin childish voice. The doctor suddenly fell silent and gazed at her. His face darkened and grew stern.

"Forgive me, Princess," he said in a dull voice. "I gave way to malice and forgot myself. It wasn't a good thing to do!"

With an embarrassed cough, forgetting to put on his hat, he walked quickly away from the Princess.

The stars were already twinkling in the sky. The moon must have risen on the other side of the monastery, for the sky was brilliantly clear, soft, and transparent. There were bats flitting noiselessly along the white monastery wall.

Slowly the clock struck three-quarters, probably a quarter to nine. The Princess got up and walked silently to the gate. She felt she had been deeply wronged, and she wept, and then it seemed to her that the trees and the stars and the bats were all pitying her, and she thought the musical chiming of the clock was an expression of sympathy for her. She wept and kept thinking how good it would be to spend her whole life in a monastery. On silent summer evenings she would wander alone along the alleyways, insulted, injured, misunderstood by people, and only God and the starry heavens would observe her tears of suffering. In the church the evening service was still going on. The Princess paused and listened to the singing. How perfect the sound of their singing in the dark and motionless air! How sweet to weep and suffer to the sound of their singing!

Returning to the hostel, she gazed in a mirror at her tear-stained face, and then she powdered her face and sat down to supper. The monks knew she liked pickled sturgeon, little mushrooms, and simple gingerbread cakes which left a taste of cypress in her mouth, and each time she came they served the things she liked. Eating the mushrooms and drinking their Málaga wine, the Princess dreamed of how in the end she would be abandoned and forsaken, and all her stewards, bailiffs, clerks, and maid-servants, for whom she had done so much, would betray her and say coarse things about her, and how everyone all over the world would attack her and speak evil of her and jeer at her. She would renounce her title of Princess, she would renounce luxury and society, and she would enter a monastery without a word of reproach to anyone; and she would pray for her enemies, and then they would all suddenly come to understand her, and seek her forgiveness, but by then it would be too late. . . .

After supper she fell on her knees in a corner of the room in front of the icon and read two chapters of the Gospels. Then her maidservant made her bed and she lay down to sleep. Stretching herself under a white blanket, she uttered a sweet and prolonged sigh, such as one utters after weeping, and she closed her eyes and fell asleep. . . .

In the morning she woke and glanced at her little clock: it was half past nine. On the carpet near her bed there lay a clear, thin streak of light made by a sunbeam which came from the window and vaguely lit the room. From behind the black window curtain came the buzzing of flies.

"It's still early," the Princess thought, and she shut her eyes.

Stretching herself out, lying comfortably in bed, she remembered her meeting with the doctor the previous day and all the thoughts with which she had fallen asleep; and she remembered she was unhappy. Then the memory of her husband, living in St. Petersburg, came back to her, and her stewards, and the doctor, and neighbors, and officials she knew . . . a long procession of familiar masculine faces marched through her imagination. She smiled, and it occurred to her that if only these people could peer into her soul and understand her, they would be at her feet. . . .

At a quarter past eleven she called her maid. "Let me get dressed now," she said languidly. "But first, tell them to harness the horses. I must go and visit Claudia Nikolayevna."

When she left the hostel and was about to get into her carriage, she had to screw up her eyes against the strong sun, and she laughed with joy: it was such a wonderfully fine day! And looking through half-closed eyes at the monks who had gathered by the steps to bid her farewell, she nodded pleasantly and said: "Good-by, my friends! Until the day after tomorrow!"

She was pleasantly surprised to find the doctor standing on the steps with the monks. His face was pale and stern.

"Princess," he said, removing his hat, "I've been waiting for you a long time. Forgive me, for God's sake! A bad, vindictive feeling came over me yesterday. I said terrible things to you . . . stupid things. I beg your forgiveness!"

The Princess smiled graciously and held out her hand to his lips. He kissed it and his face reddened.

Trying to resemble a little bird, the Princess fluttered into the carriage, nodding in all directions. Her heart was warm and bright and gay, and she thought her smile was unusually sweet and friendly. As the carriage rolled up to the gates and then along the dusty road past peasant huts and gardens, past long trains of carts and processions of pilgrims making their way to the monastery, she was still screwing up her eyes and smiling softly. She was thinking there was no greater delight than to bring joy, warmth, and light to those she met, to forgive wrongs, and to smile kindly at her enemies. The peasants bowed to her as she passed, the carriage rustled softly, clouds of dust rose from under the wheels and the wind carried them across the fields of golden rye, and it seemed to the Princess that her body was swaying not on the cushions in the carriage but on clouds, and she herself was like a light transparent little cloud. . . .

"How happy I am!" she murmured, closing her eyes. "How happy I am!"

1889

Gusev

I

IT was already dark, and would soon be night.

Gusev, a discharged soldier, sat up in his hammock and said softly: "Pavel Ivanich, are you listening to me? At Suchan there was a soldier who said a big fish came smack against his ship and tore a hole in the bottom."

He was addressing a rather nondescript individual known to everyone in sick bay as Pavel Ivanich, but there was no answer: the man seemed not to have heard.

Once more there was silence. The wind wandered over the rigging, the propeller throbbed, waves dashed against the ship, hammocks creaked, but the ear had long since grown accustomed to these sounds, and everything seemed to sleep, caught up in a trance of silence. It was boring. The three sick men—two soldiers and a sailor—had spent the day playing cards; now they slept and uttered all kinds of nonsense in their dreams.

Apparently the ship was beginning to roll. The hammock slowly rose and fell under Gusev, as though it were sighing: this happened once, twice, three times. . . . Something crashed down on the floor with a ringing sound: probably a jug had fallen.

"The wind must have slipped its chains," Gusev said, straining his ears.

This time Pavel Ivanich cleared his throat and said irritably:

"First you say a fish has smacked into the side of a ship, then you say the wind has slipped its chains. . . . Is the wind, then, an animal that it breaks loose from its chains?"

"That's what the Christians say."

"Then the Christians are know-nothings just like you. They say whatever they want to say. You should have a head on your shoulders and try to reason things out. You don't have any brains!"

Pavel Ivanich suffered from seasickness. When the sea was rough he was usually bad-tempered, and the merest trifle would reduce him to a state of complete exasperation. In Gusev's opinion there was nothing at all to be angry about. What was strange or astonishing in the story about the fish or the wind slipping its chains? Suppose the fish were as big as a mountain, suppose its backbone was as strong as a sturgeon's, and then suppose that far away, at the very end of the world, there were great walls of stone and that the furious winds were chained to these walls. If the winds had not broken loose from their chains, how do you account for the fact that they fling themselves across the sea like maniacs, and struggle to escape like dogs? If they were not chained up, what became of them when the seas were calm?

For a long time Gusev pondered those massive rusty chains and the fish as big as mountains, and then he wearied of these things and instead he summoned up the memory of his village, that village to which he was returning after five years' service in the Far East. He thought of an immense pool crusted with snow; on one side stood the potteries, which were the color of brick, with the high chimney and clouds of black smoke, and on the other side lay the village. Driving a sleigh, his brother Alexey emerged from the fifth courtyard from the end, his little son Vanka and his daughter Akulka sitting behind him, both of them wearing big felt boots. Alexey had been drinking, Vanka was laughing, and Akulka was bundled up so that it was impossible to see her face.

"Unless he's careful, the children will be frozen stiff!" Gusev thought. "Oh Lord, put some sense in their heads so that they will honor their father and mother, and not be any wiser than their father and mother. . . ."

"They need new soles for their boots," the sick sailor roared in his delirium. "Yes, they do!"

At this point Gusev's thoughts broke off, and for no reason at all the pool gave place to the head of a huge bull without eyes, and the horse and sleigh were no longer going straight ahead, but were whirling round and round in clouds of black smoke. But he was delighted to have seen his own people. Joy made him catch his breath, shivers went up and down his spine, and his fingers tingled.

"Praise the Lord, for He has granted us to see each other," he murmured feverishly, and then he opened his eyes and looked for water in the dark.

He drank some water and lay down, and once more he saw the sleigh gliding along, and once more he saw the head of the bull without eyes, and the smoke, and the clouds. And so it went on until the sun rose.

II

The first object to emerge through the darkness was a blue circle, the porthole; then little by little Gusev was able to make out the shape of the man in the next hammock, Pavel Ivanich. This man slept sitting up, as he felt suffocated lying down. He had a gray face, a long sharp nose, and eyes which seemed enormous because he was terribly emaciated; and his temples were sunken, his hair was long, and there were only a few small threads of beard. From his face no one could have told his social status, whether he was a gentleman, a merchant, or a peasant. Judging from his expression and his long hair, he might have been a hermit or a lay brother in a monastery, but no one hearing him talk would ever have regarded him as a monk. Worn out by coughing, illness, and suffocating heat, he breathed laboriously, his parched lips trembling. Seeing Gusev gazing at him, he turned his face towards him and said: "I'm beginning to guess. . . . Yes . . . I understand it perfectly now. . . ."

"What do you understand, Pavel Ivanich?"

"It's like this. . . . It has always seemed strange to me. Here you are, terribly ill, and instead of being left in peace, you are taken on board a ship where it's hot and the air's stifling and the deck is always pitching and rolling, and in fact everything threatens you with death. . . . It's all clear to me now. . . . Yes. . . . The doctors got you on the ship, to get rid of you. They were fed up with looking after you—you're only cattle. You don't pay them anything, you are a nuisance, and you spoil their statistics when you die. So, of course, you are cattle! And it's no trouble to get rid of you. All that's needed in the first place is to have no conscience or humanity, and in the second place the ship's officers can be told lies. No need to worry about the first— we are artists in all that. As for the second, you can always do it with a little practice. In a crowd of four hundred healthy soldiers and sailors, no one notices half a dozen sick ones. Well, they got you on the ship, mixed you up with the healthy ones, made a quick count, and because there was a lot of confusion no one saw anything wrong in it, but when the ship sailed they discovered there were paralytics and sick people in the last stages of consumption lying about the deck. . . ."

Gusev did not understand a single word spoken by Pavel Ivanich, and thinking he was being reprimanded, he said in self-defense: "I was lying on deck only because I didn't have the strength to stand. When we were being unloaded from the barge onto the ship, I caught a terrible chill."

"It's revolting," Pavel Ivanich went on. "The worst of it is they knew perfectly well you couldn't survive such a long journey, and yet they shove you on the ship! Let's suppose you last out as far as the Indian Ocean, what happens then? It's terrible to think about it. . . . And that's all you get for your years of faithful service with never a bad mark against you."

Pavel Ivanich's eyes flashed anger, he frowned contemptuously, and gasped out: "There are people the newspapers really ought to tear apart, till the feathers are flying!"

The two sick soldiers and the sailor were awake, and already playing cards. The sailor was half reclining on his hammock, while the soldiers sat near him on the floor in uncomfortable attitudes. One soldier had his right arm in a sling, and his wrist was so heavily bandaged that it resembled a fur cap: he kept his cards under his right armpit or in the crook of his elbow while playing with his left hand. The ship was rolling heavily. It was impossible to stand upright or drink tea or take medicine.

"What were you—an officer's servant?" Pavel Ivanich asked Gusev.

"That's right. I was an officer's orderly."

"Dear God!" said Pavel Ivanich, and he shook his head mournfully. "You tear a man from his home, drag him out of his nest, send him ten thousand miles away, let him rot with consumption, and . . . You wonder why they do it! . . . Just to make him the servant of some Captain Kopeikin or Midshipman Dirka! It doesn't make sense!"

"Being an officer's servant isn't hard work, Pavel Ivanich. You get up in the morning and clean the boots and get the samovar ready and sweep the rooms, and then there's nothing more to do. The lieutenant spends his days drawing up plans, and if you like you can say your prayers or maybe read a book or maybe go out on the street. God grant everyone such a life!"

"That's all very well. The lieutenant draws up his plans, while you spend the day sitting around the kitchen and longing for your own home. . . . Plans! . . . It's not a question of plans, but of a human life! Life doesn't come back again, and you have to treat it gently."

"Of course, Pavel Ivanich, a bad man is never well treated, either at home or in the service, but if you live right and obey orders, who wants to do you harm? The officers are educated gentlemen, they understand. . . . In five years they never once put me in the can, and they only hit me once, so help me God!"

"What did they hit you for?"

"For fighting. I've got a pair of tough hands, Pavel Ivanich. Four Chinese came into our yard, they were bringing firewood or something—I don't remember. Well, I was bored, and I beat them up, and the nose of one of them started to bleed. . . . The lieutenant watched it through a window, flew into a temper, and boxed my ears!"

"Poor stupid fool," said Pavel Ivanich. "You never understand anything."

He was completely exhausted by the rolling of the ship, and closed his eyes, and sometimes his head fell back and sometimes it dropped on his chest. Several times he tried to lie down, but he never succeeded. His breathing was labored.

"Why did you beat up those four Chinese?"

"They came into the yard and so I beat them up—that's all."

Silence followed. The cardplayers went on playing for two hours with much eagerness and angry shouting, but the rolling of the ship was finally too much even for them; they threw their cards aside, and lay down. Once again Gusev saw the large pool, the potteries, and the village. Once again the sleigh made its way over the snow, and Vanka was laughing, and Akulka in the silliest way was throwing open her fur coat and kicking out her feet, as though she were saying: "Look, good people, at my new felt boots, not like Vanka's old ones!"

"Soon she will be six years old, and she hasn't any sense in her head," Gusev murmured in his fever. "Instead of kicking out your feet, you would be spending your time better if you brought a drink to the old soldier who is your uncle, and then I'll give you a present!"

And then came Andron with his flintlock over his shoulder, carrying a hare he had shot, with the crazy Jew Issaichik coming after him and offering a bar of soap for the hare; and then there was the black calf in the passageway, and Domna was sewing a shirt and crying about something, and there came once again the bull's head without eyes, and the black smoke. . . .

Overhead someone gave a loud shout, and several sailors ran past, and there was a sound as though some heavy object was being dragged across the deck or something had burst open. Again the sailors ran past. . . . Had there been an accident? Gusev lifted his head, listened, and observed that the two soldiers and the sailor were playing cards again. Pavel Ivanich was sitting up and moving his lips. You were suffocating in the heat, you had no strength to breathe, you were thirsty, and the water was hot, disgusting. The ship was still rolling badly.

Suddenly something strange happened to one of the soldiers who was playing cards. . . . He called hearts diamonds, then he got muddled over the score, and then let the cards fall from his hands. He smiled a frightened, stupid smile, and gazed at the other cardplayers.

"I won't be a moment, fellows," he said, and lay down on the floor.

They were all astonished. They shouted at him, but he did not answer.

"Stepan, maybe you're feeling ill, eh?" the soldier with his arm in a sling said. "Maybe we should get a priest, eh?"

"Drink some water, Stepan," the sailor said. "Here, drink, brother!"

"Why do you have to knock the jug against his teeth?" Gusev exclaimed angrily. "Haven't you got eyes, cabbagehead?"

"What's that?"

"What's that?" Gusev mimicked him. "There's not a drop of breath left in him—he's dead! That's what! Lord God, how stupid can you get?"

III

The ship stopped rolling, and Pavel Ivanich grew more cheerful. He was no longer ill-tempered. His face wore a boastful, challenging, defiant look, as though he wanted to say: "Just a moment, I'll tell you something to make you split your sides with laughing!" The little round porthole was open, and a gentle breeze was blowing on Pavel Ivanich. There came the sound of voices and the splashing of oars in the water. . . . Beneath the porthole someone was droning in an unpleasant, reedy voice; it was probably a Chinese singing.

"So here we are in the harbor," Pavel Ivanich said with an ironical smile. "Only another month, and we'll be in Russia. . . . I address myself to our distinguished civilians and military men! I reach Odessa, and then make a beeline for Kharkov. In Kharkov I have a friend, a man of letters. I'll go up to him and say: 'Come, brother, put aside those abominable subjects you write about, the loves of women and the beauties of nature, and show us the two-legged vermin. There's a theme for you. . . .' "

He thought for a minute and then he said: "Gusev, do you know how I made a fool of them?"

"Made a fool of who, Pavel Ivanich?"

"Why, those people. . . . You know, there's only a first and third class on this ship, and they only allow peasants in the third class—only the scum. If you're wearing a coat and look from a distance like a gentleman or a bourgeois, then they make you travel first class. You have to put down five hundred rubles, even if it kills you. 'Why make a rule like that?' I ask them. 'Do you want to raise the prestige of the Russian intellectuals?' 'Not on your life,' they say. 'We won't let you, because a decent person won't go into the third class—it's too horrible and disgusting.' 'Sir, I congratulate you for being so considerate for the affairs of decent people. Besides, whether it is nice or horrible, I haven't got the five hundred rubles. I haven't looted the treasury, I haven't exploited natives, I never smuggled contraband, or flogged anyone to death, so judge for yourselves whether I have the right to travel first class or even the right to count myself among the Russian intellectuals.' But you can't teach logic to these fellows. I had to play a trick on them. I put on a peasant's coat and high-boots, and wore a drunken stupid expression, and went to the ticket agents and said: 'Won't you give me a little ticket, Your Excellencies?' "

"What class do you really belong to?" the sailor said.

"The ecclesiastical class. My father was an honest priest, and he always told the truth to the great ones of the world—threw it in their faces—and so we suffered a great deal."

Pavel Ivanich was exhausted with talking. He went on, gasping for breath: "Yes, I always tell them the truth straight in their faces. I'm not afraid of anyone or anything. In this respect there is a vast difference between me and you. You people are in the dark, you are blind and beaten to the ground; you see nothing, and what you do see you fail to understand. . . . They tell you the wind breaks loose from its chains, that you are beasts, savages, and you believe it. Someone punches you in the neck—you kiss his hand! A reptile in a raccoon coat strips you of everything you possess, and then tosses you a penny for your pains, and you say: 'Sir, let me kiss your hand.' You are outcasts, poor pathetic wretches. . . . I am different. I live in full consciousness of my powers. I see everything, like a hawk or an eagle hovering over the earth, and I understand everything. I am protest incarnate. When I see tyranny, I protest. When I see cant and hypocrisy, I protest. When I see swine triumphant, I protest. I cannot be silenced: no Spanish Inquisition will make me hold my tongue. No! If you cut out my tongue, I will still protest—with gestures. Bury me in a cellar, and I will shout so loud they will hear me a mile away, or else I will starve myself to death, and thus hang another weight round their black consciences. Kill me, and my ghost will haunt them! All my acquaintances say: 'You are a most insufferable fellow, Pavel Ivanich!' I am proud of my reputation. For three years I served in the Far East, and I shall be remembered there for a hundred years because I quarreled with everyone. My friends write to me from Russia: 'Don't come back!' But as you see I am going back to spite them! . . .

Yes, that's life as I understand it! That's what is called life."

Gusev was not listening: he was gazing out of the porthole. A boat, bathed in a blazing and brilliant sunlight, was swaying on a transparent and delicate turquoise-colored sea. In it naked Chinamen were holding up cages with canaries, and saying: "It sings! It sings!"

Another boat came knocking against the first; a steam pinnace darted by. There came still another boat: in it was a fat Chinaman eating rice with little sticks. The sea rolled languidly, and there were white seagulls hovering lazily in the air.

"I should like to give that fat fellow a punch in the neck," Gusev meditated, gazing at the fat Chinaman and yawning.

Then he became drowsy, and it seemed to him that all nature was falling asleep. Time flew by. Imperceptibly the daylight faded away, and imperceptibly there came the shadows of evening. . . . The ship was no longer standing still, but moving again.

IV

Two days passed. Pavel Ivanich was lying down, no longer sitting up. His eyes were closed, and his nose seemed to have grown sharper.

"Pavel Ivanich," Gusev called to him. "Hey, Pavel Ivanich."

Pavel Ivanich opened his eyes and moved his lips.

"Are you feeling ill?"

"No," Pavel Ivanich replied, gasping. "No, on the contrary. . . . I'm better. . . . As you see, I can lie down. . . . I'm a bit easier."

"Well, thank God, Pavel Ivanich."

"When I compare myself with you, I'm sorry for you poor fellows. . . . My lungs are healthy—what I've got is a stomach cough. I can stand hell, and that goes for the Red Sea. Also, I take a critical attitude toward my illness and the medicines I take. While you . . . you are in the dark. . . . It's hard for you, very, very hard!"

The ship was no longer rolling, the sea was calm, and the air was as hot and suffocating as a bathhouse: it was hard not only to speak but to listen. Gusev threw his hands round his knees, laid his head on them, and thought of home. My God, what a relief it was to think of cold weather and snow in this suffocating heat! You're riding in a sleigh, and suddenly the horses take fright at something and bolt. . . . Careless of roads, ditches and gullies, they tear like mad through the village, and over the pool by the potteries, and then across the fields. Comes the full-throated cry of the factory workers and all the others in the path of the horses: "Stop them!" Why stop them? Let the raw, cold winds beat about your face and bite your hands; let the lumps of snow flung up by the horses' hoofs fall on your fur cap, your collar, your neck, and your chest; let the runners scream on the snow and let the shafts and traces be smashed to smithereens, devil take them all! How wonderful it is when the sleigh overturns and you are sent flying headlong into a snowdrift, face to the snow, and when you rise you are white all over, no fur cap, no gloves, your belt undone, and icicles clinging to your mustache. . . . People laugh, and the dogs bark.

Pavel Ivanich half opened an eye, gazed at Gusev, and said softly: "Did your commanding officer go stealing?"

"Who knows, Pavel Ivanich? We never heard about it."

A long time passed in silence. Gusev meditated, murmured something in his fever, and kept on drinking water. It was hard for him to talk and hard for him to listen, and he was afraid of being talked at. An hour passed, then another, then a third. Evening came down, and then it was night, and he did not notice it. He sat there dreaming of the cold.

There was the sound of someone coming into the sick bay, voices were heard, but five minutes passed, and then there was only silence.

"May he enter the kingdom of Heaven and receive eternal

peace," the soldier with the arm in the sling was saying. "He was a restless man."

"Eh, what's that?" Gusev asked. "Who is this?"

"He's dead. They've just taken him up on deck."

"Oh, well," murmured Gusev, yawning. "May he enter the Kingdom of Heaven."

"What do you think?" the soldier with the sling said after a short silence. "Will he be received into the Kingdom of Heaven or not?"

"Who do you mean?"

"Pavel Ivanich."

"Yes, he will. He suffered so long. And there's another thing —he belonged to an ecclesiastical family, and those priests have many relatives. So they'll pray and he'll enter the Kingdom."

The soldier with the sling sat down on the hammock near Gusev and said in an undertone: "You, too, Gusev, you're not long for this world. You'll never reach Russia."

"Did the doctor or the orderly tell you?" Gusev asked.

"They didn't tell me, but it's obvious. You know at once when a man is close to death. You don't eat, you don't drink, you're so thin you're frightening. It's consumption all right! I'm not saying this to upset you, but because maybe you'd like to receive the sacrament and extreme unction. And too, if you've got any money you'd better give it to the senior officer."

"I haven't written home," Gusev sighed. "I'll die, and they'll never hear about it."

"They'll hear," the sick sailor said in a deep voice. "When you die, they'll write it down in the ship's log, and in Odessa they'll send a copy to the military authority, and he'll send it to the parish or somewhere. . . ."

Such conversations made Gusev uneasy, and he began to be tormented with vague yearnings. He drank water—that wasn't it; he dragged himself to the small circular window and breathed the hot moist air—that wasn't it; he tried to think of home and the cold—it wasn't that either. . . . At last it occurred to him that if he remained another minute in the sick bay, he would suffocate to death.

"The air's suffocating, brother," he said. "I'm going up on deck. Take me topsides, for Christ's sake."

"All right," agreed the soldier with the sling. "You can't do it alone. I'll carry you. Put your arms round my neck."

Gusev threw his arms round the soldier's neck, and with his healthy arm the soldier supported him, and in this way he was carried on deck where the discharged soldiers and sailors lay sleeping side by side, so many of them that it was difficult to pass.

"Get down now," the soldier with the sling said softly. "Follow me quietly, and hold on to my shirt."

It was dark, there were no lights on deck, nor on the masts, nor anywhere in the sea around. On the prow the seaman on watch was standing perfectly still like a statue, and it seemed as though he, too, were asleep. The ship appeared to be abandoned to its own devices, going wherever it desired to go.

"They'll throw Pavel Ivanich into the sea soon," said the soldier with a sling. "In a sack and then into the water."

"Yes, that's the regulation."

"It's better to lie in the earth at home. That way your mother comes to the grave and weeps over you."

"That's true."

There was a smell of dung and hay. There were oxen standing with drooping heads at the ship's rail—one, two, three, eight of them altogether! There was a little pony, too. Gusev stretched forth his hand to caress it, but it shook its head, revealed its teeth, and tried to bite his sleeve.

"You bloody brute," Gusev said angrily.

The two of them, Gusev and the soldier, made their way quietly to the ship's prow, then they stood at the rail and silently gazed out to sea. The deep sky lay over them, the clear stars, stillness and peace, and it was exactly as it was in the village at home—while below them lurked darkness and chaos. Great waves were booming; no one knew why. Every wave, whichever one you looked at, was trying to climb over the rest, hurling itself on its neighbor, crushing it down; and then there would come a third wave with a glint of light on its white mane, as ferocious and hideous as all the others, with a full-throated roar.

The sea is senseless and pitiless. If the ship had been smaller, and not made of thick iron plates, the waves would have crushed it without the slightest remorse and devoured all the people, making no distinction between saints and sinners. The ship itself possessed the same cruel expression, devoid of any meaning. This beaked monster pressed forward, cutting a pathway through a million waves, fearing neither darkness nor winds, neither space nor solitude—all these were as nothing, and if the ocean had been populated, the monster would have crushed its inhabitants, making no distinction between saints and sinners.

"Where are we now?" asked Gusev.

"I don't know. I suppose we are far out to sea."

"You can't see land?"

"None at all! They say we'll see it in a week."

The two soldiers stared at the white foam gleaming with phosphorescence and were silent, lost in thought. Gusev was the first to break the silence.

"There's nothing to be afraid of," he said. "Only it's strange, like when you sit down in a dark forest, but if—supposing they lowered a boat on the water this moment and an officer ordered me to go to a place fifty miles away across the sea to catch fish, I'd go! Or supposing a Christian fell into the water this very moment, I'd jump in after him! I wouldn't try to save a German or a Chinese, but I'd jump in after a Christian!"

"Are you afraid of dying?"

"Yes, I'm afraid. I'm full of sorrow for the farm. My brother at home, you know, there's nothing sober about him—he's a drunkard, beats his wife for no reason at all, and doesn't honor his parents. Without me everything will go to ruin, and soon, I don't wonder, my father and my old mother will be begging in the streets. But my legs won't hold me up, brother, and it's suffocating here. Let's go to sleep!"

V

Gusev returned to the sick bay and lay in his hammock. Once again he was tormented with vague yearnings, and could not understand what he wanted. There was a weight on his chest, a throbbing in his head, his mouth was so dry it was difficult for him to move his tongue. He dozed off, talked wildly in his sleep, and toward morning, worn out with nightmares, coughing, and the suffocating heat, he fell into a heavy sleep. He dreamed they were just taking the bread out of the oven in the barracks, and he climbed into the oven and took a steam bath in it, lashing himself with a bunch of birch twigs. He slept for two days, and on the third day at noon two sailors came down and carried him out of the sick bay.

They sewed him up in a sailcloth and to make him heavier they put in two iron fire bars. Sewn up in the sailcloth, he looked like a carrot or a horse-radish: broad at the head and narrow at the feet. . . . Before sunset they brought him on deck and laid him on a plank. One end of the plank lay on the ship's rail, the other on a box placed on a stool. Around him stood the ship's company and the discharged soldiers, their heads bared.

"Blessed be the name of God," the priest began, "as it was in the beginning, is now, and ever shall be!"

"Amen!" three sailors chanted.

The ship's company and the discharged soldiers crossed themselves and looked out to sea. Strange that a man should be sewn up in a sailcloth and then tossed into the waves. Was it possible that such a thing could happen to anyone?

The priest scattered earth over Gusev and bowed low. They sang "Eternal Memory."

The seaman on watch tilted the end of the plank. At first Gusev slid down slowly, then he rushed head foremost into the sea, turning a somersault in the air, then splashing. The foam enclosed him, and for a brief moment he seemed to be wrapped in lace, but this moment passed and he disappeared under the waves.

He plunged rapidly to the bottom. Did he reach it? The sea, they say, is three miles deep at this point. Falling sixty or seventy feet, he started to fall more slowly, swaying rhythmically, as though hesitating, at the mercy of the currents, sliding sideways more quickly than he sank down.

Then he fell among a shoal of pilot fish. When they saw the dark body they were astounded and rooted to the spot, and they suddenly turned tail and fled. In less than a minute they came hurrying back to him, quick as a shot, and they began zigzagging round him in the water.

Then still another dark body appeared. This was a shark. It swam below Gusev with dignity and reserve, seeming not to notice him; and when he, descending, fell against the back of the shark, then the shark turned belly upwards, basking in the warm transparent water and lazily opening its jaws with their two rows of teeth. The pilot fish were in ecstasy; they stopped to see what would happen next. After playing around with the body for a while, the shark calmly laid its jaws on it, tapped it with its teeth, and ripped open the sailcloth along the whole length of the body from head to foot; one of the fire bars fell out, frightened the pilot fish, struck the shark in the ribs, and sank rapidly to the bottom.

Meanwhile in the heavens clouds came and massed themselves against the sunset, and one cloud resembled a triumphal arch, another a lion, a third a pair of scissors. . . . There came a great beam of green light transpiercing the clouds and stretching to the center of the sky, and a little while later a violet-colored beam lay beside it, and then there was a golden beam, and then a rose-colored beam. The heavens turned lilac, very soft. Gazing up at the enchanted heavens, magnificent in their splendor, the sea fumed darkly at first, but soon assumed the sweet, joyous, passionate colors for which there are scarcely any names in the tongue of man.

December 1890

The Peasant Women

IN the village of Raibuzh, just opposite the church, there is a two-story house with stone foundations and an iron roof. The owner of the house, Philip Ivanov Kamin, and his family live in the lower story. Kamin's nickname is Dyudya. On the upper floor, where it is very hot in summer and very cold in winter, there are lodgings for officials, merchants, and country gentlemen passing through the town. Dyudya rents out some parcels of land, runs a tavern along the main road, trades in tar, honey, cattle, and magpies, and has amassed some eight thousand rubles, which he keeps in the town bank.

Fedor, his elder son, is a foreman mechanic in a factory, and as the peasants say, he has climbed so high that no one can follow after him. Fedor's wife, Sophia, is a plain sickly woman who lives at home with her father-in-law, weeps continually, and every Sunday drives over to the hospital for treatment. The second son, Alyoshka, is a hunchback and lives at home with his father. He has only lately married Varvara, a girl from a poor family, young, pretty, healthy, fond of dressing up. When officials and merchants stay at the house, they always demand that Varvara bring in the samovar and make up their beds.

One evening in June when the sun was setting and the air smelled of hay and warm manure and steaming milk, a plain cart came driving into Dyudya's courtyard with three people sitting in it. One was a man of about thirty who wore a canvas suit, and sitting beside him was a boy of seven or eight in a long black coat with big bone buttons, and there was a young fellow in a red shirt sitting on the driver's seat.

This young fellow unhitched the horses and walked them up and down the street, while the man washed himself, said a prayer with his face turned toward the church, and spreading out a fur cloak on the ground, sat down and had supper with the boy. He ate slowly, steadily, and Dyudya, who had known many travelers in his day, observed from his manners that he was a serious man with a head for business who knew his own worth.

Dyudya was sitting on the steps in his waistcoat, without a cap, waiting for a word from the stranger. He liked to listen in the evenings to travelers telling all kinds of stories as a preparation for sleep, and this had been his custom for some time. His old wife, Afanasyevna, and his daughter-in-law Sophia were milking in the cowshed, while Varvara, the other daughter-in-law, sat upstairs by an open window, eating sunflower seeds.

"I reckon that little fellow must be your son," Dyudya asked the stranger.

"Well, no. Adopted. An orphan. I took him up for the salvation of my soul."

They got to talking. The stranger seemed to be a talkative man with a gift for speech, and Dyudya learned that he belonged to the lower middle class, came from the town, owned his own house, and went by the name of Matvey Savvich. He was on his way to inspect some gardens he was renting from some German colonists. The name of the boy was Kuzka. The evening was hot and close, and no one wanted to sleep. When it grew dark and the pale stars were twinkling in the sky, Matvey Savvich began to tell the story of how he had taken up with Kuzka. Afanasyevna and Sophia stood a little way off, listening. Kuzka was away by the gate.

"It's a complicated story, grandfather—extraordinarily so," Matvey began. "If I told you everything that happened, it would

take all night. Ten years ago in our street, in a little house
next to mine, where there's now a candle factory and a creamery,
there used to live an old widow, Marfa Semyonovna Kapluntsev,
with her two sons. One was a conductor on the railroad, and the
other, Vasya, was a boy of my own age, and he lived at home
with his mother. The widow's husband had kept horses, five
pairs of them, and he used to send his drivers all over town.
The widow continued the business, and she was just as good at
managing the drivers as her husband, and so there were days
when they made a clear five-ruble profit. The young fellow, too,
was making a bit of money. He bred prize pigeons and sold them
to the fanciers. I remember him standing on the roof, throwing
up a broom and whistling, and the pigeons were high in the sky,
but not high enough for him—he wanted them to go higher.
Greenfinches and starlings, too, he caught, and he knew how to
make good cages. . . . All pretty trifling maybe, but a man
can make ten rubles a month from trifles like that. Well, time
went on, the old woman lost the use of her legs and took to her
bed. Consequently the house had no woman to look after it,
and that's about as good as being blind in both eyes! So the
old lady bestirred herself and made up her mind to get Vasya
married. They called in a matchmaker at once, and then the old
women got to talking and our Vasya went off to look at the
girls. He picked on Mashenka, the widow Samokhvalikha's
daughter. They didn't waste any time: they decided to get married on the spot, and in a week all arrangements were made.
She was quite young, just seventeen, very thin, knee-high to a
grasshopper, with a pale pretty-looking face, and all the qualities
of a young lady, and the dowry was good, too, amounting to
five hundred rubles, a cow, and a bed. . . . But the old lady
knew what was in store, and on the third day after the wedding
she departed unto the heavenly Jerusalem where there is neither
sickness nor sighing. The young ones had masses said for her
soul, and they began to live. Things went splendidly for six
months, and then suddenly another misfortune occurred. It

never rains but it pours. Vasya was summoned to draw lots as a conscript. Poor fellow, they made a soldier out of him, and they gave him no exemptions. They shaved his head and packed him off to the kingdom of Poland. It was God's will, there was nothing to be done about it. When he said good-by to his wife in the courtyard he was all right until he looked up at the pigeons in the hayloft for the last time, and then he cried as if his heart would break. It was pitiful to see him. At first Mashenka got her mother to stay with her so that she wouldn't be bored by being alone; the mother stayed until the birth of the baby, who is this very Kuzka, and then went off to stay with another married daughter in Oboyan, and Mashenka was alone with her child. There were the five drivers—drunken and mischievous peasants, all of them—and then there were the horses and carts, and fences would get broken or the soot would catch fire in the chimney—things a woman couldn't cope with—and being as how we were neighbors she would come to me for every least thing. So I would go over and put things right and give her advice. Naturally I'd go indoors and have a cup of tea and we'd fall to talking. I was a young fellow then, quite clever, and I was fond of talking on all manner of subjects, and she was refined and well-mannered. She dressed neatly—in summer she went about with a sunshade. I remember how I would start on theology or politics, and she would be flattered, and she would give me tea and jam. . . . In a word, not to make a long story out of it, I'm telling you, grandfather, a year had not passed before I was troubled with the Evil Spirit, the enemy of all mankind. I began by noticing I was getting bored and irritable on the days when I didn't see her. All the time I was trying to think up excuses for going to see her. 'It's high time,' I'd say, 'to put in the double windows for winter,' and I'd idle away a whole day putting in the windows for her and taking care to leave a couple for the next day. 'I'd better count Vasya's pigeons and see that none of them has got lost'—things like that. I was always talking to her across the fence, and in the end I made a little gate in it to avoid going all the way round. From women much evil and every abomination have come into the world. Not only we sinners, but even holy men have been seduced. Mashenka did not keep me at arm's length. Instead of thinking of her husband and taking care of herself, she fell in love with me. I began to notice how she was bored without me, and she was always walking along the fence and looking through the chinks into my yard. My head was going round in a kind of frenzy. On Thursday in Easter Week I got up early before there was any light in the sky, and when I went to market I passed close to her gate, and the Evil One was waiting for me. I watched her, looking through the trellis at the top of the gate, and she was standing there in the middle of her courtyard, already awake and feeding her ducks. I lost control over myself and called to her. She came and looked at me through the trellis. Her little face was pale, her eyes soft and sleepy-looking. . . . I loved her so much, and I began paying her compliments as though we were not standing at the gate, but visiting on name days, while she blushed and laughed and looked me straight in the eyes, not blinking. I lost my senses. I began to tell her about my real feelings for her. She opened the gate, let me in, and from that morning we began to live as man and wife."

At that moment the hunchback Alyoshka came into the yard from the street, and without paying any attention to them he ran breathlessly into the house. Soon he came running out with a concertina, and jingling some coins in his pocket and chewing sunflower seeds, he ran off and disappeared behind the gate.

"Who's that fellow?" Matvey Savvich asked.

"My son Alexey," Dyudya replied. "He's gone off to have some fun, the scoundrel! God has afflicted him with a hunchback, so we don't ask too much of him!"

"He's always out with the boys, always having fun," Afanasyevna sighed. "Before Shrovetide we married him off and thought he'd improve, but, well—he's worse than ever now!"

"There's nothing we can do," Dyudya said. "All it comes to

175

is that we are keeping another man's daughter for nothing."

From somewhere behind the church there came the sound of glorious mournful singing. The words were indistinguishable, but the voices of two tenors and a bass could be made out. Everyone was listening, and there was complete silence in the yard. Suddenly two of the singers broke off with a roar of laughter, while the third, the tenor, continued to sing in a voice so high that everyone instinctively looked up as though the voice had reached the very heights of heaven. Varvara came out of the house, shading her eyes with her hand as though blinded by the sun, and she looked toward the church.

"It's the priest's sons and the schoolmaster," she said.

Once again all three voices sang together.

Matvey Savvich sighed and went on: "Well, grandfather, that's how it was. Two years later we got a letter from Vasya in Warsaw. He wrote that the authorities were invaliding him home. He was ill. By that time I had put all foolishness out of my head, and I had a fine match arranged for me, but I didn't know how to get rid of my sweetheart. Every day I made up my mind to speak to Mashenka, but I didn't know how to approach her without her screaming her head off. The letter freed my hands. We read it together, and then she turned white as snow, and I said: 'Thank God, now you will be an honest woman again,' and then she said: 'I'm not going to live with him!' 'Well, he's your husband, isn't he?' I said. 'Is it an easy thing?' she went on. 'I never loved him, and married him against my will. My mother made me do it.' 'Don't try to get out of it, you little fool,' I said. 'Tell me this: were you married to him in church, or not?' 'I was married to him,' she answered, 'but I love you and want to live with you till I die. Let people laugh! I don't care! . . .' 'You're a God-fearing woman,' I said, 'and you have read the holy books. What does it say there?' "

"Once married, she must cleave unto her husband." Dyudya said.

"Husband and wife are one flesh," Matvey Savvich went on.

176

" 'We have sinned, you and I,' I said, 'and we must listen to our consciences and fear God. We must ask forgiveness of Vasya—he's a quiet soft sort of fellow, and he won't kill you! And it's better,' I said, 'to suffer tortures in this world at the hands of a lawful husband than to gnash your teeth on Judgment Day!' But the silly woman would not listen to me, and she kept on with her 'I love you,' and that was all she could do. Vasya came back on the Saturday before Trinity early in the morning. I saw everything from my fence. He ran into the house and a moment later emerged with Kuzka in his arms, laughing and crying at the same time, kissing Kuzka while looking up at the hayloft—he wanted to go to his pigeons, but he had no heart to put the boy down. He was a timid fellow, sentimental too. The day passed happily, quiet and decent. They were ringing the bells for the evening service when the thought came to me: 'Tomorrow is Trinity Sunday, and why haven't they decorated the gate and the fences with green boughs? Something must be wrong,' I thought. So I went over to their house. I looked in, and there he was sitting on the floor in the middle of the room, his eyes staring as though he were drunk, tears streaming down his cheeks and his hands shaking. He was pulling cracknels, necklaces, gingerbread, and all kinds of sweetmeats out of his bundle and hurling them on the floor. Three-year-old Kuzka was crawling about and chewing gingerbread, while Mashenka stood by the stove, pale and trembling, muttering to herself: 'I'm not your wife, I don't want to live with you!' and more nonsense like that. I bowed down at Vasya's feet and said: 'We have sinned grievously against you, Vasily Maximich—forgive us for Christ's sake!' Then I got up and said these words to Mashenka: 'It is your solemn duty, Maria Semyonovna, to wash Vasily's feet and drink the dirty water. Be an obedient wife to him, and pray to God's mercy that my transgressions may be forgiven unto me.' All this came to me as though inspired by an angel from heaven, and then I gave her some wise counsels, speaking with such feeling that tears came to my eyes. And two

177

days later Vasya comes up to me. 'Matvey, I forgive you, you and my wife,' he says. 'God be with you! She is a soldier's wife, all alone, and it was hard for her to take care of herself. She isn't the first and she won't be the last. Only,' he went on, 'I beseech you to live in the future as though there never had been anything between you, and not to show any signs of affection for her, while I'll do everything in my power to please her so that she'll love me again.' He shook my hand, drank some tea, and went off happily. 'Well,' I thought, 'God be praised,' and I was happy because everything had gone off so well. But no sooner had Vasya gone out of the yard than Mashenka came in. What sufferings I had to undergo! She hung on my neck, wept, and prayed. 'For God's sake, don't leave me,' she said. 'I can't go on living without you!' "

"Shameful hussy!" Dyudya sighed.

"So I swore at her and stamped my feet and took her into the hallway and latched the door and shouted at her: 'Go back to your husband! Don't shame me in front of people! Put the fear of God in your heart!' And every day there were scenes like that. One morning I was standing in the yard near the stable and mending a bridle. Suddenly I looked up and saw her running through the little gate into my yard, barefoot, wearing only a petticoat, coming straight toward me. She took hold of the bridle and got smeared with rosin. She was trembling and weeping. 'I can't live with that brute! I can't bear it! If you don't love me, kill me!' I lost patience and struck out at her with the bridle, and at that moment Vasya ran in through the gate shouting despairingly: 'Don't you hit her! Don't you hit her!' He went right up to her, and he was waving his arms and behaving like a madman, and then he began to beat her with his fists with all his strength, and then he threw her to the ground and stomped her. I tried to protect her, but he took the reins and gave her a thrashing, and all the time he was making little whinnying sounds like a colt: *hee-hee-hee!*"

"I'd take the reins and give you a taste of them!" Varvara

muttered, moving away. "Torturing one of us women, you damned brutes!"

"Shut up, you jade!" Dyudya shouted at her.

"*Hee-hee-hee!*" Matvey Savvich went on. "Then one of the drivers came running up from his yard, I called out for my workman, and between us we were able to rescue Mashenka and carry her home. What a disgrace it was! That same evening I went to see how she was. She was lying in bed, wrapped up in bandages and compresses, with only her eyes and nose visible, looking up at the ceiling. 'Well, good evening, Maria Semyonovna,' I said, and got no answer. Vasya was sitting in the next room, holding his head in his hands and blubbering. 'What a brute I am!' he was saying. 'I've ruined my life! Dear God, let me die!' I sat for half an hour with Mashenka, and gave her some sound advice. I tried to put the fear of God in her. 'Those who behave righteously,' I said, 'go to Paradise, but as for you—you will go to a Gehenna of fire, like all adultresses! Don't resist your husband! Go down on your knees before him!' But she said nary a word and did not blink an eyelid, and I might just as well have talked to a post. The next day Vasya fell ill with something like cholera, and during the evening I heard he was dead. Then they buried him. Mashenka did not go to the funeral—she did not want to let people see her shameless face and her bruises. But soon they were saying all over the place that Vasya had not died a natural death, but Mashenka had done away with him. The police soon heard about it. They dug up Vasya, slit him open, and found arsenic in his stomach. It was quite obvious he had been poisoned, so the police came and they took Mashenka away and the sweet innocent babe Kuzka, too. They put her in jail. The stupid woman had gone too far—God was punishing her! Eight months later she went on trial. She sat, I remember, on a low stool, wearing a gray gown with a white kerchief round her head, thin, pale, sharp-eyed, pitiable. Beside her there was a soldier holding a gun. She wouldn't confess her guilt. There were some in the court who said she had poisoned her husband, and there were others who argued he had poisoned himself from grief. I was one of the witnesses. When they questioned me, I told them the whole truth. 'She's guilty,' I said. 'It's no use hiding it—she didn't love her husband, and she was strong-willed. . . .' The trial began in the morning, and the same evening she was sentenced to thirteen years' penal servitude in Siberia. After the sentence Mashenka spent three months in the local jail. I used to go and see her, bringing her in simple humanity small gifts of tea and sugar. I remember how her whole body would start trembling as soon as she set eyes on me, and she would wring her hands and mutter: 'Go away! Go away!' She would clasp Kuzka to her, as though she were afraid I would take the boy away from her. 'See,' I would say, 'what you have brought upon yourself! Ah, my poor dear ruined Mashenka, you wouldn't listen to me when I was giving you advice, and so you must weep! Yes, you are guilty,' I said, 'and you have only yourself to blame!' I was offering her sound advice, but she only kept on saying: 'Go away! Go away!' as she huddled against the wall with Kuzka in her arms, trembling all over. When they were taking her off to the provincial capital, I accompanied her to the railroad station and slipped a ruble into her bundle for my soul's sake. She never reached Siberia. In the provincial capital she fell ill with a fever, and she died in the jail."

"Live like a dog, die like a dog!" Dyudya said.

"Well, Kuzka was sent back home. . . . I thought it over and then decided I would bring him up. What else could I do? He was born of a jailbird, but he had a living, Christian soul. I was sorry for him. I'll make a clerk out of him, and if I never have children of my own I'll make a merchant of him. Wherever I go now I take him with me—let him learn to work!"

All the time that Matvey Savvich was talking, Kuzka was sitting on a stone by the gate, his face cupped in his hands, gazing up at the sky; and seen from a distance in the dark, he resembled a tree stump.

"Kuzka, go to bed!" Matvey Savvich yelled at him.

"Yes, it's high time!" Dyudya said, getting up. He yawned noisily and then went on: "They think they're clever, not listening to advice, and so they come to grief!"

The moon was now floating high over the courtyard, moving in one direction while the clouds moved in another, but soon the clouds drifted away and then the moon shone clear over the courtyard. Matvey Savvich said a prayer with his face turned toward the church, bade the others good night, and lay down on the ground near the cart. Kuzka also said a prayer, lay down in the cart, and covered himself with a short coat; and for comfort he dug a hole in the straw and curled up so that his elbows touched his knees. From the yard Dyudya could be seen lighting a candle in a downstairs room, and then he put on his spectacles and stood in a corner with a book. For a long time he continued to read and bow before the icon.

The travelers fell asleep. Afanasyevna and Sophia went up to the cart and gazed down at Kuzka.

"The poor orphan sleeps," the old woman said. "He's so thin and weak, nothing but bones! He has no mother and no one to look after him on the road."

"My Grisha must be about two years older," Sophia said. "Up there in the factory, without his mother, he lives like a slave. I dare say his master beats him. When I looked at this poor orphan just now, I thought of my own Grisha, and my heart's blood turned to ice."

There was silence between them for a few moments.

"I wonder whether he remembers his mother," the old woman asked.

"How could he?"

From Sophia's eyes large tears flowed.

"He's all curled up like a kitten," she said, sobbing and laughing with tenderness and sorrow. "Poor little orphan!"

Kuzka started and opened his eyes. He saw above him an ugly, wrinkled, tear-stained face, and beside it another face, old and toothless, with a sharp chin and a humped nose, and high above them the unfathomable sky and the rushing clouds and the moon; and he screamed in terror. Sophia also screamed, echoes answered their screams, the heavy air trembled, a watchman tapped with his stick, and a dog barked. Matvey Savvich muttered in his sleep and turned over on the other side.

Late at night when Dyudya and the old woman and the watchman were all asleep, Sophia came out to the gate and sat down on a bench. The heat was stifling, and her head ached from crying. The street was wide and long; it stretched for nearly two miles to the right, and two miles to the left, and there was no end to it. The moon no longer shone over the court-yard, but from behind the church. One side of the street was flooded with moonlight, the other lay in deep darkness; and the long shadows of the poplars and the starling cotes stretched across the whole street, while the black and menacing shadows of the church spread far and wide, embracing Dyudya's gate and half his house. No one was about; only silence. From time to time there came faint strains of music from the end of the street. It was Alyoshka playing on his concertina.

Something moved in the shadows near the walls of the church: impossible to tell whether it was a man or a cow, or only a big bird rustling in the trees. And then a figure emerged out of the shadows, paused, said something in a man's voice, and dis-appeared down the church lane. A moment later another figure emerged about six feet away from the church gate, and this figure went straight from the church to the gate, and when it saw Sophia sitting on the bench, it stood still.

"Is that you, Varvara?" Sophia said.

"What if it is?"

It was Varvara. She stood perfectly still for a few moments, and then she went to the bench and sat down.

"Where have you been?" Sophia asked.

Varvara said nothing.

"You'll get into trouble if you play around, you young bride!"

Sophia said. "Did you hear what happened to Mashenka, how she was kicked and beaten with the reins? Look out, or the same thing will happen to you!"

"I don't care!" Varvara laughed into her handkerchief and whispered: "I've been having fun with the priest's son."

"You're making it up!"

"I swear to God . . ."

"It's a sin," whispered Sophia.

"I don't care! What should I be sorry for? If it's a sin, then it's a sin, and it's better to be struck dead by lightning than to live as I am doing. I'm young and healthy. I'm saddled with a horrible, hunchbacked husband, and he's worse than that damned Dyudya! Before I was married I never had enough to eat, I went barefoot, I had to get away from all that misery, and there was Alyoshka's wealth tempting me, and so I became a slave, or a fish caught in a net, and I would sooner sleep with a serpent than with that scab-covered Alyoshka! And what about your life? It's terrible to think about it! Your Fedor threw you out of the factory and sent you home to his father, and now he has taken another woman: they took your boy away and sold him into slavery. You work like a horse, and never hear a kind word! I'd rather spend my days an old maid and get half a ruble from the priest's son, I'd rather beg for a pittance, I'd rather throw myself down a well. . . ."

"It's a sin," Sophia whispered again.

"I don't care."

From somewhere behind the church came the mournful song of three voices: two tenors and a bass. And again it was impossible to distinguish the words.

"They're nightbirds all right," Varvara said, laughing.

And she began to whisper about her nightly escapades with the priest's son, and what he said to her, and what his friends were like, and how she carried on with the officials and merchants who came to the house. The mournful songs awoke in Sophia a longing for life and freedom, and she began to laugh.

For her, it was all sinful and terrible and sweet to hear about, and she envied Varvara and was sorry that she too had not been a sinner when she was young and beautiful.

From the church cemetery came the twelve strokes of the watchman's rattle, announcing midnight.

"It's time to sleep," Sophia said, getting up. "Dyudya will catch us if we don't!"

They both went quietly into the courtyard.

"I went away and never heard what happened to Mashenka afterwards," Varvara said, making her bed beneath the window.

"He said she died in prison. She poisoned her husband."

Varvara lay down beside Sophia, deep in thought, and then she said softly: "I could kill Alyoshka and never regret it."

"God help you, you are talking nonsense!"

When Sophia was dropping asleep, Varvara pressed close to her and whispered in her ear: "Let's kill Dyudya and Alyoshka!"

Sophia shuddered and said nothing, but her eyes were open wide and for a long time she gazed steadily at the sky.

"People might find out," she murmured.

"No, they would never find out. Dyudya is old, and it's time for him to die, and they'd say Alyoshka had croaked from drinking!"

"It's terrible. . . . God would strike us dead. . . ."

"I don't care."

Neither of them slept; they went on thinking in silence.

"It's cold," Sophia said, and she was beginning to shiver all over. "It will soon be light. Are you sleeping?"

"No. . . . Don't listen to me, my dear," Varvara whispered. "I get so mad with those damned swine, and sometimes I don't know what I am saying. Go to sleep—the dawn will be coming up soon. . . . Are you asleep?"

They were both quiet, and soon they grew calm and fell asleep.

Old Afanasyevna was the first to wake up. She woke Sophia, and they both went to the cowshed to milk the cows. Then the hunchback Alyoshka walked in, hopelessly drunk, without his concertina, and with his knees and chest all covered with dust and straw—he must have fallen down on the road. Swaying from side to side, he went into the cowshed, and without undressing he rolled over on a sleigh and a moment later was snoring. And when the rising sun shone with a clear flame on the gold crosses of the church, and silvered the windows, and the shadows of the trees and the wellhead were strewn across the courtyard over the dew-wet grass, then Matvey Savvich rose and attended to business.

"Kuzka, get up!" he shouted. "Time to harness the horses! Get going!"

The morning uproar was about to begin. A young Jewess in a flounced brown dress led a horse to the yard for water. The pulley of the well creaked painfully, the bucket rattled. Still tired and sleepy, his clothes covered with dew, Kuzka sat up in the cart, and lazily slipping on his overcoat, he listened to the water splashing out of the bucket into the well, and all the time he was shivering from cold.

"Auntie!" shouted Matvey Savvich. "Tell that brat of mine to harness the horses!"

At the same moment Dyudya shouted from the window: "Sophia, make that Jewess pay a kopeck for watering the horses! They're making a habit of it, the slobs!"

Up and down the street ran the bleating sheep; the peasant women were screeching at the shepherd, who played on his reed pipe, cracked his whip, and replied to them in his rough sleepy bass voice. Three sheep came running into the yard; not finding the gate, they butted the fence. Varvara was awakened by the noise, and taking up her bedding in her hands, she wandered into the house.

"You ought at least to drive the sheep out," the old woman shouted after her. "Ladylike, eh?"

"What's more, you needn't think I'm going to work for a lot of Herods," Varvara said as she entered the house.

The axles were greased and the horses harnessed. Dyudya emerged from the house with his accounts in his hands, sat down on the step, and began reckoning how much the travelers owed for oats, the night's lodging, and watering the horses.

"Grandfather, you charged a lot for the oats," Matvey Savvich said.

"If it's too much, you don't have to take it. We're not forcing you!"

Just when the travelers were about to get into the cart and ride off, an accident occurred. Kuzka lost his cap.

"Where did you put it, you little swine?" Matvey Savvich roared at the boy. "Where is it?"

Kuzka's face was contorted with terror; he searched all round the cart, and not finding it, he ran to the gate and then to the cowshed. The old woman and Sophia helped him look for it.

"I'll rip your ears off!" Matvey Savvich shouted. "Filthy little brat!"

The cap was found at the bottom of the cart. Kuzka brushed off the straw, put it on, and crawled timidly into the cart, still wearing an expression of terror on his face, as though he expected a blow from behind. Matvey Savvich crossed himself, the driver pulled on the reins, and the cart rolled slowly out of the yard.

1891

After the Theater

WHEN Nadia Zelenina came home with her mother from the theater, where they had been watching a performance of *Eugene Onegin*, she went to her own room, slipped quickly out of her dress, and wearing only a petticoat and a white bodice, sat down at the table in a great hurry and began to write a letter in the manner of Tatiana: "I love you," she wrote, "but you have no love for me—none at all!"

A moment later she burst out laughing.

She was only sixteen, and in all her life she had never been in love. She knew that Gorny, an officer, and Gruzdev, a student, were both in love with her, but now, having seen the opera, she was inclined to doubt that they loved her. To be unloved and unhappy—how interesting that was! How beautiful, poetic, and touching, when one was hopelessly in love with someone who was completely indifferent. What was interesting about Onegin was that he was incapable of loving, and what was enchanting about Tatiana was that she was hopelessly in love. If they had loved each other with an identical passion and were completely happy together, how boring!

"You must never again confess your love for me," Nadia went on writing, thinking of Gorny, the officer. "I cannot believe your words. You are clever, well educated, serious, you have a great talent, and maybe a brilliant future awaits you. As for me, I am only an insignificant and uninteresting young woman, and you yourself know perfectly well that I would only be a hindrance in your life; and though you were attracted to me, and thought you had found your ideal in me, still it was all a mistake, and even now you are saying to yourself in your despair: 'Why did I ever meet that girl?' Only your goodness of heart prevents you from admitting it!"

At this point Nadia began to feel sorry for herself. She burst into tears, but continued writing: "If it were not so hard for me to leave my mother and my brother, I would take the veil and wander away wherever my feet led me. Then you would be free to love someone else. Oh, if only I were dead!"

Through her tears she could no longer see what she had written. Tiny rainbows trembled on the floor, on the table, on the ceiling, and it seemed to Nadia that she was looking through a prism. Impossible to go on writing. She threw herself back in her armchair and began thinking of Gorny.

Goodness, how attractive, how fascinating men were! Nadia remembered Gorny's beautiful expression during a discussion on music: so compelling, so tender, so deferential, and he had difficulty subduing the passion in his voice. In society, where an icy pride and an air of indifference are the marks of a good education and fine breeding, he tried to conceal his feelings, but without success, and everyone knew how devoted he was— how passionately devoted—to music. Those never-ending discussions on music, and the loud criticisms of ignoramuses, kept him in a constant state of tension, so that he appeared to be awed, timid, and silent. He played the piano with the flair of a professional pianist, and if he had not been an officer, he would certainly have become a famous musician.

The tears dried on Nadia's cheeks. She remembered now that Gorny had declared his love for her during a symphony concert, and then again downstairs near the cloakroom, where they were chilled by the strong draft which came at them from all sides.

"I am so glad you have at last made the acquaintance of

the student Gruzdev," she wrote. "He is a very clever man, and I am sure you will be friends. Yesterday he came to see us, and stayed until two. We were all so happy—I am sorry you could not join us. He said some very remarkable things.

Nadia laid her arms on the table, and rested her head on them. Her hair fell over the letter. It occurred to her that the student Gruzdev was also in love with her, and deserved a letter as much as Gorny. But then—she wondered—perhaps after all she should be writing to Gruzdev. An unreasoning joy stirred in her heart: at first it was a very small joy, and rolled about in her heart like a little rubber ball, but it became more powerful and vaster, and at last poured out of her like a fountain. She had forgotten Gorny and Gruzdev. She was confused; but her joy grew and spread from her heart into her hands and feet, and it seemed that a gentle and refreshing wind was fanning her face and lifting her hair. Her shoulders shook with silent laughter, the table shook, the lamp chimney trembled. Her tears were sprinkled on the letter she was writing. She could not control her laughter and so, to prove that she was not laughing for no reason at all, she quickly thought of something funny.

"Oh, what an amusing poodle!" she exclaimed, feeling faint with laughter. "What an amusing poodle!"

She remembered how on the previous day Gruzdev had romped with Maxim, the family poodle, after they had taken tea together, and later he told her the story of a clever poodle who chased a raven round the garden. Suddenly the raven stopped, looked round, and said: "Stinker!" The poodle was completely unaware that the raven was trained, and became terribly confused, running away with a look of utter bewilderment. After a while he began to bark.

"No, it would be much better to fall in love with Gruzdev," Nadia decided, and she tore up the letter.

Her thoughts turned to the student, of his love for her and her love for him, and soon her thoughts went wandering, and she found herself thinking of many things: of her mother, of the street, of the pencil, of the piano. . . . She thought of all these things with joy, and it seemed to her that everything was good and splendid and beautiful, and her joy spoke to her, saying there was much more to come, and in a little while it would be still better. Soon spring would come, and then it would be summer, and she would go with her mother to Gorbiky, and then Gorny would come for the holidays, take her for walks in the garden, and flirt with her. And then Gruzdev would come. They would play croquet and bowls, and he would tell her funny stories and others that would leave her dumb with astonishment. Passionately she longed for the garden, the darkness, the clear sky, the stars. Once more her shoulders shook with laughter: the room seemed to fill with aromatic scents, and a twig was tapping against the windowpane.

She went to her bed and sat down, and then not knowing what to do with the joy that was flooding into her heart, she gazed at the icon which hung at the head of her bed, and murmured: "Dear God, dear God, dear God!"

April 1892

A Fragment

ON his retirement State Councilor Kozerogov bought a modest property in the country and settled down on it. There, partly in imitation of Cincinnatus, but also partly in imitation of Professor Kaigorodov, he toiled in the sweat of his brow and wrote down his observations of natural phenomena. After his death these writings, together with his effects, following the desire expressed in his will, fell into the possession of his housekeeper, Marfa Yevlampyevna. As is well known, this inestimable old woman tore down his manor house and in its place erected a superb tavern licensed to sell strong liquor. This tavern acquired a "special room" fitted out for passing landowners and civil servants. On a table of this room were placed the writings of the deceased, for the convenience of such of the guests who might be in need of paper. One sheet fell into my hands. Apparently it relates to the very early agricultural efforts of the deceased, and contains the following information:

March 3. The spring migration of birds has begun. Yesterday I saw sparrows. I greet you, O feathered children of the south! In your sweet chirping I seem to hear you express the wish: "Be happy, Your Excellency."

March 14. Today I asked Marfa Yevlampyevna: "Why does the cock crow so much?" She answered me: "Because he has a throat." I replied: "I, too, have a throat, but I don't crow!" So multitudinous are the mysteries of Nature! During my years of service in St. Petersburg I ate turkey more than several times, but only yesterday for the first time in my life did I observe a living turkey. A very remarkable bird indeed!

March 22. The rural officer called. For a long time we debated the subject of virtue—I sitting down, he standing. Among other things he said: "Have you ever wished, Your Excellency, to return to the days of your youth?" I replied to this question: "No, not in the least, for if I were young again, I would not be enjoying my present rank." He agreed with my point of view, and went off, visibly moved.

April 16. With my own hands I have dug up two rows in the kitchen garden and planted semolina. I said nothing about this to anyone, to surprise my Marfa Yevlampyevna, to whom I am indebted for many happy moments in my life. Yesterday at tea she grumbled bitterly about her constitution, remarking that her expanding girth prevented her from passing through the door leading to the storehouse. My observation to her was: "On the contrary, my dear, the fullness of your form serves as an embellishment and disposes me all the more favorably towards you." She blushed at this. I rose and embraced her with both arms, for it is impossible to embrace her with only one.

May 28. An old man, seeing me near the women's bathing place, asked me why I was sitting there. I answered him with the observation: "The reason I am sitting here is because I want to see that young men do not come and sit here." "Then let us watch together," the old man said, and then he sat down beside me, and we began to talk about virtue.

April 1892

In Exile

OLD Semyon, nicknamed Smarty, and a young Tartar whom nobody knew by name, were sitting by a bonfire near the river: the other three ferrymen were inside the hut. Semyon was an old man of sixty, and though gaunt and toothless he was broad in the shoulder and gave an appearance of health. He was drunk, and would have been asleep long ago if it had not been for the half bottle in his pocket and his dread that the young fellows in the hut would want his vodka. The Tartar was ill and tired, and wrapping himself up in his rags, he talked about how good it was in Simbirsk province and about the good-looking, clever wife he had left behind him. He was no more than twenty-five, but looking at his pale, sick, melancholy face in the firelight, you would have thought he was only a boy.

"You can hardly call this place Paradise," Smarty said. "You can see for yourself: water, the naked shore, clay everywhere— nothing else. . . . Holy Week is over, but the ice is still floating down the river, and there was snow this morning."

"Misery, misery!" moaned the Tartar, looking round him in terror.

Ten paces below, the river flowed darkly, muttering to itself as it dug a path between the steep clay banks and made its way to the distant sea. The dark shape of one of those huge barges which the ferrymen call a *karbass* loomed against the bank. Far-off, on the further shore, dying down and flickering up again, were little serpents of fire: they were burning last year's grasses. And behind these serpents darkness again. There could be heard the sound of little blocks of ice crashing against the barge. Dampness and cold. . . .

The Tartar looked at the sky. There were as many stars as there were at home, and the same darkness around, but something was missing. At home, in Simbirsk province, the stars were altogether different, and so was the sky.

"Misery, misery!" he repeated.

"You'll get used to it," Smarty said, laughing. "You're young and foolish now, and wet round the ears, and it's only your folly which makes you believe you are the most miserable mortal on earth, but the time will come when you will say: 'May God grant everyone such a life!' Just look at me. In a week's time the water will have fallen, and then we'll launch the small boat, and you'll go wandering around Siberia to amuse yourself, and I'll be staying here, rowing back and forth across the river. For twenty years I've been doing just that. Day and night! White salmon and pike beneath the water, and I above it! And glory be, I'm not in need of anything. God grant everyone such a life!"

The Tartar thrust some brushwood into the flames, drew closer to the fire, and said: "My father ill. When he dies, my mother, my wife come here. They have promised."

"What's the use of having a mother and a wife here?" asked Smarty. "It's all foolishness, brother. The devil is tormenting you, damn his soul. Don't listen to the accursed one. Don't surrender to him. If he talks about women, answer him: 'Don't want them.' If he talks about freedom, tell him straightway: 'Don't want it.' You don't need anything. Neither father, nor mother, nor wife, nor freedom, nor house, nor home. I don't want anything, damn their souls!"

Smarty took a swig at the bottle and went on: "Brother, I'm no peasant, I don't come from the class of slaves, I'm the son of a sexton, and when I was free in Kursk I wore a frock coat, but now I have brought myself to such a point that I can sleep naked on the earth and eat grass. God grant everyone such a life! I don't want for anything, and I don't fear anyone, and I know there is no one in the world as rich and free as I am! From the very first day they sent me here from Russia, I got into the swing of it—I wanted for nothing. The devil was at me for a wife, for a home, for freedom, but I told him: 'I want for nothing!' I tired him out, and now, as you can see, I live well and don't complain about anything. If anyone should give an inch to the devil and listen to him just once, then he's lost and there's no salvation for him: he'll sink into the bog up to his ears and never crawl out again. It's not only boys like you, poor stupid peasants, who get lost—even well-educated gentleman fall by the wayside. Fifteen years ago they sent a gentleman here from Russia. There was something he refused to share with his brothers—he had forged a will or something. They said he was a prince or a baron, but maybe he was just an official. Who knows? Well, this gentleman came here, and the first thing he did was to buy a house and some land at Mukhortinskoe. He said he wanted to live by his own labor, by the sweat of his brow, because, he said, he was no longer a gentleman but an exile.[1] So I said: 'God help you, it's the best thing you can do!' He was then a young man, a hustler, always busy, he used to mow the grass himself and ride sixty versts on horseback. And that was the cause of his trouble.

"From the very first year he would ride to the post office at Gyrino. He would be standing with me on my ferryboat, and he would say with a sigh: 'Ah, Semyon, it's a long time since they sent me any money from home.' And I'd say: 'You don't need money, Vassily Sergeich. What good is it? Throw all the past away, forget it as though it had never existed, as though it was only a dream, and begin a new life. Don't listen to the devil,' I'd say to him. 'He'll never bring you any good, he'll only tighten the noose. At present you want money,' I'd tell him, 'but in a little while you'll be wanting something more, and then

[1] He means a prisoner on parole, forced to live in Siberia.

you'll want still more, but if you have put your heart on being happy, then you'll have to learn not to want anything. Yes. . . . Already,' I'd pursue the argument, 'fate has played cruel tricks on both of us, but it's no good going down on your knees and begging his mercy—you have to despise fate, laugh in his face! Then fate will begin laughing at itself.' That's what I told him. . . . Well, two years passed, and I ferried him across to this side of the river, and one day he was rubbing his hands together and laughing. 'I'm going to Gyrino,' he said, 'to meet my wife. She has taken pity on me, and has come to join me. I have a nice kind wife.' He was breathless with joy. And the next day he arrived with his wife, a pretty young lady wearing a hat, with a little girl in her arms. And lots of luggage of all kinds. My Vassily Sergeich was spinning around her, he couldn't take his eyes away from her, and couldn't praise her enough. 'Yes, brother Semyon, even in Siberia people live!' Well, thought I, he won't always be showing a happy face to the world. From that time he went riding almost every week to Gyrino to find out whether the money was being sent from Russia. He needed a pile of money. He would tell me: 'She is ruining her youth and beauty in Siberia for my sake, and sharing my miserable fate, and so I ought to provide her with every comfort.' And to make life more cheerful for his lady, he made the acquaintance of officials and all sorts of riffraff, and of course he had to provide food and drink for the whole crowd, and there had to be a piano and a shaggy dog sitting on the sofa —a plague on such nonsense! . . . Luxury and self-indulgence, that's what it was! The lady did not stay long with him. How could she? Clay, water, cold weather, no vegetables for you, no fruit, surrounded by ignorant and drunken people, and she a pampered darling from the capital. . . . Of course she got bored. Besides, her husband was no gentleman any longer: he was in exile, and there's no honor in that. Three years later, I remember, on the eve of the Assumption, there was the sound of shouting from the other bank. I went over on the ferry and saw the lady herself—she was all muffled up, and there was a young gentleman with her, one of the officials. There was a troika, too. . . . I ferried them across, and they got into the troika and vanished into thin air! That was the last we saw of them. Toward morning Vassily Sergeich came galloping down to the ferry. 'Semyon, tell me,' he said, 'didn't my wife pass this way with a gentleman in spectacles?' 'Yes, she did,' I told him. 'Run after the wind in the fields. . . .' So he galloped after them, and for five days and nights he was pursuing them. Later, when I took him over to the other side, he flung himself down in the ferry and beat his head against the planking and howled. 'So that's how it is!' said I, and I laughed and reminded him how he had said: 'People can live even in Siberia.' And he beat his head all the more. . . . After that he began to long for his freedom. His wife had gone back to Russia, and so naturally he was drawn there, so that he could see her and take her away from her lover. And then, brother, what did he do but ride off nearly every day to the post office or the town to see the authorities. He kept sending them petitions begging them to have mercy on him and to let him return home, and he used to say he spent two hundred rubles on telegrams alone. He sold his land and mortgaged his house to a Jew. He grew gray, stooped, and his face turned yellow like a consumptive's. He would talk to you and go: *hee-hee-hee* . . . and there would be tears in his eyes. He wasted away with all those petitions for eight years, but recently he has recovered his spirits and shows a more cheerful face to the world: he has thought up a new self-indulgence. His daughter, you see, was growing up. He was always looking at her and doting on her. To tell the truth, there's nothing wrong with her—she's a pretty thing, with black eyebrows, and high-spirited. Every Sunday he would go to church with her at Gyrino. They would be standing side by side on the ferryboat, and the girl would be laughing, and he would never look away from her. 'Yes, Semyon,' he would say, 'people can live in Siberia. Even in Siberia there is happiness.

Look what a daughter I have! I don't believe that if you traveled a thousand miles you would find another like her!' And I'd say to him: 'Your daughter's all right, there's no question at all. . . .' And I'd find myself thinking: 'Wait a bit. . . . The girl is still young, the blood is dancing in her veins, she wants to live, and what kind of life is there here?' And, brother, she began to pine away. She withered and wasted away and fell into a decline until she was too weak to stand on her feet. Consumption! There's your Siberian happiness for you, a curse on it! That's how people live in Siberia. . . . Now he spends his time running after doctors and taking them home with him. As soon as he hears of a doctor or a quack two or three hundred miles away, he drives over to fetch him. It's terrible to think of the money he spends on doctors, and it's my opinion he would much better spend it on drinking. . . . She'll die anyway. She's certain to die, and then he will be finished. He'll hang himself from grief or run away to Russia, that's for sure. If he runs away, they'll catch him, there'll be a trial, he'll be sentenced to hard labor, and they'll give him the taste of the whip. . . ."

"Good, good," muttered the Tartar, shivering with cold.

"Why good?" Smarty asked.

"Wife, daughter. . . . Let suffer hard labor, let sorrow, but he seen wife, daughter. . . . You say: want nothing. But nothing is bad! Wife lived with him three years—this is gift from God. Nothing is bad, but three years is good. How not understand?"

Trembling with cold and stammering, the Tartar picked out with great difficulty the Russian words, of which he knew so few, and he went on to say that God forbid one should fall ill in a strange land, and die, and be buried in the cold, rusty earth; and if his wife should come to him even for a single day or a single hour, then for such happiness he would be willing to bear any torture whatsoever, and he would thank God for it. Better a single day of happiness than nothing at all.

Then once again he described how he had left a pretty and clever wife at home; then, clutching his head with both hands, he began to weep, assuring Semyon that he was not guilty and had in fact been falsely accused. His uncle and two brothers had run off with a peasant's horse and beaten the old man until he was half dead, but society had judged them and decided to sentence all three brothers to Siberia, while the uncle, a rich man, went scot-free.

"You'll soo-oo-oon get used to it," Semyon said.

The Tartar fell silent, turning his tearful gaze on the fire: his face expressed bewilderment and fear, as though he still failed to understand what he was doing there, in the darkness and the damp, among strangers, and far from Simbirsk province. Smarty lay beside the fire, and he laughed quietly at something, and began singing under his breath.

"What happiness can she have with her father?" he asked a few moments later. "He loves her and finds consolation with her, and all that is true. But, brother, you can't put your fingers in his mouth, as they say. He's a strict old man, and a harsh one, and what use is strictness to a young woman? What she wants is caresses and ha-ha-ha and ho-ho-ho and scents and pomades, isn't that so? Eh, eh, such troubles there are!" Semyon sighed, and he rose heavily to his feet. "The vodka has all gone, so it's time to sleep. Well, brother, I'm off to bed."

Left alone, the Tartar added more brushwood to the fire, lay down, gazed into the flames, and began to dream of his wife and village. If only his wife would come for a month or even a day, and if she wanted to, she could then go back again! Better a month or even a day than nothing. But if she kept her promise and came, how would he provide for her and where would she stay?

"How could she live without anything to eat?" he asked aloud.

They paid him only ten kopecks for working night and day at the oars. True, the passengers sometimes gave tea and vodka money, but the ferrymen shared all the money they received among themselves; they never gave any to the Tartar, and only laughed at him. Poverty made him hungry, cold, and frightened. . . . Now that his whole body was aching and shivering, he ought to have gone to the hut to lie down and sleep, but he had nothing to cover him there, and it was colder than on the banks of the river; here he had nothing to cover himself with, but at least he could make a fire. . . .

In another week the waters would have fallen, the ferryboat would put up sails, and the ferrymen, except for Semyon, would no longer be needed: then the Tartar would begin wandering from village to village, looking for work and begging for alms. His wife was only seventeen, a shy, pretty, spoiled girl—could she possibly go to the villages begging for alms, with her face unveiled? No, it was too horrible to think about. . . .

It was already growing light. The barge, the willow bushes on the water, and the ripples were clearly distinguishable, and, looking round, you could see the steep clay slopes with the small huts thatched with brown straw at the bottom, while the village huts clung to the higher ground. The cocks were already crowing in the village.

The red clay slopes, the barge, the river, the strange and evil villagers, the cold, the hunger, and the sickness—perhaps all these had no real existence. Perhaps, thought the Tartar, it was all a dream. He thought he was asleep and heard himself snoring. . . . It occurred to him that he was at home in Simbirsk province, and he had only to call his wife's name and she would answer him, and in the next room was his mother. . . . How terrible these dreams were! What are they for? The Tartar smiled and opened his eyes wide. What river was this? Was it the Volga?

Snow was falling.

"Ahoy there!" someone shouted from the other side. "*Karba-a-a-ss!*"

The Tartar awoke and went to wake his comrades, to row over to the other side. Slipping into their sheepskins as they emerged from the hut, the ferrymen came along the bank, swearing in hoarse, sleepy voices, shuddering in the cold. After their sleep, the river, with its piercing cold, seemed quite disgusting and horrifying. And they made no haste as they tumbled onto the barge. . . . Then the Tartar and the three ferrymen manned the long, broad-bladed oars, which in the darkness somehow resembled the claws of a crab, and Semyon leaned his belly against the long tiller. The shouting could still be heard from the other side, and two shots were fired from a revolver, in the belief perhaps that the ferrymen were fast asleep or had wandered off to the village tavern.

"All right, all right, you'll get over in time!" Smarty said in the tone of a man convinced that there is nothing in the world worth hurrying for, because it was all one in the end and nothing would ever come of it.

The heavy blundering barge drew away from the bank and moved through the willow bushes, only the backward motion of the willows suggesting they were not standing still, but moving. The ferrymen dipped and raised their oars evenly, in unison. Smarty pressed his belly against the tiller, his body describing an arc as he danced from one side of the boat to the other. In the darkness the men seemed to be sitting on a long-pawed prehistoric animal, floating through a cold and desolate landscape, the very same landscape we sometimes see in dreams.

They slipped beyond the willows and came out into the open river. The creaking and the measured dipping of the oars could be heard on the other bank, and a voice crying: "Hurry! Hurry!" Ten minutes passed before the barge bumped heavily against the landing stage.

"It keeps coming down," Semyon muttered, wiping the snow from his face. "And where it comes from, only God knows!"

On the bank stood a small thin man wearing a jacket lined with fox fur and a cap of white lamb's wool. He stood at some distance from the horses, motionless; he wore a melancholy and concentrated expression, as though trying to remember something, annoyed with the failing powers of his memory. Semyon approached him with a smile, doffing his cap, and the man said: "I'm in a hurry to reach Anastasyevka. My daughter is worse. There is a new doctor at Anastasyevka, they tell me."

So his carriage was dragged onto the barge, and they made their way across the river. The man whom Semyon called Vassily Sergeich stood motionless throughout the journey, his thick lips tightly compressed, his eyes fixed on one place; and when the coachman asked for permission to smoke in his presence, he made no reply; it was as though he had not heard. But Semyon, pressing his belly against the tiller, looked at him mockingly and said: "Even in Siberia people can live. Li-i-i-ive!"

On Semyon's face there was an expression of triumph, as though he had proved something and rejoiced that everything had happened as he predicted. The miserable, helpless look on the face of the man in the jacket lined with fox fur evidently afforded him great satisfaction.

"It's muddy traveling this time of the year, Vassily Sergeich," he said while they were harnessing the horses on the riverbank. "You'd have done better to wait a week or two, when it gets drier. Or better still, given up the journey. . . . It might be worthwhile if any good could come out of it, but as you know yourself, people have been driving about for ages and ages, and day and night too, and nothing ever came of it. That's the truth!"

In silence Vassily Sergeich handed them some vodka money, climbed into the carriage, and drove away.

"So he's chasing after a doctor," said Semyon, shuddering with cold. "Looking for a real doctor is like hunting the wind across the fields or taking the devil by the hind leg, damn it all! What queer fellows, eh? Lord have mercy on me!"

The Tartar went up to Semyon, looking at him with hatred and horror, trembling all over, and, mixing Tartar words with his broken Russian, said: "He is good . . . good, but you . . . you are bad! You are bad! Gentleman is good soul, fine man, you . . . you are beast, horrible! Gentleman is alive, you are carcass. . . . God created man to be alive, to be happy and sad and full of sorrow, but you . . . you want nothing. You not alive, you stone, lump of clay! Stone want nothing, and you want nothing! You are stone, and God does not love you. God loves gentleman!"

They all laughed at him, and the Tartar frowned contemptuously, and with a wave of his hand he wrapped himself in his rags and went up to the fire. Semyon and the ferrymen went off to the hut.

"It's cold," one of the ferrymen said in a hoarse voice, stretching himself on the straw which littered the damp clay floor.

"Well, it's not warm," another agreed. "It's a convict's life all right!"

They were all lying down. The door was blown open by the wind, and snow poured into the hut. No one wanted to get up and close the door; it was cold, and they were lazy.

"I'm all right," said Semyon, going off to sleep. "God give everyone such a life!"

"Seven years' hard labor, and everyone knows it. The devil himself wouldn't have you!"

From outside came a sound like a dog howling.

"What's that? Who's there?"

"It's the Tartar crying."

"Well, he's a queer one!"

"Oh, he'll get used to it," Semyon said, and he went off to sleep.

Soon all the others were asleep. And the door remained unclosed.

May 1892

Big Volodya and Little Volodya

~~~~~~~~~~~~~~~~~~~~

"PLEASE let me drive! I'll go and sit with the driver!" Sophia Lvovna said in a loud voice. "Wait a moment, driver! I'm coming to sit beside you!"

She stood up in the sleigh, and her husband, Vladimir Nikitich, and the friend of her childhood, Vladimir Mikhailovich, both held her hands to prevent her from falling. The troika was moving fast.

"I said she should never have touched the brandy," Vladimir Nikitich said in annoyance as he turned to his companion. "You're some fellow, eh?"

The colonel knew from experience that after even a moderate amount of drinking women like Sophia Lvovna often give way to hysterical laughter and then tears. He was afraid that when they reached home, instead of going to sleep, he would spend the night administering compresses and pouring out medicines.

"Whoa there!" Sophia Lvovna shouted. "I want to drive!"

She felt genuinely happy and on top of the world. For the last two months, ever since her wedding, she had tormented herself with the thought that she had married Colonel Yagich for his money and, as they say, *par dépit*; but that day, in a surburban restaurant, she came suddenly and finally to the conclusion that she loved him passionately. In spite of his fifty-four years he was so finely built, so agile and sinewy, and he was always making exquisite puns and accompanying gypsy bands. It is quite true that older men nowadays are a thousand times more interesting than the young: it seems as though age and youth have exchanged roles. The colonel was two years older than her father, but such a fact could have no significance when, to tell the truth, he had infinitely more vitality, vigor, and youthfulness than she had, and she was only twenty-three.

"Oh, my darling!" she thought. "How wonderful you are!"

In the restaurant she came to the conclusion that there was not one spark of her old feeling for her childhood friend left. For this friend, Vladimir Mikhailovich, or simply Volodya, she had felt only the day before an insane and desperate passion; now she was completely indifferent to him. All evening he had seemed stupid, dull, uninteresting, insignificant; and the way he cold-bloodedly and continually escaped paying the restaurant checks had shocked her, and so she had only just been able to resist telling him: "Why don't you stay at home, if you are so poor?" The colonel paid for everything.

Perhaps because trees, telephone poles, and snowdrifts were flitting past her eyes, all kinds of disconnected thoughts were passing through her brain. She remembered now that the check at the restaurant amounted to a hundred and twenty rubles, and there was another hundred rubles for the gypsies, and tomorrow she could throw a thousand rubles away if she wanted to, while only two months ago, before her wedding, she had not three rubles to her name, and had to beg her father for the least little thing. How things had changed!

Her thoughts were confused. It occurred to her that when she was ten years old her present husband, Colonel Yagich, was flirting with her aunt, and everyone at home said he had ruined her, and it was perfectly true that her aunt came down to dinner with tears in her eyes and was always going off somewhere; and they said of her that she would never find any peace. He was extremely handsome in those days and had extraordinary success with women, a fact widely known in the town. They said that every day he went on a round of visits among his adorers, exactly like a doctor visiting his patients. Even now, in spite of his gray hair, wrinkles, and spectacles, his lean face, especially in profile, remained handsome.

Sophia Lvovna's father was an army doctor who had once served in the same regiment as Yagich. Volodya's father was also an army doctor; at one time he had served in the same regiment as Yagich and her father. In spite of many turbulent and complicated love affairs, Volodya had been a brilliant student, and now, having completed his course at the university with great success, he was specializing in foreign literature and, as they say, writing his dissertation. He lived in the barracks with his father, the army doctor, and although he was now thirty years old he still had no means of subsistence. As children, Sophia Lvovna and he had lived under the same roof, though in different apartments, and he often came to play with her, and they learned dancing and took French lessons together. As he grew to become a well-built, exceedingly handsome young man, she began to feel shy in his presence and fell madly in love with him, and she remained in love with him right up to the moment when she married Yagich. He, too, had been extraordinarily successful with women almost from the age of fourteen, and the women who deceived their husbands with him usually justified themselves by saying that Volodya was only a boy. Recently the story got around that when he was a student living in lodgings near the university, anyone who went to call on him would hear footsteps behind the door and there would come a whispered apology: *"Pardon, je ne suis pas seul."* Yagich was enthusiastic about him, and as Derzhavin blessed Pushkin,[1] so Yagich blessed the young student, solemnly regarding him as his successor; and apparently he was very fond of him. For whole hours they played billiards or piquet together without saying a word, and if Yagich drove out on his troika he always took Volodya with him; and Yagich alone was initiated into the mysteries of

[1] The poet Gavril Derzhavin is said to have blessed the sixteen-year-old Pushkin in 1815.

his dissertation. Earlier, when the colonel was younger, they were often rivals in love, but there was never any jealousy between them. In the society in which they moved, Yagich was nicknamed Big Volodya and his friend Little Volodya.

On the sleigh, besides Sophia Lvovna, Big Volodya, and Little Volodya, there was still another person—Margarita Alexandrovna, known as Rita, a cousin of Madame Yagich, a very pale woman, over thirty, with black eyebrows and wearing pince-nez; she smoked cigarettes continually even in the bitterest frosty weather: there was always cigarette ash on her knees and on the front of her dress. She spoke through her nose, drawling out each word, a coldhearted woman who could drink any amount of liqueurs and brandy without getting drunk, and she liked telling anecdotes with *double-entendres* in a tasteless way. At home she read serious magazines from morning to night, while strewing cigarette ash all over them and eating frozen apples.

"Oh, Sonya, stop behaving like a lunatic!" she said, drawling out the words. "Really, it is too silly for words!"

When they were in sight of the town gate, the troika went more slowly, as houses and people began to flicker past; and now Sophia Lvovna grew quiet, nestling against her husband and surrendering to her own thoughts. Sitting opposite her was Little Volodya. Her happy, lighthearted thoughts were mingled with melancholy ones. She thought: "This man who is sitting opposite me knows I loved him, and it is very likely he believes the gossip that I married the colonel *par dépit*." Not once had she ever told him she was in love with him, and she had never wanted him to know this, and accordingly she had concealed her feelings; but from the expression on his face it was perfectly obvious that he had seen through her, and her pride suffered. The most humiliating thing was that ever since the wedding Little Volodya had been forcing his attentions upon her, and this had never happened before. He spent long hours with her in complete silence or talking about nothing at all, and even now in the sleigh, though he did not speak to her, he would gently touch her feet or her hands. It appeared that he wanted nothing more and was delighted with her marriage; it also appeared that he despised her and she excited in him an interest of a certain kind, as though she were an immoral, disreputable woman. And when her triumphant affection for her husband mingled in her soul with feelings of humiliation and wounded pride, she was overcome with a fierce resentment and wanted to sit in the coachman's box and whistle and scream at the horses.

They were just passing the nunnery when the huge sixteen-ton bell rang out. Rita crossed herself.

"Our Olga lives in the nunnery," Sophia Ivanovna said, and then she crossed herself and shivered.

"Why did she enter a nunnery?" the colonel asked.

"*Par dépit*," Rita said angrily, with obvious reference to Sophia Lvovna's marriage to Yagich. "*Par dépit* is all the rage now. Defy the whole world—that's what they do. She was a furious little coquette, always giggling, and she only liked balls and cavaliers and then suddenly—she had gone away, and everyone was surprised!"

"Not true at all!" said Little Volodya, turning down the collar of his fur coat and revealing his handsome face. "It wasn't *par dépit* at all, but something quite horrible, if you please. Her brother Dmitry went to penal servitude, and no one knows where he is. Her mother died of grief."

Then he turned up his collar.

"Olga did well," he added in a muffled voice. "Living as an adopted child and with that paragon of virtue Sophia Lvovna— you have to take that into account, too!"

Sophia Lvovna was well aware of the note of contempt in his voice and she wanted to say something to hurt him, but she remained silent. Once again she was overcome with a passion of remonstrance, and she rose to her feet and shouted in a tear-filled voice: "I want to go to the early service! Turn back, driver! I want to see Olga!"

They turned back, and the deep-toned nunnery bell reminded Sophia of Olga and about all Olga's life. Other church bells were also ringing. When the driver brought the troika to a stop, Sophia Lvovna jumped from the sleigh, and ran unescorted up to the gate of the nunnery.

"Please be quick!" her husband shouted after her. "We're already late!"

She went through the dark gateway and then along an avenue which led from the gateway to the largest of the churches, while the snow crackled under her feet and the church bells rang directly over her head, so that they seemed to penetrate her whole being. Then she came to the church door; there were three steps leading down, and a porch with icons on each side which smelled of incense and juniper, and then there was another door, and a dark figure opened it and bowed low to the ground. Inside the church, the service had not yet begun. One of the nuns was walking past the iconostasis and lighting the candles on the tall candlesticks, while another lit the candles on the luster. Here and there by the columns and the side chapels stood black motionless figures. "I suppose they will be standing there as they are now until tomorrow morning," Sophia Lvovna thought, and it seemed to her that everything in the church was cold, dark, and boring—more boring than a cemetery. With a bored gaze she watched those motionless figures growing colder each minute, and suddenly she felt as though a hand were squeezing her heart. She recognized Olga, who was one of the nuns, with thin shoulders, a black kerchief over her head, and quite short. She was sure she had seen her, though when Olga had entered the nunnery she was plump and seemed taller. Hesitating, completely overwhelmed by what she had seen, Sophia Lvovna went up to the nun and looked at her over her shoulder, and she was sure it was Olga.

"Olga!" she cried, and clapped her hands, and she was so tongue-tied that she could only say: "Olga!"

The nun recognized her at once, and her eyebrows rose in

surprise. Both her pure, pale, freshly washed face and the white headband she wore under the wimple seemed to be shining with joy.

"God has sent a miracle!" she cried, and she clapped her thin, pale hands.

Sophia Lvovna threw her arms fiercely around her, and then kissed her. She was afraid Olga would smell the wine she had drunk.

"We were just driving past when I remembered about you," she said, breathing deeply, as though she had been hurrying. "Lord, how pale you are! I'm so glad to see you! Tell me how you are! Are you lonely here?"

Sophia Lvovna looked round at the other nuns and said softly: "There have been so many changes at home. You know I am married to Yagich—Vladimir Nikitich Yagich. I suppose you remember him. . . . I'm very happy!"

"Praise be," Olga said. "And is your father well?"

"Yes, he's well, thank you. He often asks about you. Olga, you must come and stay with us during the holidays."

"Yes, of course," Olga said, and she smiled. "I'll come the second day of the holidays."

Sophia Lvovna did not know why she began weeping. For a whole minute she wept silently, and then she dried her eyes and said: "Rita will be very sorry not to have seen you. She is here with us. Volodya's here, too. They are near the gate. How pleased they would be if you would come out and see them! Shall we go? The service hasn't begun yet."

"Yes, let's go," Olga agreed.

She crossed herself three times and went out with Sophia Lvovna to the gate.

"Are you really happy? Are you, Sophia?" she asked as they came into the open.

"Very happy!"

"Praise be!"

Big Volodya and Little Volodya jumped out of the sleigh as

soon as they saw the nun, and they greeted her respectfully. They were both visibly touched by her pallor and the dark nun's costume, and they were both pleased because she remembered them and had come out to greet them. To prevent her from getting cold, Sophia wrapped her in a rug and covered her with a flap of fur coat. Sophia's tears of a few moments ago had cleansed and relieved her spirits, and she was happy now that this noisy, restless, and in fact thoroughly impure night could have such a pure and clear-cut sequel. To keep Olga a little longer by her side, she said: "Let's take her for a drive! Come in, Olga! We'll just have a short drive. . . ."

The men expected the nun to refuse—holy people do not ride around in troikas—but to their surprise she agreed and got into the sleigh. And when the sleigh was hurrying in the direction of the town gate they were all silent, while trying to keep her warm and comfortable, and they were all thinking about her past and her present. Her face was passionless, almost expressionless, cold, pale, transparent, as though water, not blood, were flowing through her veins. Only two or three years ago she had been plump and red-cheeked, and she had talked all the time about her beaux and giggled over every mortal thing.

Near the town gate the sleigh turned back, and ten minutes later they stopped outside the nunnery gate and Olga got out. Now the church bells were ringing again.

"May God be with you," Olga said, making a low bow as nuns always do.

"You'll come and visit us, won't you, Olga?"

"Yes, indeed!"

Then she left them and quickly disappeared through the dark gateway. Afterward the troika drove on again, and they were engulfed in a wave of melancholy. They were all silent. Sophia Lvovna felt as though her whole body had gone weak, and her spirits fell. It occurred to her that inviting a nun to sit in a sleigh and drive around with some drunken companions was stupid, tactless, and perhaps sacrilegious, and as her own drunkenness wore off, so she lost any desire to delude herself, and it became clear to her that she had no love for her husband and indeed could never love him, and it was all folly and stupidity. She had married him for his money, because, in the words of her school friends, he was madly rich, and because she was afraid of being an old maid like Rita, and because she was fed up with her father, the doctor, and because she wanted to annoy Little Volodya. If she could have known when she married her husband that her life would be hideous, dreadful, and burdensome, she would not have consented to the marriage for all the gold in the world. But the damage could never be undone, and she had to reconcile herself to it.

They went home. Lying in her warm soft bed and covering herself with her bedclothes, Sophia Lvovna remembered the dark doorway, the smell of incense, and the figures beside the columns, and she was terrified by the thought that these figures would remain motionless through the night, while she slept. The early service would go on forever, and would be followed by "the hours," and then by the mass, and then by the thanksgiving service. . . .

"Oh, there is a God, yes, there truly is a God, and I must surely die, and that is why sooner or later I must think about my soul, about eternal life, and about Olga. Olga is saved now—she has found the answers to all the questions about herself. . . . But what if there is no God? Then her life has come to nothing. But how has it come to nothing? Why?"

A moment later another thought entered her head: "Yes, there is a God, and death will surely come, and I must think about my soul. If Olga saw death before her this very minute, she would not be afraid. She is ready. The important thing is that she has solved the problem of life for herself. There is a God . . . yes. . . . But is there any other way out, except by entering a nunnery? Entering a nunnery means renouncing life, reducing it to zero. . . ."

Sophia Lvovna began to feel a bit frightened. She hid her head under a pillow.

"I mustn't think about it," she muttered. "No, I mustn't think about it. . . ."

Yagich was pacing the carpet in the adjoining room: there came the soft jingling sound of spurs as he surrendered to his contemplations. It occurred to Sophia Lvovna that this man was near and dear to her only because he bore the name of Vladimir: that was the only reason. She sat up in bed and called out tenderly: "Volodya!"

"What's the matter?" her husband answered.

"Nothing."

She lay down again. She heard the pealing of a bell, and perhaps it came from the same nunnery she had been visiting. Once again she remembered the dark gateway and the figures standing there, and there came to her the idea of God and of her own inevitable death, and she put her hands to her ears to keep out the sound of the bells. It occurred to her that a long, long life stretched before her until old age and death finally overcame her, and every day of her life she would have to live in close proximity to a man she did not love, this man who was now entering the bedroom and preparing to go to bed, and she would have to stifle her hopeless love for the other man, who was young and fascinating and in her eyes quite extraordinary. She looked up at her husband and tried to say good night to him, but instead she suddenly burst into tears. She was distraught.

"Well, here comes the music!" Yagich said, and he stressed the second syllable of "music."

She remained distraught until ten o'clock the next morning, when she finally stopped crying and trembling all over; her tears gave place to a terrible headache. Yagich was in a hurry to attend late mass; he was growling at the orderly who was helping him to dress in the next room. Once he came into the bedroom to fetch something, and his footsteps were attended by the soft jingling of spurs, and then he came in again wearing his epaulettes and medals, limping slightly from rheumatism, and it occurred to Sophia Lvovna that he looked and walked like a ravening beast.

She heard him ringing up someone on the telephone.

"Be so good as to connect me with the Vasilyevsky barracks," he said, and a minute later: "Vasilyevsky barracks? Would you please ask Dr. Salimovich to come to the telephone?" And then another minute later: "Who's speaking? Is that you, Volodya? Delighted. Dear boy, ask your father to come to the telephone at once. My wife is a bit upset after yesterday. Not at home, eh? Well, thank you very much. Excellent. Much obliged. *Merci.* . . ."

For the third time Yagich entered the bedroom, and he bent over the bed and made the sign of the cross over her and gave her his hand to kiss—the women who had loved him invariably kissed his hand, and he had fallen into the habit of doing this. Then, saying he would be back for dinner, he went out.

At noon the maid announced that Vladimir Mikhailovich had arrived. Though she was staggering with fatigue and a headache, Sophia Lvovna quietly slipped into her wonderful new lilac-colored dressing gown, which was trimmed with fur, and she hurriedly arranged her hair. In her heart she felt a surge of inexpressible tenderness, and she was trembling with joy and the fear that he might leave her. She wanted only one thing—to gaze upon him.

Little Volodya was properly attired for calling upon a lady: he wore a frock coat and a white tie. When Sophia Lvovna entered the drawing room he kissed her hand and genuinely offered his sympathy over her illness. When they sat down, he praised her dressing gown.

"I was absolutely shattered by the visit to Olga yesterday," she said. "At first I thought it was quite terrible, but now I envy her. She is like a rock which can never be destroyed, nothing can budge her. Tell me, Volodya, was there any other way out for her? Is burying oneself alive the answer to all life's problems? It is death, not life . . ."

Little Volodya's face was touched with deep emotion as he remembered Olga.

"Listen to me, Volodya, you are a clever man," Sophia Lvovna went on. "Teach me how to rise above myself, as she has done. Of course, I am not a believer and could never enter a nunnery, but surely I could do something which is equivalent. My life is not an easy one," she added after a pause. "Tell me something which will give me faith. Tell me something, even if it is only a single word."

"One word? Well—*ta-ra-ra-boom-dee-ay!*"

"Volodya, why do you despise me?" she asked, livid with anger. "You have a quite fatuous way of talking to me—I beg your pardon, but you do—people don't talk to their friends and women acquaintances like that. You are so successful and so learned, and you love science, yet you never talk to me about scientific things. Why? Am I not worthy?"

Little Volodya's brows were knit with vexation.

"Why this sudden interest in science?" he asked. "What about a discussion on the constitution—or maybe about sturgeon and horse-radish?"

"Very well. I'm an insignificant, silly, stupid woman without principles. I have an appalling number of faults. I'm a psychopath, I am utterly depraved—I should be despised for these things. But remember, you are ten years older than I am, and my husband is thirty years older. I've grown up before your eyes, and if you had wanted, you could have made anything out of me—even an angel. But instead"—and here her voice quivered —"you treated me abominably! Yagich married me when he was already an old man, but you could have . . ."

"We've had quite enough of that, haven't we?" Volodya said, sitting close to her and kissing both her hands. "Let the Schopenhauers philosophize and prove whatever they like, while I kiss your little hands . . ."

"You despise me! If only you knew how you are making me suffer!" She spoke uncertainly, knowing already that he would not believe her. "If only you knew how much I want to change and start my life afresh! I think about it with such joy!" she went on, while tears of joy actually sprang into her eyes. "Oh, to be good, honest, pure, never to lie, to have an aim in life . . ."

"Please stop putting on those silly airs—I don't like them at all," Volodya said, and his face assumed a whimsical expression. "Dear God, it's like being on the stage! Why don't we behave like ordinary people?"

She was afraid he would be angry and go away, and so she began to justify herself, and she forced herself to smile to please him, and once again she talked about Olga and how much she wanted to solve the problem of her life and become human.

"*Ta-ra-ra-boom-dee-ay,*" he sang under his breath. "*Ta-ra-ra-boom-dee-ay* . . ."

Quite suddenly he put his arm round her waist. Without knowing what she was doing she put her hands on his shoulders and for a full minute she gazed with a look of dazed rapture at his clever mocking face, his forehead, his eyes, his handsome beard.

"You have known for a long time how much I love you," she confessed to him, and she blushed painfully, and she knew her lips were twisting convulsively with shame. "I love you! Why are you torturing me?"

She closed her eyes and kissed him fiercely on the lips, and it was a full minute before she was able to put an end to the kiss, even though she knew that kissing him was improper, and that he was standing in judgment over her, and that a servant might come in at any moment.

"Oh, how you are torturing me!" she repeated.

Half an hour later, when he had got all he wanted from her, and was sitting over lunch, she knelt before him and gazed hungrily up at his face, while he told her she resembled a puppy wait-

ing for some ham to be thrown to it. Then he sat her on one knee
and danced her up and down, as though she were a child, singing: "*Ta-ra-ra-boom-dee-ay . . . Ta-ra-ra-boom-dee-ay . . .*"

When he was about to leave, she asked in passionate tones:
"When? Today? Where?"

She held out both arms toward his lips, as though she
wanted to tear out his answer with her hands.

"Today would hardly be suitable," he told her after some
thought. "Tomorrow perhaps."

And so they parted. Before dinner Sophia Lvovna went along
to the nunnery to see Olga, and was told that Olga was reading
the psalter over the dead somewhere. From the nunnery she
went off to see her father, but he was not at home, and so she
took another sleigh and drove aimlessly through the roads and
side streets until evening. For some reason she kept remembering
that aunt of hers whose eyes were filled with tears and who knew
no peace.

That night they drove again to the restaurant outside the town
in a troika and listened to the gypsies. Driving past the nunnery,
Sophia Lvovna again thought about Olga, and it terrified her
that for girls and women of her station in life there was no
solution except to go driving around in troikas and tell lies, or
else to enter a nunnery and mortify the flesh. The next day she
met her lover, and afterwards she drove around the town alone
with a coachman and thought about her aunt.

During the following week Little Volodya threw her over.
Life went on as usual, dull, miserable, sometimes even agonizing. The colonel and Little Volodya spent long hours together
at billiards or playing piquet, and Rita continued to tell her
tasteless anecdotes. Sophia Lvovna wandered around in her
hired sleigh and kept asking her husband to take her for a drive
in a troika.

Almost every day now she went to the nunnery and bored
Olga with a recital of her unbearable sufferings, and she wept

and felt she was bringing something impure and pitiable and worn-out into the cell with her, while Olga, in the tone of some-one mechanically repeating a lesson, told her that all this was of no importance, it would all pass away, and God would forgive her.

1893

The Student

AT first the weather was fine and it was very quiet. Blackbirds sang, and from the neighboring marshes something living could be heard making a pathetic moaning sound like air being blown in an empty bottle. A solitary woodcock flew up, and someone aimed, and a shot rang out vividly and joyfully on the spring air. Then as the woods grew dark a cold and penetrating wind rose unreasonably from the east, and everything was silent. Needles of ice stretched over the pools; darkness, misery, and loneliness hung over the woods. It smelled of winter.

Ivan Velikopolsky, a student in the theological seminary and the son of a sacristan, was making his way home from hunting, barefoot, taking the path through the water-logged meadows. His fingers were numbed, and his face burned by the wind. It seemed to him that the sudden fall of temperature had somehow destroyed the order and harmony of the universe, and the earth herself was in agony, and that was why the evening shadows fell more rapidly than usual. All round him there was only emptiness and a peculiar obscurity. The only light shone from the widows' gardens near the river; elsewhere, far into the distance and close to him, everything was plunged in the cold evening fog, and the village three miles away was also hidden in the fog. The student remembered that when he left home his mother was sitting on the floor in the doorway cleaning the samovar, while his father lay coughing on the stove; and because it was Good Friday, no cooking had been done in the house and the student was ferociously hungry. Oppressed by the cold, he fell to thinking that just such a wind as this had blown in the time of Rurik and in the days of Ivan the Terrible and Peter the Great, and in those days men suffered from the same terrible poverty and hunger; they had the same thatched roofs filled with holes; there was the same wretchedness, ignorance, and desolation everywhere, the same darkness, the same sense of being oppressed—all these dreadful things had existed, did exist, and would continue to exist, and in a thousand years' time life would be no better. He did not want to go home.

The widows' gardens were so called because they were kept by two widows, a mother and daughter. There a wood fire was crackling and blazing, throwing a great circle of light over the plowed earth. The widow Vasilissa, a huge, bloated old woman, was wearing a man's coat. She stood gazing dreamily at the flames while her daughter Lukerya, a little pock-marked woman with a stupid expression, sat on the ground washing a kettle and some spoons. Apparently they had just finished supper. Men's voices could be heard; they were the local farm workers watering their horses at the river.

"Well, winter's back again," the student said, going up to the fire. "Good day to you!"

Vasilissa gave a start, but she recognized him and smiled at him warmly.

"I did not recognize you at first," she said. "God bless you! You'll be rich one day!"

They went on talking. Vasilissa was a woman of experience; she had served the gentry first as a wet nurse and then as a children's nurse, and she expressed herself with refinement. A grave and gentle smile never left her lips. Her daughter Lukerya was a peasant; the life had been crushed out of her by her husband. She screwed up her eyes at the student and said nothing. She had a strange expression, like that of a deaf-mute.

"On just such a cold night as this St. Peter warmed himself

by a fire," the student said, stretching his hands over the flames. "So it must have been very cold! What a terrible night, eh? Yes, it was an extraordinarily long, sad night!"

Saying this, he gazed at the encircling shadows, gave a little convulsive shake of his head, and went on: "Tell me, have you ever attended a reading of the Twelve Gospels?"

"Yes, I have," Vasilissa answered.

"Then you'll remember that at the Last Supper, Peter said to Jesus: 'I am ready to go with thee down into darkness and death,' and the Lord answered: 'I tell thee, Peter, the cock, the bird of dawning, shall not crow this day, before that thou shalt thrice deny that thou knowest me.' After the supper Jesus suffered the agony in the garden, and prayed, but poor Peter was faint and weary of spirit, and his eyelids were heavy, and he could no longer fight against sleep. So he slept. Then, as you know, Judas came that same night and kissed Jesus and betrayed him to his tormentors. They bound him and took him to the high priest and beat him, while Peter, worn out with fear and anxiety, utterly exhausted, you understand, not yet fully awake, feeling that something terrible was about to happen on earth, followed after him. For he loved Jesus passionately and with all his soul, and he saw from afar off how they were beating him. . . ."

Lukerya dropped the spoons and looked fixedly in the direction of the student.

"They came to the house of the high priest," he went on, "and they began to interrogate Jesus, while the workmen lit a fire in the courtyard because it was cold, and they warmed themselves round the fire, and Peter stood close by the fire, and he too warmed himself, just as I am doing now. There was a woman who recognized him and said: 'This man also was with Jesus,' meaning that he too should be taken for interrogation. And all the workmen who were standing round the fire must have looked at him searchingly and suspiciously, for he was troubled and said: 'I do not know him.' After a while someone recognized him as one of the disciples of Jesus, and said: 'You were one of them.'

And again Peter denied it. And then for the third time someone turned toward him and said: 'Did I not see thee with him in
the garden?" And again Peter denied it, and at that very moment
the cock crew, and Peter gazing from afar off at Jesus remembered the words spoken to him earlier in the evening. . . . He
remembered and suddenly recovered his senses and went out
from the courtyard and wept bitterly. The Gospels say: 'He
went out and wept bitterly.' And so I imagine it—the garden
was deathly still and very dark, and in the silence there came the
sound of muffled sobbing. . . ."

The student sighed and fell into deep thought. Though her
lips still formed a smile, Vasilissa suddenly gave way to weeping, and the heavy tears rolled down her cheeks, and she hid her
face in her sleeve as though ashamed of her tears, while Lukerya, still gazing motionlessly at the student, flushed scarlet,
and her expression became strained and heavy as though she
were suffering great pain.

The farm workers returned from the river, and one who was
on horseback came near them, and the light from the fire glittered on him. The student bade good night to the widows and
went on his way. Once again the shadows crowded close around
him, and his hands froze. A cruel wind was blowing, winter had
settled in, and it was hard to believe that Easter was only the
day after tomorrow.

The student fell to thinking about Vasilissa. It occurred to
him that because she had been weeping, everything that happened to Peter on the night of the Last Supper must have a
special meaning for her. . . .

He looked round him. He could see the solitary fire gleaming
peacefully in the dark, but there was no longer anyone near it.
Once more the student thought that if Vasilissa gave way to
weeping, and her daughter was moved by his words, then it was
clear that the story he had been telling them, though it happened
nineteen centuries ago, still possessed a meaning for the present
time—to both these women, to the desolate village, to himself,

and to all people. The old woman wept, not because he was able to tell the story touchingly, but because Peter was close to her and because her whole being was deeply affected by what happened in Peter's soul.

And suddenly his soul was filled with joy, and for a moment he had to pause to recover his breath. "The past," he thought, "is linked to the present by an unbroken chain of events all flowing from one to the other." And it seemed to him that he had just seen both ends of the chain, and when he touched one end the other trembled.

When he took the raft across the river, and afterward when he was climbing the hill and looking back in the direction of his native village and toward the west, where the cold purple sunset was no more than a thin streak of light, it occurred to him that the same truth and the same beauty which reigned over humankind in the garden and in the courtyard of the high priest had endured uninterruptedly until the present time, and always they were the most important influences working on human life and everything on the earth; and the feeling of youth, health, and vigor—he was only twenty-two—and the inexpressible sweet expectation of happiness, of an unknown and secret happiness, took possession of him little by little, and life suddenly seemed to him ravishing, marvelous, and full of deep meaning.

April 1894

Anna Round the Neck

I

AFTER the wedding not even a light lunch was served. The young couple drank their champagne, changed their clothes, and set off for the station. Instead of attending a gay ball and a wedding supper, instead of music and dancing, they went off on a pilgrimage to a place a hundred and fifty miles away. There were many who approved of this, saying that Modest Alexeich was a fairly high-ranking official and no longer young, and that a noisy wedding would not have been altogether proper: music would obviously bore the fifty-two-year-old official married to a girl who had just turned eighteen. They said that Modest Alexeich, being a man of principle, really arranged this journey to a monastery so that his young bride would clearly understand that in marriage the first place must be given to religion and morality.

The couple was seen off at the station. Crowds of relatives together with the groom's colleagues stood there with champagne glasses in their hands, waiting to shout "hurrah" when the train pulled away. Pyotr Leontyich, the bride's father, stood there wearing a top hat and the frock coat of a schoolmaster, already drunk and very pale, and he kept peering up at the window with a glass in his hand, saying in an imploring voice: "Anyuta! Anna! Anna, just one last word . . ."

Anna leaned out of the window while he whispered something to her, enveloping her in the smell of brandy, blowing in her ear—she understood nothing at all—and he made the sign of the cross over her face, her breast, and her hands, his breath coming in gasps and tears shining in his eyes. Anna's brothers, the schoolboys Petya and Andryusha, were pulling at his coattails and whispering shamefacedly: "Papa, that's enough. . . . Papa, don't do it . . ."

When the train started, Anna saw her father running a little way after the carriage, staggering and spilling wine, and it seemed to her that his face was pitiful, guilty, and very kind.

"Hu-hu-hurrah!" he shouted.

Then the young couple were left alone. Modest Alexeich looked round the compartment, arranged their things on the racks, and sat down opposite his young wife. He was an official of medium height, rather stout, puffy, well fed, with long whiskers but no mustache, and his round, clean-shaven, and sharply outlined chin resembled the heel of a foot. The most characteristic thing about his face was the absence of a mustache, his freshly shaven and naked upper lip merging imperceptibly into the fat cheeks, which quivered like jelly. His deportment was dignified, his movements unhurried, his manner suave.

"At this particular moment," he said, smiling, "I cannot help recalling a certain incident. It happened five years ago when Kosorotov received the Order of St. Anna, second class, and accordingly went to proffer his thanks to His Excellency. His Excellency expressed himself in the following manner: 'So now you have three Annas,' he said. 'One in your buttonhole, and two round your neck.' I have to tell you that this incident occurred at the time when Kosorotov's wife had just returned to him—she was a quarrelsome and lightheaded woman—and, of course, her name was Anna. I hope that when the time comes for me to receive my Anna of the second class, His Excellency will have no occasion to speak to me in the same way."

He smiled with his small eyes. She, too, smiled, for she was troubled by the thought that any moment he might kiss her with his full, moist lips, and now she no longer had the right to refuse him. The sleek movements of his fat body frightened her: she was terrified and disgusted. He got up, slowly removed the order he was wearing round his neck, removed his frock coat and waistcoat, and put on a dressing gown.

"That's better," he said, sitting down beside Anna.

Anna remembered the agony of the wedding, when it seemed to her that the priest, the guests, and everyone else in the church were gazing at her sorrowfully: why, why, was this dear, charming girl marrying that elderly and uninteresting gentleman? Only that morning she was in raptures because everything had been settled so well, but during the wedding ceremony and now in the carriage she felt guilty, cheated, and ridiculous. Now she had married a rich man, but still she had no money at all, her bridal dress had been bought on credit, and when her father and brothers were saying good-by, she saw from their faces that not one of them had a kopeck to his name. Would they have any supper tonight? And tomorrow? And for some reason it seemed to her that her father and the boys were suffering from hunger and they knew the same misery that weighed down upon them on the evening of their mother's funeral.

"Oh, how unhappy I am," she thought. "Why am I so unhappy?"

With the awkwardness of a man of dignity, unaccustomed to dealing with women, Modest Alexeich touched her waist and petted her on the shoulder while she continued to think of money, of her mother, and of her mother's death. When her mother died, her father, Pyotr Leontyich, a teacher of calligraphy and drawing in the high school, took to drinking and knew real poverty; the boys were without boots or galoshes; her father was brought before the magistrate; a court officer came and seized the furniture for debt. . . . What a disgrace! Anna had to look after her drunken father, darn her brothers' stockings, do the marketing, and when she was complimented on her youth, her beauty, her elegant manners, then it seemed to her that the whole world was only looking at her cheap hat and the holes in her shoes which she concealed with ink. At night she wept, troubled by the persistent thought that her father would soon, very soon, be dismissed from the high school because of this weakness of his, and he would be unable to endure his dismissal, and he would die as her mother had died. But then some ladies of their acquaintance began to take an interest in her and began to look for a good husband for her. Soon they found this Modest Alexeich, who was neither young nor handsome—but he had money. He had in fact a hundred thousand rubles in the bank and a family estate which he had rented to a tenant. He was a man of principles and His Excellency thought highly of him; and Anna was told that nothing would be easier than to arrange for His Excellency to send a note to the principal or to the trustee of the high school, so that Pyotr Leontyich would not be dismissed . . .

While she was remembering these things, the strains of music and the sound of voices suddenly burst in through the window. The train had stopped at a small wayside station. Beyond the platform there was a crowd of people listening to an accordion and a cheap squeaking fiddle playing lively tunes, and from behind the tall birches and poplars and the country cottages flooded with moonlight there came the sound of a military band: obviously it was dance night in the village. The summer visitors and the town people who came out here in fine weather to breathe the fresh air were walking up and down the platform. Among them was Artynov, the very rich, stout, dark-haired owner of the summer cottages. He had prominent eyes, looked like an Armenian, and wore a strange costume: his shirt was unbuttoned, revealing his chest, and he wore boots with spurs, and from his shoulders hung a black cloak which trailed like a train. Two borzois followed him, their pointed muzzles hanging low to the ground.

The tears were still glistening in Anna's eyes, but she was no longer thinking about money, or her mother, or her marriage. She was shaking hands with the schoolboys and officers she knew, laughing gaily and saying quickly: "How are you? How do you do?"

She walked out on the platform in the moonlight and stood so that they could all see her in her new finery.

"Why are we stopping here?" she asked.

"This is a siding," they told her. "We are waiting for the mail train to pass."

Observing that Artynov was watching her closely, she winked coquettishly and began talking loudly in French, and because her voice was so beautiful, and because she heard music, and because the moon was reflected in a pool, and because Artynov, a notorious Don Juan and man of the world, was gazing at her eagerly and inquisitively, and because everyone was gay, she suddenly felt a great happiness, and when the train started and the officers she knew saluted her by snapping their hands to their caps, she was humming the polka which was being played by the military band somewhere beyond the trees, and she returned to the compartment with the feeling that she had received here, at the wayside station, proof that she would be happy in spite of everything.

They spent two days at the monastery and then returned to the town. They lived in an apartment provided by the government. When Modest Alexeich went to his office, Anna played the piano, or wept out of sheer boredom, or lay down on the sofa, or read novels, or looked through the fashion magazines. At dinner Modest Alexeich ate a great deal, and talked about politics, appointments, staff transfers, special remunerations; he observed that it was necessary for men to work very hard, and further that family life was not a pleasure but a duty, and that if you take care of the kopecks the rubles will take care of themselves. He said he placed religion and morality above everything in the world. Holding a knife in his hand, like a sword, he declared: "Everyone should perform his duties!"

Anna listened in fear and trembling; she could not bring herself to eat; and usually she rose hungry from the table. After dinner her husband took a nap, snoring loudly, while she went off to see her own people. Her father and the boys looked at her in a peculiar way, as though just a few minutes before she arrived they were blaming her for having married that tiresome man for money—a man she did not love. Her bracelets, her dress, which made a beautiful rustling sound, and her stylish appearance embarrassed and offended them; and in her presence they were a little confused, and did not know what to talk about; but they still loved her as before and had not yet grown accustomed to having dinner without her. She sat down and ate cabbage soup, porridge, and potatoes fried in mutton dripping, which smelled of tallow candles. With trembling hands Pyotr Leontyich filled his glass from a decanter and drank quickly, greedily, with disgust, and then he filled another glass, and then another. Petya and Andryusha, thin, pale little boys with large eyes, took the decanter away and said with embarrassment: "You shouldn't, Papa. . . . It's enough, Papa. . . ."

Anna was dismayed. She begged him not to drink any more, and he suddenly flew into a wild temper and struck the table with his fist.

"I won't let anyone tell me what to do!" he roared at her. "My children are all guttersnipes! I've a good mind to throw you all out of the house!"

But there was a note of weakness and good nature in his voice, and no one was afraid of him. After dinner it was his habit to wear his best clothes. Pale, with cuts on his chin from shaving, he would stand in front of the mirror for half an hour, combing his hair, twisting his black mustache, and sprinkling himself with perfume. Finally he would tie his cravat in a bow, slip on his gloves, put on his top hat, and go off to give private lessons. If it was a holiday, he remained at home and painted or played the harmonium, which hissed and growled; he would try to wrestle melodic and harmonious sounds from it, and he would sing to the music, or else he would roar at the boys: "Vile creatures! Good-for-nothings! They have ruined the instrument!"

In the evening Anna's husband played cards with his colleagues who lived under the same roof at the government-owned house. While they were playing cards, the wives of the officials would come in—ugly, tastelessly dressed, coarse as cooks—and the gossip that circulated through the apartment was as ugly and tasteless as the women themselves. Sometimes it happened that Modest Alexeich took Anna to the theater. During the entr'acte he would not let her move an inch from his side, but walked with her on his arm in the foyer and in the corridors. Whenever he bowed to anyone he would immediately whisper to Anna: "He's a State Councilor . . . attends the receptions of His Excellency," or "Very well-to-do . . . has a house of his own." Passing the buffet, Anna was overwhelmed with a desire for sweets; she loved chocolate and apple tarts, but she had no money and did not like to ask her husband. He would take up a pear, pinch it with his fingers, and ask uncertainly: "How much?"

"Twenty-five kopecks."

"Good heavens!" he would say, replacing the pear, but as it was awkward to leave the buffet without buying anything he would order a bottle of seltzer water and drink it all himself, while tears would come to his eyes. At such times Anna loathed him. Or else, suddenly blushing scarlet, he would say quickly: "Bow to that old lady!"

"But I've never been introduced to her."

"It doesn't matter. She's the wife of the director of the local treasury. Yes, I'm talking to you—bow to her!" he would grumble insistently. "Your head won't fall off!"

Anna bowed, and her head did not fall off, but it was sheer torture. She did everything her husband wanted her to do, and was furious with herself for letting him deceive her like the

silliest little fool. She had only married him for his money, and
yet she had less money now than before her marriage. Formerly
her father would sometimes give her a twenty-kopeck piece, but
now she did not have a kopeck to her name. She could not bring
herself to steal money or ask for it: she was afraid of her husband
and trembled before him. She felt as though she had been
afraid of him for many years. In her childhood the most imposing
and terrifying person had been the principal of her high school,
a man who swept down on her like a thundercloud or a steam
engine about to crush her. Another great power, often discussed
by her family and inordinately feared, was His Excellency.
Among the dozen less formidable powers were her high-school
teachers, stern and implacable, with their shaved upper lips. But
now she feared Modest Alexeich most of all, that man of principle, whose face even resembled the face of her high-school
principal. In Anna's imagination all these powers merged into
one single power which took the form of a huge and terrifying
white bear which attacked the guilty and those who were weak
like her father. The thought of contradicting her husband terrified her, and so she smiled her strained smile and pretended to
be pleased when he caressed her in a coarse way or defiled her
with his embraces, which filled her with horror.

Only once did Pyotr Leontyich make bold to ask him for a
loan of fifty rubles to pay off a most unpleasant debt, but what
agony it was!

"Very well, I shall give you the money," Modest Alexeich
said after a moment's thought, "but I warn you—it will be impossible for me to help you again until you give up drinking!
Such a weakness in a man who is in government service is a
downright disgrace! I must remind you of the well-established
fact that many capable people have been ruined by this addic-
tion, and they were people, moreover, who might have reached
very high rank if they had acquired the gift of temperance!"

There followed long-winded paragraphs—"whereas," "in the

measure of," "in view of the aforesaid"—and all the time poor Pyotr Leontyich suffered agonies of humiliation and an intense craving for a drink.

When the boys came to visit Anna, usually in broken boots and threadbare trousers, they too had to listen to his sermons.

"Everyone has a duty to perform!" Modest Alexeich would say.

He never gave them any money. But he gave Anna rings, bracelets, and brooches, explaining that they would come in usefully on a rainy day. Often he would open her chest of drawers for a formal inspection: to see whether they were still safe.

II

Meanwhile winter was coming on. Long before Christmas there was an announcement in the local newspaper to the effect that on December 29 the usual winter ball would be held in the Hall of Nobles. In excited whispers Modest Alexeich would confer with the wives of his colleagues after the evening game of cards. He would glance anxiously at Anna, and then for a long time he would pace across the room, sunk in thought. At last, late one evening, he stood quite still in front of Anna and said: "You really must have a ball dress made. Do you understand me? Only please consult Marya Grigoryevna and Natalya Kuzminishna."

He gave her a hundred rubles. She took the money, but when ordering the gown she consulted no one, and spoke only with her father, and she tried to imagine how her mother would have dressed for a ball. Her lamented mother had always dressed her in the latest fashion, taking trouble over her clothes, dressing her daintily like a doll, teaching her to speak French and to dance the mazurka superbly. (She had been a governess for five years before her marriage.) Like her mother, Anna could make a new dress out of an old one, clean gloves with benzine, and rent jewels. Like her mother, she knew how to squint, speak with a lisp, assume ravishing poses, and whenever it was necessary she could get wildly enthusiastic or look mysterious and melancholy. From her father she had inherited her dark hair and dark eyes, her nervous temperament, and her habit of always appearing at her best.

Half an hour before leaving for the ball Modest Alexeich came into her bedroom, coatless. He wanted to put his order round his neck in front of her mirror. He was so dazzled by her beauty and by the splendor of her fresh, gossamer-like gown that he complacently stroked his side whiskers and said: "So that's what my wife looks like. . . . Look at you, Anyuta!" Suddenly assuming a solemn tone, he went on: "Anna, my dear, I have given you happiness, and today you have the opportunity to give me happiness. I am begging you to obtain an introduction to the wife of His Excellency! For God's sake do this for me! Through her I may be able to get the post of senior reporter!"

They drove to the ball. There was a uniformed doorman in the lobby of the Hall of Nobles. The vestibule was a sea of fur coats, hatstands, hurrying lackeys, and décolleté ladies hiding behind their fans to avoid the drafts: the place smelled of illuminating gas and soldiers. Walking up the stairs on her husband's arm, Anna heard music and caught a glimpse of herself in an immense mirror in the glow of innumerable lamps, and there came a rush of joy to her heart and she knew the same presentiment of happiness which had come to her on a moonlit night at the railway station. She walked proudly, sure of herself, and for the first time felt she was no longer a girl, but a lady, and unconsciously she found herself imitating her mother in her walk and in her manner. For the first time in her life she felt rich and free. Even the presence of her husband did not embarrass her, for as she passed through the entrance leading into the Hall of Nobles she had instinctively guessed that the presence of an elderly husband did not in the least detract from her; on the contrary, it gave her an air of seductive mystery, which is always pleasing to men. The orchestra had already struck up in the ballroom, and the dances had begun. After their apartment, Anna was overwhelmed by the lights, the bright colors, the music, the noise, and looking round the ballroom, she thought: "Oh, how adorable!" and immediately she recognized in the crowd the acquaintances she had met at parties and picnics: officers, teachers, lawyers, officials, landowners, His Excellency, Artynov, and also those very décolleté ladies dressed in their finery, the hideous and the beautiful, and they were already in their places in the pavilions and booths which made up the charity bazaar, and they were all ready to sell things for the benefit of the poor. A huge officer with epaulettes—she had been introduced to him once before in Old Kiev Street when she was attending high school, but she could no longer remember his name—this officer seemed to rise out of the ground to ask her for a waltz, and she flew away from her husband, feeling like someone caught in the midst of a violent storm in a sailing boat, while her husband was left far behind on the shore. . . . She danced a waltz, and then a polka, and then a quadrille with passionate eagerness, passing from one partner to another, dizzy with the music and noise, mixing Russian with French, laughing, lisping, never thinking about her husband, never thinking at all. She was a great success among the men—that was self-evident, and it could not have been otherwise: she was breathless with excitement and squeezed her fan convulsively in her hand, and wanted something to drink. Her father, Pyotr Leontyich, wearing a crumpled dress coat which smelled of benzine, came up to her and offered her a plate of pink ice cream.

"You are so enchanting this evening," he said, gazing at her in rapture. "Never have I so deeply regretted that you were in a hurry to get married. Why did you do it? Oh, I know you did it for us, but . . ." With trembling hands he drew out a roll of banknotes and said: "Today I got the money they owed me for my lessons. I can pay back the debt I owe your husband."

She thrust the plate back into his hands, and was snatched away by someone who carried her far into the distance. Over her partner's shoulders she caught a glimpse of her father gliding over the parquet floor, putting his arm around a lady, and whirling her across the ballroom.

"How sweet he is when he is sober," she thought.

She danced the mazurka with the same huge officer, who moved gravely and heavily, a carcass in uniform, twitching his shoulders and chest, languidly stamping his feet—he felt fearfully disinclined to dance—but she fluttered round him, provoking him with her beauty, with her bare neck; her eyes were on fire, and her movements were passionate. The officer, however, grew increasingly indifferent, holding out his hands to her graciously, like a king.

"Bravo, bravo!" people were shouting at them.

Little by little the huge officer caught the excitement. He stirred into life, became intoxicated by the dance, and yielded to her fascination. Carried away, he danced lightly, youthfully, while she merely moved her shoulders and gazed at him slyly, as though she were a queen and he were her slave. At that moment it seemed to her that the whole ballroom was watching them, and that all those people were thrilled and envious of them. The huge officer had scarcely thanked her for the dance when the crowd suddenly parted and the men drew themselves up in an odd way, with their hands at their sides. His Excellency, with two stars on his dress coat, came walking up to her. Yes, His Excellency was making his way straight up to her and gazing straight into her eyes and smiling in the sweetest way, licking his lips as he always did when he saw a pretty woman.

"Delighted, delighted," he began. "I shall have to put your husband in the guardhouse for keeping such a treasure hidden from me. I have come to you on an errand from my wife," he went on, offering his arm. "Really you must help me! M-m-yes. We should give you a prize for beauty, as they do in America. M-m-m-yes. . . . The Americans. . . . My wife is most anxious to meet you. . . ."

He led her to a booth and presented her to an elderly lady, the lower part of whose face was disproportionately large, so that she looked as though she were holding an enormous stone in her mouth.

"Oh, you must help me!" the elderly lady said through her nose in a singsong voice. "All our pretty women are working for the charity bazaar, and you are having a fine time all by yourself. Now why won't you help us?"

She went away, and Anna took her place beside the cups and the silver samovar. She was soon doing a tremendous trade in tea. She charged no less than a ruble for a cup of tea, and she made the huge officer drink three cups in a row. Artynov, the very rich and short-winded man with the bulging eyes, came up too. He was no longer dressed in the costume he wore when Anna saw him at the station during the summer: now he wore a dress coat like everyone else. Without looking away from Anna, he drank a glass of champagne and paid a hundred rubles for it, and then he drank a cup of tea and gave her another hundred— all this in silence, because of his asthma. Anna solicited customers and got money from them. She was now firmly convinced that her smiles and glances gave these people only the greatest pleasure. She saw now that she had been created exclusively for this noisy, glittering existence, filled with music, laughter, dancing, admirers, and her former fear of a power swooping down on her and threatening to crush her now seemed ridiculous: she was afraid of no one, and only sorry her mother was not there to enjoy her success.

Pyotr Leontyich, who had grown pale but still held himself well, came to her booth and demanded a glass of brandy. Anna turned crimson, expecting him to say something silly—she was already ashamed of having such a poor and undistinguished father—but he drank down the brandy, removed ten rubles from his roll of banknotes, and walked away with great dignity, in perfect silence. A little while later she saw him dancing in *le grand rond*, but by this time he was staggering and shouting, to the embarrassment of his partner, and Anna remembered the ball which took place three years ago and how he had staggered and shouted in exactly the same way—it all ended when a police officer took him home to bed, and on the following day the principal of the school threatened to dismiss him from his post. But how silly these memories were!

When the samovars in the booths had grown cold and the weary charity workers had handed their takings to the lady with the stone in her mouth, Artynov took Anna by the arm and led her away to the hall where supper was served to all who had been working for the charity bazaar. There were twenty people at the supper, no more, and they were very noisy. His Excellency proposed a toast, saying: "There is no finer place than this magnificent dining room for drinking a toast to the success of our charity kitchens, which are of course the object of today's bazaar." And a brigadier general proposed a toast to "the force which overcomes even the artillery," and thereupon all the men clinked glasses with the ladies. It was very, very gay!

When Anna was escorted home, it was already daylight and the cooks were on their way to market. Elated, intoxicated, full of new sensations and completely exhausted, she undressed, fell on the bed, and immediately fell asleep.

Sometime after one o'clock in the afternoon the maid woke her and announced that Mr. Artynov had come to call on her. She dressed hurriedly and went into the drawing room. Soon after Artynov had made his departure His Excellency came to thank her for all the help she had given at the charity bazaar. With his sugary smile, running his tongue over his lips, he kissed her hand and begged permission to return. When he took leave of her, she was standing in the middle of the drawing room, amazed, enchanted, incapable of believing that this change, this marvelous change, had taken place in her life so quickly. And at that precise moment Modest Alexeich walked in. . . . He stood there in front of her with a sweet, ingratiating, servile expression—the same expression which she was accustomed to see on his face whenever he was in the presence of the illustrious and powerful; and with rapture, with indignation and contempt, in the full confidence that no harm could befall her, she said, articulating each word distinctly: "Get out, you blockhead!"

After that Anna never spent a single day alone. She was continually going to picnics, excursions, and theatricals. Every day she came home in the early hours of the morning and lay down on the floor of the drawing room, and afterwards she told everyone touchingly how she had slept under the flowers. She needed a lot of money. No longer afraid of Modest Alexeich, she spent his money as though it were her own, and she did not ask or demand it, she simply sent him the bills or scribbled notes saying: "Give bearer 200 rubles," or else "Pay 100 rubles without delay."

At Easter, Modest Alexeich received the Order of St. Anna, second class. When he went to offer thanks, His Excellency laid aside his newspaper and settled deep in the armchair.

"So now you have three Annas," His Excellency said, examining his white hands with their pink fingernails. "One in your buttonhole and two round your neck."

Modest Alexeich put two fingers to his lips to prevent himself from laughing out loud.

"It only remains for me to await the arrival of a little Vladimir," he said. "I make bold to suggest that Your Excellency might be disposed to act as godfather."

He was alluding to the Order of St. Vladimir, fourth class, and he was already imagining how he would soon be telling everyone about his little witticism, so felicitously apt and audacious, and now again he wanted to say something equally felicitous, but His Excellency was buried in his newspaper and merely gave him a nod.

Meanwhile Anna continued to drive around in troikas; she went hunting with Artynov, performed in one-act plays, attended supper parties, and spent less and less time with her own family. They now dined alone. As for Pyotr Leontyich, he was drinking more heavily than ever; he had no money, and had long ago sold the harmonium to pay his debts. The boys did not let him go out alone in the streets, and they always followed him for fear he would fall; and when they met Anna driving down Old Kiev Street in a carriage drawn by two horses with Artynov sitting in the coachman's box, Pyotr Leontyich would sweep off his top hat and try to shout something, but Petya and Andryusha would hold him by the arms and say imploringly:

"No, Papa! No, you really mustn't!"

1895

The House with the Mezzanine

〰〰〰〰〰

AN ARTIST'S STORY

I

SOME six or seven years ago, when I was living in T—— province, I stayed on the estate of a young landowner called Belokurov, a man who always rose very early, dressed himself in one of those sleeveless jackets worn by peasants, drank beer in the evenings, and perpetually complained to me that he could never find anyone who sympathized with him. He lived in a little house in the garden, while I lived in the old mansion in the huge columned ballroom with no furniture except the wide sofa on which I slept and the table on which I played patience. Even on calm days there was always the sound of moaning in the ancient stoves, and during a thunderstorm the whole house shook as though on the point of collapse; and it was rather terrifying, especially at night, when the ten great windows blazed in the flashes of lightning.

I was doomed by fate to a life of permanent idleness, and did nothing whatever. For whole hours I gazed out of the windows at the sky, the birds, the avenues of trees, and read whatever the mails brought me, and slept. Sometimes I slipped away from the house and wandered about aimlessly until late at night.

Once on my way home I happened upon an estate I had never seen before. The sun was already setting, and the evening shadows lay over the ripening rye. There were two rows of ancient, towering fir trees, planted so close together that they formed two parallel walls enclosing an avenue of somber beauty. I climbed easily over a fence and walked down the avenue, my feet slipping on a two-inch-thick carpet of fir needles. It was quiet and dark but for the occasional gleams of golden light shimmering high in the treetops, painting the spiders' webs in rainbow colors. Suffocating and overpowering was the fragrance of the pines. I soon turned into a long avenue of lime trees. Here, too, everything spoke of neglect and age. Last year's leaves rustled mournfully beneath my feet, and shadows lurked in the twilight between the trees. From an ancient orchard on my right a goldhammer sang feebly and listlessly; it gave the impression of being very old. And then the lime trees came to an end, and I went past a white house with a terrace and a mezzanine, and quite suddenly there unfolded before my eyes a view of the manorial courtyard with a large pond, a bathhouse, a huddle of green willows, and a village beyond the pond dominated by a high and slender belfry crowned with a cross blazing in the light of the setting sun. For a moment I was under the spell of something very dear and familiar to me: it was as though I had seen this same scene in the days of my childhood.

An old and sturdy gate, the white stone gateposts adorned with lions, led from the courtyard into open fields; here two young women were standing. The older of the two was thin and pale and very pretty, with great masses of chestnut hair piled high on her head, and she had a small straight mouth and a severe expression. She scarcely glanced at me. The other was still quite young, hardly more than seventeen or eighteen, and she too was thin and pale, but her lips were full and her enormous eyes followed me with a look of surprise as I walked past. She said some words in English and looked embarrassed. I felt I had known these charming faces all my life. I went home with the feeling that I had experienced a pleasant dream.

Soon afterwards, around noon, I was walking with Belokurov near the house when the grass rustled beneath a spring carriage as it came into our courtyard; the older of the two girls was sitting in it. She had come to collect subscriptions in aid of the victims of a fire. Without looking at us, she spoke gravely and in great detail about the number of houses which had burned down in the village of Siyanovo, the number of men, women, and children rendered homeless, and the measures proposed by the committee for the relief of the victims, for she was herself a member of the committee. She gave us the subscription list so that we could write down our names, then she put the list away, and prepared to take her leave.

"You have completely forgotten us, Pyotr Petrovich." She addressed Belokurov, offering him her hand. "Do come and visit with us, and if Monsieur N. [she mentioned my name] would like to see how his admirers live, and if he would care to come, then Mama and I would be only too pleased."

I bowed.

When she had gone, Pyotr Petrovich began to tell me about her. According to him, she was a young woman of good family, her name was Lydia Volchaninova, and the estate on which she lived with her mother and sister was called Shelkovka, like the village on the other side of the pond. Her father had occupied an important post in Moscow, and held the rank of privy councilor when he died. Although they possessed considerable wealth, the Volchaninovs lived in the country all the year round, never leaving the estate. Lydia was a teacher in the zemstvo [1] school in her home village of Shelkovka, and earned twenty-five rubles a month. This was all the money she spent on herself, and she was proud of earning her own living.

"They're an interesting family," said Belokurov. "We might go over and see them. They will be delighted to see you."

One afternoon on a holiday we remembered the Volchaninovs and drove over to see them. The mother and the two daughters

---

[1] The zemstvo was the elective district council in pre-revolutionary Russia.

were at home. It was obvious that Yekaterina Pavlovna, the
mother, had once been pretty, but she had become more bloated
than her years warranted, and she was short-winded, melancholy, and absent-minded. She tried to entertain me with talk
about painting. Learning from her daughter that I might visit
Shelkovka, she hurriedly called to mind two or three landscapes of mine she had seen on exhibition in Moscow, and now
asked me what I was attempting to express in them. Lydia, or,
as she was called at home, Leda, talked more to Belokurov than
to me. Grave and unsmiling, she asked him why he did not work
in the zemstvo, and why he had never attended a single one of its
meetings.

"It's not right, Pyotr Petrovich," she said reproachfully. "It's
not right at all—it's a shame!"

"True, Leda, true," her mother agreed. "It's a shame!"

"All of our district is in Balagin's hands," Leda went on, turning to me. "He is the chairman of the local council, and all official business in the district goes to his nephews and brothers-in-
law, and he does exactly as he pleases. We must fight him! We
young people ought to form a strong party, but you see what
kind of young people we have among us. For shame, Pyotr
Petrovich!"

The younger sister, Zhenia, remained silent during the conversation about the zemstvo. She never took part in serious conversations, not being considered grown-up in the family, and they always called her by the pet name Missy, because she used to call
her governess Miss when she was a child. All the time she ex-
amined me curiously, and when I was turning the pages of the
photograph album she kept saying: "There's my uncle . . .
there's my godfather . . ." and she kept pointing at the photographs. In her childish way she pressed her shoulder against
mine, and I clearly saw her small undeveloped breasts, her thin
shoulders, her braided hair, and her slim waist tightly drawn
in by a belt.

We played croquet and lawn tennis, wandered about the garden, drank tea, and sat a long while over supper. After the high-columned empty ballroom where I lived, I felt pleasantly comfortable in this small cozy house where there were no oleographs hanging on the walls, and the servants were addressed as "you," and not as "thou," and everything seemed pure and youthful thanks to the presence of Leda and Missy, and the atmosphere breathed a sense of order. At supper Leda again talked to Belokurov about the zemstvo, about Balagin, about school libraries. She was a lively, sincere, and persuasive young woman, and it was interesting to listen to her although she spoke in a loud voice a great deal, perhaps because she was accustomed to speaking in this way at school. On the other hand, my friend Pyotr Petrovich still clung to the habit of his student days, reducing all discussion to argument. He spoke in a bored and languid voice, at vast length, with an obvious desire to be taken for a man of intelligence and progressive views. Gesticulating, he knocked a sauceboat over with his cuff, and it made a large pool on the tablecloth, but it seemed that no one noticed it except me.

When we made our way home, the night was dark and still.

"I call it good breeding," Belokurov sighed, "not so much when you don't upset a sauceboat over the tablecloth, but when you don't notice it if someone else does. Yes, they are an admirably cultured family. I'm out of touch with nice people—terribly out of touch. It's all the fault of business, business!"

He went on to discuss all the hard work which goes with being a landed proprietor. And I thought: "What a ponderous, lazy, good-for-nothing he is!" Whenever he spoke seriously, he kept saying "Er—er—" painfully drawling out his hesitations, and he worked exactly as he talked, slowly, always getting behindhand, never on time. Nor did I have any great belief in his business sense, for the letters I gave him to post remained in his pocket for weeks.

"The worst of it is," he muttered as we walked along together, "the worst of it is that you go on working and no one has any sympathy for you. No sympathy at all!"

II

Soon I started calling on the Volchaninovs. Usually I sat on the bottom step of the terrace. I was oppressed with a sense of vague discontent and dissatisfaction with my own life, which was passing so quickly and uninterestingly, and I kept thinking it would be a good thing if I could tear my heart out of my breast, that heart which had grown so weary of life. All the time they would be talking on the terrace, and I would hear the rustle of skirts and the whispering sound of pages being turned. I soon grew accustomed to the sight of Leda receiving patients during the day, giving out books, and going off to the village bareheaded under a sunshade, while in the evenings she would declaim in a loud voice about the zemstvo and about schools. She was a beautiful, slender, unfailingly correct young woman with thin, sensitive lips, and whenever a serious discussion got under way she would say to me coldly: "This won't interest you."

I was unsympathetic to her. She disapproved of me because I was a landscape painter and my paintings did not represent the needs of the people, and she felt therefore that I was indifferent to all her deepest beliefs. I remember riding along the shores of Lake Baikal and meeting a Buryat girl on horseback. She wore a shirt and blue sailcloth trousers. I asked her to sell me her pipe, and while we were talking, she gazed contemptuously at my European features and my hat. A moment later, bored with my conversation, she uttered a wild yell and galloped away. In exactly the same way Leda despised me as a stranger. Outwardly she showed no signs of her dislike, but I could feel it, and sitting on the bottom step of the terrace, I gave way to my sense of irritation and said that to treat peasants without being a doctor was to deceive them, and it was easy to be charitable if one was the owner of five thousand acres.

Her sister Missy had no such cares and spent her life in complete idleness, as I did. When she awoke in the morning she would take a book onto the terrace and read it in a deep armchair, her feet scarcely touching the ground, or she would hide away with the book somewhere in the avenue of lime trees, or she would pass through the gate into the open fields. She spent the day reading, her eyes glued avidly on the page, and only an occasional weary and listless glance, and her extreme pallor, showed how exhausted she became from reading. When I came on the scene and when she saw me, she would blush a little, put the book aside, and gazing at me with her enormous eyes, she would tell me in her high-spirited way about everything that had happened: how the chimney in the servants' quarters had caught fire or how one of the workmen had caught a big fish in the pond. On weekdays she usually wore a light-colored blouse and a dark-blue skirt. We took walks together and gathered cherries to make into preserves or went boating together, and when she jumped up to reach the cherries or pulled on the oars, her thin and delicate arms gleamed through her wide sleeves. Or else I sketched, and she would stand there beside me, watching breathlessly.

One Sunday at the end of July, I went over to see the Volchaninovs around nine o'clock in the morning. I went through the park, staying far from the house, looking for white mushrooms, which were very plentiful that summer, marking the places where I found them so that I could pick them later with Zhenia. A warm wind was blowing. I could see Zhenia and her mother coming back from church, both wearing light holiday dresses, and Zhenia was holding on to her hat because of the strong wind. Afterwards I heard them having tea on the terrace.

Being a man without any care in the world, always seeking some justification for a life of perpetual idleness, I found these mornings on summer holidays on the estate especially charming. When the gardens were all green and wet with dew, shining joyously in the sun, and when the oleanders and the mignonettes spread their perfume all round the house, and when the young people have just returned from church and are drinking tea in the garden, and when they are all joyful and charmingly dressed, and when you know that all these healthy, beautiful, well-fed people will be doing nothing all day, at such times I long for life to be always like this. So I thought as I wandered about the garden, ready to pursue my careless wanderings all day and all summer.

Zhenia came from the house carrying a basket. She had an expression on her face suggesting that she knew, or felt, she would find me in the garden. We gathered mushrooms and talked, and whenever she asked me a question she went ahead of me so that she could see my face.

"Yesterday," she said, "a miracle happened in our village. Pelageya, the cripple, has been ill for a whole year, and no doctors or medicines were any use to her, but yesterday an old woman whispered something over her, and she has recovered."

"This is of no importance," I said. "No need to go to old women or sick people to find miracles. Isn't health a miracle? And life itself? Whatever is beyond our understanding is a miracle."

"Aren't you afraid of things you can't understand?"

"No, I march boldly up to the incomprehensible, and refuse to submit to it. I am superior to all these phenomena. Men should realize they are superior to lions and tigers and stars, they are greater than anything in nature, greater than the things they profess not to understand which they call miracles. Otherwise we are not men, but mice, afraid of everything."

Zhenia supposed that because I was a painter I must know a good deal and could accurately divine anything I did not know. She longed for me to lead her into the realm of the eternal and the beautiful, into that higher world where she thought I was at home, and she talked to me about God, about life everlasting, and about the miraculous. And I, who refuse to believe that I and my imagination will perish forever after my death, would

247

reply: "Yes, people are immortal." "Yes, eternal life awaits us." And she would listen and believe and never demand proof.

We were going home when she suddenly paused and said: "Our Leda is a remarkable person, isn't she? I adore her passionately and I would lay down my life for her at any moment. Tell me"—Zhenia touched my sleeve with her finger—"tell me why you are always arguing with her? Why do you get so irritated?"

"Because she is wrong."

Zhenia gave her head a protesting shake, and tears came to her eyes. "That's incomprehensible!" she said.

At that very moment Leda had just returned from somewhere and was standing near the steps with a riding whip in her hands, a slender beautiful figure in the streaming sunlight. She was giving orders to one of the laborers. Then, in a great hurry and talking loudly, she received two or three patients, and with a businesslike, preoccupied air she went through all the rooms of the house, opening one cupboard after another, and then she went to the mezzanine; it took some time to find her and call her for dinner, and by the time she came down we had already finished the soup. Somehow I remember all these little details and love to dwell on them, and I remember everything that happened that day even though nothing of great importance occurred. After lunch Zhenia read, lying in a deep armchair, while I sat on the lowest step of the terrace. We were silent. The whole sky was overcast, and a fine, thin rain began to fall. It was warm, the wind had dropped, and it seemed the day would never come to an end. Yekaterina Pavlovna came out on the terrace with a fan. She was very sleepy.

"Oh, Mama," Zhenia said, kissing her hand. "It's not good for you to sleep during the day."

They adored each other. When one went into the garden the other would stand on the terrace and call out: "Hello, Zhenia!" or "Mama, where are you?" They always prayed together, and they shared the same beliefs, and understood each other very

well, even when they said nothing. And their attitude toward
people was exactly the same. Yekaterina Pavlovna soon grew accustomed to my presence and became fond of me, and when I
did not come for two or three days, she would send out to ask
whether I was well. And she had an enthusiastic way of looking
at my drawings, and she would relate what was happening as
openly and freely as Missy, and she often confided her domestic
secrets to me.

She was in awe of her elder daughter. Leda never cared for
endearments, and always spoke seriously: she lived her own
life, and to her mother and sister she was as sacred and mysterious as an admiral sitting in his cabin is to his sailors.

"Our Leda is a remarkable person, isn't she?" her mother
used to say.

Now as the rain fell softly we spoke about Leda.

"Yes, she is a remarkable person," her mother said, adding in
a low conspiratorial voice, with a nervous glance over her shoulder: "You have to search far and wide for people like that. Even
so, I am beginning to be a bit worried. The school, the dispensary, books—they are all very well, but why go to extremes? She
is twenty-four, and it is time she was thinking seriously about
herself. If you spend your time with books and dispensaries, you
find that life slips by without your being aware of it. . . . She
ought to be married."

Zhenia, pale from reading and with her hair in disorder, lifted
her head and said, as though to herself, but looking at her
mother: "Mama dear, it is all in the hands of God!"

Then she plunged back into her book.

Belokurov came over, wearing a peasant jacket and an embroidered shirt. We played croquet and lawn tennis, and when it
grew dark we spent a long time over supper, and once more Leda
spoke about her schools and about Balagin, who had the whole
district under his thumb. When I left the Volchaninovs that
evening, I carried away an impression of a long, long idle day
with the melancholy consciousness that everything in the world

comes to an end, however long it may last. Zhenia saw us to the gate, and perhaps because I had spent the whole day with her from morning to night, I felt strangely lonely and bored without her, and I realized how dear to me this charming family had become, and for the first time during all that summer I was overcome with the desire to paint.

"Tell me, why do you lead such a boring, colorless life?" I asked Belokurov as we were walking home. "As for me, my life is difficult, boring, and monotonous because I am a painter, different from other people, and I have been eaten up with envy and dissatisfaction with myself and misgivings over my work ever since I was quite young. I shall always be poor, and a vagabond, but as for you—you are a normal, healthy man, a landowner, a gentleman—why then is your life so uninteresting? Why do you get so little out of life? Why, for instance, don't you fall in love with Leda or Zhenia?"

"You forget I love another woman," Belokurov answered.

He was referring to his friend, Lyubov Ivanovna, who lived with him in the little house. I used to see the lady every day. She would be walking in the garden, plump and massive, pompous as a fatted goose, wearing Russian costume with strings of beads, always carrying a sunshade, and the servants would call her for meals and tea. Some three years before this she had taken one of the small houses for the summer, and she had stayed on with Belukurov, and apparently she proposed to stay there forever. She was ten years older than he was, and she kept a strict watch over him, so much so that when he left the house he had to ask her permission. She often gave way to deep, masculine sobs, and then I would send word to her that unless she stopped, I would have to give up my apartment; and she always stopped.

When we came home, Belokurov sat down on my sofa, brooding and frowning, while I began pacing up and down the carpet, aware of a sweet emotion stirring in me, exactly like the stirring of love. I felt a desire to talk about the Volchaninovs.

"Leda could only fall in love with a zemstvo worker, someone who is just as fascinated by hospitals and schools as she is," I said. "For the sake of a young woman like that a man should be prepared to become a zemstvo worker, and even wear out a pair of iron boots, as in the fairy story. And then there's Missy! What an adorable person she is!"

Then Belokurov began to talk at great length, with his drawling "er-er-er," about the disease of the age—pessimism. He spoke with confidence, and by his tone it might be thought I was having an argument with him. Hundreds of miles of empty, monotonous, burned-out steppe were no drearier than this man who sat and talked and gave no sign of ever going away.

"It's not a question of pessimism or optimism," I said irritably. "It's just that ninety-nine out of a hundred people don't have any brains."

Belukurov took this as a personal remark, and he walked out, deeply insulted.

III

"The prince is staying at Malozyomovo and sends you his greetings," Leda said, coming in and taking off her gloves. "He had a lot of interesting things to say. He promised to raise the question of a medical center at Malozyomovo at the provincial assembly, but he says there's not much hope." And then, turning to me, she said: "Please excuse me, I was forgetting that this cannot be of the slightest interest to you."

I was irritated by her remark.

"Why shouldn't it be interesting to me?" I asked with a shrug. "You don't care to know my opinion, but I assure you the question interests me greatly."

"Yes?"

"It does indeed. In my opinion a medical center at Malozyomovo is quite unnecessary."

My irritation was communicated to her. She looked at me, half closed her eyes, and said: "Then what is necessary? Paintings of landscapes?"

"No, landscapes aren't necessary. You don't need anything there!"

She finished taking off her gloves and opened a newspaper, which had just come in the mail. A moment later she said quietly, evidently restraining her deep feelings: "Last week Anna died in childbirth. If there had been a medical center near by, she would still be alive. Even landscape painters, I should think, might have convictions on this subject."

"I have very definite convictions, I assure you," I answered, while she took refuge behind her newspaper as though unwilling to listen to me. "In my opinion, medical centers, schools, libraries, dispensaries—all these under present conditions only serve to keep the people enslaved. They are being held down with heavy chains, and you are not breaking the chains, you are only adding new links to them. That's what I think!"

She raised her eyes to me and smiled scornfully, but I went on, trying to catch the thread of my ideas: "What matters is not that Anna died in childbirth, but that all those Annas, Mouras, Pelageyas, bend their backs from early morning to late at night, fall ill from working beyond their strength, spend their whole lives worrying about their sick and starving children, always dreading death and disease, always having to doctor themselves, fading early and aging quickly and dying in foul-smelling filth! Their children grow up, and then it is the same story all over again, and hundreds of years pass by, and millions of people are still living worse than the beasts—in perpetual fear, for the sake of a crust of bread. The whole horror of their position lies in their never having time to think about their souls, never having time to remember they are made in the image and likeness of God. Cold, hunger, animal fear, the heavy burden of toil—these are like the drifts of snow, cutting them off from the pathways leading them to spiritual activity, to everything that distinguishes a man from a beast, to the only thing that makes life worth living. You come to their aid with your hospitals and schools, but you are not delivering them from their shackles. On the contrary, you are forcing them deeper and deeper into slavery, for by introducing new prejudices into their lives you increase the number of their wants, not to mention the fact that they have to pay the zemstvo for the drugs and the books, and so they have to work harder than ever!"

"I'm not going to argue with you," Leda said, putting down her newspaper. "I've heard all that before. I will say only one thing—it is no good sitting with folded arms. True, we are not saving mankind, and perhaps we are making a great many mistakes, but we do what we can, and—we are right! The great and holy task of a civilized man is to serve his neighbors, and we are trying to serve them as best we can. You may not like it, but it is impossible to please everyone."

"True, Leda, true," said her mother.

Her mother's courage always failed her in Leda's presence, and while she was talking she would look timidly at her daughter, afraid of saying anything superfluous or inappropriate, and she never contradicted her, but would always agree with her: "True, Leda, true!"

"Teaching the peasants to read and write, giving them books full of wretched moralizings and quaint adages, and building medical centers can no more diminish their ignorance or decrease the death rate than the lamp in your window can light up the whole of your vast garden," I said. "You are not giving them anything by interfering in their lives. You only create new wants, and make them have to work more."

"Good heavens, something has to be done!" Leda said angrily, and I could tell from her voice that she thought my arguments completely worthless, and despised them.

"You must free people from hard physical labor," I said. "Their yoke must be lifted from them, they must be given a breathing space so that they don't have to spend their whole lives at the stove and the washtub and in the fields. They should have time to think about their souls and about God, and time to develop their spiritual faculties. The salvation of every human being lies in spiritual activity—in the continual search for truth and the meaning of life. Make it unnecessary for them to work at rough physical labor, let them feel themselves free, and then you will see what a mockery all these books and dispensaries really are! Once a man is aware of his true vocation, he can only be satisfied with religion, science, and art—not with those other trifles!"

"Free them from work?" Leda gave a smile. "Is that possible?"

"Yes, if we take upon ourselves a share of the work. If all of us, townspeople and country people alike, all without exception, agreed to share the work which is expended to satisfy the physical needs of mankind, then perhaps none of us would have to work more than two or three hours a day. If all of us, rich and poor, worked only three hours a day, then the rest of our time would be free. And then, in order to be still less dependent upon our bodies and upon physical labor, imagine that we invent machines which will take the place of labor, and imagine that we make an effort to reduce our requirements to the minimum. We should harden ourselves and our children, so that they would no longer fear hunger and cold, and then we wouldn't be perpetually worrying about health, as the Annas, Mouras, and Pelageyas of the world worry! If we didn't take medicines and maintain dispensaries, tobacco factories, and distilleries—what a lot of free time we would have after all! We would all—all of us together —devote our leisure to science and art. Just as the peasants sometimes work communally to repair and mend the roads, so all of us together, the whole community, would search together for truth and the meaning of life, and—I am sure of it—the truth would be very soon discovered, and man would be delivered from his continual, agonizing, oppressive fear of death, and even death itself might be conquered."

"But you are contradicting yourself," Leda said. "You keep talking about science while denying the need for literacy."

"What is the good of literacy when men have nothing to read

but the signs on public houses and occasional books which they don't understand? We have had that kind of literacy since the days of Rurik.[2] Gogol's Petrushka has been reading for a long time now, but the villages haven't changed since the time of Rurik. What is needed is not literacy, but freedom for the full development of men's spiritual faculties. What we need is not schools, but universities."

"So you are opposed to medicine too?"

"Yes, medicine should be required only for the study of diseases as natural phenomena, not for their cure. It is no use treating diseases, unless we treat the causes. Remove the chief cause, physical labor, and there will be no diseases. I don't admit the existence of a science that cures diseases!" I went on excitedly. "True science and true art are not directed toward temporary or partial ends, but they are directed toward the eternal and the universal—they seek the truth and the meaning of life, they seek after God and the soul, and when they are harnessed to our everyday evils and necessities—when they are harnessed to dispensaries and libraries—then they only complicate and burden life! We have plenty of doctors, chemists, lawyers, and we have plenty of literate people, but we have no biologists, mathematicians, philosophers, and poets. All our intelligence, all our spiritual energy is wasted on temporary passing needs. . . . Scientists, writers, and painters are hard at work, and thanks to them the comforts of life are increasing daily. The demands of the body multiply, but the truth is still far away, and man continues to be an entirely rapacious and filthy animal, and everything is tending toward the degeneration of the greater part of mankind and the decay of human vitality. Under such conditions the life of an artist becomes meaningless, and the more talented he is, the stranger and more incomprehensible becomes the role he plays in society, for he would appear to be working only for the amusement of rapacious and filthy animals while he sup-

[2] The Varangian chieftain who settled in Novgorov in 862 and is regarded as the founder of Russia.

ports the established order. I have no desire to work, and I won't work! . . . Nothing is any use! Let the world go reeling to hell!"

"Missy, leave the room," Leda said to her sister, apparently thinking my words would have a bad effect on a young girl.

Zhenia looked sadly at her mother and sister, and went out.

"People usually say these charming things when they want to justify their own callousness," Leda said. "Denying the usefulness of hospitals and schools is easier than curing diseases and teaching."

"True, Leda, true," her mother agreed.

"You were threatening to give up working," Leda went on. "Apparently you place a high value on your works of art. Let us give up arguing, for we shall never agree on anything, and I regard the most imperfect library or dispensary as of infinitely greater value than all the landscapes in the world." Suddenly she turned to her mother and began speaking in an entirely different tone of voice. "The prince is very thin, and he has changed a lot since he was last here. The doctors are sending him to Vichy."

She went on talking to her mother about the prince to avoid talking to me. Her face was burning, and to conceal her agitation she bent low over the table as though she were nearsighted, and made a show of reading the newspaper. My presence was distasteful to her. I took my leave and went home.

IV

It was very quiet outside. The village on the further side of the pond was already asleep, and there was not a light anywhere to be seen. Only on the pond lay the pale reflection of the glimmering stars. At the gate with the lions Zhenia was waiting to accompany me on my walk.

"They've all gone to sleep in the village," I said, trying to make out her face in the darkness. I could see her dark mournful eyes gazing at me fixedly. "The innkeeper and the horse thieves are fast asleep, at peace, while we, who should know better, quarrel and antagonize one another."

It was a melancholy August night—melancholy because there was already a breath of autumn in the air. The moon was rising behind a purple cloud, shedding scarcely any light along the road and the dark fields of winter wheat stretching away on both sides. At times a shooting star would fall. Zhenia walked beside me, and she avoided looking up at the sky so as not to see the falling stars, which for some reason frightened her.

"I think you are right," she said, trembling in the damp night air. "If all the people were to devote themselves to spiritual activities, they would soon come to know everything."

"Of course. We are higher beings, and if we really realized the full power of human genius and lived only for higher things, then we would ultimately become like gods. But it will never happen. Mankind will degenerate and no traces of that genius will ever be found."

When we could no longer see the gates, Zhenia paused and hurriedly pressed my hand.

"Good night," she said, trembling. She had nothing but the thin blouse over her shoulders, and she was shivering with cold. "Come tomorrow."

I felt wretched at the thought of being left alone in a mood of irritation and annoyance with myself and others, and I too tried not to look at the falling stars.

"Please stay with me a little longer," I said. "Please."

I was in love with Zhenia. I must have loved her because she met me when I came and always walked with me a little way when I went home, and because she looked at me with tender, admiring glances. Her pale face, her slender neck, her thin hands, her delicacy and her laziness and her books—all these held a wistful appeal for me. And her intelligence? I surmised she had a remarkable intelligence and I was fascinated with the breadth of her views, perhaps because she thought differently from the austere and beautiful Leda, who had no love for me. Zhenia liked me because I was a painter. I had conquered her heart with my talent, and I longed passionately to paint only for her, and I dreamed of her as my little queen who would one day inherit with me all these trees, fields, mists, and dawns, all those miraculous and enchanting scenes from nature where until now I had felt so hopelessly lonely and unwanted.

"Please stay a little longer," I begged her. "Only a little longer."

I took off my overcoat and covered her shivering shoulders; and becase she was afraid of looking funny and ugly in a man's coat she laughed and threw it off, and then I put my arms round her and began to cover her face, her shoulders, her hands, with kisses.

"Until tomorrow," she whispered, and gently, as though afraid of breaking the silence of the night, she embraced me. "We have no secrets from each other now. Quickly I must tell everything to Mama and my sister. . . . I'm so afraid! I'm not afraid of Mama, for she loves you, but my sister . . ."

Then she ran toward the gates.

"Good-by!" she called back.

Then for some moments I heard her running. I had no desire to return home, and there was nothing to return home for. For a while I stood there lost in thought, and then I turned slowly back to look once more at the house she lived in, that house which was so old and innocent and dear to me; and the windows of the mezzanine looked down on me like eyes, seeming to understand everything. I walked past the terrace and sat on a bench by the lawn-tennis court, in the darkness of an ancient elm, and once again I gazed up at the house. I could see the windows of the mezzanine, where Missy slept, and the bright light shining there, but this light turned later to a faintly glowing green—she had pulled a shade over the lamp. Shadows stirred. . . . I was filled with a sense of tenderness and calm contentment—a contentment which came with my discovery that I had fallen helplessly in love, and at the same time I felt uneasy with the knowledge that Leda, who disliked and perhaps hated me, was lying in bed in one of those rooms only a few yards away. I sat there, straining my ears, waiting to see whether Zhenia would come out, and I fancied I heard voices coming from the mezzanine.

An hour passed. The green lamp went out, and no more shadows could be seen. The moon rode high over the house, shining on the pathways and the sleeping garden. The dahlias and roses in the flower bed in front of the house could be seen distinctly, and everything seemed to be of one color. It grew very cold. I left the garden, picked up my coat from the road, and made my way slowly home.

The following day when I went to see the Volchaninovs after dinner, the glass door leading to the garden was wide open. I sat down for a while on the terrace, expecting to see Zhenia appear from behind the flower beds or along one of the pathways, or perhaps I would hear the sound of her voice coming from the house. Then I went through the drawing room and the dining room. There was no one to be seen. From the dining room I walked down a long corridor that led to the reception room, and back again. Several doors opened on the corridor, and from behind one of them came the voice of Leda.

"To the crow somewhere . . . God . . ." she was saying in a loud, singsong voice, probably dictating. "God sent a piece of cheese . . . To the crow . . . somewhere . . . Who's there?" she called out suddenly, hearing my footsteps.

"It is I."

"Oh, excuse me, I cannot come out just now. I am giving Dasha her lesson."

"Is Yekaterina Pavlovna in the garden?"

"No, she left this morning with my sister. They are going to stay with an aunt in Penza province, and in the winter they will probably go abroad." She added after a moment's pause: "God sent . . . the cr-ow . . . so-me-where . . . a pie-ce of chee-se . . . Have you written it down?"

I went out in the reception room without a thought in my head, gazing at the pond and the village in the distance, while her voice followed me: "A pie-ce of chee-se . . . God sent the crow somewhere a piece of cheese . . ."

And I went back by the way I had come on the day when I first visited the house, only this time in reverse. I went from the courtyard into the garden and along the side of the house until I reached the avenue of lime trees. . . . There I was overtaken by a small boy who gave me a note which read: "I told my sister everything, and she says I must never see you again. I'm weak, and dare not anger her by disobeying her. God grant you happiness. Forgive me. If only you knew how many bitter tears Mama and I have shed!"

I went down the dark avenue of firs past the rotting fence. . . . In the fields where the rye was once ripening and the quail were screaming, now hobbled horses and cows were grazing. Here and there on the low hills the winter crops were already showing green. A sobering mood took hold of me, the things I had said at the Volchaninovs' filled me with shame, and I was as bored with life as I ever was before. When I reached home, I packed my things, and I left that evening for St. Petersburg.

I never saw the Volchaninovs again. Not long ago, when on my way to the Crimea, I met Belokurov on the train. He was wearing the familiar peasant jacket and embroidered shirt, and when I asked after his health, he replied: "Thank you for your good wishes." We fell into conversation. He had sold his old estate and bought another, smaller one in Lyubov Ivanovna's name. There was little he could tell me about the Volchaninovs. He told me Leda was still living at Shelkovka, teaching children at her school. Little by little she had succeeded in gathering around her a circle of friends who agreed with her and who were able to form a strong party, and at the last zemstvo election they had "gotten rid" of Balagin, the man who had kept the whole dis-

trict under his thumb in the old days. As for Zhenia, all he knew
was that she had left home, and he did not know where she was.

I am beginning to forget the house with the mezzanine, but
sometimes when I am painting or reading, for no reason at all,
quite suddenly, I find myself remembering the green lamp at the
window and the sound of my footsteps echoing through the fields
of the night as I walked home on the day I was in love, rubbing
my hands to keep them warm. And sometimes too—but this happens more rarely—when I am weighed down with melancholy
and loneliness, I am the prey of other confused thoughts, and it
seems to me that I, too, am being remembered, and she is waiting for me, and we shall meet again. . . .

Missy, where are you?

1896

In the Horsecart

~~~~~~~~~~

AT half past eight in the morning they drove out of town.

The highway was dry, a splendid April sun was shedding a fierce warmth on the earth, but there was still snow in the ditches and the forests. The long, dark, cruel winter had only just come to an end, spring came suddenly, but for Maria Vasilyevna sitting in the horsecart, there was nothing new or interesting in the warmth of the sun, or in the languid, luminous forests warmed with the breath of spring, or in the flocks of dark birds flying over the puddles in the fields—puddles as large as lakes—or in the marvelous and unfathomable sky into which it seemed one could plunge with such joy. For thirteen years she had been a schoolteacher, and during the course of these years she had gone so often to the town for her salary that the times were past counting; and whether it was spring, as now, or a rainy autumn evening, or winter, it was all the same to her, and she always and invariably longed for only one thing: to get there as quickly as possible.

She felt she had been living here for a long, long time, for a hundred years, and it seemed to her that she knew every stone, every tree on the road from the town to her school. Here was her past and her present, and she could imagine no other future than the school, the road to the town and back again, and again the school and again the road.

Of all that had happened to her before her appointment as a schoolteacher, she remembered very little. She had forgotten nearly everything. Once she had a father and mother—they lived in Moscow in a large apartment near the Red Gate—but of this period in her life the memories were as fluid and confused as dreams. Her father died when she was ten years old; her mother soon afterward. . . . She had a brother, an officer; at first they wrote to each other, and then he lost the habit of answering her letters. Of her former possessions only the photograph of her mother remained, but the damp air at school had faded it, and now nothing could be seen except the hair and eyebrows.

They had driven for two miles along the road when old Semyon, who held the reins, turned to her and said: "They've caught one of the town officials—taken him away somewhere. Said he and some Germans killed Alexeyev, the mayor, in Moscow."

"Who told you?"

"I heard someone read it in the newspaper at Ivan Ionov's tavern."

There followed another long silence. Maria Vasilyevna thought about her school, and the examinations which would soon be coming along, and the four boys and one girl who would take part in them. She was still pondering these examinations when they were overtaken by a man driving in a carriage harnessed to four horses. The man was a landowner called Khanov, and he had in fact been the examiner at her school the year before. He drew alongside, recognized her, and bowed.

"Good morning," he said. "I reckon you must be on your way home."

Khanov was a man about forty years old, with a languid air and a face which showed signs of wear; he was rapidly aging, though he was still handsome and attractive to women. He lived alone on a large estate, and took no part in government service; they said he did nothing at home except whistle as he paced up and down the room, or else he played chess with an old footman. They said, too, that he drank a great deal. Indeed, during the examinations the year before, the very papers he brought with him smelled of wine and perfume. On that occasion he was dressed in brand-new clothes, and Maria Vasilyevna thought him very attractive: she was embarrassed and confused when she sat beside him. She was accustomed to receiving the visits of chilling, hardheaded examiners, but this particular examiner could not remember a single prayer, did not know what questions to ask, and was extraordinarily courteous and kind, giving all the children good marks.

"I am going to visit Bakvist," he went on, still addressing Maria Vasilyevna, "but it occurs to me that he may not be at home."

They turned off the highway into a narrow lane, Khanov leading the way and Semyon coming up behind. The four-horse team moved at a walking pace, straining to drag the heavy carriage out of the mud. Semyon followed a more erratic course, leaving the road to avoid a hump in his path or to skirt a puddle, and sometimes he would jump down from the cart to help the horse. Maria Vasilyevna was still thinking about the school: she was wondering whether the questions at the examination would be difficult or easy. Also, she was annoyed with the zemstvo council, which she had visited the previous day only to find no one there. What lack of principle! For the last two years she had been asking them to dismiss the janitor, who did nothing, was rude to her, and beat up the school children; but no one paid any attention to her. The chairman of the board was rarely at the office, and when he was, he would say with tears in his eyes that he had no time to spare; the inspector visited the school once in three years and knew nothing about the business, having previously served in the excise department and having received his present post through patronage. The school board rarely met, no one knew where. The trustee was an almost illiterate peasant who owned a tannery: a coarse, stupid fellow, bosom companion to the janitor—only God knew to whom she should turn when there were complaints to be made or wrongs to be put right.

"He really is handsome," she thought, glancing at Khanov.

The road was becoming worse and worse. . . . They drove
into the forest. Here there was no possibility of leaving the road,
the ruts were deep, and water flowed and gurgled through
them. Sharp twigs struck across their faces.

"What a road, eh?" Khanov said, and laughed.

The schoolmistress gazed at him, wondering why the strange
fellow ever came to live here. What good was this God-forsaken
place with its mud and boredom to a man of wealth and refinement and an attractive presence? Life was granting him no special privileges here. Like Semyon, he was jogging along slowly
over an appalling road, enduring exactly the same hardships.
Why live here, when there was the possibility of living in St.
Petersburg or abroad? One would have thought it a simple matter for a rich man to build a fine road instead of this awful one;
in this way he would avoid all the horror of the journey and the
sight of the despair written on the faces of Semyon and of his
own coachman. But he only laughed; apparently it was all one to
him, and he wanted no better life. He was kind, gentle, unso-
phisticated, and was ignorant of the hard facts of life just as he
was ignorant of the proper prayers to be offered at an examination. His only gifts to the school were globes; therefore he sincerely came to regard himself as a useful person and a prominent
fighter for the cause of popular education. And what use were his
globes anyway?

"Sit tight, Vasilyevna!" Semyon shouted.

The cart lurched violently, and was on the point of upsetting.
Something heavy hurtled down on Maria Vasilyevna's feet—the
purchases she had made in town. There followed a steep climb
up a clayey hill, with streams of water roaring down winding
ditches and gnawing the road away—how could one possibly
climb the hill? The horses were breathing heavily. Khanov got
out of his carriage and walked along the edge of the road in his
long overcoat. He was hot.

"What a road, eh?" he exclaimed, and laughed again. "Soon
the whole carriage will be smashed to bits!"

"Who told you to go driving about in this weather?" Semyon said sharply. "Why didn't you stay at home?"

"It's boring to stay at home, old fellow. I don't like it."

He looked strong and well built as he walked beside old Semyon, but there was something barely perceptible in his gait which revealed a person already touched by decay, weak, and nearing his end. The forest suddenly smelled of wine. Maria Vasilyevna shuddered, and began to feel pity for this man who was going to ruin for no good reason, and it occurred to her that if she were his wife or sister she would devote her whole life to saving him. His wife? But he had so ordered his life that he had come to live alone on a vast estate, while she lived out her life in an obscure little village, and so the mere thought of them meeting as equals and becoming intimate seemed impossible and absurd. In reality, life was so ordered and human relationships were so infinitely various and complex that if you thought about them at all, you would be overwhelmed with terror and your heart would stop beating!

"It is beyond all understanding," she thought, "why God gives beauty and charm and gentle, melancholy eyes to weak, unhappy, useless mortals—why are they so charming?"

"I'll be turning off to the right here," Khanov said, jumping into his carriage. "Good-by, and a pleasant journey to you!"

And now once again she thought of her pupils, of the examination, of the janitor and the school board; and when the wind blowing from the right brought her the rumbling of the departing carriage, these thoughts were mingled with others. She wanted to dream of his beautiful eyes, of love, of the happiness that would never come to her.

And if she became his wife! It was cold in the morning, there was no one to heat the stove, the janitor was away somewhere, and the school children came in as soon as it was light, making a good deal of noise, bringing in mud and snow. Everything was so bleak and uncomfortable. Her quarters consisted of one little room and a kitchen. Every day after school hours she had a headache, and after dinner a burning sensation over her heart. She had to collect money from the children for firewood and for the janitor, and this money had to be turned over to the trustee, and then she had to implore this man—this insolent, over-stuffed peasant—for God's sake to send her some of the firewood. At night she dreamed of examinations, peasants, snowdrifts. This life had aged and coarsened her, making her ugly, awk-ward, and gaunt, so that she looked as though lead had been poured into her veins. She was afraid of everything, and always stood up in the presence of the trustee or a member of the zemstvo council, and when she had cause to mention any of them she always referred to them deferentially, never using their names; it was always "they said this, they did that." No one found her attractive, and life continued to be boring, with no show of affection, no friendly sharing of interests, no interesting acquaintances. In her situation, how terrible it would be if she fell in love!

"Sit tight, Vasilyevna!"

Once again there was another steep climb.

She had become a schoolteacher out of necessity, without any vocation for it. She had in fact never thought of a vocation, or of the usefulness of education: the most important part of her work, she thought, lay not in the children or in enlightening their minds, but in examinations. And when, pray, did she ever have time to think of a vocation or of the advantages of education? Schoolteachers and ill-paid doctors and their assistants, for all their arduous work, never have even the consolation of thinking they are serving the people or an idea—they are thinking about the next crust of bread, about firewood, about bad roads, about illnesses. Their lives are hard and uninteresting, and only plod-ding silent cart horses like Maria Vasilyevna can bear such servi-tude for long. Lively, sensitive, impressionable people who talk of a vocation and service to an idea soon grow weary and throw up the task.

To find the driest and shortest road Semyon sometimes struck out across a meadow or behind cottages, but the peasants would not always let him pass: if he came to priests' land, there would be no free passage, and it was the same when he came to a plot of land which Ivan Ionov had bought from a landowner and surrounded with a ditch. In each case they had to turn back.

They reached Nizhneye Gorodishche. Near the tavern horse-carts loaded with great bottles of sulfuric acid stood about the dung-strewn earth, still covered with snow. There were a great many people in the tavern, all of them drivers, and the place smelled of vodka, tobacco, and sheepskins. The roar of conversation was sometimes interrupted by the banging of a swing door. The sound of an accordion came through the partition wall, an endless sound. Maria Vasilyevna sat down and drank her tea, while the peasants at the next table swilled down vodka and beer, perspiring freely from the tea they had already drunk and the suffocating heat of the tavern.

Voices kept shouting confusedly: "Did you hear that, Kuzma?" "What's up, eh?" "Lord save us!" "Ivan Dementyich, I'll get you!" "Look there, brother!"

A very small pock-marked peasant with a black beard, quite drunk, was suddenly surprised by something or other, and exploded into a torrent of foul language.

"What do you mean by all that dirty language, eh?" Semyon shouted angrily. He was sitting at the far end of the room. "Can't you see there's a young lady present?"

"What's that, a young lady, eh?" someone jeered from another corner.

"What a swine!"

"I didn't mean any harm," the very small peasant said confusedly. "Excuse me. I lays down my money, and the young lady lays hers. Good morning, ma'am."

"Good morning," replied the schoolteacher.

"Very well, thank you kindly."

Maria Vasilyevna enjoyed her tea, and soon her face was as

red as the others, and once more she fell to thinking about the
janitor, about firewood. . . .

She heard a voice from the next table: "Just look over there,
brother. That's the schoolmistress from Vyazovye. I recognize
her. She's a fine young lady. . . ."

"She's all right."

The swing door was continually banging, and people were
continually coming in and going out. Maria Vasilyevna sat there
absorbed in her thoughts, but the accordion on the other side of
the wall kept playing and playing. Patches of sunlight which had
lain on the floor when she came in moved up to the counter, then
up the wall, and then vanished altogether: it meant it was now
afternoon. The peasants at the next table were getting ready to
go. The very small peasant went up to Maria Vasilyevna, swaying slightly. He thrust out his hand; and seeing him, all the other
peasants came up to her and shook hands and went out one by
one. The door banged and whined nine times.

"Vasilyevna, get ready!" Semyon called to her.

They drove away, and again the horse went at a walking pace.

"A while back they were building a school here in their
Nizhneye Gorodishche," said Semyon, turning round. "And
they did something wicked."

"What did they do?"

"The chairman put a thousand in his pocket, and the trustee
put a thousand, and the teacher put five hundred."

"You shouldn't slander people, grandfather. The whole school
only cost a thousand. It's all nonsense what you say!"

"I wouldn't know. . . . I'm only telling you what they tell
me."

It was quite clear that Semyon did not believe the schoolmistress. The peasants, too, did not believe her. They always
thought her salary was too large, twenty-one rubles a month—
five rubles, in their estimation, would have been sufficient—and
they thought she kept the greater part of the money she re-

ceived for firewood and for the janitor. The trustee thought like the rest, though he made a profit out of the firewood and received a salary from the peasants for acting as trustee, and all this in secret without the knowledge of the authorities.

But now, thank God, they had left the forest behind them, and it was level ground all the way to Vyazovye. They had only a little further to go—a river to cross, then a railroad track, and then they would be in Vyazovye.

"Where are you going now?" Maria Vasilyevna asked Semyon. "Why don't you take the road to the right across the bridge?"

"What's wrong with this road? The water's not very deep."

"Be careful you don't drown the horse!"

"What's that?"

"Why, there's Khanov driving over the bridge," Maria Vasilyevna said, seeing the carriage and four horses far to the right. "It is him, isn't it?"

"It's him for sure. Reckon he didn't find Bakvist at home after all. God in heaven, he's a fool to drive all that way, when it's all of two miles nearer this way."

They came to the river. In summer the river was only a shallow stream which you could walk across easily. Usually in August it was dried up, but now, after the spring floods, it had grown to be a torrent of swift, cold, muddy water fifty feet wide. There were fresh wheel tracks visible on the bank up to the water's edge: evidently carts had been going over.

"Giddap!" Semyon shouted angrily and anxiously, tugging violently at the reins and flapping his arms like a pair of wings. "Giddap!"

The horse waded into the water up to his belly, stopped, and then plunged on again, straining to the utmost, and Maria Vasilyevna felt the shock of cold water lapping her feet.

"Get up!" she shouted, rising to her feet. "Get up!"

They came to the opposite bank.

"What a business, eh? Good Lord!" muttered Semyon, setting

the harness straight. "Those zemstvo people plague the devil out of us!"

Her shoes and galoshes were full of water; the hem of her skirt and her coat and one sleeve were drenched and dripping. The bags of sugar and flour she had bought were soaked, and this was harder to bear than all the rest. In her despair Maria Vasilyevna only clasped her hands together and murmured: "Oh, Semyon, Semyon, how could you . . . really?"

The barrier was down at the railroad crossing: an express train was leaving the station. Maria Vasilyevna stood at the crossing waiting for the train to pass, her whole body trembling with cold. From where they were, they could see Vyazovye, the green roof over the school and the church with the blazing crosses reflecting the rays of the setting sun; and the station windows were also ablaze, and rose-colored smoke came from the engine. . . . And it seemed to her that everything in the world was shivering with cold.

At last the train appeared, the windows aflame like the crosses on the church: it made her eyes ache to look at them. Maria Vasilyevna caught a quick glimpse of a lady standing on the platform of a first-class carriage. It was her mother! There was an extraordinary resemblance. The same glorious hair, the same forehead, the same inclination of the head. With amazing clarity, for the first time in thirty years, there came to her vivid images of her mother, her father, her brother, their apartment in Moscow, the aquarium with the little fishes, everything to the smallest detail. There came to her the sound of someone playing on the grand piano, and the voice of her father, and she saw herself young and pretty and well dressed in a warm and brilliantly lit room, with her whole family around her. A great joy and happiness welled up in her heart, and she pressed her hands to her temples in rapture, crying softly and imploringly: "Mother!"

And she began to cry, for no reason. At that moment Khanov drove up with his four-in-hand, and seeing him, she imagined such happiness as had never been, and she smiled and nodded to him as though they possessed equal stations in life and were intimate with one another, and it seemed to her that the whole sky, the trees, and all the windows were glowing with her happiness and her triumph. No! Her father and mother had never died, and she herself had never been a schoolteacher: there had been a long, strange, tortured dream, but now she was wide awake.

"Vasilyevna, get up in the cart!"

Suddenly it all vanished. The barrier slowly rose. Trembling, numb with cold, Maria Vasilyevna took her place in the cart. The carriage with the four horses crossed the railroad track, and Semyon followed it. The guard at the crossing lifted his cap.

"Here is Vyazovye! We have arrived!"

1897

On Love

AT breakfast the next day they served very tasty *pirozhki*, cray-fish, and mutton cutlets, and while we were eating, Nicanor the cook came in to ask what the guests would like for dinner. He was a man of middle height with a puffy face and small eyes, and though clean-shaven he somehow looked as though his mustache had been plucked rather than shaved.

Alyokhin told us that the beautiful Pelageya was in love with Nicanor. As he was a drunkard with a violent temper, she did not want him for a husband, but was prepared to live with him. He was a very devout man, and his religious convictions did not permit him to live in this way, and so he insisted upon marriage and refused any other solution, and when he was drunk he used to curse her and even beat her. Sometimes she would hide up-stairs and fall into fits of weeping, and on such occasions Alyokhin and the servants remained in the house to defend her if it should become necessary.

They started talking about love.

"How love is born," Alyokhin was saying, "why Pelageya has not fallen in love with someone closer to her both inwardly and outwardly, why she fell in love with 'Dog-face' Nicanor—for we all call him 'Dog-face'—and to what extent personal happiness counts in love—all these things are unknown and you can argue about them as much as you please. So far there has been only one incontestably true statement made on the subject of love, and that is the statement that love is the most wonderful thing in the world: everything else which has been written or spoken on the subject of love is incomplete and inconclusive, nothing more than a list of unanswered questions. The explanation which seems to fit one case fails to fit a dozen others, and in my opinion the very best thing is to offer explanations in particular cases rather than generalizations. As the doctors say, each case should receive individual treatment."

"Perfectly true," Burkin assented.

"We educated Russians have a partiality for unanswered questions. We usually poeticize love, prettifying it with roses and nightingales, and so we Russians prettify our love affairs with these fatal questions, and usually we choose the least interesting questions. In Moscow when I was a student I had a girl, a charming creature, who was always thinking about the monthly allowance I would give her and the price of a pound of beef whenever I embraced her. So, too, when we are in love, we never weary of asking ourselves questions about whether it is honorable or dishonorable, sensible or stupid, and where this love affair will lead us, and things like that. I don't know whether this is a good thing or not, but I do know these questions get in the way, and are irritating and unsatisfying."

He had the appearance of a man who wants to tell a story. People who lead lonely lives always have something on their minds they are eager to talk about. Bachelors living in town visit bathhouses and restaurants for no other reason except to talk, and sometimes they tell exceedingly interesting stories to the waiters and bathhouse attendants; and in the country they will usually pour out their hearts to their guests. Through a window we could see a gray sky and trees drenched in rain. It was the kind of weather which makes it impossible to go anywhere, when the only thing to do is to tell stories and to listen to them. So Alyokhin began his story:

I have been living and farming at Sofino for a long time, ever since I finished at the university. By education I belong to the class of idlers, and by avocation to the study. When I came here I found the estate heavily mortgaged, and since my father had got into debt partly because he had spent so much money on my education, I decided to remain and work until the debt was paid off. That was what I decided to do, but I must confess that I did not settle down to work without some repugnance. The land here does not yield very much, and unless you are going to farm at a loss you have to employ serfs and hired hands, which is about the same thing, or else you have to work like the peasants— I mean, you and your whole family working in the fields. There is no middle way. But in those days I wasn't concerned with such subtleties. I did not leave a single clod of earth unturned, I gathered together all the peasants and the peasant women from the neighboring villages, and work went on at a furious pace. I myself plowed, sowed, and reaped, and was bored by it all, and frowned with disgust, like a village cat driven by hunger to eat cucumbers in the kitchen garden. My body ached, and I would fall asleep while walking. At first I thought it would be easy to reconcile my life as a toiler with my educated habits. To do this, I thought, it was only necessary to lead an outwardly orderly life. So I settled down here, upstairs in the best rooms, and bade them serve me coffee and liqueurs after breakfast and dinner, and every night when I went to bed I read *The Messenger of Europe*. But one day our priest, Father Ivan, came on a visit and at one sitting he drank up my entire supply of liqueurs, and *The Messenger of Europe* went to the priest's daughters, because in summer and especially at mowing time, I never succeeded in getting to bed at all, but slept on a sleigh in the barn or in the forester's hut in the woods: so how could I do any reading? Then little by little I moved downstairs and began eating in the servants' kitchen, and of all my former luxury nothing is left except the servants who were once in my father's service or those it was too painful to discharge.

During those first years I was elected honorary justice of the peace. Sometimes I would have to go to town to take part in the assizes—the circuit courts—and this pleased and delighted me. When you have lived here for two or three months without ever leaving the place, then—and this happens especially in winter—you finally come to yearn for the sight of a black coat. Now, uniforms and black coats and frock coats were in evidence at the circuit courts; they were worn by lawyers, who are men who have received a liberal education; and there were people to talk to. After sleeping in a sleigh and eating in the servants' kitchen it was the purest luxury to sit in an armchair wearing clean linen and soft boots, with a chain of office round one's neck.

I was warmly received in the town, and eagerly made friends. Of these friendships the most intimate and, to speak truthfully, the most delightful for me was my friendship with Luganovich, the vice-chairman of the circuit court. You both know him, of course—a wonderfully charming fellow. All this happened after a celebrated case of arson. The preliminary investigation lasted two days, leaving us exhausted. Luganovich looked over to me and said: "Look here, come and have dinner with me."

This was an unexpected invitation because I scarcely knew Luganovich except in his official capacity, and I had never been to his house. I returned to my hotel room for a few moments to change, and then went off to dinner. And there it happened that I met Anna Alexeyevna, Luganovich's wife. In those days she was still a very young woman, no more than twenty-two, and her first child had been born only six months before. This all happened a long time ago, and nowadays I would find it hard to understand what was so remarkable about her, and what attracted me to her, but during the dinner it was all perfectly clear to me. I saw a young woman who was kind, beautiful, clever, fascinating, such as I had never met before. I felt her as a being who was close to me, and already familiar to me: it was as though I had seen her face and those friendly intelligent eyes long ago in the days of my childhood, in the album which lay on my mother's chest of drawers.

In the arson case, four Jews, said to be members of a gang,

were placed on trial; in my opinion they were completely innocent. At dinner I was very much agitated and disturbed, and I
no longer remember what I said. All I recall is that Anna
Alexeyevna kept shaking her head and saying to her husband:
"Dmitry, how can this be?"

Luganovich was a good-natured fellow, one of those simple-
minded people who hold firmly to the opinion that once a man
is brought before the court he must be guilty, and that one
should not express any doubts about the correctness of a judgment unless all legal formalities have been complied with, and
never over a dinner or in the course of a private conversation.

"You and I did not set fire to the place," he said softly, "and
as you see, we are not on trial, and we are not in prison."

Both the husband and the wife tried to make me eat and drink
as much as possible. From little things that happened—for
example, the way they made coffee together, the way they understood one another without finishing their words or sentences
—I came to the conclusion they were living peacefully and in
harmony together, and were glad to welcome a visitor. After
dinner they played a duet on the piano, then it grew dark and I
drove home. It was then the beginning of spring. After that I
spent the whole summer at Sofino without a break, and I had no
time even to think of the town, but the memory of that handsome
fair-haired woman remained with me through all those days. I
did not think about her, but it was as though her shadow lay
lightly over my soul.

In the late autumn a theatrical performance was given for
charity in the town. I went to the governor's box, having been
invited during the entr'acte, and looked and saw Anna Alexeyevna sitting with the governor's wife; and again there was the
same overwhelming and irresistible impression of beauty, and
the adorable caressing eyes, and again the same feeling of close-
ness.

We sat side by side, and later went out in the foyer.

"You have grown thinner," she said. "Have you been ill?"

"Yes, I have had rheumatism in my shoulder, and in rainy weather I sleep atrociously."

"You look worn out. When you came to dinner with us in the spring, you seemed younger, livelier. You were excited, and you talked a good deal, and you were very interesting, and I confess I was a little carried away by you. For some reason during the summer I often found myself thinking about you, and today when I was getting ready for the theater I felt sure I would see you."

And she laughed.

"You look tired tonight," she repeated. "It makes you look older."

The next day I had lunch at the Luganoviches', and after lunch they drove out to their summer villa to make arrangements for the winter, and I went with them. And then we all returned to town, and at midnight drank tea together in quiet domesticity, while the fire blazed and the young mother kept going to see if her little girl was asleep. And after that, whenever I went to town, I would always visit with the Luganoviches. They became accustomed to me, and I to them. I would usually go unannounced, as one of the family.

"Who is there?" would come a voice from some distant room, a soft lingering voice which seemed very sweet to me.

"It is Pavel Konstantinovich," the maid or the nurse would answer.

And then Anna Alexeyevna would come out to meet me with a preoccupied air, and invariably she would say: "Why is it so long since you came? Is something wrong?"

Her gaze, and the elegant, aristocratic hands she offered me, her house dress, her hair style, her voice, her step, all these always produced on me the impression of something new and quite extraordinary in my life, and very meaningful. We would talk for a long time, and for a long time we would surrender to silences, thinking our own thoughts, or else she would play for me on the piano. If there was no one at home, I stayed and waited till they returned, talked to the nurse, played with the child, or lay down on the Turkish divan in the study to read the newspaper, and when Anna Alexeyevna returned I would go out and meet her in the hall and take all her parcels from her, and for some reason I always found myself carrying these parcels with as much love, as much pride, as though I were a boy.

There is a proverb which runs: "Women with no worries go off and buy pigs." The Luganoviches had no worries, so they made friends with me. If there were long intervals between my visits to town, they would think I was ill or something had happened to me, and they would be worried to death. It distressed them that I, an educated man with a knowledge of languages, instead of devoting myself to scholarship or literary work, lived in the country, ran around like a squirrel in a cage, and worked hard without a penny to show for it. They thought I was unhappy, and that I only talked, laughed, and ate in order to conceal my sufferings, and even during those happy moments when everything went well with me, I was aware of their searching gaze. They were especially touching at times when I was really depressed, when I was being hounded by creditors, or when it happened that I was unable to make a payment which fell due. Then husband and wife could be seen whispering together by the window, and afterward they would come over to me with grave faces and say: "If you are in any need of money, Pavel Konstantinovich, I and my wife beg you not to stand on ceremony, and to borrow from us."

As he spoke, his ears would turn red with emotion. Sometimes, after whispering with her at the window, he would approach me with red ears and say: "My wife and I earnestly beg you to accept this little present from us."

Then he would give me studs, a cigar case, or a lamp, and in return I would send them flowers, poultry, and butter from the country. Both of them, by the way, possessed considerable private means. In those early days I was often borrowing money and was not very particular where it came from, borrowing wherever I could, but nothing in the world would have induced me to borrow from the Luganoviches. But why talk about that?

I was unhappy. At home, in the fields, in the barn, I would find myself dreaming about her and trying to understand the mystery of a beautiful and intelligent young woman marrying such a dull man verging on old age (her husband was over forty) and having children by him—to understand the mystery of this dull, kindly, simple-minded man, who reasoned with such a boring and wholesome good sense, and who at balls and evening parties kept close to the solid citizens, looking listless and superfluous, wearing a submissive and apathetic expression, as though he had been brought there to be put on sale, even though he believed in his right to happiness, his right to have children by her; and I kept trying to understand why she had met him first and not me, and why it was necessary that such a terrible mistake should have occurred in our lives.

Every time I came to town I saw in her eyes that she had been waiting for me, and she would confess to me herself that from the early morning she had had a peculiar feeling and had guessed that I would come. We talked for a long time and fell into silences, and we never confessed our love for one another, but instead timidly and jealously concealed it. We were afraid of everything that would reveal our secret even to ourselves. I loved her tenderly, deeply, but I reflected and kept asking myself what our love could lead to if we lacked the strength to fight against it: it seemed to me beyond belief that my gentle and melancholy love could crudely obliterate the happy course of their lives, the lives of her husband and her children and the entire household where I was loved and trusted. Would it be honorable? She would go away with me, but where? Where could I take her? It would have been a different matter if I led a beautiful and interesting life, or if I had been struggling for the emancipation of my country, or if I were a famous scholar, actor, or painter; but as things stood, it meant removing her from one humdrum life to another which was equally humdrum, or perhaps more so. How long would our happiness last? What would happen to her if I became ill or died, or if we no longer loved one another?

I had the feeling that she was reasoning in the same way. She thought of her husband, her children, and her mother, who loved the husband like a son. If she surrendered to her feelings, she would be forced to lie or tell the truth, and in her position both would have been equally inconvenient and terrible. She was tormented, too, by the question whether her love would bring me happiness—whether she would not complicate my life, which was already difficult enough and filled with all sorts of troubles. She imagined she was not young enough for me, nor sufficiently energetic and industrious to begin a new life, and she often spoke to her husband about how I needed to marry some worthy and intelligent girl who would make a good housekeeper and companion for me—and she would immediately add that such a girl was unlikely to be found in the whole town.

Meanwhile the years passed. Anna Alexeyevna already had two children. Whenever I arrived at the Luganoviches', the servants put on cheerful smiles, the children shouted that Uncle Pavel Konstantinovich had come, and hung on my neck; everyone was happy. They did not understand what was going on inside me, and thought that I, too, must be happy. They all regarded me as a gentlemanly person. Grownups and children alike felt that a fine gentleman was walking about the room, and this gave a peculiar charm to their relationship with me, as though in my presence their lives became purer and more beautiful. Anna Alexeyevna and I would go to the theater together, always on foot, and we would sit side by side, our shoulders touching, and without saying a word I would take the opera glasses from her hands, and feel her very close to me, knowing she was mine and that we could not live without one another, but when we left the theater, by some misunderstanding, we always said good-by and went our separate ways like complete strangers. God knows what people were saying about us in the town, but there was not a word of truth in it all.

In later years Anna Alexeyevna paid frequent visits to her mother and sister, suffered from spells of melancholia, and came to realize that there were no satisfactions in her life, which was now ruined, and at such times she had no desire to see either her husband or her children. She was also being treated for a nervous breakdown.

We continued to say nothing, to be silent, and in the presence of strangers she displayed toward me a strange irritation: she would contradict everything I said, no matter what it was, and if I engaged in an argument, she would take the side of my opponent. If I dropped something, she would say coldly: "Congratulations!" Or else if I forgot to take the opera glasses when we were going to the theater, she would say later: "I knew you would forget!"

Luckily or unluckily there is nothing in our lives which does not sooner or later come to an end. At last the time for parting came, when Luganovich was appointed chief justice in one of the western provinces. They sold their furniture, their summer villa, and their horses. When for the last time they drove out to the villa and then turned and looked back at the garden and the green roof, everyone was sad, and I realized that the time had come to say good-by not only to the villa. It was decided that at the end of August we should see Anna Alexeyevna off to the Crimea, where the doctors were sending her, and a little while later Luganovich and the children would set off for the western province.

A great crowd of us came to see Anna Alexeyevna off. She said good-by to her husband and children, and then there were only a few moments left before the ringing of the third bell, and I ran into her compartment to put on the rack one of her baskets which she had almost forgotten; and then it was time to say good-by. There, in the compartment, our eyes met, our spiritual fortitude deserted us, I threw my arms round her, and she pressed her face against my chest, and wept. Kissing her face, her shoulders, her hands all wet with tears—oh, how unhappy we were!—I confessed my love for her, and with a burning pain in my heart I realized how needless and petty and deceptive were all those things which had kept us from loving one another. I came to realize that when you are in love, then in all your judgments about love you should start from something higher and more important than happiness or unhappiness, virtue and sin in all their accepted meanings, or you should make no judgments at all.

I kissed her for the last time, pressed her hand, and we parted—forever. The train was already in motion. I went into the next compartment, which was empty, and stayed there crying until we came to the next station. Then I got out and walked back to Sofino.

While Alyokhin was telling his story, the rain stopped and the sun came out. Burkin and Ivan Ivanich went out on the balcony, and from there gazed on the beautiful view over the garden and the river gleaming in the sun like a mirror. They admired the view, and at the same time they were full of pity for the man with the kind, intelligent eyes who had told them his story with so much forthrightness, and they were sorry he was rushing hither and thither over his vast estate like a squirrel in a cage instead of devoting himself to science or to some similar occupation which would have made his life more pleasant; and they thought of the sorrowful face the young woman must have shown when he said good-by to her in the compartment and kissed her face and shoulders. Both of them had met her in the town, and Burkin was well acquainted with her and thought her quite beautiful.

1898

The Lady with the Pet Dog

I

THEY were saying a new face had been seen on the esplanade: a lady with a pet dog. Dmitry Dmitrich Gurov, who had already spent two weeks in Yalta and regarded himself as an old hand, was beginning to show an interest in new faces. He was sitting in Vernet's coffeehouse when he saw a young lady, blonde and fairly tall, wearing a beret and walking along the esplanade. A white Pomeranian was trotting behind her.

Later he encountered her several times a day in the public gardens or in the square. She walked alone, always wearing the same beret, and always accompanied by the Pomeranian. No one knew who she was, and people called her simply "the lady with the pet dog."

"If she is here alone without a husband or any friends," thought Gurov, "then it wouldn't be a bad idea to make her acquaintance."

He was under forty, but he already had a twelve-year-old daughter and two boys at school. He had married young, when still a second-year student at college, and by now his wife looked nearly twice as old as he did. She was a tall, erect woman with dark eyebrows, dignified and imposing, who called herself a thinking person. She read a good deal, used simplified spelling in her letters, and called her husband Dimitry instead of Dmitry. Though he secretly regarded her as a woman of limited intelligence, narrow-minded and rather dowdy, he stood in awe of her and disliked being at home. Long ago he had begun being unfaithful to her, and he was now constantly unfaithful, and perhaps that was why he nearly always spoke ill of women, and whenever they were discussed in his presence he would call them "the lower race."

It seemed to him that he had been so schooled by bitter experience that he was entitled to call them anything he liked, but he was unable to live for even two days without "the lower race." In the company of men he was bored, cold, ill at ease, and uncommunicative, but felt at home among women, and knew what to say to them and how to behave; and even when he was silent in their presence he felt at ease. In his appearance, in his character, in his whole nature, there was something charming and elusive, which made him attractive to women and cast a spell over them. He knew this, and was himself attracted to them by some mysterious power.

Repeated and bitter experience had taught him that every fresh intimacy, which at first seems to give the spice of variety to life and a sense of delightful and easy conquest, inevitably ends by introducing excessively complicated problems, and creating intolerable situations—this is particularly true of the well-intentioned Moscow people, who are irresolute and slow to embark on adventures. But with every new encounter with an interesting woman he forgot all about his former experiences, and the desire to live surged in him, and everything suddenly seemed simple and amusing.

One evening when he was dining in the public gardens, the lady in the beret came strolling up and sat down at the next table. Her expression, her clothes, her way of walking, the way she did her hair, suggested that she belonged to the upper classes, that she was married, that she was paying her first visit to Yalta, and that she was alone and bored. . . . Stories told about immorality in Yalta are largely untrue, and for his part Gurov despised them, knowing they were mostly invented by people who were only too ready to sin, if they had the chance. . . . But when the lady sat down at the next table a few yards away from him, he remembered all those stories of easy conquests and trips to the mountains, and he was suddenly possessed with the tempting thought of a quick and temporary liaison, a romance with an unknown woman of whose very name he was ignorant.

He beckoned invitingly at the Pomeranian, and when the little dog came up to him, he shook his finger at it. The Pomeranian began to bark. Then Gurov wagged his finger again.

The lady glanced up at him and immediately lowered her eyes.

"He doesn't bite!" she said, and blushed.

"May I give him a bone?" Gurov said, and when she nodded, he asked politely: "Have you been long in Yalta?"

"Five days."

"And I am dragging through my second week."

There was silence for a while.

"Time passes so quickly, and it is so dull here," she said without looking at him.

"It's quite the fashion to say it is boring here," he replied. "People who live out their lives in places like Belevo or Zhizdro are not bored, but when they come here they say: 'How dull! All this dust!' One would think they live in Granada!"

She laughed. Then they both went on eating in silence, like complete strangers, but after dinner they walked off together and began to converse lightly and playfully like people who are completely at their ease and contented with themselves, and it is all the same to them where they go or what they talk about. They walked and talked about the strange light of the sea, the soft warm lilac color of the water, and the golden pathway made by the moonlight. They talked of how sultry it was after a hot day. Gurov told her he came from Moscow, that he had been trained as a philologist, though he now worked in a bank, that at one time he had trained to be an opera singer, but had given it up, and he told her about the two houses he owned in Moscow. From her he learned that she grew up in St. Petersburg and had been married in the town of S——, where she had been living for the past two years, that she would stay another month in Yalta, and perhaps her husband, who also needed a rest, would come to join her. She was not sure whether her husband was a member of a government board or on the zemstvo council, and this amused her. Gurov learned that her name was Anna Sergeyevna.

Afterwards in his room at the hotel he thought about her, and how they would surely meet on the following day. It was inevitable. Getting into bed, he recalled that only a little while ago she was a schoolgirl, doing lessons like his own daughter, and he remembered how awkward and timid she was in her laughter and in her manner of talking with a stranger—it was probably the first time in her life that she had found herself alone, in a situation where men followed her, gazed at her, and talked with her, always with a secret purpose she could not fail to guess. He thought of her slender and delicate throat and her lovely gray eyes.

"There's something pathetic about her," he thought, as he fell asleep.

II

A week had passed since they met. It was a holiday. Indoors it was oppressively hot, but the dust rose in clouds out of doors, and the people's hats whirled away. All day long Gurov was plagued with thirst, and kept going to the soft-drink stand to offer Anna Sergeyevna a soft drink or an ice cream. There was no refuge from the heat.

In the evening when the wind dropped they walked to the pier to watch the steamer come in. There were a great many people strolling along the pier: they had come to welcome friends, and they carried bunches of flowers. Two peculiarities of a festive Yalta crowd stood out distinctly: the elderly ladies were dressed like young women, and there were innumerable generals.

Because there was a heavy sea, the steamer was late, and already the sun was going down. The steamer had to maneuver for a long time before it could take its place beside the jetty. Anna Sergeyevna scanned the steamer and the passengers through her lorgnette, as though searching for someone she knew, and when she turned to Gurov her eyes were shining. She talked a good deal, with sudden abrupt questions, and quickly forgot what she had been saying; and then she lost her lorgnette in the crush.

The smartly dressed people went away, and it was now too dark to recognize faces. The wind had dropped, but Gurov and Anna Sergeyevna still stood there as though waiting for someone to come off the steamer. Anna Sergeyevna had fallen silent, and every now and then she would smell her flowers. She did not look at Gurov.

"The weather is better this evening," he said. "Where shall we go now? We might go for a drive."

He gazed at her intently and suddenly embraced her and kissed her on the lips, overwhelmed by the perfume and moisture of the flowers. And then, frightened, he looked around —had anyone observed them?

"Let us go to your . . ." he said softly.

They walked away quickly.

Her room was oppressively hot, and there was the scent of the perfume she had bought at a Japanese shop. Gurov gazed at her, and all the while he was thinking: "How strange are our meetings!" Out of the past there came to him the memory of other careless, good-natured women, happy in their love-making, grateful for the joy he gave them, however short, and then he remembered other women, like his wife, whose caresses were insincere and who talked endlessly in an affected and hysterical manner, with an expression which said this was not love or passion but something far more meaningful; and then he thought of the few very beautiful cold women on whose faces there would suddenly appear the glow of a fierce flame, a stubborn desire to take, to wring from life more than it can give: women who were no longer in their first youth, capricious, imprudent, unreflecting, and domineering, and when Gurov grew cold to them, their beauty aroused his hatred, and the lace trimming of their lingerie reminded him of fish scales.

But here there was all the shyness and awkwardness of inexperienced youth: a feeling of embarrassment, as though someone had suddenly knocked on the door. Anna Sergeyevna, "the lady with the pet dog," accepted what had happened in her own special way, gravely and seriously, as though she had accomplished her own downfall, an attitude which he found odd and disconcerting. Her features faded and drooped away, and on both sides of her face the long hair hung mournfully down, while she sat musing disconsolately like an adulteress in an antique painting.

"It's not right," she said. "You're the first person not to respect me."

There was a watermelon on the table. Gurov cut off a slice and began eating it slowly. For at least half an hour they were silent.

There was something touching about Anna Sergeyevna, revealing the purity of a simple and naïve woman who knew very little about life. The single candle burning on the table barely illumined her face, but it was clear that she was deeply unhappy.

"Why should I not respect you?" Gurov said. "You don't know what you are saying."

"God forgive me!" she said, and her eyes filled with tears. "It's terrible!"

"You don't have to justify yourself."

"How can I justify myself? No, I am a wicked, fallen woman! I despise myself, and have no desire to justify myself! It isn't my husband I have deceived, but myself! And not only now, I have been deceiving myself for a long time. My husband may be a good, honest man, but he is also a flunky! I don't know what work he does, but I know he is a flunky! When I married him I was twenty. I was devoured with curiosity. I longed for something better! Surely, I told myself, there is another kind of life! I wanted to live! To live, only to live! I was burning with curiosity. You won't understand, but I swear by God I was no longer in control of myself! Something strange was going on in me. I could not hold back. I told my husband I was ill, and I came here. . . . And now I have been walking about as though in a daze, like someone who has gone out of his senses. . . . And now I am nothing else but a low, common woman, and anyone may despise me!"

Gurov listened to her, bored to death. He was irritated with her naïve tone, and with her remorse, so unexpected and so out of place. But for the tears in her eyes, he would have thought she was joking or playing a part.

"I don't understand," he said gently. "What do you want?"

She laid her face against his chest and pressed close to him.

"Believe me, believe me, I beg you," she said. "I love all that is honest and pure in life, and sin is hateful to me. I don't know what I am doing. There are simple people who say: 'The Evil One led her astray,' and now I can say of myself that the Evil One has led me astray."

"Don't say such things," he murmured.

Then he gazed into her frightened, staring eyes, kissed her, spoke softly and affectionately, and gradually he was able to quieten her, and she was happy again; and then they both began to laugh.

Afterwards when they went out, there was not a soul on the esplanade. The town with its cypresses looked like a city of the dead, but the sea still roared and hurled itself against the shore. A single boat was rocking on the waves, and the lantern on it shone with a sleepy light.

They found a cab and drove to Oreanda.

"I discovered your name in the foyer just now," he said. "It was written up on the board—von Diederichs. Is your husband German?"

"No, I believe his grandfather was German, but he himself is an Orthodox Russian."

At Oreanda they sat on a bench not far from the church and gazed below at the sea and were lost in silence. Yalta was scarcely visible through the morning mist. Motionless white clouds covered the mountaintops. No leaves rustled, but the cicadas sang, and the monotonous muffled thunder of the sea, coming up from below, spoke of the peace, the eternal sleep awaiting us. This muffled thunder rose from the sea when neither Yalta nor Oreanda existed, and so it roars and will roar, dully, indifferently, after we have passed away. In this constancy of the sea, in her perfect indifference to our living and dying, there lies perhaps the promise of our eternal salvation, the unbroken stream of life on earth, and its unceasing movement toward perfection. Sitting beside the young woman, who looked so beautiful in the dawn, Gurov was soothed and enchanted by the fairylike scene—the sea and the mountains, the clouds and the broad sky. He pondered how everything in the universe, if properly understood, would be entirely beautiful, but for our own thoughts and actions when we lose sight of the higher purposes of life and our human dignity.

Someone came up to them—probably a coast guard—looked at them and then walked away. His coming seemed full of mystery and beauty. Then in the glow of the early dawn they saw the steamer coming from Feodossia, its lights already doused.

"There is dew on the grass," said Anna Sergeyevna after a silence.

"Yes, it's time to go home."

They went back to the town.

Thereafter they met every day at noon on the esplanade, lunched and dined together, went out on excursions, and admired the sea. She complained of sleeping badly and of the violent beating of her heart, and she kept asking the same questions over and over again, alternately surrendering to jealousy and the fear that he did not really respect her. And often in the square or in the public gardens, when there was no one near, he would suddenly draw her to him and kiss her passionately. Their perfect idleness, those kisses in the full light of day, exchanged circumspectly and furtively for fear that anyone should see them, the heat, the smell of the sea, the continual glittering procession of idle, fashionable, well-fed people—all this seemed to give him a new lease of life. He kept telling Anna Sergeyevna how beautiful and seductive she was; he was impatient and passionate for her; and he never left her side, while she brooded continually, always trying to make him confess that he had no respect for her, did not love her at all, and saw in her nothing but a loose woman. Almost every evening at a late hour they would leave the town and drive out to Oreanda or to the waterfall, and these excursions were invariably a success, while the sensations they enjoyed were invariably beautiful and sublime.

All this time they were waiting for her husband to come, but he sent a letter saying he was having trouble with his eyes and imploring her to come home as soon as possible. Anna Sergeyevna made haste to obey.

"It's a good thing I am going away," she told Gurov. "It is fate."

She took a carriage to the railroad station, and he went with her. The drive took nearly a whole day. When she had taken her seat in the express train, and when the second bell had rung, she said: "Let me have one more look at you! Just one more! Like that!"

She did not cry, but looked sad and ill, and her face trembled.

"I shall always think of you and remember you," she said. "God be with you! Think kindly of me! We shall never meet again—that's all for the good, for we should never have met. God bless you!"

The train moved off rapidly, and soon its lights vanished, and in a few moments the sound of the engine grew silent, as though everything were conspiring to put an end to this sweet oblivion, this madness. Alone on the platform, gazing into the dark distance, Gurov listened to the crying of the cicadas and the humming of the telegraph wires with the feeling that he had only just this moment woken up. And he told himself that this was just one more of the many adventures in his life, and it was now over, and there remained only a memory. . . . He was confused, sad, and filled with a faint sensation of remorse. After all, this young woman whom he would never meet again, had not been happy with him. He had been affectionate and sincere, but in his manner, his tone, his caresses, there had always been a suggestion of irony, the insulting arrogance of a successful male who was almost twice her age. And always she had called him kind, exceptional, noble: obviously he had seemed to her different from what he really was, and unintentionally he had deceived her. . . .

Here at the railroad station there was the scent of autumn in the air; and the evening was cold.

"It's time for me to go north, too," Gurov thought as he left the platform. "High time!"

III

At home in Moscow winter was already at hand. The stoves were heated, and it was still dark when the children got up to go to school, and the nurse would light the lamp for a short while. Already there was frost. When the first snow falls, and people go out for the first time on sleighs, it is good to see the white ground, the white roofs: one breathes easily and lightly, and one remembers the days of one's youth. The old lime trees and birches have a kindly look about them: they lie closer to one's heart than cypresses and palms; and below their branches one has no desire to dream of mountains and the sea.

Gurov, a native of Moscow, arrived there on a fine, frosty day, and when he put on his fur coat and warm gloves and went for a stroll along the Petrovka, and when on Saturday evening he heard the church bells ringing, then his recent travels and all the places he had visited lost their charm for him. Little by little he became immersed in Moscow life, eagerly read three newspapers a day, and declared that on principle he never read Moscow newspapers. Once more he was caught up in a whirl of restaurants, clubs, banquets, and celebrations, and it was flattering to have famous lawyers and actors visiting his house, and flattering to play cards with a professor at the doctors' club. He could eat a whole portion of *selyanka*, a cabbage stew, straight off the frying pan. . . .

So a month would pass, and the image of Anna Sergeyevna, he thought, would vanish into the mists of memory, and only rarely would she visit his dreams with her touching smile, like the other women who appeared in his dreams. But more than a month went by, soon it was the dead of winter, and the memory of Anna Sergeyevna remained as vivid as if he had parted from her only the day before. And these memories kept glowing with an even stronger flame. Whether it was in the silence of the evening when he was in his study and heard the voices of his children preparing their lessons, or listening to a song or the music in a restaurant or a storm howling in the chimney, suddenly all his memories would spring to life again: what happened on the pier, the misty mountains in the early morning, the steamer coming in from Feodossia, their kisses. He would pace up and down the room for a long while, remembering it all and smiling to himself, and later these memories would fill his dreams, and in his imagination the past would mingle with the future. When he closed his eyes, he saw her as though she were standing before him in the flesh, younger, lovelier, tenderer than she had really been; and he imagined himself a finer person than he had been in Yalta. In the evenings she peered at him from the bookshelves, the fireplace, a corner of the room; he heard her breathing and the soft rustle of her skirts. In the street he followed the women with his eyes, looking for someone who resembled her.

He began to feel an overwhelming desire to share his memories with someone. But in his home it was impossible for him to talk of his love, and away from home—there was no one. The tenants who lived in his house and his colleagues at the bank were equally useless. And what could he tell them? Had he really been in love? Was there anything beautiful, poetic, edifying, or even interesting, in his relations with Anna Sergeyevna? He found himself talking about women and love in vague generalities, and nobody guessed what he meant, and only his wife twitched her dark eyebrows and said: "Really, Dimitry, the role of a coxcomb does not suit you at all!"

One evening he was coming out of the doctors' club with one of his card partners, a government official, and he could not prevent himself from saying: "If you only knew what a fascinating woman I met in Yalta!"

The official sat down in the sleigh, and was driving away when he suddenly turned round and shouted: "Dmitry Dmitrich!"

"What?"

"You were quite right just now! The sturgeon wasn't fresh!"

These words, in themselves so commonplace, for some reason aroused Gurov's indignation: they seemed somehow dirty and degrading. What savage manners, what awful faces! What wasted nights, what dull days devoid of interest! Frenzied card playing, gluttony, drunkenness, endless conversations about the same thing. Futile pursuits and conversations about the same topics taking up the greater part of the day and the greater part of a man's strength, so that he was left to live out a curtailed, bobtailed life with his wings clipped—an idiotic mess—impos-

sible to run away or escape—one might as well be in a madhouse
or a convict settlement.

Gurov, boiling with indignation, did not sleep a wink that
night, and all the next day he suffered from a headache. On the
following nights, too, he slept badly, sitting up in bed, thinking,
or pacing the floor of his room. He was fed up with his children,
fed up with the bank, and had not the slightest desire to go
anywhere or talk about anything.

During the December holidays he decided to go on a journey
and told his wife he had to go to St. Petersburg on some business
connected with a certain young friend of his. Instead he went
to the town of S——. Why? He hardly knew himself. He wanted
to see Anna Sergeyevna and talk with her and if possible arrange
a rendezvous.

He arrived at S—— during the morning and took the best
room in the hotel, where the floor was covered with gray army
cloth and on the table there was an inkstand, gray with dust,
topped by a headless rider holding a hat in his raised hand. The
porter gave him the necessary information: von Diederichs lived
on Old Goncharnaya Street in a house of his own not far from
the hotel; lived on a grand scale, luxuriously, and kept his own
horses; the whole town knew him. The porter pronounced the
name "Driderits."

He was in no hurry. He walked along Old Goncharnaya
Street and found the house. In front of the house stretched a long
gray fence studded with nails.

"You'd run away from a fence like that," Gurov thought,
glancing now at the windows of the house, now at the fence.

He thought: "Today is a holiday, and her husband is probably
at home. In any case it would be tactless to go up to the house
and upset her. And if I sent her a note it might fall into her
husband's hands and bring about a catastrophe! The best thing
is to trust to chance." So he kept walking up and down the
street by the fence, waiting for the chance. He saw a beggar
entering the gates, only to be attacked by dogs, and about an

hour later he heard someone playing on a piano, but the sounds were very faint and indistinct. Probably Anna Sergeyevna was playing. Suddenly the front door opened, and an old woman came out, followed by the familiar white Pomeranian. Gurov thought of calling out to the dog, but his heart suddenly began to beat violently and he was so excited he could not remember the dog's name.

As he walked on, he came to hate the gray fence more and more, and it occurred to him with a sense of irritation that Anna Sergeyevna had forgotten him and was perhaps amusing herself with another man, and that was very natural in a young woman who had nothing to look at from morning to night but that damned fence. He went back to his hotel room and for a long while sat on the sofa, not knowing what to do. Then he ordered dinner and took a long nap.

"How absurd and tiresome it is!" he thought when he woke and looked at the dark windows, for evening had fallen. "Well, I've had some sleep, and what is there to do tonight?"

He sat up in the bed, which was covered with a cheap gray blanket of the kind seen in hospitals, and he taunted himself with anger and vexation.

"You and your lady with the pet dog. . . . There's a fine adventure for you! You're in a nice fix now!"

However, at the railroad station that morning his eye had been caught by a playbill advertising in enormous letters the first performance of *The Geisha*. He remembered this, and drove to the theater.

"It's very likely that she goes to first nights," he told himself.

The theater was full. There, as so often in provincial theaters, a thick haze hung above the chandeliers, and the crowds in the gallery were fidgeting noisily. In the first row of the orchestra the local dandies were standing with their hands behind their backs, waiting for the curtain to rise, while in the governor's box the governor's daughter, wearing a boa, sat in front, the governor himself sitting modestly behind the drapes, with only his hands visible. The curtain was swaying; the orchestra spent a long time tuning up. While the audience was coming in and taking their seats, Gurov was looking impatiently around him.

And then Anna Sergeyevna came in. She sat in the third row, and when Gurov looked at her his heart seemed to stop, and he understood clearly that the whole world contained no one nearer, dearer, and more important than Anna. This slight woman, lost amid a provincial rabble, in no way remarkable, with her silly lorgnette in her hands, filled his whole life: she was his sorrow and his joy, the only happiness he desired for himself; and to the sounds of the wretched orchestra, with its feeble provincial violins, he thought how beautiful she was. He thought and dreamed.

There came with Anna Sergeyevna a young man with small side whiskers, very tall and stooped, who inclined his head at every step and seemed to be continually bowing. Probably this was the husband she once described as a flunky one day in Yalta when she was in a bitter mood. And indeed in his lanky figure, his side whiskers, his small bald patch, there was something of a flunky's servility. He smiled sweetly, and in his buttonhole there was an academic badge like the number worn by a waiter.

During the first intermission the husband went away to smoke, and she remained in her seat. Gurov, who was also sitting in the orchestra, went up to her and said in a trembling voice, with a forced smile: "How are you?"

She looked up at him and turned pale, then glanced at him again in horror, unable to believe her eyes, tightly gripping the fan and the lorgnette, evidently fighting to overcome a feeling of faintness. Both were silent. She sat, he stood, and he was frightened by her distress, and did not dare sit beside her. The violins and flutes sang out as they were tuned. Suddenly he was afraid, as it occurred to him that all the people in the boxes were staring down at them. She stood up and walked quickly to the exit; he followed her, and both of them walked aimlessly up and down the corridors, while crowds of lawyers, teachers, and civil servants, all wearing the appropriate uniforms and badges, flashed past; and the ladies, and the fur coats hanging from pegs, also flashed past; and the draft blew through the place, bringing with it the odor of cigar stubs. Gurov, whose heart was beating wildly, thought: "Oh Lord, why are these people here and this orchestra?"

At that moment he recalled how, when he saw Anna Sergeyevna off at the station in the evening, he had told himself it was all over and they would never meet again. But how far away the end seemed to be now!

Anna paused on a narrow dark stairway which bore the inscription: "This way to the upper balcony."

"How you frightened me!" she said, breathing heavily, pale and stunned. "How you frightened me! I am half dead! Why did you come? Why?"

"Do try to understand, Anna—please understand . . ." he said in a hurried whisper. "I implore you, please understand . . ."

She looked at him with dread, with entreaty, with love, intently, to retain his features all the more firmly in her memory.

"I've been so unhappy," she went on, not listening to him. "All this time I've thought only of you, I've lived on thoughts of you. I tried to forget, to forget—why, why have you come?"

A pair of schoolboys were standing on the landing above them, smoking and peering down, but Gurov did not care, and drawing Anna to him, he began kissing her face, her cheeks, her hands.

"What are you doing? What are you doing?" she said in terror, pushing him away from her. "We have both lost our senses! Go away now—tonight! . . . I implore you by everything you hold sacred. . . . Someone is coming!"

Someone was climbing up the stairs.

"You must go away . . ." Anna Sergeyevna went on in a whisper. "Do you hear, Dmitry Dmitrich? I'll come and visit you in Moscow. I have never been happy. I am miserable now, and I shall never be happy again, never! Don't make me suffer any more! I swear I'll come to Moscow! We must separate now. My dear precious darling, we have to separate!"

She pressed his hand and went quickly down the stairs, all the while gazing back at him, and it was clear from the expression in her eyes that she was miserable. For a while Gurov stood there, listening to her footsteps, and then all sounds faded away, and he went to look for his coat and left the theater.

IV

And Anna Sergeyevna began coming to see him in Moscow. Every two or three months she would leave the town of S——, telling her husband she was going to consult a specialist in women's disorders, and her husband neither believed her nor disbelieved her. In Moscow she always stayed at the Slavyansky Bazaar Hotel, and the moment she arrived she would send a red-capped hotel messenger to Gurov. He would visit her, and no one in Moscow ever knew about their meetings.

One winter morning he was going to visit her as usual. (The messenger from the hotel had come the evening before, but he was out.) His daughter accompanied him. He was taking her to school, and the school lay on the way to the hotel. Great wet flakes of snow were falling.

"Three degrees above freezing, and it's still snowing," he told his daughter. "That's only the surface temperature of the earth— the other layers of the atmosphere have other temperatures."

"Yes, Papa. But why are there no thunderstorms in winter?"

He explained that, too. He talked, and all the while he was thinking about his meeting with the beloved, and not a living soul knew of it, and probably no one would ever know. He was living a double life: an open and public life visible to all who had any need to know, full of conventional truth and conventional lies, exactly like the lives of his friends and acquaintances, and another which followed a secret course. And by one of those

strange and perhaps accidental circumstances everything that
was to him meaningful, urgent, and important, everything about
which he felt sincerely and did not deceive himself, everything
that went to shape the very core of his existence, was concealed
from others, while everything that was false and the shell where
he hid in order to hide the truth about himself—his work at
the bank, discussions at the club, conversations about women as
"an inferior race," and attending anniversary celebrations with
his wife—all this was on the surface. Judging others by himself,
he refused to believe the evidence of his eyes, and therefore he
imagined that all men led their real and meaningful lives under
a veil of mystery and under cover of darkness. Every man's
intimate existence revolved around mysterious secrets, and it
was perhaps partly for this reason that all civilized men were
so nervously anxious to protect their privacy.

Leaving his daughter at the school, Gurov went on to the
Slavyansky Bazaar Hotel. He removed his fur coat in the lobby,
and then went upstairs and knocked softly on the door. Anna
Sergeyevna had been exhausted by the journey and the suspense
of waiting for his arrival—she had in fact expected him the
previous evening. She was wearing her favorite gray dress.
She was pale, and she looked at him without smiling, and he
had scarcely entered the room when she threw herself in his
arms. Their kisses were lingering and prolonged, as though
two years had passed since they had seen each other.

"How were things down there?" he said. "Anything new?"

"Please wait. . . . I'll tell you in a moment. . . . I can't
speak yet!"

She could not speak because she was crying. She turned away
from him, pressing a handkerchief to her eyes.

"Let her have her cry," he thought. "I'll sit down and wait."
And he sat down in an armchair.

Then he rang and ordered tea, and while he drank the tea she
remained standing with her face turned to the window. . . .
She was crying from the depth of her emotions, in the bitter

knowledge that their life together was so weighed down with sadness, because they could only meet in secret and were always hiding from people like thieves. And that meant surely that their lives were shattered!

"Oh, do stop crying!" he said.

It was evident to him that their love affair would not soon be over, and there was no end in sight. Anna Sergeyevna was growing more and more passionately fond of him, and it was beyond belief that he would ever tell her it must one day end; and if he had told her, she would not have believed him.

He went up to her and put his hands on her shoulders, intending to console her with some meaningless words and to fondle her; and then he saw himself in the mirror.

His hair was turning gray. It struck him as strange that he should have aged so much in these last years, and lost his good looks. Her shoulders were warm and trembling at his touch. He felt pity for her, who was so warm and beautiful, though probably it would not be long before she would begin to fade and wither, as he had done. Why did she love him so much? Women had always believed him to be other than what he was, and they loved in him not himself but the creature who came to life in their imagination, the man they had been seeking eagerly all their lives, and when they had discovered their mistake, they went on loving him. And not one of them was ever happy with him. Time passed, he met other women, became intimate with them, parted from them, never having loved them. It was anything you please, but it was not love.

And now at last, when his hair was turning gray, he had fallen in love—real love—for the first time in his life.

Anna Sergeyevna and he loved one another as people who are very close and dear love one another: they were like deeply devoted friends, like husband and wife. It seemed to them that Fate had intended them for one another, and it was beyond understanding that one had a wife, the other a husband. It was as though they were two birds of passage, one male, one female, who had been trapped and were now compelled to live in different cages. They had forgiven one another for all they were ashamed of in the past, they forgave everything in the present, and felt that this love of theirs changed them both.

Formerly in moments of depression he had consoled himself with the first argument that came into his head, but now all such arguments were foreign to him. He felt a deep compassion for her, and desired to be tender and sincere. . . .

"Don't cry, my darling," he said. "You've cried enough. Now let us talk, and we'll think of something. . . ."

Then they talked it over for a long time, trying to discover some way of avoiding secrecy and deception, and living in different towns, and being separated for long periods. How could they free themselves from their intolerable chains?

"How? How?" he asked, holding his head in his hands. "How?"

And it seemed as though in a little while the solution would be found and a lovely new life would begin for them; and to both of them it was clear that the end was still very far away, and the hardest and most difficult part was only beginning.

1899

The Bishop

I

VESPERS were being sung on the eve of Palm Sunday in the Old Petrovsky convent. When they began distributing the pussy willows, it was nearly ten o'clock, the candles were shedding only a dim light and the wicks wanted snuffing out: it was like being in a fog. In the twilight of the church the crowd heaved like a sea, and to His Eminence Bishop Peter, who had been ill for three days, it seemed that all those faces—men and women, old and young—were exactly the same, and all those who came up to receive the pussy willows had the same expression in their eyes. He could not see the doors through the haze, the crowd kept moving, and it looked as though there was no end to it and there would never be an end to it. A choir of women's voices was singing, and a nun was reading the prayers of the day.

How hot and close the air was! The service seemed interminable. The Bishop was tired. His breathing was labored, dry, and rapid, his shoulders ached with weariness, his legs were trembling. He was also unpleasantly disturbed by one of God's fools who kept screaming from the gallery. Suddenly, as though in a dream or in delirium, the Bishop thought he saw Maria Timofeyevna, his own mother, whom he had not seen in nine years, coming up to him in the crowd, or perhaps it was only an old woman who resembled his mother. She took a pussy willow

304

from him, gazing joyfully after him, a sweet and gentle smile on her lips, until she was lost in the crowd. For some reason tears began to flow down his cheeks. His soul was at rest, everything was at peace, while he kept gazing fixedly at the choir on the left, where the prayers were being read and where amid the evening shadows it was impossible to distinguish any human beings at all; and as he looked, he wept. The tears glistened on his cheeks and on his beard. Soon someone near him began to weep, and then someone farther away, and then still others wept, and gradually the whole church was full of the soft sound of weeping. After about five minutes the nuns' choir began singing, there was no more weeping, and everything went on as before.

Soon afterward the service came to an end. The Bishop got into his carriage and drove home, listening to the joyous and harmonious chimes of the heavy church bells, which he loved and which filled the whole garden in the moonlight. White walls, white crosses on the tombs, white birches and black shadows, and the moon afar off, yet hanging directly over the convent roof —all these things seemed to be living their own lives, remote and incomprehensible, and very close to mankind. It was early in April, but it had turned chilly after the warm spring day, with a light frost falling. The breath of spring could still be felt in the soft cool air. The road from the convent to the town was sandy, and the horses were obliged to go at a walking pace. Bathed in a clear and peaceful moonlight, the pilgrims were trudging home through the sand on both sides of the carriage. All were silent, deep in thought. Everything around looked familiar and friendly and young—trees and sky and even the moon itself—so that one longed to believe it would endure forever.

At last the carriage drove through the town, rumbling along the main street. All the stores except Yerakin's were shut. Yerakin was a millionaire who was trying out the new electric lamps, and these flickered so brilliantly that a crowd had gathered round the store. There followed wide, dark, deserted streets in endless procession; then came the highway, the fields, and the smell of pines. Suddenly there rose before the Bishop's eyes a white crenelated wall, behind it a tall bell tower flanked by five large golden cupolas on fire with moonlight. This was the Pankratievsky Monastery, where the Bishop lived. Here, too, high above the monastery there floated a silent moon lost in thought. The carriage drove through the gates, crunching over sand. Here and there dark monastic shapes hovered in the moonlight, and footsteps rang out over the flagstones. . . .

"Did you know, Your Eminence, that your mother came here while you were away?" A lay brother spoke to the Bishop as he entered his room.

"My mother? When did she come?"

"Before vespers. She first asked where you were, and then drove to the convent."

"Then I must have seen her in the church. Dear Lord!"

And the Bishop laughed with joy.

"She bade me tell Your Eminence," the lay brother went on, "that she will be coming back tomorrow. There was a little girl with her, I suppose a granddaughter. They are staying at Ovsyabnikov's inn for the night."

"What time is it?"

"A little after eleven."

"Oh, what a shame!"

The Bishop sat for a while in his living room, pondering. He could scarcely bring himself to believe it was so late. His legs and arms were stiff, the back of his neck ached. He felt hot and uncomfortable. After resting a few moments he went into his bedroom, and there too he sat down and gave himself up to thoughts of his mother. He heard the lay brother walking away and Father Sisoi coughing in the next room. The monastery clock chimed the quarter.

The Bishop undressed and recited the prayers before going to sleep. He uttered those old and long-familiar words with scrupulous attention, and yet all the time he was thinking about his mother. She had nine children, and perhaps forty grandchildren. She had spent most of her life in a poor village with her husband, who was a deacon; she had lived there for a very long time, from the age of seventeen to the age of sixty. The Bishop had memories of her going back to his earliest childhood, almost from the age of three. How he had loved her! Dear, precious, unforgettable childhood! Why was it that those far-off days, which would never return, seemed brighter, gayer, and richer than they really were! How gentle and good his mother had been to him when he fell ill during childhood, and in his youth! And now his prayers mingled with memories which shone ever more luminously like a flame, and they did not hinder him from thinking of his mother.

After his prayers the Bishop finished undressing and lay down, and as soon as he became aware of being in darkness there rose before him the image of his dead father, his mother, and his native village, which was called Lyesopolye. Wheels creaking, sheep bleating, church bells on clear summer mornings, gypsies beneath the window—how sweet to dream of such things! He remembered Father Simeon, the priest at Lyesopolye, a decent, gentle, good-natured man, small and lean, with a son studying for the priesthood—the son was a huge strapping fellow with a ferocious bass voice. Once the young seminarian flew into a rage at the cook and thundered: "Jehu's ass—that's what you are!" And Father Simeon heard him and said nothing, ashamed because he could no longer remember where the existence of such an ass was recorded in holy scripture. The priest who followed Father Simeon at Lyesopolye was called Father Demian. Because he drank heavily and sometimes saw green snakes, this priest was sometimes called "Demian the Snake Seer." The schoolmaster at Lyesopolye was called Matvey Nikolaich. He, too, had been a divinity student. Though kindly and intelligent, he was a drunkard. He never beat his students, but for some reason or other he always kept a bundle of birch twigs hanging on the wall, and underneath it there was the wholly unintelligible inscription: *Betula kinderbalsamica secuta.* He also had a shaggy black dog who went by the name of Syntax.

The Bishop laughed. Some five miles from Lyesopolye lay the village of Obnino with its wonder-working icon. In summer they would take the icon in procession, leaving Obnino to make the rounds of the neighboring villages, so that the church bells rang all day, now in one place, now in another, and to the Bishop it seemed as though the air itself had trembled with joy as he followed behind the icon, barefoot and hatless, with a simple smile on his lips and a simple faith in his heart. He had been immeasurably happy in those days, when he was known as Little Paul. Now he remembered that there were always crowds of people in Obnino, and in those days the priest, Father Alexey, in order to allow time for the offertory, made his deaf nephew read out the names of those for whom special prayers were asked "for the peace of their souls" or "for the health of their bodies." Ilarion would read out the list of names, receiving an occasional five- or ten-kopeck coin for his services, and it was only when he had grown gray and bald, and was close to death, that he suddenly noticed on one of the slips of paper the words: "What a fool you are, Ilarion!" Until the age of fifteen Little Paul showed few signs of promise, and his schoolwork was so bad that his parents thought of removing him from the ecclesiastical school and putting him to work in a store. One day, calling at the Obnino post office for letters, he stared for a long time at the clerks and said: "Excuse me, how are you paid, every month or every day?"

The Bishop crossed himself and turned over on the other side, hoping to put his thoughts to rest, hoping to sleep.

"My mother has come," he remembered, and laughed.

The moon glittered through the window, the floor shone white with moonlight, and the shadows lay over him. A cricket chirped. Through the wall came the sound of Father Sisoi snoring in the next room, and the old man's snores somehow suggested loneliness, forlornness, a strange wandering. Once Father Sisoi had been the housekeeper of the diocesan bishop, and so they called him "the former Father Housekeeper." He was seventy years old, and sometimes he lived in the monastery twelve miles out of town, and sometimes he remained in the town. Just three days before he had turned up at the Pankratievsky Monastery, and the Bishop was keeping him there to discuss some affairs and business with him at his leisure.

The bell for matins rang at half past one. Father Sisoi coughed, muttered something in a disgruntled voice, and then got up and went wandering barefoot through the rooms.

"Father Sisoi," the Bishop called.

Father Sisoi returned to his room and a little later reappeared, wearing boots and carrying a candle, with a cassock over his underclothes and an old, small, faded skullcap on his head.

"I can't sleep," the Bishop said, sitting up. "I must be ill. I don't know what it is. Fever!"

"You may have caught cold, Your Eminence. You should get yourself rubbed with tallow."

Father Sisoi stood there for a while and yawned: "O Lord, forgive me, a poor sinner . . ."

"I saw the electric lamps in Yerakin's store," the Bishop went on. "I don't like them at all."

Father Sisoi was old, lean, bent, always dissatisfied with something or other, and his eyes were angry and prominent like a crab's.

"I don't like it either," he said, going away. "I don't like it at all. O Lord, what a mess!"

II

On the following day, Palm Sunday, the Bishop took the service in the cathedral in the town. Afterward he paid a visit to the archbishop, called upon the widow of a general who was very ill, and then drove home. Around two o'clock he entertained two beloved guests for lunch—his aged mother and his niece Katya, who was eight years old. All through lunch the spring sunshine streamed through the windows from the courtyard, shining sweetly on the white tablecloth and on Katya's red hair. Through the double windowpanes there could be heard the cawing of rooks and the singing of starlings in the garden.

"It's all of nine years since we saw one another," the old woman was saying, "but when I caught sight of you at the convent yesterday, dear Lord, you hadn't changed even a little bit, though maybe you're a bit thinner and your beard is longer! Oh, Holy Mother, Queen of Heaven! Why, yesterday at the evening service there wasn't anybody who could hold back his tears—they all wept, and as soon as I saw you, I wept too, though God knows what I was weeping for. It's God's holy will!"

Yet in spite of the affectionate tone in which she spoke to him, it was clear that she was not at her ease, did not know whether to address him with the familiar "thou" or the more formal "you," or whether she should laugh or not, and she seemed to feel more like the widow of a deacon than his mother, while Katya sat there with her eyes glued on her uncle the Bishop, as though trying to make out what manner of man he was. Her hair had escaped from the comb and the velvet ribbon, and stood around her head like a halo; she had a turned-up nose, and her eyes were shifty, a little sly. Before they sat down to dinner she had broken a wineglass, and while talking her grandmother kept moving glasses and tumblers away from her. The Bishop listened to his mother, remembering how many, many years before, she had taken him and his brothers and sisters to visit relatives who were reputed to be rich. In those days she was busy with her own children, and now she was busy with her grandchildren, and she had brought Katya to see him. . . .

"Your sister Varenka has four children now," she was saying. "Katya is the oldest. Your brother-in-law, Father Ivan, fell ill— God knows why these things happen—and he died three days before the Feast of the Assumption, and so my poor Varenka was thrown out into a cold world . . ."

"How is Nikanor?" The Bishop asked about his oldest brother.

"Pretty well, thank God. Well enough, praise the Lord, to have some breath in his body. There's one thing though: his son Nikolasha—that's my grandson—didn't want to enter the Church and he's gone to the university instead to study medicine. He thinks it's the best thing, but who really knows? It's all God's holy will!"

"Nikolasha cuts up dead people," Katya said, spilling water over her lap.

"Sit still, child," her grandmother said gently, and she removed the glass from the child's hand. "Say a prayer, and eat!"

"It's such a long time since we met!" the Bishop said, tenderly stroking his mother's hand and shoulder. "I missed you when I was abroad, Mother. I missed you dreadfully."

"Thank you."

"In the evenings I used to sit by the open window, and I was terribly alone, and the band was playing, and suddenly I would be overcome with homesickness, and I would have given everything in the world to be home again, and seeing you. . . ."

His mother smiled and beamed, and then her face assumed a serious expression, and she said: "Thank you."

Abruptly the Bishop's mood changed. He gazed at his mother and could not understand how she had come by that timid, deferential expression of face and voice, and he could not understand what lay behind it, and he did not recognize her. He felt sad and hurt. He was still suffering from the headache of the day before, and his legs were aching horribly, and the fish he was eating seemed stale and insipid, and all the time he was very thirsty.

After dinner two rich ladies, landowners, came and sat for an hour and a half, pulling long faces, never uttering a word. Then the archimandrite, a gloomy, taciturn man, came on business. Then they rang the bells for vespers, and the sun set behind the woods, and the day was over. Returning from church, the Bishop said his prayers hurriedly, went to bed, and drew up the covers to keep as warm as possible.

It disturbed him to remember the fish he had eaten at dinner. The moonlight too disturbed him, and the sound of voices came to his ears. In a nearby room, probably the guest room, Father Sisoi was talking politics.

"They're fighting in Japan now," he was saying. "The Japanese are just like the Montenegrins, you know, they're the same race. They were both under the Turkish yoke, don't you know?"

And then came the voice of Maria Timofeyevna: "We said our prayers and had a cup of tea, and then we went off to see Father Yegor at Novokhatnoye, and then we . . ."

She kept saying: "We had a cup of tea" or "We drank tea," until it seemed that her whole life was devoted to tea drinking. Slowly, drowsily, the Bishop found himself surrendering to recollections of the seminary where he had studied. For three years he had taught Greek in the seminary, until he could no longer read without glasses; he became a monk, and later was made school inspector. Then he took the examination for a degree. At thirty-two he became rector of a seminary and was consecrated archimandrite. In those days his life flowed so peacefully and pleasantly, and seemed to stretch far into the future with no end in sight. Then his health began to fail, he became very thin and nearly blind, and his doctors advised him to give up everything and live abroad.

"And what did you do then?" Father Sisoi was saying in the next room.

"Then we had a cup of tea," Maria Timofeyevna answered.

"Oh, Father, look, your beard is green!" Katya exclaimed suddenly in surprise, and she burst out laughing.

The Bishop remembered that old gray-haired Father Sisoi's beard really did have a touch of green, and he, too, laughed.

"God have mercy on us, what a nuisance the girl is!" Father

Sisoi shouted in an angry voice. "You're a spoiled brat! Sit still, will you?"

New recollections came to the Bishop—he remembered the white church, all perfectly new, in which he held services when he went abroad, and the roaring of the warm sea. His apartment there contained five lofty rooms, well lit, with a brand-new writing table in his study and a whole library of books. He read a great deal and wrote a lot. He remembered how homesick he had been for his native land, and he remembered a blind beggar woman playing on a guitar underneath his window and singing about love, and whenever he listened to her, he always found himself for some reason meditating on the past. Eight years slipped away before he was recalled to Russia, and now he was a suffragan bishop, and the past was already fading into the far-off mists, as though it were a dream.

Father Sisoi came into the bedroom with a candle in his hand.

"Well, well," he said, surprised. "So you went to sleep early, Your Eminence."

"What's that?"

"It's still very early, only ten o'clock! I bought a candle this evening. I want to rub you with tallow!"

"I have a fever," the Bishop said, sitting up. "I really should do something about it. My head feels queer. . . ."

Father Sisoi removed the Bishop's shirt and began rubbing his chest and back with tallow.

"There . . . there," he said. "Oh, Lord Jesus Christ! There! I went to the town today and met—what's his name?—yes, Archpresbyter Sidonsky. I had a cup of tea with him. I don't like him. Oh, Lord Jesus Christ! There! I don't like him one little bit!"

III

The archbishop was an old man, very fat, and for more than a month he had kept to his bed, suffering from rheumatism or gout. Bishop Peter went to see him almost every day, and he also saw all those who had been going to the archbishop as suppliants. Now that he was unwell, he was troubled by the triviality and emptiness of everything they asked for, everything that made them weep, and he was distressed by their ignorance and cowardice. And all these useless, trivial requests oppressed him by their sheer weight, and now at last he felt he understood the man who wrote in his early days a treatise on the freedom of the will, and now seemed to be absorbed in trivialities, to have forgotten everything, and to have put thoughts of God aside. It occurred to the Bishop that he must have grown out of touch with Russian life while abroad; it was no longer easy for him; the people seemed coarse, the women who came for guidance seemed dull and stupid, the seminarians and their teachers uncultured and sometimes savage. And the documents which came in and went out could be counted in the tens of thousands! What documents they were! The ecclesiastical superintendents were giving marks to all the priests in the diocese; the young and old priests, and their wives and children, all were given marks according to their behavior—five, four, sometimes three—and he was obliged to talk and read and write serious reports on the subject. There was not a moment he could call his own, his soul was troubled all day, and he was at peace with himself only in church.

He could not grow accustomed to the terror he inspired unwittingly among people in spite of his quiet and modest ways. Everyone in the province seemed to shrivel and show demonstrable signs of guilt and fear the moment he glanced at them. Everyone, even the old archpresbyters, trembled in his presence; they all threw themselves at his feet, and not long ago an old lady, the wife of a village priest, came to him and was so overcome with awe that she was unable to utter a word, and went away without asking for anything. And he, who was incapable of uttering a harsh word against people in his sermons, and who never blamed people because he pitied them so, was moved to fury by these suppliants; he lost his temper and hurled their petitions to the floor. In all the time he had been there not one single person had spoken to him genuinely, simply, humanly. Even his old mother had changed—had in fact changed more than most! Why did she chatter incessantly with Father Sisoi, and laugh so much with him, while maintaining a strange seriousness and reserve and constraint in the presence of her son? It was not like her. The only person who behaved naturally and said whatever came into his head was old Father Sisoi, who had lived with bishops all his life and had outlasted eleven of them. And so Bishop Peter was at ease with him, although, of course, he was a horrible and empty-headed little man.

After the service on Tuesday, Bishop Peter went to the archbishop's house and received petitions; he grew excited, lost his temper, and drove home. He felt as unwell as before, and longed for his bed, but he was hardly in the house when he was informed that the young merchant Yerakin, a benefactor of the church, had come to see him on important business. The Bishop was obliged to receive him. Yerakin stayed about an hour, talking in a loud voice, almost screaming, and it was difficult to understand what he said.

"May God grant it!" the merchant said as he went away. "It's absolutely necessary, too! According to the circumstances, Your Eminence! Oh, I do hope it comes to pass!"

After him came the mother superior of a distant convent. And when she had gone, the bells were ringing for vespers and he had to go to the church.

That evening the monks sang in harmony and as though inspired, while a young black-bearded priest officiated; and the Bishop, listening as they sang of the Bridegroom who entered at midnight into the chamber adorned for Him, felt no sorrow over his sins, nor any grief, only a great sense of peace and tranquillity, and in his imagination he was being swept back into the distant past, to the days of his childhood and youth, when they also sang of the Bridegroom entering the chamber, and now the past rose up before him, vivid, beautiful, and joyful, as in all likelihood it had never been. And perhaps in the other world, in the life to come, we shall remember the distant past, our life on earth, with the same feeling. Who knows? The Bishop sat near the altar, where the shadows were deepest, while tears trickled down his cheeks, and he thought of how he had attained everything a man of his position could attain; he had faith, but not everything was clear to him. Something was lacking, and he did not want to die. He felt he had failed to discover the most important thing of all, something which he had glimpsed obscurely in dreams in the past, and he was still troubled by the same hopes for the future he had felt as a child, and at the seminary, and when he was abroad.

"How beautifully they are singing today," he thought, listening to the hymns. "Oh, how beautifully!"

IV

On Thursday he celebrated mass in the cathedral. It was the Washing of the Feet. When the service was over and the people had gone home, the warm sun was shining merrily, the water was streaming noisily in the gutters, and the perpetual trilling of larks came floating in from the fields outside the city, speaking of peace and tenderness. The trees were already awakening and smiling a welcome, and over them stretched the unfathomable, the immeasurable blue sky.

As soon as he reached home Bishop Peter drank some tea, changed his clothes, lay down on the bed, and told the lay brother to close the shutters. The bedroom grew dark. But what weariness he suffered, what pain there was in his legs and back, a heavy chilling pain, what noises in his ears! For a long time he had not slept—it seemed to him now a very long time indeed—and there was something completely nonsensical which tickled his brain as soon as he closed his eyes, preventing him from sleeping. As on the previous day, there came to him from

the next room the sound of voices, the ringing sound of glasses
and teaspoons. . . . Maria Timofeyevna was gaily recounting
an anecdote to Father Sisoi, with many a quaint turn of phrase,
and sometimes the old man would answer in a gruff, ill-
tempered voice: "Well, and what then? Did they do that? And
what next?" And once more the Bishop felt first annoyed and
then hurt that in the presence of others his old mother should
behave so naturally and simply, while with him, her son, she
was awkward, spoke little, and did not say what she intended
to say, and during all those days he was sure she had been
trying to find some pretext for standing, as though embarrassed
to be seated in his presence. And his father? He, too, if he had
been alive, would probably have been incapable of uttering a
word. . . .

Something in the next room crashed to the floor. Katya must
have dropped a cup or saucer, for Father Sisoi suddenly rumbled
and shouted angrily: "The child is an awful nuisance. Lord,
forgive me my sins, but you can't put anything in her hands!"

Then it was quiet, the only sounds coming from outside.
When at last the Bishop opened his eyes, he saw Katya standing
motionless in the room, gazing at him.

"Is that you, Katya?" he asked. "Who's opening and shutting
doors downstairs?"

"I can't hear anything," Katya said, listening.

"There, someone just walked by."

"Uncle, that was a noise from your stomach!"

He laughed and stroked her head.

"So brother Nikolasha cuts up dead people?" he said after a
while.

"Yes, he's studying."

"Is he good to you?"

"He's very good, Uncle, but he drinks a terrible lot of vodka."

"What did your father die of?"

"He felt poorly and got awful thin, and then suddenly there
was something wrong with his throat. I was ill, too, and so was

my brother Fedya. We all had sore throats. Papa died, but we got well."

Her chin quivered, and tears filled her eyes and went trickling down her cheeks.

"Your Eminence!" she cried in a shrill voice, weeping bitterly. "Uncle dear, we're all so unhappy—our mother and all of us. . . . Do give us a little money. . . . Do be good to us, Uncle dear!"

Then he too began weeping, and for a long time he was too moved to speak. He caressed her hair and patted her shoulders and said: "Very good, my child. Wait till Easter comes, and then we'll talk about it. I'll help you. I'll help. . . ."

His mother came quietly and timidly into the room, and prayed before the icon. Seeing that he was not sleeping, she said: "Wouldn't you like some soup?"

"No, thank you," he answered. "I'm not hungry."

"You don't look well to me. You mustn't fall ill, you know. All day on your legs, all day—God knows it makes my heart ache just to look at you. Well, Easter isn't on the other side of the hills, as they say, and then you'll rest, and then, God willing, we'll have time for a talk, but now I'm not going to keep you awake with my chatter. Come along, Katenka! Let His Eminence have a bit of sleep!"

And he remembered how long ago, when he was a boy, he had spoken to high dignitaries of the Church in exactly the same way, playfully and respectfully. Only by noticing her strangely tender eyes and the troubled glance she shot at him as she left the room could anyone have guessed that she was his mother. He closed his eyes and seemed to sleep, but he could hear Father Sisoi coughing on the other side of the wall, and he heard the clock strike twice. His mother came in again, and for a long moment she gazed at him timidly. Then he heard someone driving up to the front steps either in a carriage or an open cart. Suddenly there came a knock, a door banged, the lay brother entered the bedroom.

"Your Eminence!"

"Yes, what is it?"

"The horses have come. It's time to go to Our Lord's Passion."

"What time is it?"

"A quarter past seven."

He dressed and drove to the cathedral. During the reading of the Twelve Gospels he had to stand motionless in the middle of the church, and the first gospel, which is the longest and most beautiful, he read himself. A mood of confidence and courage took hold of him. That first gospel—"Now is the Son of Man glorified"—he knew by heart, and as he read he sometimes raised his eyes and saw a perfect sea of lights all round him, and he heard the spluttering of the candles, but as happened in the past he was unable to see the people. It occurred to him that they were perhaps the same people who had been around him in the days of his childhood and youth, and they would always be there year after year until such time as God provided.

His father had been a deacon, his grandfather a priest, his great-grandfather a deacon, and perhaps his whole family from the days when Christianity first entered Russia had belonged to the Church, and his love for the holy services, for the priesthood, and for the sound of church bells was ineradicably born in him. In church, especially when he was conducting the service, he felt vividly alive, vigorous, and happy. So it was with him now. Only when the eighth gospel had been read, he felt his voice had grown weak, even his coughing had become inaudible. His head was aching horribly, and he was overwhelmed by the fear of a sudden collapse. His legs had grown quite numb, all the feeling gradually going out of them, and he could not imagine how he was able to stand or what he was standing on, and why he did not fall down. . . .

It was a quarter to twelve when the service came to an end. As soon as he reached home the Bishop undressed and went to bed without even saying his prayers. He could not speak, and he was sure he could not stand. When he pulled the blanket over him, he felt a sudden longing to be abroad, a deep and passionate longing. He imagined he would give his whole life not to see those cheap pitiful shutters, the low ceilings, not to breathe the overwhelming smell of the monastery. If only there was one person he could talk to, and to whom he could unburden his soul!

For a long time he heard footsteps in the next room, and could not tell whose they were. At last the door opened and Father Sisoi came in with a teacup in one hand and a candle in the other.

"So you're in bed already, Your Eminence?" Father Sisoi said. "I've come to rub you down with vodka and vinegar. A thorough rubbing will do you good! Lord Jesus Christ! There! There! I've just come from our monastery. . . . I don't like it a bit! . . . I'll be leaving tomorrow, Your Eminence, because I've had enough of it. Lord Jesus Christ! Well, that's how it is! . . ."

Father Sisoi could never stay long in one place, and he felt as though he had been a whole year in the Pankratievsky Monastery. It was hard to tell from what he said where his home was, whether there was anyone or anything he loved, whether he believed in God. He did not know himself why he had become a monk, but he never thought about it, and the time when he took his vows had long since faded from his memory. Perhaps he had been born into the monastery.

"I'm leaving them tomorrow, and may God have them!" Father Sisoi said.

"I've been wanting to talk to you," the Bishop said. "I never seem to have the time." His voice came in whispers, and he was making a great effort. "I don't know anyone or anything here."

"Then I'll stay till Sunday if you like. So be it, but no longer. I have to leave that place. . . ."

"What sort of bishop am I?" the Bishop went on in a very faint voice. "I should have been a village priest or a deacon or just a simple monk. All this is choking me—choking me . . ."

"What? Oh, Lord Jesus Christ! There, go to sleep now, Your Eminence. What's up with you? What's it all about, eh? Well, good night!"

All night the Bishop lay awake. In the morning at eight o'clock he began to hemorrhage from the bowels. The lay brother was alarmed and ran first to the archimandrite and then to Ivan Andreyich, the monastery doctor, who lived in the town. The doctor, a stout old man with a long gray beard, gazed for a long while at the Bishop, shook his head, frowned, and said: "Do you know, Your Eminence, you are suffering from typhus?"

For about an hour the Bishop continued to hemorrhage. He grew paler, thinner, was visibly wasting away. His face was covered with wrinkles and his eyes were enormous: it was as though he was grown old and shriveled. He felt that he was becoming thinner and weaker and more insignificant than anyone in the world, and it seemed to him that everything that had ever happened in the past was vanishing into the distance and would never come back again.

"How good!" he thought. "Oh, how good!"

His old mother came into the room. Seeing his wrinkled face and enormous eyes, she was frightened and fell on her knees by the bed and began to kiss his face, his shoulders, and his hands. And to her it seemed that he had grown thinner, weaker, and more insignificant than he had ever been, and she forgot he was a bishop, and she kissed him as though he were a child very close and dear to her.

"Little Paul, my dearest," she said. "How dear you are to me! My son, my son! . . . What has happened? Pavlusha, talk to me!"

Katya, pale and serious, stood beside her, and she could not understand what was happening to her uncle or why there was such a look of suffering on her grandmother's face or why she said such heart-rending things. The Bishop could no longer formulate words, and no longer understood what was happening around him. He imagined he was a simple, ordinary fellow striding joyfully across the fields, swinging his cane, free as a bird to wander wherever he pleased under the broad spaces of the sunlit sky.

"Pavlusha, my darling, talk to me!" the old woman was saying. "What has happened? My dear boy, my son . . ."

"You shouldn't disturb His Eminence," Father Sisoi exclaimed angrily, striding up and down the room. "Let him sleep! There's nothing we can do now. . . ."

Three doctors came, went into consultation, and took their leave. The day grew unbelievably long, and was followed by an excruciatingly long night. Toward dawn on Saturday the lay brother went up to the old woman, who was lying on a couch in the sitting room, and bade her go into the bedroom. The Bishop was dead.

The next day was Easter. There are forty-two churches and two monasteries in the town; and from morning to evening the deep, happy notes of the church bells hovered over the town, never silent, quivering in the spring air. Birds were singing, and the bright sun was shining. The great market square was full of noise: seesaws were swinging, barrel organs were playing, concertinas were screaming, and there was a roar of drunken voices. In a word, everything was lighthearted and frolicsome, just as it had been during the previous year and as it doubtless would be in the years to come.

A month later a new bishop was installed, and no one gave a thought to Bishop Peter. Soon he was completely forgotten. His old mother, who is living today in a remote little country town with her son-in-law the deacon, goes out toward evening to bring her cow in, and sometimes she will pause and talk with the other women in the fields about her children and grandchildren and her son who became a bishop, and she speaks very softly and shyly, afraid that no one will believe her.

And indeed there are some who do not believe her.

April 1902

The Bride

I

IT was about ten o'clock in the evening, and a full moon was
shining over the garden. In the Shumins' house the evening
service, held because the grandmother, Marfa Mikhailovna,
wanted it, was only just over, and now Nadya—who had slipped
out into the garden for a minute—could see the table being laid
for supper in the dining room, and her grandmother bustling
about in a magnificent silk dress, while Father Andrey, the
archpresbyter of the cathedral, was discussing something with
Nina Ivanovna, Nadya's mother, who for some reason looked
very young when seen through the window in the evening light.
Beside Nina Ivanovna stood Andrey Andreyich, Father Andrey's
son, who was listening attentively.

It was quiet and cool in the garden, where the dark peaceful
shadows lay on the earth. From a long way away, probably
from outside the town, came the croaking of frogs. There was a
feeling of May, sweet May, in the air. You found yourself
breathing deeply, and you imagined that somewhere else, somewhere beneath the sky and above the treetops, somewhere in the
open fields and the forests far from the town—somewhere there
the spring was burgeoning with its own mysterious and beautiful life, full of riches and holiness, beyond the comprehension of
weak, sinful man. And for some reason you found yourself
wanting to cry.

Nadya was already twenty-three, and ever since she was six-teen she had been passionately dreaming of marriage: now at last she was betrothed to Andrey Andreyich, whom she could see clearly through the window. She liked him, the wedding had been arranged for the seventh of July, but she felt no joy in her heart, slept badly at night, and all her happiness had gone from her. Through the open windows of the kitchen in the basement, she heard the servants scurrying about, the clatter of knives, the banging of the swinging door; there was the smell of roast tur-key and marinated cherries. And for some reason it seemed to her that it would always be like this, unchanging till the end of time.

Someone came out of the house and stood on the steps. It was Alexander Timofeyich, known as Sasha, who had arrived from Moscow about ten days before for a visit. Many years ago there had come to the grandmother's house a certain distant relative, Maria Petrovna, a widowed gentlewoman, begging charity. She was small and thin, and suffered from some illness, and was very poor. Sasha was her son. For some reason people said of him that he would make a fine artist, and when his mother died, Grandmother, for the salvation of her own soul, sent him to study at the Komissarov school in Moscow. A year or so later he went on to study at a school of painting, where he remained for about fifteen years, just managing to scrape through his final ex-aminations in architecture, but he never practiced as an archi-tect. Instead he went to work at a lithography shop in Moscow. He used to spend nearly every summer with Nadya's grand-mother, usually very ill, to rest and recuperate.

He wore a tightly buttoned frock coat and shabby canvas trousers crumpled at the hems. His shirt had not been ironed, and there was something soiled about him. He wore a beard, was very thin, with enormous eyes, long lean fingers, and his skin was dark; in spite of this, he was handsome. At the Shu-mins' he was regarded as one of the family, and felt himself at home. For a long time the room where he lived when he visited them had been known as Sasha's room.

Standing on the porch, he caught sight of Nadya and went up to her.

"It's nice here," he said.

"It's really nice. You ought to stay until the autumn."

"Yes, I know. Probably I'll have to. I may stay with you till September."

He burst out laughing for no reason at all, and then sat down beside her.

"I've been sitting here and gazing at Mother," said Nadya. "She looks so young from here. Of course, she has her weaknesses," she added after a pause, "but she is still a most unusual woman."

"Yes, she's very nice," Sasha agreed. "In her own way, of course. She's good and kind, but somehow . . . How shall I put it? Early this morning I went down to your kitchen. I saw four maidservants sleeping right there on the floor, no beds, just a few rags for bedclothes, stench, bedbugs, cockroaches. . . . It was like that twenty years ago, and since then there's been no change at all. It's no use blaming your grandmother, God bless her soul, but your mother speaks French and acts in amateur theatricals. . . . You'd think she'd understand about these things."

While Sasha talked, he held out two long bony fingers in front of Nadya's face.

"Everything here looks strange to me," he went on. "Maybe it's because I'm not used to it. God in heaven, no one ever does anything! Your mother does nothing all day but walk about like a duchess, your grandmother does nothing either, and you're the same. And your fiancé, Andrey Andreyich, does nothing either!"

Nadya had heard all this the year before, and she thought she had heard it the year before that: she knew that was how

Sasha's mind worked. Once these speeches had amused her, but now for some reason they irritated her.

"It's old stuff," she said, and got up. "I wish you'd say something new."

He laughed and got up too, and they walked together to the house. She was tall, beautiful, well formed, and looked almost offensively healthy and stylishly dressed beside him; she was even conscious of this herself, and felt sorry for him, and strangely awkward.

"You talk a lot of nonsense!" she said. "Look what you just said about my Andrey—you really don't know him at all!"

"*My* Andrey! . . . Never mind *your* Andrey! . . . It's your youth I'm sorry for!"

When they reached the dining room, everyone was already at supper. The grandmother—"Granny" to everyone in the house—was a very corpulent, plain old lady with thick eyebrows and a tiny mustache, who talked in a loud voice: from her voice and manner of speaking it was obvious that she was the most important woman in the household. She owned a row of stalls in the market place, the old house with its pillars and garden was hers, and every morning she prayed tearfully to God to spare her from ruin. Her daughter-in-law, Nadya's mother, Nina Ivanovna, was a tightly corseted blonde who wore pince-nez and rings on all her fingers. Father Andrey was a lean toothless old man who wore an expression which suggested that he was always about to say something amusing, and his son Andrey Andreyich, Nadya's fiancé, was a plump handsome creature with curly hair, who resembled an actor or a painter. They were all talking about hypnotism.

"You'll be well again in a week here," Granny said, turning to Sasha. "Only you must eat more. Just look at you," she sighed. "You look dreadful! Why, you look like the Prodigal Son, and that's the truth!"

"He wasted his substance in riotous living," Father Andrey

said slowly, his eyes lighting up with amusement. "And it was his curse to feed with the unmitigated swine!"

"I admire my old man," Andrey Andreyich said, patting his father's shoulder. "He's really a splendid old fellow. Very decent."

They were silent for a while. Sasha suddenly burst out laughing, and covered his mouth with his napkin.

"So you believe in hypnotism?" Father Andrey asked Nina Ivanovna.

"No, I can't exactly say I believe in it," Nina Ivanovna replied, assuming a very grave, almost harsh expression. "Still, I must admit there is a good deal that remains mysterious and incomprehensible in nature."

"I am entirely of your opinion, though I would add that for us faith decidedly narrows the sphere of the mysterious."

A huge, immensely fat turkey was being served. Father Andrey and Nina Ivanovna continued their conversation. The diamonds on Nina Ivanovna's fingers sparkled, but soon tears came to gleam in her eyes, and she was overcome with emotion.

"Yes, yes," she said. "I wouldn't dream of arguing with you, but you must agree that there are many insoluble riddles to life!"

"Well, I don't know *one* insoluble riddle!"

After supper Andrey Andreyich played the violin, Nina Ivanovna accompanying him on the piano. Ten years previously he had graduated from the faculty of philology at the university, but he never entered government service, never worked at a definite occupation; he merely played at occasional concerts given for charity. In the town, people spoke of him as an artist.

Andrey Andreyich played, and they listened in silence. The samovar steamed quietly on the table, but Sasha was the only one to drink tea. When it struck twelve, a violin string suddenly snapped, and they all laughed. Then they bustled about, and soon they were saying good-by.

After taking leave of her fiancé, Nadya went upstairs to the apartment she shared with her mother—the lower floor was occupied by her grandmother. Down below, in the drawing room, they were putting out the lights, but Sasha was still there, drinking tea. He always spent a long time over his tea, in the Moscow fashion, drinking up to seven glasses at a sitting. Long after she had undressed and gone to bed, Nadya could hear the servants clearing away and Granny talking angrily. At last silence reigned over the house, and there was no sound except the occasional coughing which came from somewhere below, from Sasha's room.

II

It must have been about two o'clock when Nadya awoke. The dawn was coming up. The night watchman's rattle could be heard in the distance. Nadya could not sleep: her bed felt soft and uncomfortable. She sat up in bed and gave herself up to her thoughts, as she had done during all the previous nights of May. Her thoughts were the same as on the night before: monotonous, futile, insistent—thoughts of how Andrey Andreyich courted and proposed to her, and how she had accepted him and gradually learned to appreciate this good and intelligent man. Yet for some reason, now, a month before the wedding, she began to experience a sense of fear and uneasiness, as though something vague and oppressive lay in wait for her.

"Tick-tock, tick-tock . . ." came the lazy tapping of the night watchman. "Tick-tock . . ."

Through the big old-fashioned window she could see the garden, and beyond the garden lay the lilac bushes heavy with bloom, drowsy and languid in the cold air, and a heavy white mist suddenly swept up to the lilacs, as though determined to drown them. The drowsy rooks were cawing in the distant trees.

"My God, why am I so depressed?"

Perhaps all brides feel the same before their weddings? Who knows? Or could it be the influence of Sasha? But for several years now Sasha had been repeating the same outworn phrases, like a copybook, and when he spoke to her now, he seemed naïve and strange to her. Why couldn't she get the thought of Sasha out of her head? Why?

The night watchman had stopped tapping long ago. The birds were twittering beneath her window, and in the garden the mist vanished, so that everything glittered and seemed to be smiling in the spring sunshine. Soon the whole garden, warmed and caressed by the sun, sprang to life, and drops of dew gleamed like jewels on the leaves; and the ancient, long-neglected garden looked young and beautifully arrayed in the morning light.

Granny was already awake. Sasha's deep coughing could be heard. From below came the sound of the servants setting up the samovar and arranging the chairs.

The hours passed slowly. Nadya had risen long ago, and for a long time she had been walking about the garden, and still the morning dragged on.

Then Nina Ivanovna appeared, her face tear-stained, a glass of mineral water in her hand. She went in for spiritualism and homeopathy, read a great deal, and loved talking about the doubts which continually assailed her, and Nadya supposed that all this possessed a profound and mysterious significance. She kissed her mother and walked beside her.

"What are you crying for, Mama?" she asked.

"I started a novel last night—it was about an old man and his daughter. The old man worked in an office, and the boss fell in love with the daughter. I never finished it, but I came to a place where I couldn't prevent myself from crying," Nina Ivanovna said, and she took a sip from the glass. "And then this morning I remembered it again, and it made me cry."

"I've been so depressed these nights," Nadya said after a silence. "I wish I knew why I can't sleep."

"I don't know, dear. When I can't sleep I shut my eyes very, very tight—like this—and then I try to imagine how Anna Karenina walked and talked, or else I try to imagine something historical, something from ancient times. . . ."

329

Nadya felt that her mother did not understand her, and was incapable of understanding her. She had never felt this before, and it frightened her. She wanted to hide, and went back to her room.

At two o'clock they sat down to dinner. It was Wednesday, a fast day, and Granny was served meatless *borshch* and bream with porridge.

To tease the grandmother, Sasha ate the meat soup as well as the vegetable soup. He joked all through the meal, but his jokes were labored and invariably directed toward a moral, and there was nothing amusing in his habit of lifting up his long, lean, deathly fingers before making some witty remark, nor was there anything amusing in the thought that he was very ill and perhaps not long for this world. At such times you felt so sorry for him that tears sprang to the eyes.

After dinner the grandmother went to her room to rest. Nina Ivanovna played for a while on the piano, and then she too went to her room.

"Oh, dearest Nadya," Sasha started his usual after-dinner conversation. "If only you would listen to me! If only you would!"

She was sitting back in an old-fashioned armchair, her eyes closed, while he paced up and down the room.

"If only you would go away and study!" he said. "Only the enlightened and holy people are interesting—they are the only ones needed. The more such people there are, the quicker will the Kingdom of Heaven descend on earth. Then it will happen little by little that not one stone will be left standing, in this town of yours everything will be shaken to its foundations, and everything will be changed, as though by magic. There will be immense and utterly magnificent houses, marvelous gardens, glorious fountains, extraordinary people. . . . But this is not the important thing! The most important thing is that the masses, as we understand the word, giving it its present-day meaning—they will disappear, this evil will vanish, and every man will know what he is living for, and no one any longer will look for support among the masses. My dearest darling, go away! Show them that you are sick to the stomach of this stagnant, dull, sinful life of yours! At least prove it for yourself!"

"No, Sasha, I can't! I'm going to be married."

"Never mind! Who cares about that?"

They went into the garden and strolled for a while.

"Anyhow, my dearest, you simply must think, you must realize how immoral and unclean your idle life is," Sasha went on. "Can't you realize that to enable you and your mother and your grandmother to live a life of leisure, others have to work for you, and you are devouring their lives? Is that right? Isn't it a filthy thing to do?"

Nadya wanted to say: "Yes, you are right." She wanted to say she understood perfectly, but tears came to her eyes, and suddenly she fell silent, and she shrank into herself, and went to her room.

Toward evening Andrey Andreyich arrived, and as usual he played the violin for a long time. He was by nature taciturn, and perhaps he enjoyed playing the violin because there was no need to speak while playing it. At eleven o'clock he had put on his overcoat and was about to go home when he took Nadya in his arms and passionately kissed her face, her shoulders, her hands.

"My dear, beautiful darling," he murmured. "Oh, how happy I am! I am out of my mind with happiness!"

And it seemed to her that she had heard these same words long ago, or perhaps she had read them somewhere . . . in an old dog-eared novel thrown away a long time ago.

In the drawing room Sasha was sitting at table drinking tea, the saucer poised on his five long fingers, while Granny was spreading out the cards for a game of patience, and Nina Ivanovna was reading. The flame spluttered in the icon lamp, and it seemed that everyone was quietly happy. Nadya said good night and went upstairs to her room, and lying down on the bed, she immediately fell asleep. But just as on the night before, she awoke with the first light of dawn. She could not sleep: a restless and oppressive spirit moved in her. She sat up in bed, resting her head on her knees, and thinking about her fiancé and her wedding. . . . For some reason she remembered that her mother had never loved her father, and now the mother possessed nothing of her own, and was completely dependent on Granny, her mother-in-law. And try as she would, Nadya could not understand why she had always regarded her mother as an exceptional and remarkable person, and why it had never occurred to her that her mother was only a simple, quite ordinary, and unhappy woman.

And Sasha, too, was awake—she heard him coughing downstairs. "What a strange naïve person he is," Nadya thought, "and those dreams of his—those marvelous gardens and glorious fountains—how absurd they are!" But for some reason she found so much that was beautiful in his naïveté and his absurdity, and the moment she permitted herself to dream of going away and studying, cold shivers bathed her whole heart and breast, and she was overwhelmed with sensations of joy and ecstasy.

"Better not to think about it," she whispered. "No, one shouldn't think about such things."

"Tick-tock . . ." the night watchman was rapping with his stick far away. "Tick-tock . . . tick-tock . . ."

III

Toward the middle of June, Sasha was suddenly overcome with boredom and made up his mind to return to Moscow.

"I can't go on living in this town," he said moodily. "No running water, no drains! I can hardly force myself to eat dinner—the kitchen is so indescribably filthy!"

"Wait a little while, Prodigal Son," Grandmother said, and for some reason she lowered her voice to a whisper. "The wedding is on the seventh."

"I don't want to wait!"

"Didn't you say you intended to stay until September?"

"I don't want to any more. I want to go and work!"

The summer had turned cold and wet, the trees were damp, the garden looked somber and uninviting, and none of this caused anyone to desire to work. Unfamiliar female voices were heard in all the rooms upstairs and downstairs, and they could hear the clatter of the sewing machine in Grandmother's room: they were rushing to get the trousseau ready. Of fur coats alone, Nadya was to have six, and the cheapest of them, according to Grandmother, cost three hundred rubles! The fuss irritated Sasha, who remained in his room, fuming with anger; but they talked him into staying, and he promised not to leave before the first of July.

Time passed quickly. On St. Peter's day Andrey Andreyich took Nadya to Moscow Street after dinner, to have yet another look at the house which had long since been rented and made ready for the young couple. It was a two-story house, but so far only the upper floor had been furnished. On the gleaming floor of the hall, painted to resemble parquet, stood bentwood chairs, a grand piano, a music stand for the violin. There was the smell of paint. On the wall hung a large oil painting in a gold frame—a picture of a naked woman beside a lilac-colored vase with a broken handle.

"Wonderful painting," said Andrey Andreyich with an awed sigh. "It's by Shishmachevsky."

Then there was the drawing room with a round table, a sofa, and armchairs upholstered in some bright blue material. Above the sofa hung a large photograph of Father Andrey in priestly skullcap and wearing his decorations. They passed into the dining room, where there was a sideboard, then into the bedroom, where two beds could be seen side by side in the half dusk: it seemed as though the bedroom had been furnished in such a way that life there would always be happy and could never be anything else. Andrey Andreyich led Nadya through the rooms, never taking his arm from her waist; but all the time she felt weak and conscience-stricken, hating these rooms and beds and armchairs, nauseated by the painting of the naked woman. Already it had become transparently clear to her that she no longer loved Andrey Andreyich, and perhaps had never loved him; but she did not—and could not—understand how to say this and to whom to say it and why she should say it, even though she thought about it all day and all night. . . . He had put his arm round her waist, and was talking so courteously and modestly, and was so happy as he walked around his house, but in all this she saw only vulgarity, stupid, naïve, intolerable vulgarity, and his arm round her waist felt rough and cold like an iron hoop. Every moment she was on the point of running away, bursting into sobs, throwing herself out of the window. Andrey Andreyich led her into the bathroom, and there he touched a tap set in the wall, and at once water flowed out.

"Just look at that!" he said, and burst out laughing. "I had them put up a cistern in the loft with a hundred gallons of water. So you see, we now have running water!"

They walked across a yard and out into the street, and hailed a cab. The dust rose in thick clouds, and it looked as though it would rain.

"You're not cold?" Andrey Andreyich asked, screwing up his eyes against the dust.

She did not answer.

"Remember how yesterday Sasha reproached me for not doing anything?" he said after a brief silence. "Well, he's right! He's absolutely right! I do nothing, and don't know how to do anything! And why is that, my dear? Why is it that I hate the thought of one day putting a cockade in my cap and going into government service? Why is it that I can't stand the sight of a lawyer, or a teacher of Latin, or a town councilor? O Mother Russia! O Mother Russia! What a burden of idle and useless people you carry along with you! O long-suffering Mother Russia, how many there are like me!"

And he continued to make generalizations about his own idleness, seeing it as a sign of the times.

"When we are married, my darling," he went on, "we'll go and live in the country, and we'll get down to work! We'll buy a small plot of land with a garden and a stream, and we'll work and observe life. . . . How splendid it will be!"

He removed his hat, and his hair waved in the wind, while she listened and thought: "Oh God, I want to go home! Oh God!" They were near the house when they caught up with Father Andrey.

"Look, there's Father!" Andrey said joyfully, and he waved his hat. "I love my old man, I really do," he said, paying off the cab driver. "He is a splendid old fellow. Really splendid."

Nadya went into the house, feeling ill and out of humor, remembering that visitors would be arriving in the evening and she would have to entertain them, smile, listen to the violin, listen to all kinds of idiocies, and talk only about the wedding. There would be her grandmother sitting by the samovar, stiff and magnificent in silk, looking very proud, as she always seemed to be in the presence of guests. Father Andrey came into the room with a sly smile.

"I have the pleasure and blessed consolation of seeing you in excellent health," he said to Grandmother, and it was hard to say whether he spoke in earnest or in jest.

IV

The wind was knocking on the windowpanes and on the roof; whistling sounds were heard; and you could hear the hobgoblin in the chimney singing his melancholy, plaintive song. It was after midnight, everyone was in bed, but no one could sleep. Nadya thought someone was still playing on the violin downstairs. A minute later Nina Ivanovna entered the room in her nightgown, holding a candle.

"What was that knocking sound, Nadya?" she asked.

Her mother, her hair in a single plait, a timid smile on her face, looked older, uglier, and shorter than ever on this stormy night. Nadya remembered how, quite recently, she had regarded her mother as a remarkable woman and listened with pride to the things she said, but now she could no longer remember those words she had spoken—the only ones that came back to her seemed feeble and affected.

She thought she could hear deep-throated voices singing in the chimney, even thought she could distinguish the words "Oh, my Go-o-o-d!" She sat up in bed, suddenly clutched fiercely at her hair, and burst into sobs.

"Mama, Mama!" she exclaimed. "My own dear mother, if only you knew what was happening to me! I beg you, I implore you—let me go away from here!"

"Where to?" Nina Ivanovna asked in surprise, and she sat down on the bed. "Where to?"

Nadya cried for a long time and could not utter a word.

"Let me leave town," she said at last. "The wedding mustn't —won't happen! Please understand that! I don't love him! . . . I can't bear to talk about him!"

"No, my darling, no!" Nina Ivanovna said quickly, frightened out of her wits. "Calm yourself. You're in low spirits, but it will pass. It often happens. Probably you've been quarreling with Andrey, but then lovers' quarrels always end in smiles!"

"Go away, Mama, go away!" Nadya sobbed.

"Yes," said Nina Ivanovna after a pause. "Only a little while ago you were a baby, a little girl, and now you are almost a bride. In nature there are always these transformations. Before you know where you are, you will be a mother and then an old woman, with a stubborn daughter like mine on your hands!"

"My dear sweet mother, you are clever and unhappy," said Nadya. "You are so very unhappy—why do you say such vulgar, commonplace things? For God's sake why?"

Nina Ivanovna tried to say something but could not utter a word, and went sobbing back to her own room. Once again deep-throated voices droned in the chimney, and Nadya suddenly felt frightened. She jumped out of bed and ran to her mother. Nina Ivanovna's eyes were red with weeping. She lay on the bed wrapped in a blue blanket, a book in her hands.

"Mama, listen to me!" Nadya cried. "I implore you—try to understand! If you only understood how petty and degrading our life is! My eyes have been opened and I see it all now. And what about your Andrey Andreyich? He's not a bit clever, Mama! Oh God, he's nothing more than a fool!"

Nina Ivanovna sat up with a jerk.

"You and your grandmother keep torturing me," she sobbed. "I want to live—to live!" she repeated, and she struck her breast twice with her little fist. "Let me free! I'm still young and I want to live, and you're making an old woman out of me!"

She cried bitterly and lay down, rolling herself up in the blanket, looking very silly, small, and pathetic. Nadya went to her room, dressed, and sat at the window to wait for the dawn. All night she sat there thinking, while someone down below in the courtyard seemed to be tapping the shutters and whistling.

The next morning Grandmother complained that during the night the wind had blown down all the apples in the garden and thrown down an old plum tree. It was a dull gray desolate day: one of those mornings when you want to light the lamps; everyone complained of the cold, and the raindrops kept tapping on the windowpanes. After breakfast Nadya went to Sasha's room, and without saying a word she fell on her knees before a chair in the corner and covered her face with her hands.

"What's the matter?" Sasha asked.

"I can't go on," she said. "I don't know how I was able to live here before. I don't understand it. I despise my fiancé, I despise myself, I despise all idle, nonsensical life!"

"What's come over you?" said Sasha, who was still unable to understand what it was all about. "You know . . . everything will turn out all right."

"I am disgusted with my life," Nadya went on. "I can't endure the thought of another day here! I'm leaving here tomorrow. Take me with you, for God's sake!"

For a moment Sasha gazed at her in astonishment. At last the truth dawned on him, and he was as delighted as a child. He waved his arms and began to shuffle around the room in his slippers, like someone dancing for joy.

"Wonderful!" he said, rubbing his hands together. "God, how wonderful!"

And she gazed at him steadily with wide-open eyes full of love, like someone spellbound, and she waited for him to say something important, something which would have infinite meaning for her. He had told her nothing yet, but already it seemed to her that something new and great, something she had never known before, was opening before her, and already she was gazing at him with a look of expectation, prepared for everything, even for death.

"I'm leaving tomorrow," he told her after some thought. "You can come to the station to see me off. . . . I'll have your baggage in my trunk and get your ticket, and then when the third bell rings you can jump on the train, and we'll go away. You can come with me to Moscow and then go off alone to St. Petersburg. Have you a passport?"

"Yes."

"I swear you'll never regret it, never repent," Sasha said with enthusiasm. "You can leave here and study, and then go whereever fate beckons. When your life is completely revolutionized, then everything will change. The important thing is to revolutionize your life, and nothing else is of any importance. Shall we leave tomorrow?"

"Yes, for God's sake, let's leave tomorrow!"

Nadya, who imagined that she was deeply moved and that her heart had never felt so heavy, was quite sure she would spend all the time before her departure in anguish and torment. Yet she had scarcely reached her room and lain down on the bed when she was overcome with sleep; and she slept soundly, her face wet with tears and a smile on her lips, till evening came.

V

They sent for a cab. Nadya went upstairs, in her hat and coat, to take one last look at her mother, at all the things that had belonged to her for so long. First she went to her own room and stood beside the bed, which was still warm, and for a while she looked around her; then she went softly into her mother's room. After kissing her mother and smoothing her hair, she remained there a few moments before walking slowly downstairs.

A heavy rain fell. In front of the porch stood a droshky, the hood up, drenched with rain.

"There's no room for you, Nadya," said Grandmother while a servant was stowing the luggage. "I wonder you want to see him off in this weather! Much better to stay at home! Oh, look at the rain!"

Nadya tried to say something, but words failed her. Sasha helped her into the droshky, and covered her legs with a rug. Then he sat down beside her.

"Good luck! May God keep you!" Grandmother shouted from the steps. "Write to us when you get to Moscow!"

"Yes, of course. Good-by, Granny!"

"May the Queen of Heaven have you in her keeping."

"What rotten weather!" Sasha said.

At this point Nadya burst out sobbing. Now for the first time she realized she was really going away, and this was something she had not permitted herself to believe when she was gazing at her mother or saying good-by to her grandmother. Good-by, town! It all came back to her with a rush: Andrey, the father, the new house, the naked lady with the vase; but these things no longer oppressed her, no longer frightened her, but on the contrary seemed naïve and unimportant, fading deeper and deeper into the distance. And when they were sitting in the railroad carriage and the train started, the whole of the past, once so huge and imposing, shrank almost to nothing: instead the broad roads of the future, scarcely perceptible until this moment, opened out to her. The rain rapped on the carriage windows, nothing could be seen but the green fields and the telegraph poles flashing past—the birds sitting on the wires. Quite suddenly she found she was almost choking with joy. It seemed to her she would soon enter her freedom, spending her time studying, "running wild," as people used to say. She was simultaneously laughing and crying and saying her prayers.

"Everything is going to be all right," Sasha was saying with a broad smile. "You'll see. . . ."

VI

Autumn had gone, and winter, too, had passed away. Nadya was now very homesick, and every day she thought of her mother and her grandmother; she thought of Sasha, too. Letters from home were resigned and kindly, everything seemed to have been forgiven and forgotten. In May after the examinations she went home in good health and high spirits, breaking her journey in Moscow to see Sasha. He had changed very little since the previous summer—the same beard, the same disheveled hair, the same large and beautiful eyes, and he wore the same coat and the same canvas trousers. Yet he looked ill and troubled, and seemed much older and thinner, and coughed incessantly. He struck Nadya at first as oddly colorless and provincial.

"Good heavens, Nadya is here!" he exclaimed with a burst of gay laughter. "My dear child . . ."

They sat in the lithography shop, which was full of tobacco smoke and the suffocating smell of paint and India ink, and then they went to his room, which was filthy and also reeked of tobacco. The samovar on the table had turned cold; beside it lay a shattered plate with dark paper on it, and there were heaps of dead flies on the table and on the floor. Everything about the room suggested that Sasha led a completely slovenly existence, living anyhow, and despising comfort; and if anyone had spoken to him about his private joys, about his personal life and whether anyone loved him, he would have understood nothing and would only have laughed.

"Everything went off all right," Nadya said hurriedly. "Mama came to see me in Petersburg during the autumn. She tells me Granny isn't angry any more, but keeps going to my room and making the sign of the cross over the walls."

Sasha seemed cheerful, but he coughed continually and spoke in an oddly broken voice. Nadya was watching him closely, unable to make up her mind whether he was seriously ill or whether she was just imagining it.

"Dear Sasha," she said. "How ill you are!"

"Nonsense. Maybe I'm not well, but I'm all right!"

"Dear God!" Nadya exclaimed, suddenly overwhelmed. "You ought to see a doctor. Why don't you take care of yourself? Oh, dear darling Sasha," she said as tears rushed to her eyes, and for some reason she thought of Andrey Andreyich and the naked lady with the vase and the whole of her past life, which seemed as distant as childhood, and she began to cry because Sasha no longer seemed so original, so intelligent, and so interesting as the year before. "Sasha dear, you are very, very ill. I don't know what I wouldn't do to keep you from being thin and pale. I owe you so much! Dear kind Sasha, you can't imagine how much you have done for me! Your are really the closest and dearest person in my whole life!"

They sat there and went on talking. After her winter in St. Petersburg she found his words, his smile, the man himself and everything about him, curiously old-fashioned and out of date, as though the time of maturity had passed long ago, and perhaps he was already in his grave.

"I'm going down the Volga the day after tomorrow," Sasha said. "That way I can drink some koumiss. I'm going to try koumiss seriously. A friend of mine and his wife are coming with me. His wife is wonderful. I've been trying to make her study. I think she ought to revolutionize herself."

When they had talked themselves to a standstill, Sasha drove her to the station. He treated her to tea and bought her apples, and when the train began to move out he smiled and waved his handkerchief, but even his thin legs showed that he was very ill and not long for this world.

Nadya arrived at her native town at midday. As she drove home from the station, the streets seemed unusually wide, but the houses looked curiously squat and very small. There were no people about, and the only person she met was the German piano tuner with the rust-colored coat. All the houses seemed covered in dust. Her grandmother, who looked very old, and as fat and ugly as ever, threw her arms round Nadya and wept interminably, with her face against Nadya's shoulder, and she was completely unable to tear herself away. Nina Ivanovna looked much older and plainer; she seemed shrunken and as strait-laced as ever; and the diamonds glittered on her fingers.

"My dearest," she said, trembling all over. "My darling . . ."

Then they sat down and wept silently together. It was evident that both the mother and the grandmother realized that the past would never return, was irrevocably lost: their social position, their prestige in the community, their right to invite guests to stay with them, all this had gone. So it happens sometimes that the police burst into a house at night, one of those houses accustomed to an easy, leisurely existence, and the master of the house is discovered to be a forger and an embezzler, and then farewell forever to the easy, leisurely existence!

Nadya went upstairs and saw the familiar bed, the familiar windows and simple white curtains, and from the windows there could be seen the familiar view of the garden, brilliant with sunshine, gay and clamorous with birdsong. She ran her fingers over the table, sat down, and fell to thinking. She had enjoyed a good dinner, and the tea was served with delicious thick cream, but something was missing. She was aware of the emptiness of the room, and the ceilings were very low. In the evening when she went to bed, covering herself with the bedclothes, it somehow seemed absurd to be lying in that warm, very soft bed.

Nina Ivanovna came in for a moment and sat down, as people do when they feel guilty. She was timid and kept glancing round her.

"Tell me, Nadya, how is everything?" she asked after a moment's silence. "Are you contented? Quite contented?"

"Yes, Mama."

Nina Ivanovna rose and made the sign of the cross over Nadya and over the window.

"As you see, I have grown deeply religious," she said. "You know, I am studying philosophy now, and I am always thinking, thinking. . . . And many things are clear as daylight now. It seems to me now that what is necessary above all is that life should pass as it were through a prism."

"Mama, tell me, how is Grandmother?"

"Oh, she's all right. When you went away with Sasha, and then when your telegram came, your grandmother read it and fell to the ground, and for three days she lay in bed without moving. After that she was always praying and weeping. But now it's over."

She got up and walked around the room.

"Tick-tock . . ." came the tapping of the night watchman. "Tick-tock, tick-tock . . ."

"What is necessary above all is that life should as it were pass through a prism," she said. "In other words, what is necessary is that our life in consciousness should be analyzed into its simplest elements, as though into the seven primary colors, and each element must be studied separately."

What else Nina Ivanovna said, and when she went away, Nadya did not know, for she soon fell asleep.

May passed, and June came. Nadya had grown accustomed to being at home. Grandmother fussed over the samovar, and gave deep sighs, while Nina Ivanovna spent her evenings talking about philosophy; she still lived in the house like a poor cousin, and she had to ask Grandmother for every twenty-kopeck piece. There were heaps of flies in the house, and the ceilings seemed to be falling lower and lower. For fear of meeting Father Andrey and Andrey Andreyich, Granny and Nina Ivanovna never went out into the streets. Nadya wandered through the garden and strolled down the streets, gazing at the houses and the gray fences, and it seemed to her that everything in the town had been growing old for a long time, and the town itself had outlived its day and was now waiting either for the end or for the beginning of something fresh and young. Oh, if only this new pure life would come more quickly, a life where one could look one's fate in the eyes boldly and straightforwardly, sure of being right, joyful and free! Sooner or later this life would come! The time would come when there would be nothing left of her grandmother's house, that house where everything was so arranged that the four servants could only live in the basement in a single filthy room—the time would come when no trace of the house would remain, when it would be forgotten and no one would remember it. Nadya's only distraction came from the little boys next door: when she wandered in the garden, they banged on the fence and shouted with glee: "The bride! The bride!"

A letter from Sasha arrived from Saratov. In his happy, dancing handwriting he wrote that the journey down the Volga was a complete success, but he had fallen rather ill in Saratov, and had lost his voice and was spending these last two weeks in the hospital. She knew what this meant, and she was overwhelmed with a foreboding which amounted to a complete certainty. It hurt her that her foreboding and her thoughts about Sasha did not distress her, as once they would have done. She passionately wanted to live and she longed to be in St. Petersburg, and her friendship with Sasha, although still sweet, seemed to belong to a far-distant past. She could not sleep all night, and in the morning she sat by the window, listening. And she did hear voices coming from downstairs: her grandmother was asking questions in rapid, querulous tones, and someone was weeping. . . . When Nadya went down, her grandmother was standing in a corner of the room praying, and her face was wet with tears. On the table lay a telegram.

For a long while Nadya paced up and down the room, listening to her grandmother's sobs; then she picked up the telegram and read it. The telegram said that on the previous morning, in Saratov, Alexander Timofeyich, Sasha for short, had died of consumption.

Grandmother and Nina Ivanovna went to the church to order a service for the dead, while Nadya remained in her room, deep in thought. She realized clearly that her life had been revolutionized, as Sasha had wished, and she was a stranger here, lonely and unwanted, and there was nothing she wanted here. She realized, too, that the past had been ripped away from her and had now vanished altogether, as though it had been burned and the ashes had been scattered in the winds. She went into Sasha's room and stood there.

"Good-by, dear Sasha," she murmured.

In her imagination life stretched before her, a new, vast, infinitely spacious life, and this life, though still obscure and full of mysteries, lured and attracted her.

She went upstairs to her own room to pack, and the next morning said good-by to her family, and left the town. She was full of life and high spirits, and she expected never to return.

1903

A Note about the Translator

ROBERT PAYNE studied Russian language and literature under Dr. Bruce Boswell at Liverpool University, and he had already translated the short stories of Boris Pasternak by 1937, printing them in Singapore, just before the outbreak of the war in the Pacific. He has since published *The Three Worlds of Boris Pasternak* (1961). His first published work was a translation of Yuri Olyesha's *Envy* (1937), published by Virginia and Leonard Woolf in London, and he has also translated Olyesha's short stories. His book *The Terrorists* (1957) was a study of Russian political movements in the last years of the nineteenth century. His *Dostoyevsky: A Human Portrait* (1961) also contains much original translation from the Russian.

Born in Cornwall, England, in 1911, Robert Payne was educated at St. Paul's School, London, and at the universities of Capetown, Liverpool, Munich, and the Sorbonne. Among his many published books are *Forever China* (1945), *The White Pony* (1947), *The Three Worlds of Albert Schweitzer* (1957), *The Splendor of Persia* (1957), *The Gold of Troy* (1958), a Book-of-the-Month Club choice, *The Shepherd* (1959), *The Life and Death of Lenin* (1964), *The Fortress* (1967), and *Marx* (1968). Prior to settling in New York, where he makes his home, Mr. Payne lived in many parts of Europe, in Africa, and in Asia.

A Note on the Type

THE TEXT of this book is set in *Monticello*, a Linotype revival of the original Binny & Ronaldson Roman No. 1, cut by Archibald Binny and cast in 1796 by that Philadelphia type foundry. The face was named Monticello in honor of its use in the monumental fifty-volume *Papers of Thomas Jefferson*, published by Princeton University Press. Monticello is a transitional type design, embodying certain features of Bulmer and Baskerville, but it is a distinguished face in its own right.

Typography and binding design by
GEORGE SALTER